JOOLZ DENI

Joolz Denby is Britain's foremost wom
the last twenty years she has travellec
readings, performances, lectures and se
a novel, *Stone Baby*, three collections of poetry and stories and has appeared regularly on both television and radio.

Her interests range from working with cult rock band New Model Army, through to researching and studying such topics as mythology, body art, forensic psychology, Wilfred Owen and the Brontë sisters. She is based in Bradford, where she writes, reads and tries – unsuccessfully – to catch up on her sleep.

Acclaim for *Stone Baby*:

'By turns burningly sincere, tough and tender, funny and acute. What makes a woman fall for a ripper? Read Joolz and find out'
Michèle Roberts, *New Statesman*

'*Stone Baby* uses the ingredients of the serial killer novel without any of the slick exploitative thrills of much of the genre to reveal the harm that ripples out from the damaged and damaging mind of a psychopath. It is an extraordinary achievement'
Natasha Cooper, *Express on Sunday*

'The book proceeds to its dramatic conclusion with a terrible inevitability . . . but Denby never loses control of her sensitive material, refusing to sensationalise, and remaining compassionate throughout . . . It's hard to imagine how anyone can read this book and remain unmoved'
Val McDermid, *Glasgow Herald*

'A story of raw and often uncomfortable power . . . An unusual and remarkable debut'
Andrew Taylor, *Crime Time*

'Denby unsparingly writes her characters into the abyss to show that the cost of murder is limitless, that the worst stories never end. In doing so, her tough, tender, edgy novel is characterized by savage compassion'
Big Issue

'Joolz Denby in *Stone Baby* mixes vignettes of the northern stand-up comedy and music scene with low-life on the mean streets of Bradford to produce a passionately written thriller about a modern Ripper'
Financial Times

By the same author

STONE BABY

Corazon

—— ✦ ——

Joolz Denby

HarperCollins*Publishers*

This novel is entirely a work of fiction. The names, characters and incidents portrayed in it are the work of the author's imagination. Any resemblance to actual persons, living or dead, events or localities is entirely coincidental.

HarperCollins*Publishers*
77–85 Fulham Palace Road, London W6 8JB

The HarperCollins website address is:
www.**fire**and**water**.com/crime

First published in Great Britain
in 2001 by HarperCollins

1 3 5 7 9 10 8 6 4 2

A catalogue record for this book
is available from the British Library

ISBN 0 00 226104 9

Set in Linotype PostScript Meridien by
Rowland Phototypesetting Ltd, Bury St Edmunds, Suffolk

Printed and bound in Great Britain by
Clays Ltd, St Ives plc

Dedicated unreservedly and with deep gratitude
to Justin Sullivan and Warren Hogg

Acknowledgements

I would like to thank the following for their invaluable help and support:

Jaime Boyd for the weather reports from Ronda. Dr Rosemary Wisdom and Alison Merrick for medical information and comment. Warren Deane (Perforations, Brighton), Sarah Strong (Pro-Body Piercing, Bradford), Russell Beeney (Wildcat Collection, Brighton) for information about body piercing, and Adam Dutton (Temple Tatu, Brighton) for creating my Virgin and additional tattoo information. Many thanks to Ben and Vic Stone, Rev Hammer, Brett Selby and Donelda McKechnie for their unflagging kindness and to the Richmond family for the house in La Indiana. My thanks to Julia Wisdom, Catherine Dey, Debbie Collings and Anne O'Brien of HarperCollins and to Gregory & Radice, my agents. I am also most grateful to the staff of Waterstones at the Wool Exchange, Bradford, for their unstinting support, and to Starbucks café. To Finn and Screamer for being – well, cats. As ever, my respect and thanks to the Goddess.

And to you, reading this book, welcome . . .

BOOK I

'Quos Deus vult perdere, prius dementat' Proverb

Prologue

He could hear the sound of the drums and the chanting. The noise rolled through the rock, wave after wave – they were calling Him; if only He could be with them, *join* with them, lead them forward through the dark maze to the light . . .

But it was no use. When He tried to rise from the great bed, the pain twined through Him, wrenching at His ruined bones like the roots of a malevolent tree thrusting itself into the iron earth. He dragged Himself up and clawed at the bed-curtains, almost pulling them down; His mouth opening in a rictus of agony. Then, just as He thought He couldn't bear the hideous torment any more, it ceased miraculously. He felt Himself soar out of His body and the visions flooded His mind, the ancient truths He'd witnessed all those years ago in the fiery cradle of His initiation and re-birth. They unfolded and bloomed in His brain like the Mystic Rose. It was so beautiful – so *primal*. Poor, foolish humanity had forgotten the glorious heritage He had suffered and witnessed in His long, long search through the scattered remnants of lost cultures and bought at such cost to His physical self, in the degenerate rituals of ruined tribes.

But it was worth it – oh, a thousand times over! He *knew*! He knew the Truth! It was ordained from the Beginning of All Things that He should be born, one half of a perfect whole, that He should suffer –

and through His terrible suffering, attain this, this *rapture*.

He floated weightlessly in the crimson amniotic fluid of His visions – this was bliss beyond the world's imagining. As if from very far away He felt the pain excoriating His body, but nothing mattered here, in the peace of His perfection.

But then, suddenly, it came again, redoubled, laying waste the dream. He felt the pain turn His crumbling spine into a white-hot rod of torment, felt it crush His joints in a brutal vice and erupt in His tattered, bubbling skin. He cried out, stricken. He screamed for her to help Him, to stop the pain, as she had so many times before in their long life together.

Then at last, He felt her cool hand on His burning forehead, heard the low, gentle tones of her voice soothing Him, comforting Him. He struggled to make out the words she spoke, so He could answer her.

Yes, yes, my love, my dearest, yes, it is time. But first, first, beloved, tell me what you have seen so I can serve your Way. Let me be your First Witness so I can share your Communion with the Children – they need your wisdom, your guidance . . . Hear them . . . Do you hear them, beloved? They are calling you . . .

He heard Himself screaming again. The raw, savage noise echoed in the darkness like a beast's voice – braying, inhuman, brutal.

'The Heart, the Mother's Heart – naked She embraces the Serpent! Oh, listen to me, listen to me for I have seen beyond the Veil that should never be lifted! It is the Blood and only the Blood that can lead us through the Gateway to the New Beginning! We will be as Shining Towers and our flesh will be purified; we will know the Truth and be free! Embrace the pain, it is the Holy Ecstasy that will lead you to the Great Translation. Be washed in the Blood of the Mother and be as one in the Passion. Oh, my Children, the Children of my soul,

I am your Prophet, your Teacher, your Father – my love for you is beyond all earthly love because I am the Sacrifice and the voice of the Dream! I know you are afraid, I know you have doubts – but cast these things aside! Cast aside the poison of unbelief! I know the world has hurt you – but here, my Children, you are safe, you are cradled in love, this is your sanctuary and you are the true and glorious Chosen! Embrace your birthright, do not fear the Ordeal. Embrace the pain and share the Dream with Us . . .'

The woman sighed and signalled for the young man who accompanied her to slide the needle into one of The Prophet's remaining viable veins. Then she turned the DAT recorder off. Tonight, at least, the Children would be happy. They would hear their Father's voice, perhaps for the last time. A tear slid down her cheek as she looked at her beloved, at peace in his drugged sleep. The young man saw her distress and knelt in front of her, taking her hand and kissing it, a look of passionate devotion on his handsome face. She laid her other hand on his head and murmured the blessing, but her eyes were on the figure in the bed.

My poor Children, she thought, *what will they do, what will become of them here in the world without their Father?*

But then she remembered, and smiled . . .

1

I knew something was up the moment I stepped through the front door. Nothing I could put my finger on, you know, just a creepy feeling. A smell, or an absence of smell; a sound – or was it the cold thud of silence? Yeah, something was definitely *wrong*. Christ, I've told this tale so often now you'd think I'd be used to it, wouldn't you? But it still makes me – urrgh, God – it makes me feel, I don't know, something between grief and fury, I suppose.

I'd got back from Whitby that morning, after spending the weekend at an academic beanfeast – whoops, sorry: important academic seminar – with my boss, Laura. She'd dropped me at the Uni and I'd gone swimming. I swim nearly every day and don't like to miss it. Then after wafting my usual perfume-of-choice, Eau De Chlorine, around the library for a bit, I'd packed up and sloped off home.

I can't say I'd been looking forward to it – getting home, that is. I'd be a liar if I let on Phillip and I were even speaking any more. That's why I spent so much time at the pool or in the library. The marriage – if you could call it that – had been a big mistake and we both knew it. I also knew he had a bit on the side, and I couldn't have cared less, frankly. Like I'd said to The Ems, if it makes him happy and gets him off my case, fair enough. I knew we'd have to split – known it for ages – but Jesus Christ, not like *this*.

Sorry, sorry. OK, no, I'm fine – I can do this. It's just, along with my other peculiarities, I get a bit asthmatic if I'm wound up. Right. So, I got home and the first thing I noticed is – no great big old moggy cattermongering round the door begging for food and attention. Usually Wellington was at the threshold like a fat, hairy shot at the merest turn of a key. I went into the kitchen calling for him, and there on the counter top was the note.

It was word processed, naturally. Phillip can't *do* handwriting since he got computerized. I thought at first it was the usual 'Gone out, don't wait up, get some milk' sort of thing. It wasn't.

It was the kiss-off letter. It started with the usual stupid 'Dear . . .' That made me snort. I certainly wasn't Phillip's dear anything. 'Dear Alma', it went on. Typical. Only Phillip and my parents called me 'Alma'. Nearly everyone else calls me Al. 'You can call me Al – and I'll be your long lost friend . . .' You know the song and the video; Paul Simon, Chevy Chase – no? Oh, never mind, it's ancient. So anyway, I scanned the rest of the note in a sort of daze, barely taking in the bits about his wanting to 'effect closure' and 'regain' his life – the sort of twaddle you'd expect from a psych lecturer. I got pretty pissed off about him instructing me to vacate his house and get myself a lawyer, so pissed off that I didn't take in the final paragraph at first. Then I read it again, to make sure.

> As you have proved to be incapable of behaving in a mature manner, or accepting responsibility of any kind, I made the painful decision to have Wellington put to sleep. Whilst this is obviously distressing, I felt it was the only option under the circumstances. He was increasingly infirm and becoming more and more costly in regard to vet's bills, etc. I doubt whether you would be capable

of successfully caring for him and so I did what I thought best.

I have it by heart. I can't . . . I mean, there aren't words. I felt like I'd been hit in the guts, all the wind knocked out of me. He'd murdered my cat. The bastard had *murdered* my cat.

I thought I was going to faint or something, really. The kitchen seemed to recede like a tracking shot in a movie and goldy-coloured spots flickered in front of my eyes. I had to grab hold of the counter top because it felt like someone had pulled the bones out of my legs – I sort of slithered to the floor and exploded with tears.

You know when you were a kid, and something happened that was just so bloody *unfair* the whole world seemed to turn dark and the sun go ashy and cold? Remember that terrible crying that seemed to come from the pit of your belly? Those big, wet, tearing sobs that snatched your breath and stoppered your nose with snot? Well, that's how I cried for my cat. Shivering and retching on the sodding black-and-white chequered vinyl tiles that smelt of antiseptic where my *husband* had swabbed them with Dettol. I hawked and spat, strings of gunk spiralling like silvery spider's silk on to the gleaming floor, my face burning, my heart freezing.

I don't know how long I crouched there, gasping for breath. Was it five minutes, or five hours? I really don't know. Time seemed to get loose from its moorings, go crazy. Eventually, I got sort of numb in my head and the room seemed to fade, like an old photograph of somewhere you used to live, years ago – in another life. It wasn't real any more, nothing was. The only creature I'd really loved, since Jack, was dead. And it was my fault. That's what I thought. OK, I may not have done the actual deed, but if I'd been more careful, more together, Wellington and I would have been holed up together in some cosy flat cuddling and watching telly. Now he was dead. No goodbyes, no last kiss, nothing. I'd failed him, like I failed at everything. It was unbearable. I felt like, like – *scum*.

I had to get out of there. It was either that or burn it down. I remember scrabbling about for my specs and my bag, and struggling into my old jacket. Then I seemed to go on to autopilot.

I sort of wandered around the kitchen for a bit, feeling like I couldn't find the door. Then, as I stood there, gawking at nothing in particular, trying to breathe properly, my eye fell on the rack of knives and kitchen implements by the cooker. I saw the big Solingen shears and – I know this sounds totally weird, right, but I swear, it seemed perfectly logical at the time – I picked them up and, taking hold of my long plait, I hacked it off at the base of my skull.

The braid lay in my hand like a dead snake, silky and damp, smelling of swimming. My head felt suddenly light and free. I think I smiled, in a grim sort of way. For some reason, I thought, *That'll show them!* I know, I know – who? But honestly, it just seemed the right thing to do . . .

Stuffing the plait in my pocket, I left. The awfulness and shock of it all kept dinning in my head – I mean, how could I ever have married that twat? How could I have lived this fucking half-life for five whole years – especially after knowing *Jack*? Yeah, well, with hindsight, it's easy to say the dread word 'rebound', but in a twisted sort of way I suppose it's true. Or maybe it was a sort of suttee.

I staggered out of the front door into a flurry of chilly spring rain. Very seasonal. Believe me, I had no idea where I was going and it was a wonder I didn't get knocked down as I weaved across the Leeds Road like a zombie on jellies. A sporty yellow car swerved to avoid me, the fella driving it leaning hard on the horn, Tupac blaring from the speakers: 'Only God Can Judge Me Now'. *You an' me both,* I thought. *Oh my God, what am I going to do? Where am I going to go?* My heart was pounding and the rain was messing up my glasses, dazzling and refracting the thin, silvery light until it made my head ache. It was like there was a horrible, tight sort of membrane separating me from the world, like psychic cling-film, and I couldn't break through it and pull myself together.

I kept thinking of Wellington – my Wells, my Prince of Cats, my old bruiser with his pugilistic, yellow stare and raggy ears. The warm bear smell of his fur, the cracked leather of his pads with their vicious, hooky claws; the way he always knew when I was blue, and would snug up to me in an off-hand, Yorkshirey way. Jack had brought Wellington home one night; he'd been piss drunk as usual and had some tale about a fella in a pub with a pocket full of kittens. It was love at first sight; I was infatuated with Wells from his first furious meow. Now my last connection with Jack was gone. Phillip had his revenge at last. Christ, how he'd hated anything to do with Jack, it was the one thing that got him riled.

'You still love him, don't you? Don't you? Bloody Jack Collier, the bloody Boy Wonder, eh? Eh? Christ!'

Of course I still loved him. I suppose I still do and, in a way, I always will. Well, who wouldn't? You can't *not* love the likes of Jack, that's the problem.

Anyway, to get on, I was so full of all this *stuff* that I found I'd walked the three miles into Town without really noticing. I walk most places, not being a driver, so it wasn't a big deal to me. But it was unsettling to lose the time like that, as if it had just folded me from here to there. I also realized I was soaking, rain dripping off my shorn hair and down my neck like perishing little fingers. I was wet right through, too, the seams of my old hiking jacket let in water chronic. My Nikes were totally sodden, as were my joggers. I felt completely miserable.

I headed instinctively for the Jazz Café, near the campus. I didn't fancy Cha-Cha's, it was too public. I just wanted somewhere to sit a moment and think what to do.

I must have looked a complete sight. My hands were shaking like an alkie after a night on the Red Biddy and I nigh on dropped the coins I managed to fumble out of my purse. You could see the trendy little geezer behind the counter was thinking about not serving me; like, who was this mumbling, sodden woman with her cheap, ugly clothes, horrible old specs and institution haircut, right? But I gave him the hard stare and he lost his nerve. Just twitched and tutted instead. I really, really did not care.

I sat by the big window and stared out into the rain, snot mixing saltily with my latte. At least the mug was warm, even if the coffee was crap. My mind kept on spiralling round and round and back again. I couldn't seem to make sense of anything. All I could think was, God, I'm alone, with nowhere to go . . . Then it suddenly struck me. What do they say? 'Home is where they *have* to take you in.'

Millie. I'd go to Millie's. She'd get hold of Maz and they'd . . . I didn't quite know what they'd do, but they'd think of something. The Ems. Right – sorted.

I got up and walked through the downpour to sanctuary.

2

I have two best friends. The same two I've had since first school. Millicent Li – Millie, or Bruce, to us – and Marzena Sielicki – Maz. I headed through Town, up the hill and out along the Lane to Millie's bachelor-girl flat. Well, semi-bachelor-girl, anyway, now she was sort of living with Lief, the world's handsomest bloke; which he is, being half Danish and half Senegalese. They like each other because they both got pretty sick early on in life of being everybody's idea of an exotic fuck. Fortunately for me, Lief was away on a job in Paris, setting up an exhibition of Pre-Raphaelite paintings.

That meant the spare room was free, and Millie would take me in. I mean, of course she'd take me in anyway, but at least it would be easier this way. Millie's place isn't exactly huge, but it's nice – she's a good housewife. Not like me, who barely notices if the dust is two-foot thick and the cobwebs so dense the house looks like a Goth-band video. Naturally, Phillip's house had been fully *done* when I moved in, since he'd already been there for a couple of years. No alterations to the black leather and chrome minimalist décor wanted, thank you.

Bruce's flat is round by the park, in one of those tremendous upright nineteenth-century townhouses, once so beloved of the Yorkshire Wool Riche. The houses had fallen into neglect during the sixties and seventies, but now they were being divided into des-res apartments and rising again as Ingleside became gentrified.

Bruce loves it because it's dead close to her office, five minutes away across the weedy, muck-and-syringe strewn reaches of the park. Still, all that apart, you can glimpse the treetops from her living-room window. Almost country, for the likes of us urban types.

By the time I got there, I was exhausted. I don't know why I didn't get the bus, but it didn't occur to me. I practically fell up the couple of steps into the porch and leant on the intercom bell. I was in a right state, crying and freezing cold. I rang and rang the bell until I realized she wasn't in. Total panic. What if she'd gone away without telling me? What would I do? Maz lived with her kid, Tatum, and her parents out in Sykebeck – miles away. Christ, it was a mess. I just couldn't *cope*. I gave up and, hugging my daysack to my chest, slid down into the corner of the porch, shaking and sobbing. All I could think to do was wait. All night, if need be. That's how fucked up I was.

Again, with the time thing, I can't say how long I crouched there blubbing. But after a while, a young woman bounded up the steps. My heart leapt, thinking it was Bruce. But it wasn't anyone I knew. The woman leant across me nervously and prodded a bell. I ignored her, just shuffled out of her road. A voice burbled out of the intercom and the door clicked open. Without thinking, I got up and made as if to go in. Major faux pas. The woman *froze*. Then she spoke, her voice nervous and thready.

'Umm, you can't – look, I'm sorry, but you can't . . . you can't come in here. God, I . . . I'm, er, really sorry but . . . this is a private house, for residents only . . . you know, people who *live* here. Oh God, here –' Wedging her neat pump in the door, she took her purse out of her shoulder bag, *and handed me a pound coin*! Even in my confused state, I was gobsmacked. I sat holding the coin in the palm of my hand and stared at it.

She was flushed now, her cheeks flaming under her foundation. 'I'm sorry, but you can't umm *sleep* here or anything . . . OK?'

Christ Almighty, I thought. Well, that's the fucking icing on the cake. It really is. I felt like laughing, in a sour, nauseous sort of way. The silly cow had assumed I was a dosser looking for a flop. I think I felt angry at first and she must have sensed it because she slid into the house molto pronto, like an eel into a trap. But then I just felt sad. I did; really sad. I mean, she'd meant well, after all. She could have screamed or something, and caused a big palaver. But she'd given me money – and money was kindness to her sort. By her lights, she'd been decent to a bit of society's flotsam that had fetched up in her porch. In the eyes of the world, it was me that was the fuck-up, sitting here like a heap of shit, snivelling – not that poor little madam in her smart navy suit, square-heeled pumps and immaculate white blouse.

I just hoped she wouldn't recant her charitable instinct and call the Plod. That was all I needed, a night in the cells.

I scrunched up in the corner again and wondered how long I should wait. I felt really thirsty, and the cold and damp seemed to exhale like a mist out of the gritty sandstone. It was starting to make my legs go numb, but I didn't seem to have the will to move; in fact, I was almost asleep, or half-conscious. That'd be great – if I died of exposure on a spring evening in Bradford . . . Possible, though.

My thoughts kept slipping away from me all the time, like gleaming, half-seen goldfish in a murky pond. I'd no sooner get hold of one than off it would shoot into the depths again. I suppose some folk would say I was over-reacting. You know, getting so worked up over a *pet.* Not as if Wells had been *human.* And the break-up of my marriage – come on, hardly unexpected. Just making a fuss. That's what Vi always said: *Alma, stop making a fuss. You're too sensitive, you've got an over-developed imagination. Don't take things to heart so much. You're upsetting everyone. Calm down.* That was rich, coming from her, the Queen of the Over-Wrought School of Landscape Painting. The only woman living who can make the Lake District look vulval. Thanks, Mum, I'll bear it in mind next time someone kills my cat and throws me out on my ear, I'll just fucking *calm down.*

I felt the tears – of fury, this time – trickling down my face, hot against my cold cheeks. The anger that I kept tightly contained all my life juddered through me like whizz. I had to fight it, get in control of it again, but I was so, so tired. Then I felt the adrenaline wave subside in the face of the grinding fatigue that kept me pinned in this stupid porch. Hah, small mercies. My glasses steamed up but I couldn't be arsed to clean them again. What did it matter if I could see or not? I could see in my mind – I had my memories to pore over like I always did. Memories of Jack, his face, his smile, his rolling, cowboy gait, his smell – sweet, vanillery and warm from his flesh; faintly musky from his thick, wavy hair. Jack, my Jack. I'd forgotten nothing, nothing at all. It was all fixed in my heart like a scar that wouldn't heal. Everything – yeah, like the first time I ever clapped eyes on him, the *infamous* Jack Collier . . .

3

I only applied for one university course. I could have gone anywhere: Oxford, Cambridge – the world was my academic langoustine, apparently. Oh, yeah, I'm supposed to be very *clever*. You'd think that was great, wouldn't you? And it would be, unless the rest of your family were extremely brilliant (and in my brother's case, a genius), in which case 'clever' simply doesn't cut it. Not at all. Just my luck.

But I didn't fancy all that snotty Oxbridge crap, though I did fancy Uni. I had (don't laugh, I was only nineteen) secret dreams of it being all brilliant conversation and witty repartee about Things That Matter in dimly lit bars, with terrifically intense young guns who would set the world to rights whilst quaffing rough but satisfying plonk. Not like the university life my father had lived, full of desiccated scholars shuffling through dusty corridors maundering on about Spenser and his pigging *Faerie Queene*. No, my imagined university world was young, modern, vibrant and totally *cool*. Yeah, right.

Also, I didn't want to leave the Bradford area and be parted from Millie and Maz, who were at the Tech doing Business Studies and Hairdressing respectively. So I applied for Modular Humanities at the Ridings University. It had lots to recommend it, like, it was notoriously liberal and the vibe was that the crazier your thesis, the better chance you had of getting a First. Recent submissions had included 'The Klingon Language as a Post-Modern Textual Peace Interface', and the immortal 'Pooh Bear – a Metaphor for the Oppression of Pre-Adults in a Piaget-Dominated Society'. Plus, my Dad despised it. *How* cool?

I got in so easily it was joke. I mean, having the illustrious scholar Freddy Greer as a father, the great muse and artist Violet Trelannon-Greer as a mother and the scandalous, wild-child computer prodigy Frankie Greer as an older brother sort of guarantees you entry to a provincial university. Any university, actually. Christ, the lecturer who interviewed me even asked me if I could get Freddy to autograph his copy of *Red Earth*, Dad's great study of the Moorish influence on the poetry of Lorca. I said, *Sure, no probs* . . . Yeah, right.

So I entered the hallowed portals of Modular Humanities. I was a student – I was *grown-up*! However, just to put the mockers on things good stylee, shortly after I started my first term, the BBC screened Freddy's monumental series on Spain and Spanish culture. You remember it, right? *Sol y Sombre*. It was a smash hit, they're always repeating it and it got all sorts of awards. I was so embarrassed I didn't go into the department for a month solid. I mean, being at Uni is all about anonymity, not being pointed out as 'that telly bloke' Freddy Greer's bloody kid.

Well, not that I went in that often anyway after the novelty wore off, which it did, quicker than gilt off the gingerbread. It wasn't like the course work was difficult or anything. The first-year essays were a piece of piss – only 1,500 words, most of 'em – and a (wow, faint) 5,000 words or so one at the end of term. I wrote more than that to my French pen-pal Sylvie when I was eleven. I mean, doing a quick critique on Post-Freudian imagery in the work of Sylvia Plath, after a lifetime of unstinting and obsessively analytic intellectualism at home, where each and every fucking comma and sodding subtext of the current Freddy opus was dissected over beans on toast . . . Well, it was child's play. Hell, I could knock out stuff like that before breakfast.

But worse – much, much worse – I *enjoyed* it. I enjoyed learning. I enjoyed studying. The course was simple, sure, but I loved it. You could doss through it if you wanted – and most people did – but if you took it at all seriously it was fab. It wasn't the department's fault it had got such a bad rep. They never seemed to twig when some cynical shysters after an effortless degree took advantage of their naïveté. Times had changed, and the idea of a funky, explorative Arts course was old hat, if not faintly ridiculous in the increasingly conservative corporate world. So sad. But I had no end of fun – well, my kind of fun. The course work directed me up little highways and byways of knowledge that, left to myself, I wouldn't have bothered with. Which would have been a great shame, as they led eventually to my fascination with the Brontës, which in turn made me think I could write a book about them. Horribly obscure, I know. Should have tried a gardening book or a thriller, then I'd never have got into so much bloody trouble and – but I'm getting ahead of myself.

So, back in dear old Uni, rabbiting on about what a lorra, lorra larfs this studying lark was . . . Well, fatal. I think I got labelled a weirdo swot in the first week. The first day, even. My rep was in tatters. A mere flimsy veil barely covering the naked pudenda of my disgusting swothood, in fact.

OK, OK. I'll be fair about it, I didn't exactly have a lot in common with the majority of the students on MH. I mean, I already had a social life in Town, I didn't have to cling to the campus like a drowning matelot. Freddy and Vi had given me a front-door key years ago – what did they care about what I got up to, as long as I didn't puke on the kilim? I mean, after what Frankie had got up to in his wild youth, anything I could manage looked pathetic by comparison . . . No, I was all alone in my post-Goth finery, trotting like a little (well, biggish) lost waif round the various nooks and crannies of the Uni, fairly boiling with disappointment and restlessness. I was bang on and ripe for a little *entertainment.*

So you can imagine how pissed off I was when the girls point-blank refused to come with me to the departmental Christmas shindig. I thought it would be a hoot and we could do some whizz and stand around looking knowing and worldly while all these nerdy students, lecturers and past graduates made dicks of themselves. I really wanted to go. I wanted to show the rest of my year I was cool, streetwise, that I didn't need them or their approval. Yeah, they'd hurt my feelings and I wanted to stick it to 'em. You don't need to be a psych to work that one out – but you do need to be older than nineteen.

But The Ems wouldn't hack it. To be fair, Millie had raging flu and her mother, the fell and scary Mrs Li – a woman who made Fu Manchu's legendary Lotus Blossom look like Mother Teresa – was dosing her with boiled essence of Dong Quai or something on the hour every hour. Strict bed-rest, sod it. Maz just plain old wouldn't. University parties – yeuch; no *way,* José! *Students* – worse, *lecturers!* Puke-a-*rama*! We compromised, and agreed to meet up in our usual after-hours boozing hole, Brandy's, after the party finished, or I got bored, whichever came first. Maz wouldn't be lonely, there'd be the crowd we hung with in there propping up the slimy bar, like usual.

I decided to go with Sam O'Donnel, the only other Brain on the course and a stone punk rocker in the traditional mould. Sam and I sat next to each other in lectures, when we made it in. Problem was, he was an anarchist; politics were his bag and, though he enjoyed literature, he would keep trying to re-cast *Wuthering Heights* in anarcho-symbolic terms. Heathcliffe as a primitive, pre-Revolutionary force, that sort of thing. I just knew he thought I had strayed from the path of righteousness into Decadence and he hoped to convert me, given time.

So it was me an' Sam in the Guevara Bar, whizzless, cheerless and skint, sitting grimly at a tiny table on the raised part at the back of the long, narrow room, studying the beery maelstrom on the dance floor and feeling more than a tad downcast. Because naturally, no one noticed us – me – at all. They had better things to do, like boogie wildly with the Head of Department, a cheery cove who was full to the brim with goodwill to all persons. The place was crawling with MH graduates who couldn't bring themselves to cut the cord and be born into the world; they mooched around like overgrown puppies, tripping over their neuroses and swigging Tetleys. God, and I'd spent hours ragging up my hair, too.

Sam was regaling me with an in-depth dissertation on Gramsci's theory of hegemony, when my attention was caught by a raucous knot of Third Years skirmishing at the bar. Naturally, having left my specs at home due to the vanity of youth, and so seeing everything in an Impressionistic blur, I couldn't make that much out. But I could hear them. They were being very, very loud on purpose. I nudged Sam, and pointed.

'. . . so basically, it's a situation where a sort of alliance of, like, certain social groups can get control, authority, if you like, over subordinate social groups by kind of making it seem like it's totally natural they should be, like, dominant – what? Oh, them, that's Mad Jack's lot. Fuck, I hate wankers like that. Just 'cos he's had that book out, they're all over him like a rash. Groupies.' Sammy scowled ferociously.

'Who's had a book out?' I asked, puzzled. Surely they

were all students? Students didn't publish. Christ Almighty, most of the *lecturers* didn't *publish.*

'Jack Collier – a book of poetry, came out last month. He's the department's golden boy now – Mad Jack. Drinks like a fuckin' fish, scraps all the time; a real piece of work. He's always in here, pissing it up. It got reviewed in the posh papers, his book. Said he was a fuckin' wonderboy. I read some of it – it's fuckin' blunt, anyways, an' clever, dead clever. I tell you what, though, he doesn't mince his words like some of 'em.' Sammy nodded sagely.

'Some of who?'

'*Poets*!' Sammy screamed over the roar of the cranky sound system as it ground out some ancient, groovy tune, like 'Bad Moon Rising', or whatever. 'Poets – you know, it's all wank usually, but not him. He tells it straight. I liked it. I might nick it from the bookshop if I get a chance.'

I pondered a moment. Poetry, eh? Hmmm. 'What's it called?' I said. 'What's it called – that lad's book?' I shouted into Sam's filthy ear'ole.

'*The Ice Pick for Heroes.* It's a reference to, y'know, Trotsky . . .'

'What?'

'THE ICE PICK FOR HEROES . . .'

And of course, at that exact moment, the record stopped and the whole place turned to stare at the nutter screaming at the top of his lungs. The bunch at the bar paused with their glasses raised to their curling lips. Then a stocky, odd-looking fella detached himself from them and walked across to us.

'Oh fuck, Mad Jack . . .' hissed Sammy.

Mad Jack stopped in front of us. He stared at Sammy pointedly and said, 'You gotta problem, mate?' *May-yut* – his North-east accent was sing-song, his voice husky with drink, as I thought. Later I found out he always spoke that way, like burning honey.

That was the first time I clapped eyes on Jack. But, like, I didn't *see* him, just some big-headed wanker who was bullying my friend. All the anger and disappointment – fuelled by vodka-and-lime – that I felt about the bolloxed-up evening, and university, and everything, boiled suddenly in my blood. What a tosser! Who the fuck did he think he was?

Sammy was stuttering and squirming. 'Er, no, no, mate. I was just – I was tellin' my friend about your book. She didn't know . . .' He was puce with embarrassment.

Jack laughed, a short, contemptuous sound. Then he leant forward and prodded his outstretched finger right in Sammy's bony chest. I was *livid.* My mouth opened and the words exited without me even thinking what the possible consequences might be. I didn't care, anyway. I was on a roll.

'You let him alone, you great bully. Fuck *off.*'

That's when he noticed me – Jack noticed me. In films, he'd have noticed me because I was a gorgeous, sultry babe. But I'm not, and he didn't. Jack noticed me because I fucked him off.

He swung his gaze to me, and we locked eyes in one of those childish staring contests. Only it didn't seem childish; it seemed like part of some dance we'd done a million times before, like we already knew each other. Barmy, I know, but that's how it felt. It really threw me for a moment. Then he laughed again and looked away. I felt a silly thrill of victory, but Jack seemed troubled, as if it had knocked him off kilter.

'Oh, well, I'm so sorry, milady . . .' he faked a posh voice. 'I didn't mean to *upset* yer fella here, but he did take my name in vain . . .' His clique, who had moved closer to watch the divertissement, sniggered inanely.

Well, that was *it,* really – the braying fuckers. Light the blue touch paper and *ree-tire,* as Frankie would say.

'Right, that's enough – just you fuck off and take those

giggling wankers with you, d'you hear? Fuck OFF. He isn't *my fella*, you bastard, he's my friend – and worth ten of you, not that it's any business of *yours*, you dickhead . . .' While I ranted on, I became uncomfortably aware that the whole room was staring at this scene in silence. The expressions on the faces floating like spoiled pearls in the poisonous ciggie-haze around me were shocked and horrified. After all, MH was a liberal arts-type course, not a school for pugilists.

If I'd thought to impress them by coming to this party, I had. But not in the way I'd planned, ooooohhh no. I faltered to a stop, panting for breath. Sammy was staring into his beer, mortified. I felt my face go scarlet and a cold sweat ran down my back.

Jack turned so he faced me directly. We were exactly the same height, about five foot eight. Close to – the joy of myopia – I saw his eyes were pale, leaf green, edged in dark jade. They were strange, almond-shaped and slightly tilted in an odd, foreign-looking way. His face was broad, almost crudely made with strong bones and a neat, squared-off cleft chin. He wasn't handsome. His face was too brutal, his bone structure too primitive. But he was . . . compelling. He stood there and stared as if he was studying me. I tried to look away, but found I couldn't. I noticed his hair was short, a true hazelnut brown and unruly, springing back from a small widow's peak. His dark eyebrows met slightly in the middle over his heavy brow-ridge. Weren't you supposed to beware of blokes whose eyebrows met in the middle – or was that in a film? I was *sweating*. My heart was pounding and I felt a right wheeze coming on. God, it was so, so crap . . .

I felt Sammy tugging my sleeve nervously. 'Al, Al, leave it. It don't matter. He's radged, he is – mental. Let it go . . .'

Jack smiled, showing his strong, uneven teeth. 'Yer

man's right, pet – I am mental, me . . . So what now, eh? Shall we scrap, or shall we be pals?'

He was laughing at me, and so were his cronies. I felt the last dam break inside my heart and a hot, dark wave of fury wash over me. The bastard! God, I hated him! All I could hear was that mocking, Geordie voice and the sickening hum of scandalized voices behind it.

I reached out and slapped him hard across the face.

You could hear the collective intake of breath. The mark of my hand went white, then brilliant red on his cheek. He looked absolutely furious and he grabbed my wrist, hurting me. I braced myself for the blow.

But it didn't come. Instead he jerked me closer to him and smiled. His eyes – those strange eyes – were full of something like, well, *tenderness.*

'Well, well,' he said. 'At last, an opponent. My fightin' Venus . . .'

OK, that was enough. Totally weirded out, I pulled away from his grip and legged it. I had to escape, to get away from this madman who looked at me as if we were long-lost lovers instead of two strangers who'd had a barney in a bar. It was freaky. He was crackers. Talk about Mad Jack – Christ.

I leant against the wall outside and rubbed my wrist. The night was deep blue and icy, with a vicious little nippy wind making the rubbish dance. I felt shaky from the adrenaline and horribly embarrassed. I mean, a bit of an argy-bargy was nothing, but a full-scale set-to with the departmental Beau Ideal in front of *everyone* . . . Then, with a stab of horror, I realized I'd left my bag inside. Oh, great, just *great.* The perfect end to a perfect evening. I knew, completely and unquestioningly, I couldn't go back in there, I couldn't. I could *not.* God, no. I turned to face the wall and pressed my hot face against the cold stone. That Geordie *bastard.* It was all his fault. I'd have to leave the bag. Maybe Sam would see it and keep it. I'd go to Brandy's and find Maz and . . .

I felt a tap on my shoulder. I swung round – and there was Jack, my bag dangling from his hand. He seemed sober, suddenly, his strange face like an ancient carving in ivory. Not modern, not of this time at all. I sort of searched inside to feel cross. But I didn't. The rush didn't come. Instead, I looked into his curious, alien eyes that gazed at me with such intensity – and I knew I loved him. I just did. Bang, bang, bang. It was like finding your lost twin, as if we were related in some way.

No one ever believes me about this, but it's true. And it was the same for him. Only, it didn't mean the same to him as it did to me – but that all came later. At this point, I was standing there in the sub-zero breeze gawking like a milk-calf. Then I regained some measure of consciousness and listened to what he was saying.

'Hey, you left your bag. Don't run off – y'don't want to, do yer? Y'feel it, I know y'do, I can see it in yer beautiful eyes. I'm not afraid of yer – I'm not afraid of yer anger like them fools, pet. Christ, I feel it meself. Always have. Don't that make us brother an' sister, Venus, eh? Oh, man, I've waited fer yer so long, so fuckin' long, an' I knew yer, I did, straight off, the minute I set eyes on yer. 'Ere, let's go fer a walk . . . Nay, don't worry, I won't hurt yer – I'll never hurt yer, you belong ter me . . .'

And after that, well, we were never parted. He fascinated me. I mean, we couldn't have had more different families, upbringing, education and such, but it seemed we felt the same about things. He was twenty-two, full of life, full of a kind of raging flame that burnt in him night and day, consuming him. We talked and talked, about everything you can think of. Ideas were like drugs to him, he gorged himself on them and came up shouting like a god.

That night, though, I dragged him to Brandy's and

made sure Maz was OK – and trust me, she wasn't impressed at being kissed off for 'some fella'. At that time, she'd already begun her lifelong romance with Billy Whizz – which for me was never more than a mild flirtation – and when we arrived she was as whippy and jumpy as a feral cat. She looked at Jack as if she wished he'd spontaneously combust. It wasn't an auspicious start and, it has to be said, they never got on. But I smoothed her ruffled fur somewhat and leaving her with a few of our equally wired acquaintances, Jack and I went to the house he shared near the Uni with some other student lads. We lay in his bed, wrapped in the mucky old quilts and just talked, holding each other close as we could – it was fucking freezing in that shitey back-to-back – while the words fell from us like water.

He didn't even try to fuck me that first night. Oh, I would have; God knows I wasn't a *virgin*. I'd been shagging since I was fourteen. Boys who hadn't even pretended to be interested after they'd rolled off me. Who lied to me as a matter of course while I believed them like a child. For years I'd been so bloody grateful when some lad actually showed an interest in me I dropped my pants like a red-hot rivet. It took me *for ever* to realize most lads would fuck a snake if they could get someone to hold its head. None of this made me hate men, or even particularly dislike them, but it did make me divide them into friends and shags. It really hadn't seemed possible to be friends, in the laughing, easy-going way I enjoyed so much with my male mates, with people who seemed to get as much pleasure out of fucking you up as they did fucking you. For a while, when I was about sixteen, I wondered if I was a lesbian, because I loved Maz and Mills so much; but in the end, it was the sheer *otherness* of blokes I liked. Anyway, I finally got the idea you could be friends with your lover. With Jack, anyway. But anything was possible with Jack. Anything.

I won't make out I wasn't surprised he didn't want to do it. I asked him to, in fact. He smiled and kissed me again, then said, in that tawny velvet voice, that we had all the time in the world; sex could wait until we were good and ready because we'd be together for ever. And when he said those trite, Valentine's card words, they became fresh and clean again, as if they'd never been spoken before by anyone, ever, and I had to turn away from him so he wouldn't see me cry. I mean, he could have had anyone, absolutely anyone, that's the honest truth. He had a quality of passion, of being filled to the brim with *life*, that attracted people to him. But he wanted *me*, needed *me*. And he really did think I was beautiful; inside and out. I can't tell you what that meant to me, to be valued, to be *visible* to someone. It was an epiphany, and Jack was my religion. I loved everything about him: his humour – and he could be very funny sometimes, he wasn't the grim, sour Mellors type at all. I adored his brilliant, unconventional mind, and his body; so stocky and muscular from real work, not from bloody 'sports' or hours in the gym like the boys of my own class. I even loved his hands, so square and strong, the way they were always slightly curved and callused because of the hard labouring he'd done to earn money.

In a month, I'd moved in with him. My parents muttered slightly, out of form, but I knew that they were impressed with his reviews. They could say (and they did), *'Oh yes, Alma is living with that new poet, Jack Collier. Far too young, of course, but girls these days . . . They're terribly in love, it's rather touching . . .'* And their lit-crit chums would smile knowingly and store it away for future reference. We had dinner with them a couple of times. Vi totally fell for him and flirted in her bosomy, antique manner, while Freddy got increasingly upper-upper and played the intellectual as he downed the Beaujolais Nouveau. Jack smiled that slight smile of his that gave away absolutely nothing and twiddled his wine glass round and round. I got pissed and watched, like I always did. Yeah, Little Miss I-Am-A-Camera.

I never met his family. He kept saying he'd take me up to see them, then he'd back down. I nagged him about it for a while, and then, to be honest, I just forgot. We were so . . . so enclosed, a sealed unit in our own scene. The family thing never mattered, except I suppose it was one of the things that bonded us together – the fact that neither of us were 'good enough' for our parents. Me because I couldn't – wouldn't – compete with all that fucking excellence, and him because his family thought he was too bloody clever for his own good, and he should have been a miner like his dad. Maybe they were right, as it turned out.

Mind you, Maz and Millie weren't too impressed with all this deathless passion. Maz was very combative with Jack. They genuinely disliked each other and were always on the point of really rowing. Millie never understood my obsession with him; she reckoned he was trouble in a skin. He upset her desire for order, he was too intense, he made her jumpy. But they made a sort of pact to tolerate him, as we always did for each other if one of us went out with a bloke the others thought was a fuck-up. It hurt me, though. I wanted them all to like each other; for The Ems to see the bright, unclouded flame of brilliance I saw in Jack, and for Jack to see The Ems as my sisters, my real family. It never happened. But The Ems let me get on with it, thinking, as I found out later, that it was a crush, a flash in the pan, and it would be over in a little while.

But it wasn't. That January he wrote 'My Fighting Venus' for me – about me. It was like I fed the pyre that burned in him; he gave me everything he wrote to 'look at' first, before anyone else. He said he trusted me completely about his work; that I wasn't like all the others who would say it was great just to please him. I swore I'd never lie to him about whether it was good or not, and I didn't, even when he threw fits and vanished for days on the piss, scrapping and creating hell round Town because I'd said it wasn't up to scratch. He always came home, skint and with a black eye or bloody knuckles. It drove me insane with worry, but I kept my promise. Unlike his pissed-up, blockhead mates, and thanks to Freddy's rigorous training, I knew what good writing was. I might not be able to write poetry myself but, by Christ, I knew what was *real* and what was lies and whore's cant, done for money and fame. Still, it took us completely by surprise when the *Guardian* published 'Venus' as that year's 'alternative Valentine'.

It made his rep solid gold. It was a sensation. Suddenly, his name was everywhere. You see, poetry in England – well, talk about a niche market. Usually it's four pretentious wankers and their token wankerette in a pub in Huddersfield droning about their tedious private lives in that weird sing-song 'recitation' voice tossers like that put on to do readings. I mean, how crap? No one had paid any real attention to it for *decades*. The time was ripe for a revival and what the media wanted was a Bad Boy. They got it, in spades. Jack was the word-up gangsta of Britspeak. He was badgered to do readings all over the country and when he did they were sold out. He was good at it, too, very good. He had that beautiful voice and he came across as completely genuine; he was charismatic, intense. He got a following, like a band or something. You know, fans, proper ones. Sacks of fan-mail as well, asking for his advice, or telling him he was wonderful, the voice of their secret hearts. There were even Jack Collier websites. It was crazy. There'd been nothing like him in British poetry for centuries, not since that club-footed pin-up flyboy Georgie Byron. Jack was a buzzword for hip. We thought it was hilarious, at first.

Then it became a prison we couldn't escape from. Everywhere we turned there were critiques, analyses, articles for and against; features in the Sunday supplements, mentions in columns, discussions on the radio. Finally, there was the big TV interview on Channel 4's major Arts programme *Nexus*. The one that capped it all.

I know everyone said he did it for publicity, for a scam, but that's not true. He didn't mean to walk out like that – I know, I was there. He'd been in a strange mood for days and nothing I did could get the black dog off his heels. He loathed the TV studio, the faffing, the mincing, the shallow fools poking and handling him, trying to put make-up on him. He was getting more and more wound up, hitting the free booze in the Green Room and snarling at me when I tried to stop him. In the end, he couldn't stand that atmosphere of self-satisfied patronage – the fat, middle-class 'welcome to the club, old chap' smugness of the Establishment *danse macabre*. Me, I was used to it, I'd lived with it all my life. I ignored it, same as I ignored them calling me Jack's 'Muse', the tossers. But he couldn't hack it. I could see his flesh tightening on his bones with irritation. I tried to speak to him but it was too late, the cameras were rolling. Then that presenter – you know, Eldon Grosse, oh yeah, sorry, *Sir* Eldon Grosse, as he is now – smirked once too often and boom! Off went the time bomb that was always ticking in Jack's head. He stood up, knocking his chair over, railing and ranting against their hypocrisy, their stupidity. Everyone around me was frozen, gobsmacked. Then, his face stark white and seared with fury, Jack took a step towards Grosse, who was cowering opposite him. I thought – well, everyone did, for a moment – that he was going to deck Grosse. You could see the abject fear on the older man's flabby, spoiled face. I felt sorry for him, to be honest. But Jack just snarled and stalked out, brushing all the twittering idiots aside.

We thought it was all over, his career ruined. How naïve. Fuelled by the 'scandal' – it was a slow season – the whole mad media chainsaw circus went ballistic. Even the *Sun* did a spread on 'People's Poet Jack Blows Stack on Snob TV', going on about what a decent working lad he was and how he'd refused to be talked down to by the poncey arty-farty types. They approved, apparently.

Depending on which rag you read, Jack Collier was the dark, driven genius of a new revolution/the media's darling wild boy/the prophet of the New Age/the true People's Poet/the greatest working-class hero since Lennon/the intellectual's idol, etc, etc, etc. Pick which label suits your own personal agenda. Whatever. One guy in particular, Leonard somebody-or-other, hounded us constantly. He was always ringing up wanting me to dish the dirt. Kiss and tell. Like, as *if.* Wanker. One thing all the pundits agreed on, though, was that Jack Collier was a total phenomenon, a one-off. He was destined for real greatness and he was set to spearhead the government's huge new Millennium Arts Imperative. Jack was a genius, he could do no wrong. He was the *Messiah.*

Barely two years later, he was dead.

4

Oh, oh, it still hurt so much – a hot, squeezing pain that made me grab my knees and rock back and forth on the freezing porch like a fool. I can't tell you how fucked up I'd been after Jack died – I mean, I even stopped eating, and believe me, it was a running gag that normally I'd eat a Flake if I was having my *leg* cut off. I dropped over a stone in weight and my mind unravelled like a badly stitched frock. I missed him so much, so much. It was like I'd been cut in half.

Wheeze, wheeze – I couldn't get the air into my congested lungs. It always happened if I thought about that night. The doctors say it's 'just stress'. Yeah, *just* stress. You see, the fact is, we'd had an argument. One of an increasing number. Things had got really bad. The rows seemed to start from nothing and explode into – he – I mean . . . It was really shitty, you know. Nasty, no holds barred. He was in a real mood most days at that time, writing things then ripping them up and going out to get pissed; doing the same thing the next day, and the next. I couldn't talk to him, it was killing me. So we rowed. Always about the same things. I thought all this hype was putting his writing in danger, distracting him. I was jealous, too. I thought I was losing him to his new-found London friends with their skinny, coke-fuelled fast-track lifestyles. Every weekend he was off down there, and soon the weekend started on Wednesday. I stayed in

Bradford, in our cruddy room, making like I wasn't bothered and hanging out with The Ems. And mighty impressed they were with all this, I can tell you. They nagged and nagged me to blow him out, get rid – but I couldn't. I knew if I hung on tight it'd all be OK in the end. And it would have been. It would.

That night, it had started as usual. There was this woman kept ringing him up, and if I answered the phone, she hung up. She'd done it again that night, twice. Second time, he picked up the phone and they talked for ages, or so it seemed to me as I huddled by the door, listening. Sasha, her name was – it sounded like a kiss, the way he said it. Or was it in my imagination? He certainly thought so. Apparently, she worked for a major publisher and could do him good. I said I'd thought he wasn't interested in that sort of careerist stuff. He wouldn't answer me; so it went on and on, round and round, getting more and more vicious. In the end, after . . . Well, he just fucked off; slammed out the door laughing. But there was no happiness in that laughter. It was dark, jagged and cold. It frightened me. I expected he'd get arseholed and stagger in the next day full of apologies like usual . . . But he didn't. I never saw him alive again.

At the inquest, Mike and Terry said he'd stepped off the kerb into the path of that lorry laughing, his arms outstretched, that savage laughter ringing from him like a curse. They were all piss-drunk, of course. It was put down as an accident. It was an accident. It was. Jack had promised he'd never leave me, we'd be together for ever. *It was an accident.*

I wept in the porch, invisible. I wept for my lost love. I wept in a ritual of grief I'd repeated over and over and over. It was comforting, in a bizarre kind of way.

I had just managed to get it under control and stop crying when the door opened and a man stepped out, leaving the door ajar. I snuffled and peered up at him blankly.

He spoke. 'Look, er, you can't stay here, it's simply out of the question. I'm sorry . . . You've been asked to leave once and so, well, if you don't go I'll be forced to call the police . . . I don't want to, but . . .'

I was about to open my mouth and reply to this, when I was pre-empted. Millie's voice cut across the bloke's burbling like a sword.

'Excuse me – Tim, what's going on here?'

I looked up gratefully and tried to stagger to my feet, but I was all over the shop, my legs having gone totally numb. Millie clocked me.

'Al! My *God*! Al! Christ, are you all right? You look *awful*! Here, give me your bag, what . . . Oh, do stop *chuntering*, Tim – it's Al, my friend, you remember her . . . Obviously there's been some sort of emergency – my God, you're *freezing*, Alma. How long have you been . . .Yes, yes, I'll take care of her now, Tim. No, of *course* you and Sara didn't realize . . . It's *quite* all right, really. Hold the door a minute while I . . . No, really, it's fine. Don't *worry* . . .'

As Millie hustled me into the hall, I reached into my pocket and pulled out the pound coin the lass had given me.

'Here, your friend, she – she gave me this . . . I don't need it . . .'

He went puce with embarrassment, and shot back into his flat muttering 'sorry' like a mantra.

Mills was incensed. All the way up the stairs, into the flat and through to the kitchen she muttered about 'Thatcher's Children' and 'Blairite Britain'.

'Giving you *money*! My God, that's their answer to *everything*, absolutely *everything*. He didn't even look at you once, did you see that? Typical. Absolutely *soulless*, like bloody *robots*, the lot of them. Money, money, *money*, that's all they care about . . .'

When Millie got mad she never raised her voice – she *italicized.*

I slumped into a chair and, taking off my specs, laid my head on my arms on the wooden kitchen table. I felt like someone had beaten me all over with a baseball bat. I just listened to Mills fulminating against the world and heard the comforting domestic sounds of the kettle going on, the teapot being fettled and smelt the sugary vanilla of the biscuit tin being opened. What a girl Bruce was. If Satan himself in all his sulphurous glory appeared to her, she'd put the kettle on and ask him if he wanted milk and sugar.

'. . . I mean, I do *wonder* where it's all *going.* Here, drink this . . . I'm going to run a bath for you, Al; you're soaked through . . .You can borrow some of Leif's clean things. I don't know about undies, though. Mine won't fit you and . . .'

'It's OK, I . . . I've got some clean pants in my bag. I was at that conference with Laura, in Whitby – I told you . . .' I couldn't seem to get a grip on the words properly, my mouth felt ropy and numb.

Mills paused in her bustling and leant against the worktop. Putting her hands on her hips, she regarded me narrowly. I suppose I must have seemed totally whacked and out of it. More than usual, I mean. I looked back at her and tried to smile, but my phased-out lips wouldn't hack it. They just did a wobbly, tremulous tic. Mills sighed in exasperation and raised one of her faint, smudgy eyebrows. Her eyes were so black you couldn't make out the pupil, but you could see what she was thinking; her brain was calculating what best to do, what was practical, sensible. Like always. That was my Millie, my Iron Lotus.

I snuffled pathetically, then sneezed like a freight train.

'Right, that's *it.* Into the bath with you before *pneumonia* sets in. Have a good, long soak, there's plenty of hot water with the new boiler.' She waved her little hand imperiously. 'No, no – don't tell me *anything* until you've had your bath. I'm going to phone Maz. She'll know what to do.'

I lay in the bath sweating, the steam thick with rose-geranium and lavender. Every so often I twiddled a trickle of hot water in with my big toe and felt my bones heat up. I always felt better in water – baths, or swimming, or the sea. Not lakes or rivers, though; I don't like the dank smell. Freshwater spirits are always tricky, in stories. Phillip proposed to me by the river at Kettlewell. I should have twigged.

Sighing at the thought of my stupid Phillip-years, and poor, poor old Wellington, I hauled my parboiled carcass out of the tub. I stood swaying dizzily for a moment then wrapped myself in one of Millie's fluffy pink bath-sheets to dry. Taking a wad of loo-paper, I wiped the mirror and studied myself. Well, I wouldn't exactly be appearing in next month's *Vogue* with that haircut – or maybe I would, given the current state of fashion.

The trouble was, frivolous though it might seem under the circumstances, I looked so fucking boring these days. The fact that I'd let myself go pissed me off not because I suddenly wanted to be some Wonderbra'd club chick, but because of what it *meant*. I'd given up. Given in. For the last few years I'd let Phillip 'suggest' and 'advise' me on what to wear, what to say, what to think. Not that he ever *dictated* to me – oh no. Phillip never, ever made a definite statement about things, he just put on a certain expression and 'wondered' if I was 'aware' of the impression I was creating. If my choice of whatever was 'mature'. Believe me, it was easier to be *mature* in the end, rather than be frozen out for weeks. The result was I'd turned into a Grade-A frump. If it wasn't trackie bottoms and trainers, I wasn't bothered. For 'special occasions' I had two truly gross 'proper' frocks in shades of sludge. I even replaced my triple set of earrings and nose-ring with practically invisible pin-head studs. As for my tattoo – well, I needn't tell you I hadn't worn anything sleeveless for years.

It was a great tattoo as well. Jack and I had the same one, on the left upper arm. A big black full-blown rose, tribal style, with lovely faint grey swirls of shading wrapped around the thorny stem. We'd gone all the way to Birmingham for it, to Van Burgess, the top guy in the country. Jack had insisted. *No fucking scratch is going to mess up my Venus,* he'd said, kissing me, *Only the very best for us.* The roses had bloomed out of the blood like a promise, like they'd grown out of our flesh, not been drawn by the needles. Everyone had been a bit, well, shocked when we'd shown them off; tattooing wasn't as mainstream as it is now. *How romantic,* they'd cooed when they got over the initial frisson. *How sweet.*

But it wasn't romantic, at least, not what they'd meant by that silly, overused word. Jack had talked about it for hours: the exact symbolism, the meaning, the subcultural implications – our personal reasons for choosing that particular design. *A black rose, eh, pet? Black as the rage that drives us both, eh? Sure, the world will think it's cute, but we'll know. Oh aye, we'll know, my Venus. It's a covenant . . . our pledge. We'll never be parted . . .*

Phillip said it was self-mutilation. A neurotic behaviour akin to cutting up, or anorexia. He liked to cite the statistics on the proportion of criminals who have tattoos. He said this showed that only alienated, marginalized individuals with low self-esteem felt the need to mark themselves in this primitive and repulsive manner. He suggested I take steps towards a *mature* resolution of my inner conflict by saving up to have it removed, and by having anger-management counselling. Then – at least in the early days of our relationship –

he'd remind me he really *cared* for me despite the tattoo, despite everything, in fact. *Despite.* What a cruel word. What an ugly, cruel word.

I heaved a huge, wheezy sigh, dropped the towel and peered myopically into the misty glass, trying to see who I was. I favour my mother not my father – our Frankie took after him. I've got Vi's short nose, medium sort of mouth, ovalish face. As an American I once knew always said: *Alma, honey, you're so English-looking, you couldn't be from anywhere else!* She meant it as a compliment. Reddy-brown hair, light hazel eyes – the usual Northern white-girl pallid, sun-starved complexion. Long hands and feet. I rather like my hands and feet, as it goes. My nails are a nice shape, with good half-moons. Big shoulders, big hips, narrow waist, muscles covered in a smooth fat layer from swimming. The normal amount of cellulite and unexplainable lumpy bits. Absolutely unfashionable. A bit like a human seal, really.

But I never enjoyed looking at myself. No, I mean it, I avoid mirrors like a vampire. Truth is, I've never . . . How can I put it? I never got *used* to myself. I just don't like the way I look; but with my bone structure, no amount of dieting would make me Kate Moss, so fuck it. Been there, done that, starved myself until my gums bled. I still looked like me, only less so. I'd always felt lumpen, ugly – until I met Jack.

Shivering despite the central heating, I got dressed in Leif's XL grey marl joggers and hideous 'Viva Picasso!' sweat-shirt as quickly as possible. God, I was getting really morbid. A twitch ran over my skin like when a fly lands on a horse. Brrr. I wandered out into the kitchen carrying my soggy clothes.

'Mills, is there anywhere I can dry these?'

'Give them to me and I'll wash them . . . No, if I don't they'll go mouldy and disgusting. Talking of which, I put your *horrible* coat in the hall to dry. No one will steal it, *believe* me. When *will* you get a decent one? I mean, you've had that rag for *years*, it's totally past it, I . . .'

I burst into tears. I couldn't help it; it just happened, involuntarily. Millie was mortified. Sobbing like a kid, I told her everything, only pausing to have a suck on my Ventolin when I got to the bit about Wellington. It was crap and I hated telling it, but I knew I'd have to get used to that; maybe repetition would blunt the pain. I hoped so.

Anyways, Mills was livid. I'd seldom seen her so cross. Generally, like a lot of Chinese folk, she disliked displays of strong emotion, and you could only tell she was narked by the way she spoke – her italics – and then only if you knew her well. But this time, she was royally pissed off. Her round, amiable face that always reminded me of a friendly porcelain piggy-bank, set into hard planes and angles. Her eyes glittered like obsidian and her mouth was like a pale, tightly compressed peony. In fact, she looked more than a tad like her mother, which was a bit scary.

'The absolute *bastard*! What – that's – God! *Wellington*! I can't believe – I mean, I *do*, but . . . How can anyone do something like *that*? It's awful – *awful* . . .' She paced around the room in her sticky-socked feet like a miniature lioness. 'Wait – I mean, just *wait* until Maz hears this. She'll be *furious*! You know what she – well, and me too, to be honest – you know what we thought about *Phillip*. God! It's . . . Divorce is one thing, but *Wellington*, a poor defenceless *animal* – that's *murder*!'

I snivelled and nodded glumly. 'I don't give a shit about splitting up with him, Mills, I really don't, but Wellington . . . God, Mills, I always thought Phillip saw me as a bloody disappointment; a nothing, you know, a *mistake*, but he must really *hate* me to do something as cruel as that . . .'

Millie stopped pacing and looked at me, sharply. 'Is

that what you think? That he wasn't bothered about you? Come *on*, he was jealous as hell. You had everything he wanted: the posh academic family, famous parents – all the things you couldn't care less about and he thought he deserved. Worst of all there was *Jack*, who he could *never* live up to. God! I'd feel *sorry* for him if he wasn't such a *bastard*! I said as much to Maz at the wedding. We were worried *stiff* about you. I don't know how your parents could have let it go on, I really don't. I thought you were going to *faint*, you looked so awful. But there we are; no use crying over spilt milk.'

Millie automatically put the kettle on again and rinsed the cups under the tap, her back stiff with indignation. My mind drifted back to pick at the memory of my wedding. Mills was right, it had been a bloody travesty. A quick, furtive ceremony at the shabby register office, me feeling like shit in Phillip's choice of a suitable wedding outfit. A pale green suit, a gross meringue of a hat, girl's shoes and a *handbag*. No bridesmaids, because Phillip didn't want a 'fuss' – i.e., he thoroughly disapproved of The Ems. It was like a bad dream, one you can't wake from. The reception was worse; an incredibly expensive do at the Carlton Hotel Empress Suite in Leeds. The guests were chosen for their value to Phillip in his relentless clamber up the academic ladder and, he hoped, into the same spotlight as Freddy. Still hopes, for all I know. As I watched him schmooze, I realized why he'd married me. Not because we were 'intellectual equals', or because he thought I needed to be 'nurtured' and 'cared for', as he put it in our brief courtship. That was a crock. He'd married my family. He'd wanted an entrée into their world, and I was the price he had to pay. Well, I suppose I'd suspected as much, but I'd longed to be looked after, protected; to lay down my weapons and my grief and rest while someone else sorted things out for a change. Phillip told me what I wanted to hear. Maybe he meant it all – at first. God knows he liked having control over everything.

I felt relief the sham was over at last. But *why* hadn't I had the gumption to do it myself and save Wellington? Sometimes, I seemed to lack the willpower, the moral courage, to confront things. I was fine at anything impersonal: politics, literature, work. I'd stand up to anyone. I was always getting into it with stupid fucks who told racist jokes and thought that was OK. But personal things, no. I was crap. Like at Jack's funeral.

Mike had told me about it. He'd been invited because he was Jack's oldest mate, though it was a strictly family affair. There'd been talk about making it a big media event with the great and good putting on black ties, but the family vetoed it. They'd never got to grips with Jack's fame, and as for his work, they hated it. Thought it was peculiar and not very nice, apparently. They wanted him back how he'd been. The eldest son. The boy. Anyhow, Mike wasn't going; as far as he was concerned it was way too heavy, he couldn't handle it, man. I wasn't going to go either – but I did.

I had to get three trains and then a taxi to the crematorium in the small town on the north-east coast where Jack was from. It was cold, and the wind off the sea was salt and bitter. I thought I'd missed it at first; running in panic up the drive to the horrible, squat building. A fringe of reporters huddled smoking moodily in their cars, talking into mobiles, or trying to get into the service. They didn't notice me and I slipped by them as quick as I could. I told an attendant I was family and, without question, he showed me to the right room. Perhaps he saw the look in my eyes, I don't know. I slipped unnoticed into a chair at the very back and studied the mourners greedily. I caught glimpses of profiles: an eye like Jack's, the corner of a mouth similar to his. The faces so oddly familiar with their Scandinavian bones, the remnants of Vikings stamping the past into the future in those tilted eyes and ivory skins. It knotted my heart to see them – to see him in them; his sisters, his father and mother . . .

The vicar jabbered on about 'a brilliant scholar', 'a great loss' 'a good son'. The usual platitudes. He didn't seem to know who Jack *was*. Never mentioned his poetry. It made me furious. I went out before he finished and waited, out of sight of the journos, trying to summon up the courage to introduce myself to the family. To make a connection.

I failed. They were so united, so close-knit in their grief. I heard his father snarl something at the jostling knot of reporters in his thick, sing-song accent, and heard his mother and sisters sobbing. I couldn't stick myself into their grief. What would I say? *'Hi, you don't know me, but I'm Jack's live-in girlfriend. You know, the one he never brought to meet you . . .'* Sure. I watched them trail away to their cars, then I left. They hadn't even noticed me. No one had. I was a widow, but not in anyone's eyes except my own. I was invisible again, even in this. I felt as dry and bleached-out as the driftwood on the beach nearby. It was over. All that was left was this terrible, brutal ache in my heart that wouldn't go away.

Millie tapped me on the shoulder, startling me out of my reverie. 'Al – *Al*! Here, more tea. Maz says she'll be over around eight with pizza, so have a biscuit to put you on. Her mum's got Tatum, so it'll just be us. We can get all this sorted out. I *didn't* tell her about your *hair* – but you *wait* . . .'

5

'Jesus H. Christ, A – what the *fuck* 'ave you done to your *'air*? Yer not right, you. What did yer do, 'ack it off wi't pinking shears? Give me strength . . .'

Maz bridled like an outraged mill-lass, her skinny frame undulating like a strand of cooked spaghetti. Her voice – like Marge Simpson's only Bradford – rose an incredulous notch. She simultaneously sucked her cheeks in, wobbled her head and heaved a deep, pained sigh. She was seriously freaked.

Grovelling was my only option. 'Soz, Maz, but . . .'

'Don't get on at her, Maz. It's awful what she's been through. Tell her, Al love . . . Go into the living room and sit down, I'll bring the food through. You tell Maz *everything* . . .' Millie hustled us out of the kitchen.

I told her. And when I got to the bit about Wellington, her language was as blue as her contact lenses. Maz swore like a trooper, but only outside work – she said it was her safety-valve. Mind you, this time, even I learned some new and interesting linguistic combinations.

Maz stretched out on the IKEA rug, propped up against Millie's knees, stuffing pizza in her mouth. She had a new hairstyle, a short, shaggy page-boy bleached white and tinted lilac at the ends. It flickered and flipped as she nodded her head and grunted encouragement through mouthfuls of greasy dough. Eventually, the pizza was gone – she'd eaten most of ours too – and I'd finished my tale.

'What a cunt,' said Maz calmly.

'*Maz*!' Millie hated what she called the C-word.

'Well, he is – you know it, I know it and she' – a long, bony finger, its acrylic talon lacquered jade green, pointed at me accusingly – 'had the fuckin' benefit of it. Am I right? I think you'll find I'm not wrong.'

We agreed she was not wrong. Millie struggled out of her chair while Maz took off her huge flap-fronted trainers then rubbed her distended stomach. She looked like a python that had just swallowed a goat. I felt totally washed out and shivery again – all I needed was flu, but that's what it felt like, bugger it.

I only half heard Maz counting off tried-and-tested revenge tactics, and Millie telling her violence was never the answer.

'His bad deeds will return to him six times over – at least. His karma will see to that. I mean, whatever we did to him – or yes, OK, *had* done to him – wouldn't, you know, be as bad as what he'll bring on himself.' Millie folded her arms and looked inscrutable.

'What *are* you on, Bruce?' said Maz.

'No,' I said woozily, 'she's right – like, he's a cunt and cunts get trait like cunts – just not always straight away, if you see what I mean. He'll get his, yeah?'

'Well, I wouldn't exactly have put it like that,' said Mills primly. 'But yes, he'll get his.'

'In the meantime, before fuckface decides to do anything funky, A, get Matty to do your lawyerin'. Go see 'im tomorrow. Hit Mr Slimy Twat in his fuckin' wallet, where it 'urts.'

'She's right, Al. Matthew will take care of everything. He'd love to, I'm sure. I'll ring him first thing and make an appointment.'

Matthew was Millie's eldest, and favourite, brother. Their father had died years ago, when Millie was a nipper, so Matty was the one she turned to first if there was any trouble. He was a respected partner in the law firm of Singh, Li & Craven who had mucho fancy offices in the middle of Town. Matty was doing well and going far – and good luck to him; he was a very nice fella.

I knew I'd have to be sensible about the split. The Ems were right, as usual. I felt irked that everyone seemed to know what was best for me better than I did, but there was no point being childish about it. Phillip might be forgetful at the moment, but he wouldn't stay that way, oh no. Underneath that mature, *caring* exterior lurked the little boy with a splinter of ice in his heart. Everything that had gone wrong with our marriage would be my fault entirely. He would never give an inch. I had to be *sensible*, or he'd pull me inside out and chuck me in the bin like an old sock. So I agreed: Matty would be my lawyer. The Ems were pleased and Maz rolled one of her skinny little spliffs to celebrate.

The evening progressed like so many evenings we had spent together. We talked, mostly about the same things, going back and forth over the same subjects until they were worn and soft with use. I sometimes think it was like we were weaving a cloth out of talk, all the strands of our lives threading back and forth, up and down, making a dense, intricate sort of pattern that we repeated and repeated until we could understand it. We never got bored of it, we were so easy with each other, wrapped up in these conversations that had gone on for years.

Millie talked about her family: Mark, her younger brother, was opening a hyper-cool café-bar in Leeds called 'Wok Around The Clock' to go with his lunch-time place near the Uni – 'Wok And Roll'. But the Great Matriarch Mrs Li wasn't pleased about the style one bit. Too modern, not traditional. But she liked the huge wads of cash the places generated and at least it deflected her from railing at Mills about her only daughter living with a *black man*.

Maz gave us the low-down on Tatum, now six and creating havoc wherever her little Kiddie Nike'd foot trod, apparently. Mrs Sielicki worshipped her granddaughter. Tatum was learning to speak both Yorkshire and Polish as her nana hadn't much English, even after all these years, though Maz's dad, Thomaz, was as near to a perfect Yorkshireman as you could get for someone born and raised in Kracow. The child was a comfort to the Sielickis as Maz' younger sister Olga had died a couple of months before Jack of a heroin overdose. Olga's death still freaked us out; we'd had no idea she was a smackhead, like, *none*. Of course, Maz blamed herself, on account of her doing whizz, spliff and nowadays, the coke. Not that she'd ever touched skag or anything, or let her recreational habits interfere with her work, but she felt she'd set a bad example. God, Olga . . . Such a fucking waste and such a horrible death. No one found her for *eight whole days*; she just lay in her bedsit in Leeds 6 all alone. Puts cogs on me to think of it, even now. Poor fucked-up Ollie . . . Then Maz fell for Tatum and, despite the 'shame' of her being an unwed mother, her parents thought it was God giving them Olga back again. We knew Maz felt guilty about how little time she spent with her child, but she worked all hours at her hair salon – 'Le Salon' – making enough money to support her daughter and sub her parents, who were getting on. Tatum's dada was Rom, another second-generation Polish Bradfordian. He was dead charming, but, man, what a waster – no help from that quarter. He was a DJ at present, but Maz was lucky if he remembered his daughter's *birthday*, never mind child support. Maz and Rom had run an on/off relationship since school. At present, it was on. Sort of.

Anyways, finally, after we'd smoked a bit more and had more tea and KitKats for the munchies, Maz said she was off to Rom's and issued me strict instructions I was to be at Le Salon by eight thirty the next morning for repairs. Millie said she'd phone Matty about an appointment and would call Laura to tell her I wouldn't be in to work for a couple of days because I had flu. Laura would know what was up, of course, academia being what it is – a hotbed of gossip and intrigue – but I wanted a cover story for a while until I got my head together. I said thank you, thank you, thank you, until Maz chucked a cushion at me and told me to shut it.

We saw Maz out, then turned in. We didn't do kissy-huggy things like in movies – we're from Bradford. People'd think we were queer . . .

Outside, it was raining again and I fell on to the narrow futon and listened to the familiar pattering and the humming counterpoint of the traffic. I knew the city so well; I knew what it would look like outside – the shining gun-metal streets webbing away into the night, stitched with lights and twitching with the dark and the unknowableness of thousands of lives. I strained my ears and heard cars and the roar of a bike; then the sound of a drunk singing himself home followed by the rise and fall of Asian voices coming closer and then fading as they passed. Lads, I thought, a bunch of lads on their way back from somewhere in Town. The bed linen smelt sweetly of fabric conditioner and I wished I was as organized as Mills. I knew I wouldn't sleep. How could I *sleep* after all this?

Then the alarm shrieked and it was seven a.m.

6

One of the many things I admire about Maz is Le Salon. She isn't what you'd call educated; she never, ever reads a book and she cannot understand why I love reading. She thinks the devil makes work for idle hands and therefore books belong to Satan. Well, OK, not really, but you get the idea. She hates anything 'arty', too, despite being so creative about hair and stuff. In fact, she gets quite narky if I say anything like that. 'It's work,' she says, '*work* – nothing else.' Le Salon, though . . . She really went for it after college, worked like a bastard, seven days a week doing mobile hairdressing on top of her salon job until she'd raised the necessary ackers to get the place together. It paid off. It wasn't a big place, but it was ultra-cool. Clients came from *Leeds* to have their hair and nails done. Incredible, but true. A big booster was when *Vogue* did a hip new provincial salons feature and Le Salon got a mensh as being a 'style-conscious sanctuary for the Northern babe'. Maz personally was booked two months in advance and the bamboo-and-bleached-wood interior, with its white orchids in stone pots, and white accessories, was always heaving with hipsters. Somehow or other, Maz knew instinctively what was *now*.

So, there I was, feeling totally cack outside the door at eight twenty-five exactly, waiting for Queen Bee. Huddled in the doorway with me was Chloë, the head stylist, and two shampoo girls, Chanel and Kerry. Chloë was smoking in her lugubrious way, her tiny blanched hand scissoring the ciggie, her pretty, delicate face nipped with cold. She coughed resoundingly – the bubbling hack of a lifelong smoker – and glared balefully into the rain like an irritated china doll, then waved her fag in the general direction of my head.

'Trouble wi't fella, then?'

I was taken aback. 'Er, yeah. How . . . ?'

'No offence, like, but it's dead common. Y'see it all the time in this line o'work. Trouble wi't fella and off comes the hair. At least you dint shave yer head wi' a Bic razor, like I seen once. Wanted me to "fix it" – hah! You'll be all right, you got loads left. Nice, thick hair, too.' She nodded approvingly and I felt a disproportionate glow of pleasure.

The shampoo girls snuffled and fidgeted, their unformed puppy faces white with fatigue. Chloë took a last, deep drag on her Benson's then heaved it into the gutter and sighed heavily. The rain pinged off the grey, metallic-smelling pavement. We waited.

''Ey up –' I heard Chloë say mournfully – ''ere's Madam. Look lively.'

Maz uncoiled from her Jeep and, with a lot of fumbling, chuntering and disabling of alarm systems, let us in. I hung around the product display admiring the funky packaging until, suddenly, Maz threw a bulging bin-bag at me. I caught it before it knocked the Fudge stand over.

'Some clothes for yer. I bin meanin' to give you 'em for ages, but I didn't think *hubby* would approve. Still, there you are. It's an ill wind . . .'

'Er, thanks . . .' I started to rummage in the bag.

'Don't get excited. It's some o' that urban combat stuff. Looks shit on me. Too baggy, too flappy round me legs, I look like a scarecrow. It's either you or t'Oxfam – so it may as well be you.'

It was all practically brand new. There was a jacket, a grey Womble-fur hooded Hooch, the sort of thing I'd always wanted . . . Plus a creamy, flecked zip-up hoodie fleece, a Quicksilver one, really nice; two skinny black T-shirts; a white strappy vest with 'Le Salon' on it in funky seventies pink glitter lettering; and some charcoal peachskin baggies.

'Don't mek a fuss, you done enough of that for a bit. I couldn't stand that bloody old jacket of yours no more. Bruce says she found yer bloody *hair* in the pocket. Honest, you do me in. Now, sit 'ere an' let Chanel shampoo yer. Kettle on, Kerry – hop to it! Chlo's got a lady at nine fifteen . . .'

Maz cut my hair extremely short and spiky, then I watched in a kind of trance as she bleached it and tinted it pale, pale blue. I mean, I wanted her to do it, she didn't make me, but there's something about hairdressers that robs me of all willpower. I phase out, hypnotized. Sometimes I fall straight to sleep. Still, this time I managed to stay awake, but pliable, throughout the whole thing.

When I was completed to her satisfaction, Maz had Kerry practise nails on me. She gave me a manicure then lacquered my nails sky blue with sparkles.

Maz sauntered over, scissors in hand. 'Mmmm, not bad, but yer gotta stop grunting while y'work, Kez. Breathe, breathe – else you'll drop dead or summat. Nice nails, though. What d'yer think, A?'

I looked at myself in the big mirror. A stranger looked back at me. Not a frumpy-dumpy-lumpy Invisible Woman, but a bright, shiny *Interesting* Woman. That did it – I lost it totally and burst into tears.

Everyone was really sweet and rushed round getting me coffee. Even the clients were nice. One woman said I looked like she'd like to but daren't for fear of what her husband would say. Maz scolded me, and told me I was useless. Then, putting her coat on, she decided we needed another coffee – but this time at Cha-Cha's. Maz leaving the salon was unheard of, but her twelve thirty lady had cancelled and . . . Getting her out the door was a nightmare, mind – talk about Napoleon's retreat from Moscow.

'Go, go – get out, Maz. Honest, I'll call you on yer mobile if we need yer – which we *won't*. Go on, you've only got forty-five minutes – *go*!' Chloë herded us out into the drizzle, while the rest of the girls laughed at us.

We sat in Cha-Cha's amid the splattery paintings by local artists, the crappy sub-funky hand-decorated wobbly tables and the fake-fur-framed mirrors drinking hot chocolate instead of coffee, with cream and sprinkles. After wiping her mouth with the back of her hand, Maz lit a fag and stared at me meaningfully. I couldn't believe how tired I was and stifled a yawn with my sparkly, blue-tipped hand. I realized Maz was still looking meaningful through her veil of fag smoke.

'What?' I queried, busy with my drink.

'Money. No, not for the hair, stupid! I mean, *your* money – 'ave y'got any? Did you an' fuckwit 'ave a joint account?' Maz could get very annoyed with me about money. She thought – rightly – that I didn't take enough interest in it.

'Er, yeah. For the housekeeping and such. He did all the bills an' that by direct debit. Said it was the modern way of doing things. There's his car money account, and I think he's got a stash fund, but I was never that bothered. Oh, and I think I've got about two hundred pounds in an old building society account – for emergencies an' that. Why?'

'Get yersel down t'bank today – straight away – an' take out half the cash in the joint account. At *least* half, mind. If it were me, I'd 'ave the lot. Else he'll shut yer down an' you'll 'ave hell on getting any dosh outta him.'

'I can't do that . . .'

'Yes yer can. 'E owes yer – good stylee. 'E's fucked yer off outta the 'ouse, murdered yer cat – an' that's gonna look well in court, the fucker ... You never shagged about or owt like that, yer kept 'ouse for 'im, yer helped 'im wi' 'is career, did typin' for 'im, all sorts. Am I right?'

'Well, yeah – but ...'

'No fuckin' "buts", Missie. 'E'll screw yer over if 'e can – an' 'is new squeeze will 'elp. They'll do it all very nicey-nicey, like – all very fuckin' *civilized* – but you'll be t'loser, mark my words. You mean jack shit to 'im now yer no use to 'im. 'E'll do yer like he did yer cat, 'e's that sort. Cold. So get down t'bank an' tek half. Let 'im squeal. You put all yer savin's in, dint yer? Get it an' put it in a sock under t'bed. It's yours be rights.'

'I don't know, Maz ... I just don't *do* stuff like that ...'

Maz drew on her fag and looked fierce. 'Then it's about fuckin' time yer did. It's about fuckin' time yer grew up, A. Yer can't moon around being Jack fuckin' Collier's widow fer ever, tendin' 'is bloody shrine. Look where it's gotten yer.'

I near jumped out of my skin. Maz must have clocked my expression because she stubbed her fag out and gave a short, mirthless laugh.

'You thought no one noticed? Get a life. You bury yer nose in them books and off you trot to fuckin' La-La Land. All high principles an' no fuckin' common sense, that's you, A. You've not bin right since that bas–, since Jack died. That's 'ow y'ended up wi' fuckbritches. Jus' 'cos yer mam an' dad dint pay no mind to t'state you were in, dint mean me an' Bruce dint. An' Frankie, fer that matter.'

'Frankie? What ...'

''E e-mails Bruce at work now an' again, askin' after yer, checkin' up on the old 'ome town an' that. That's one of 'er little perks, Bruce – 'er bein' global at the Arty Buggers expense, seein' as she's fuckin' *in-dis-pen-sible* in that office, like. Not daft, our Bruce. Anyroad, Frankie, 'e knows more'n 'e lets on ter *you*, believe me. Sound as a pound, our Frankie. Wish 'e were *my* bro.'

I was gobsmacked. I'd assumed that no one was interested, no one *cared* . . .

'Oh, buck up. Just be 'appy people love yer, stupid. Everythin's gonna be all right. Now yer rid o' needledick y'can get a whole new start, like. Do what you want ter do, not kow-tow to anyone. Now, I'm off back. Take this t'pay for that muck we supped – no, my shout, your turn next time – an' *don't worry*. It'll be all right, I swear. Just you get yersel' down t'bank and do as I say. Honest t'God, you arty types, how the *fuck* d'yer manage?'

I looked at her narrow, triangular face, so intense and white, her contact lenses blazing sapphire and her lips painted iridescent violet, and I thought: this is my best mate and I don't have a clue about her, or Millie – or *anyone*. I don't know anything – nowt about owt, in fact.

I finished my watery chocolate and wandered towards the bank, as instructed. There was something going on in Centenary Square, the big new piazza in front of the Town Hall. Well, it's not new now, and the big paving slabs are polka-dotted with discarded chewing gum but it still feels new. It's nice, though, on the whole; very Continental. Trees with little lights on an' all that. Grassy knolls. You know the kind of thing. If they pulled down the fucking monstrosity of a seventies high-rise office complex opposite it would be positively *designer*. I couldn't really make out what was happening, some sort of Gas-and-Lecky Board promo with info wagons and enamelled-looking girls in silly corporate fun outfits leafleting the stragglers who trekked agoraphobically across the still-unaccustomed wide-open space. I paused and sat on a bench, my brain whirling.

The weather seemed to echo how I felt, with patchy clouds swept across the sky by the stiff breeze, little stabs and leaps of warm sun bouncing across the ground like cosmic super-balls. Mixed-up weather, like my mixed-up head. For a moment, I watched a young couple flirting. The girl sat on her boyfriend's knee, her long perm pulled up into a high topknot, her platform trainers pistoning as she wriggled in pretend outrage at something he said. He looked at her, his dark eyes shining, as if she was Helen of Troy, not a little estate lass from the arse-end of nowhere. It made me feel about one million years old and dead inside – ashes and cinders and cold, cold, cold. My life was over; at least, that sort of life – love, romance, call it what you like. All gone. I'd never be as carelessly happy and as in love as that couple, ever again.

I got up slowly and went to the bank. I didn't want to have anything to do with the money. My pride told me to ignore it, but if I did, how would I live? How would I find the deposit money for a bedsit? The money I earned working part-time for Laura was fine for a married woman wanting a bit extra, but it wouldn't stand any big demands. No, I'd have to do as Maz said and get in there before Phillip nobbled it.

When I got the mini-statement, I realized that he'd done a bit of petty nobbling already. The last time I'd checked, two weeks ago, there'd been just under ten grand in our joint account. Now there was roughly six and a half. What had he done with it? Taken his squeeze to the friggin' Bahamas? I suddenly had the creepy feeling he'd been planning this break for a long, long time. Well, of course he had, but it hadn't struck home till now.

The bank lady was very nice and explained I'd have to have the bulk of the money I wanted in a banker's cheque, so I said, Yeah, whatever – only give me five hundred in cash. Then I sprinted up the hill and stuck it all in my old building society account and arranged to get a new Link card. For me, this amounted to high finance.

The cash was burning a hole in my pocket, badly. Retail therapy was the only option. For so long I'd been 'good' about never getting anything new, I was desperate. New hair – yeah! New specs – perfect! I turned into the big opticians on the corner and chose a pair of cool lightweight, rectangular silver frames, plastic Reactolite lenses, the works. I gave Millie's number and wondered if I could manage to wait a whole week to get 'em.

High as a kite and manic as hell, I almost ran to the Body Piercing Studio. I always have been a bit prey to mood-swings. Put me under any stress *et voilà* – the Big Dipper. But, to my mind, extreme circumstances called for extreme measures. It seemed perfectly logical. I mean, how many times had I yearned to go in and get something done? Now, I could do what the fuck I liked. *What the fuck I liked*. The piercing girl was a bit taken aback at my hyper-hyper burbling, but she agreed to enlarge my existing piercings, put proper ball closure rings in them, and pierce my lip.

I know some people will go, *'How can you be so casual about something like that? Ugh!'* Well, I can, I don't know why. Nothing like that – piercing, tattooing, weird hair things – ever bugged me. I think if I hadn't done the Phillip thing I'd have been all over with tattoos and piercings. I don't *get* all the girly shriekings and flutterings about bodies. All that pathetic 'Oooh, does my bum look big in this?' And that crap about women don't fart, or smell, or have – God forbid – *body hair*. It's a sort of wincey, fey girliness that I find irritating, personally.

Anyway, I digress, as my old English teacher used to say. The piercings . . . Well, yeah, the enlarging hurt a bit – all that shoving and wriggling with an *instrument*. But after a bit of sweating and chuffing we got there, and I thought the effect was much improved. The lip – labret, I should say – I got an anaesthetic spray for that and felt nowt. Just a hardish push and a faint, slightly sinister crunching noise. But what a head rush; talk about adrenaline! Got to beat bungy-jumping, any day. I felt a great wave of some inexplicable feeling *drench* my whole body, then my mind seemed to fill with light and clarity. I imagine it was the endorphins kicking in, or whatever they are. Some natural body chemical that lets you deal with pain. I tell you, if they bottled it, they'd make a fortune. I loved it.

My chin was a bit red – from the numbing spray mostly – but I looked at myself and thought, *yes*. It was rather dashing, like a beauty spot. I wanted more straight away, but the lass said no. Give this lot time to heal up. Relax, clean them in weak salt-water, chill out and come back in a fortnight for my tragus and belly-button. She seemed concerned about me, and suggested I take a zinc supplement as well. I said yeah, yeah, whatever; but my mind wasn't on anything except this high rolling wave of . . . hysteria, I suppose, if I'm truthful.

I rushed to the little flower booth outside the Arndale and bought a huge bunch of trumpet lilies and eucalyptus for Millie. Then I went to Thorntons and got a big box of Continentals for Maz. Still buzzing, and having to manage flowers, choccies and a bin-bag of clothes I thought, *Sod the bus,* and fell into a taxi.

Millie did her tits when she saw me at tea-time. I'd come down off my natural high by then and had started to cough, a nasty little raspy cough that punctuated my wheeze. Millie blamed Maz for leading me astray.

'Oh, for God's *sake* – you two! I should have come with you, I really should. You're not fit to be let out alone, never mind with *her*. I told her to give you something neat and manageable – and what happens? You look like a . . . a *raver*!'

I hacked becomingly and felt my fever notch up a little.

'And *listen* to that cough! You're not well. What *possessed* you to stick bits of metal in your face?' Millie fumed as I struggled not to cough again. Then she sighed heavily and put her hand on her forehead.

'Sorry. *Sorry*. No, really. God, I sound like my *mother*. Honestly, sometimes I open my mouth and her voice comes out – it's *awful*. It's just that I worry about everything. I shouldn't get angry though, it's not . . . acceptable. But I do worry, you know. About you, about Maz, about my brothers – everything. I can't help it. Sorry. Sorry. But, Al, you really *aren't* well. You should rest in bed until you get on a more even keel, you really *should*. You've had a big shock. It's no wonder you feel weird. Please, *promise* me you'll rest? Please?'

I nodded and mumbled, 'I'm sorry, I should try and . . . get steady, calm down. I don't know. Look, the flowers – they're for you, Mills. I don't want to upset you – you've been totally brilliant to me, you really have. I just . . . one minute I'm high as a kite, the next I feel like the lowest scum in the universe.' I laughed weakly and rubbed my head. 'I will rest, I swear. You're right – I'm wrong. Soz. Double soz, in fact – triple, even.'

She pressed her lips together tightly in a sorry-smile and shook her head, ponytail bobbing, escaped wisps of black hair floating round her flushed face. 'They're beautiful, thank you. Now, you stay here while I arrange them properly in my big vase and we'll have some pasta for tea and watch telly – how about that? A quiet night in, just us two?'

'Sorted.'

7

I woke up crying the next morning. Have you ever done that? It's shit. I thought Wellington was lying on my legs, like he always did, taking up half the bed. But, of course, he wasn't. It was only the mess of quilt and bedspread I'd raggled into a heap during the night. I'd had terrible dreams, claustrophobic and full of a horrible, sinister atmosphere.

I didn't want to get up. My mouth felt like it had been lined in old carpet underlay and I could smell my own breath, it was that bad. The room, Millie's fragrant boudoir, was fusty with farts and sour sweat smell. Charming. I had a raging thirst on, though, so I crawled off the futon and, staggering to my feet, opened the window. Fortunately, it was quite nice outside, almost warm and sunny. An efficient little breeze bustled through the curtains and freshened things a bit. I decided that as soon as I'd had a cuppa I'd strip the bed and wash the linen. Even thinking about it exhausted me, but I fumbled for my specs and dragged myself into the kitchen.

Ah, tea – the Protestant's chicken soup. Even the bitter, vegetal smell of it made me feel better. Since I'd virtually packed in drinking – except the odd glass of red wine with dinner – and drugs, apart from a little grass, caffeine was my drug of choice. If I could have it intravenously, I would.

I slormed about eating some toast and feeling decidedly gross. It had to be flu; my chest was sore and tight with infection. Of course, Mills was right, as ever. I should stay in bed. I'd no sooner decided to be sensible and do that when I realized it was Thursday. It was Thursday, and it was ten thirty. Shit, I should have been at work an hour ago; I'd had two days off already.

I stumbled to the phone and rang Laura's number. It rang so long I was about to give it up as a bad job when Laura answered. I started to mumble something about how sorry I was, but I had trouble at home, and . . .

'I know what's happened, my dear,' Laura cut in. 'Phillip's back from his . . . well, shall we say his *holidays*, and he's playing the wounded soldier. Says you've done a bunk.'

'God, Laura, that's not true. He chucked me out and . . . and . . .' I couldn't say it over the phone. Wellington's presence was still with me from my dream. I was totally choked.

'Oh, please – nothing Phillip does surprises me. Why don't you come in this afternoon, say, two thirty, and we'll have a little chat? Please don't worry yourself, my dear, we'll sort something out. Got to dash now – that little Simmonds girl is *weeping* in the corridor . . .'

I replaced the receiver feeling nauseous. What a lying toad. I might have guessed he'd twist things to suit himself. He'd be wanting me out of the department. What was it they always said about office romances? That the bloke never left, it was always the woman who cleared out? Well, Phillip wanted me out of his life, full stop, and he'd do it by a little aside here, an inference there; that was his style.

I sat at the table and tried to think. I couldn't stay here for ever, Lief was due back in three weeks and the flat was way too small for three people. Not that they'd ever ask me to go; they weren't like that. But I couldn't stay, dripping around like the ghost at the wedding, moaning about how miserable I was. No. I had to get my shit together or top myself. Either or.

I thought about it.

Actually, I'd thought about it a lot over the years. I know it sounds morbid, but I used to wonder if this whole life business was all it's cracked up to be. Like, what would it *really* matter if I did the deed? Who'd miss me – a nobody from nowhere who'd never even finished writing her precious book. Never had a proper, successful relationship, with children and stuff. Never been travelling, or seen the Taj Mahal, or swum in the Pacific. Never got famous or did anything interesting. Apart from The Ems – and my family – who'd give a shit? I used to plan my funeral, too. It was great; huge loads of white flowers, black velvet-draped catafalque, crowds of people weeping. *'I suppose that I shall have to die beyond my means,'* as Oscar said. Oh yeah, I'd thought about suicide often, but I never tried it. Why not? Because I knew damn well that the moment I shuffled off this mortal coil an invitation to the party of a lifetime (where I'd meet Mr Fantastic and a publisher would coo, *'My dear, I'm fascinated. Send me your manuscript!'*) would plop through the letterbox and it would be too late, *because I'd be dead.*

So, yet again, dying didn't seem like a good option. Well, I could save it for later if things got worse. I coughed loudly and spat up something nasty. At this rate I'd be dead soon anyway. Oh shit, life it was, then. As she is lived by useless buggers like me. I washed, put on my new clothes and decided that I'd go get my stuff from the cottage.

Not that I was being dead brave or anything. Thursdays were Phillip's busy days, so I could be pretty sure he wouldn't be at home. It wasn't like I had much, anyway: a couple of bags of crap clothes, a few 'bits and bobs', as Millie would say, my laptop, my books – most of which were in Laura's office – and my collection of

Virgin Mary figurines. Yeah, well, everyone collects something . . .

I got a taxi. Hey, why not? I was loaded.

Phillip's precious Audi wasn't in its usual place so I paid the taxi-man and got out feeling fairly secure.

The struggling lilac tree was beginning to come into bloom, straining its skinniness towards the hazy sun, its tightly folded greeny-purple flower cones mingling with the floppy leaf-tassels of the laburnum next to it. I paused for a moment underneath them and breathed in the mingled sharp green and dusty rank scents. I'd always meant to do something with the bit of garden we had, but somehow . . . Now it was too late. I said a silent goodbye to the two scraggy city trees.

Feeling like a burglar, I opened the front door. The whole place seemed . . . different. A faint chemical–floral perfume lingered hazily in the hall. At first I thought it was the trees outside, but it was too synthetic, too sour-sharp. I've always had a tremendous sense of smell, really extreme. My hearing is also uncannily good. 'Bat-lugs', Maz calls me. And my sense of taste is excellent, too. For food, at any rate. Makes up for being so short-sighted, I suppose. Anyways, the 'scent' was coming from a rather nasty greeny-black nylon devoré scarf hanging on one of the coat-hooks. Miss Priss's, I supposed. She certainly hadn't wasted any time.

My heart gave a lurch – what if she was here, tucking into a Ryvita and cottage cheese, or whatever women like that did at lunch-time? Peeling a grape with her hair in Carmens. Waxing her bikini line. I don't know.

I called out in a falsely cheery voice, *'Anyone ho-ome?'*

My voice echoed in that hollow, empty house way. Safe. I went to the kitchen. It stank of bleach; some sort of exorcism ritual? Banish the evil spirit with the cleansing fumes of Domestos? I laughed grimly, in what I hoped was a hard-bitten, cynical way.

Then I noticed the enormous bunch of flowers on the worktop. A florist's bouquet of crappy pastel carnations, gyp, crysanths and pallid, still-born roses, all faded and browny. I took the card from the glaucous greenery.

'To my darling little Kitty-Kat from her loving Mr Tiger XXXXXX GRRRRR!'

Mr Tiger? Kitty-Kat? Oh my good God! I sniggered silently – then felt oddly aggrieved. Phillip had never bought me a bunch of flowers, not even on our wedding day. Or given me a pet name. Now he was *Mr Tiger*. Justice might be blind but she obviously had a sense of humour. I resisted the temptation to take the card and show The Ems. Grrrrrrrrrr.

The rest of the house reflected Phillip's new-found sensitivity too. The central heating was up a couple of notches and on the black leather sofa there sat a huge, fluffy pink teddy; the nauseating flat-faced cartooney type, not the nice, snouty sort. Another smaller, fresher bunch of flowers was on the window sill. Where had he got the vases from? This was beginning to be creepy.

Upstairs in the big bedroom, a taupe polyester (OK, I'm a snob) slip-nightie lay across the immaculately made bed and the bathroom was well stocked with make-up in varying shades of beige by Clinique. I looked in the laundry bin. She wore lacy thong knickers. Pul-*ease.*

I could have bitched all night, I could have bitched all night and still have bitched some more, as Frankie would say. But I felt sick, as if I'd never existed, as if I was in a total stranger's house by accident. Then I had another minor heart attack – my computer, my disks – Christ!

I shot into the spare room, my 'study'. The oubliette, as I called it due to its extreme tinyness and lack of natural light. All my clothes, including my good winter coat, lay crumpled in a heap on the narrow bed. I dumped them on the floor in a panic and there, to my intense relief, was my laptop in its carry case and my box of disks.

As I stepped back, something crunched on the wooden floor under my trainer and I looked down to find the broken shards of one of my Virgin Marys, the first one I'd ever bought. It had obviously been dropped and now lay in two pieces; all I'd done was crush it further. Brightly coloured bits of crude terracotta had been ground into the floorboards, and only the sweetly smiling head was intact. Phillip had done did this on purpose, I *knew* it; his little revenge. Just an accident-on-purpose, unless you were a Freudian. Which he was. How he'd hated the Virgins. Primitive, superstitious, ugly, he'd called them. *You're not a Catholic,* he'd snap at me. *For God's sake, get rid of them.*

But I wouldn't, and now the remaining seven gazed serenely at me from the window ledge with their grave, tender expressions. *You're coming with me, ladies,* I thought. *Don't you fret.* I bent down and picked up the little head, putting it in my pocket. I remembered buying her, my first Virgin. I'd have been about thirteen. I don't know why, but I had to have her. She wasn't expensive – dirt cheap, in fact – but I'd spent all my pocket money on ice-cream so I had to beg the cash off Freddy. I got her in a little shop near the cathedral in Seville. All the way back to La Morena, Frankie and I had been subjected to a long disquisition on the influence of mystical Catholicism on the work of Lorca and lesser known Spanish authors like the prolific and daring Emilia Pardo Bazán and the Basque, Bernardo Atxaga. Then Violet had chimed in with a ramble about the Virgin in Art, the eternal Mother, a symbol of ancient fertility and powerfully iconic in the Jungian sense, distorted into a vapid sweetheart for the masses by a vicious and brutally oppressive patriarchal church . . . It went on and on and on until I threw up from the heat, the ice-cream and the jouncing car. Frankie was so grateful to me for stopping the Parents *lecturing* he bought me a Mars bar the next day in Ronda.

Yeah, Frankie – I missed him, but it was better for him in America, especially after all the scandal. I felt a chilly shiver run through me and hurriedly picked the clothes I wanted and wrapped up the Virgins in bits of a sheet I ripped up, packing them tightly in a knackered old suitcase, stuffing any spaces so they were snug as bugs. It didn't take me long to pack the rest. In fact it was pathetic how little I had. A second-hand laptop, a bin-bag of clothes – the bulk of which was my winter coat – and trainers, with a sponge bag chucked in for luck. Plus the suitcase full of Virgins. Oh, and a fabulously ancient frame rucksack that once belonged to Freddy. I filled that with the books and papers I'd kept in the house. Done and dusted. Sorted for fuck all.

I felt washed out by all this *excitement,* so I dragged the stuff downstairs, put the lecky kettle on and shoved a teabag in a cup. I rummaged round in the 'things' drawer for Ibuprofen and necked two tabs with a swig of water. Then I checked the Ansaphone.

There were a couple of messages from Phillip's colleagues about work stuff, and a cryptic message for me from Laura about the Leeds Medical Museum. I'd sort that out this afternoon. And there was a message from Frankie.

'Frank calling Earnest, Frank calling Earnest, come *in,* Earnest – yeah, it's me, honeypie. Call me *right back,* you know I *hate* being kept wai-*ting*. It's been ages and *ages,* you bad sib, you. And, hey, love to Phil baby, *natch.* Byeeeeeeee.'

Frankie's voice had a note of genuine concern under the sing-song campy voice he liked to affect and which he considered ironic – you know: that's how straights think gay men are supposed to be, so that's how he'd be, then, only more so. It wasn't his sexuality that was warped, it was his sense of humour. It was true I hadn't phoned him for yonks and I felt a stab of guilt. I decided to ring him back, on Phillip's phone bill. I reckoned it would be about midnight in San Francisco, but that didn't matter, Frankie stayed up all night. In fact he always said he'd moved to San Francisco because they have an all-night stationery store. Among other things.

I dialled.

The phone picked up almost instantaneously and a gruff, manly voice answered. It was Thom – or *Th*om, as I always called him privately – Frankie's boyfriend.

'Hi, this is the Gartner–Greer residence, how may I help you?'

'Th– er, Thom, it's Earnest, uh, Al . . . Is Frankie . . . ?'

'Oh, honey, we were *so* worried about you! He'll be thrilled. Now, you hold on, don't move an *inch,* and I'll fetch him for you . . .'

I heard him pad heavily away – he's a big guy – and call Frankie. I held the receiver and wondered, as I always did, at the vast distances involved. I could picture Frankie's long, bony face with its hawkish, prominent nose and intense blue eyes, like a young version of Freddy only with a super-neat flat-top. The same quizzical expression as our father's, too, and the same big, skinny, knuckley hands. I could almost smell the clean, spicy scent he used and feel his lanky frame folding me into a hug.

His voice jerked me back to reality. 'Well, aren't we quite the Greta Garbo. Where have *you* been, Miss?'

'Frank, something – something bad's happened, I . . .'

His voice lost its Transatlantic queeniness and he suddenly sounded exactly like Freddy. 'Alma, are you all right? Are you hurt?'

'No, no, I'm OK, it's just . . . Oh, Frankie . . .' And I told him the whole sorry shebang.

Frankie always was a good listener. He never interrupted or tried to rush you, just ummed at the appropriate times. This time he did mutter 'bastard' when I told him about Wellington, but that was all.

'Have you told Mum and Dad?' he said in a business-like way when I'd finished.

'Christ, no. I hadn't even thought about that. I . . . you know . . .'

'Well, you should. In fact, I think you have to, before one of Freddy's delightful cronies does it for you – you know what these *scholars* are. Then get your little butt on a jetplane and come right over here for a long vacation. No! I mean it – Thom means it, too. You know how much he loves guests. It's a huge apartment, plenty of room; we won't get in each other's way. I'll pay for your ticket. I'm loaded – and I mean *American* loaded, not Euro-loaded. I landed the contract for the new Paramount websites – yeah, it's great, *mucho dineros, mucho mucho*. Come *on*, Al, it'll be like old times – remember Windermere? I bet you *do*!'

'I . . . thanks Frankie – and thank Thom for me . . .' We both knew I wouldn't go. Don't get me wrong, I adore my brother and I miss him loads, but *America* . . . Too far, too *far-out*. Maybe some time when I was more together; like, when I was *ninety-six*, at this rate.

'OK. Come when you like – no pressure. My house is your house, and all that. We really do want you to come stay. If you need me urgently, get that poppet Millie to e-mail me. I'm going to send you an internal modem for that crappy laptop of yours. It's perks – I get all sorts of things free, don't worry. Then you can get online and Bob's your Auntie.'

'How often do you e-mail Millie, then?'

'Oh, now and then, now and then. You know, I like to keep up with the gossip. She's a dark horse, your friend, quite the little global tripster. Bet you didn't know *that,* did you? See, the benefits of the Web are *manifold, my dear, manifold.'* This last bit was an imitation of Freddy we used to do as kids and we both laughed at the same time.

'Actually, Maz did mention that Millie was a bit of a techno wizard, but it was news to me . . . Yes, she's fine too, same as ever, still mental. Baby's fine, the salon's fine – very cool. Everything's fine . . . well, except, you know . . . It'll be all right, it will, honestly. It's this flu thing's getting me down a bit . . . Yeah, I'll take some Vitamin C, I promise. Look, love you to bits . . . Yeah, and *pieces.* Bye – say bye to Thom . . .'

I put the phone down. Why the *fuck* was America so far away?

8

I got a taxi back to Millie's, hauled my kit up the stairs and dumped it in my room. I was starting to think of it as 'my' room which, under the circumstances, wasn't very useful. Pausing only to rub some of Millie's prune-coloured going-out lippie on my chapped lips – and very fetching it looked, too – I shot out of the flat again and, getting *another* taxi, I set off for the Uni. A three-taxi day, wow.

When we pulled up, I practically fell out of the knackered Metro. Everything seemed to be wavering in a very disconcerting way and, although it wasn't warm, a trickle of sweat ran down my back. I knew the feeling only too well, having been chesty – and not in the Pamela Anderson way – since a child. Bollocks and double bollocks.

I shouldered my way through a knot of smoking students on the front steps and into the department. The familiar smell of sweat, dirty cleaning rags and cheap deodorant assailed me as I staggered up to Laura's office on the first floor. I paused, futily attempted to steady my breathing, then knocked sharply on her door, trying to look composed.

'Enter,' Laura called, and I pushed the door open. She wasn't alone. Her PhD student, Imogen, was with her and it was pretty obvious they'd been 'having words'.

Laura and Imogen glanced up perfunctorily and Laura

said, 'I'm sorry, do you mind – consultation hours *are* posted on the door . . .'

'It's me, Laura – Al . . .' They both looked up again with big round eyes. Laura recovered first.

'Ah, so it is.' She seemed not to want to comment on my changed appearance in front of Imogen, who was frankly, and unkindly, goggling. You could practically see the gossip machine whirring in her narrow skull.

I made a shall-I-stay-or-shall-I-go gesture and Laura raised her hand, indicating I should stay.

'Imogen was just leaving, Al. I will take your comments on board, Imogen. I am fully aware of your position, but now, if you'll excuse me . . .'

Laura began shuffling papers dismissively, her face impassive. Imogen was livid. Turning on her stack heel, she picked up her bulging briefcase. As she went past me she paused, glared at me and then spoke, her flat, Estuary voice sliding out of her thin lips like a dull blade.

'Oh, Alma, *so* sorry to hear the bad news, but you'll bounce back, won't you? You always *do* . . .'

She slammed the door shut behind her and I sank into the spare chair feeling murderous. What a *bitch*.

Laura sat with her eyes shut and the heel of her hand pressed to her forehead. One of her headaches in the making, no doubt. I'd always admired Laura; she was the perfect older woman, in my opinion, with her loose capsule outfits in neutral shades and her gleaming silver hair cut in a neat blunt bob just below chin-level. The room smelt pleasantly of the light, floral cologne she favoured. She had a brilliant mind too, even Freddy said so. Currently she was researching her great theory about the relationship between genius and syphilis in the major artists and writers of the past.

When I first heard about it, I'd thought, *What?* I mean, it sounds so crazy. What possible connection could there be between bacteria and art? But as I did more research for her, and she explained things to me, it all seemed to fall into place. It's pretty complex, but to put it as simply as possible . . . We – Westerners, that is – have no natural predators. Nothing scaly with claws is going to drag you into an alley and rip your gizzards out. We're safe. Or so we think.

Because, you see, we've been looking for predators in the wrong place. Wrong size, even. Alter the scale: not big, hairy monsters, but microscopic *germs*. They're our predators. They prey on us, they use us. They might not *think* the way we do, but they certainly survive pretty damn well. I mean, what's consciousness anyway? Viruses get along very well without the TV, or books, or maths, or music . . . They breed, they multiply, they succeed. And they never totally kill us off. They always leave enough of us alive to continue the cycle. We may fight back with drugs, but they simply adapt and become immune to our weapons. Look at MDRTB – Multiple Drug Resistant TB. The White Plague, they call it. No drug can control it and it's spreading like billy-o in deprived areas. That's bacteria 1, humans 0.

And maybe, just maybe, the viruses, germs, bacteria or whatever, are like farmers, too. Tending us, their cattle. Especially that great survivor, syphilis. And like a good master, it rewards us, same as you'd give a horse an apple. Only our treat is *visions*. The fantastic, demented, syphilitic visions that result from extended, untreated syphilitic damage to the brain. OK, you don't see it these days, what with the cures we have – until the thing gets itself immune again, of course. But in the past, when there were no drugs to combat syphilis . . . Take Nietzsche, for example, or Blake, or Joyce. Way, way beyond the common herd – *dazzled* by visions, by insights and inspirations that seemed to whirl them into the absolute extremities of human thinking and creativity. And syphilis – God, it was absolutely epidemic in previous centuries; a bigger threat than AIDS – and as incurable. Nietzsche suffered all his adult life and died a raving lunatic because of it; Blake was terrified of it, as was Joyce, who may even have passed it to his daughter. Even that macho blow-hard *Picasso* was shit scared of it; look at the *Demoiselles d'Avignon* . . . puh-lease.

The connection was there, but proving it . . . I mean, it was a lot more complex than that, obviously, but that was the basic principle. It was a beautiful theory, exquisite.

Mind you, it got poor old Laura into no end of hassle. A lot of academics preferred to consider themselves the Lords of Creation and their reverence for genius was blind and unquestioning. They didn't want to think a bloody *germ* was responsible for *Ulysses*.

Laura was under pressure to change direction. She'd got her grant because the concept was so daring and the presentation so cogent, but increasingly, in these conservative times, the subject matter was considered 'disgusting' and 'unsuitable'. There were people – like Phillip, for example – who whispered it was bringing the department into disrepute. I felt really sorry for her because I thought it was a fantastic idea and perfectly possible, even though it meant I had to troll through some incredibly gross pictures of syphilitics with big holes eaten in their dicks and no noses. I used to wake up every morning thanking God I didn't have it. Enough to put you off sex for life, those pics. Perhaps I should e-mail some to Phillip . . .

Anyways, to get on. I sat quietly until she'd recovered herself a bit, and then suggested I put the kettle on. We drank our coffee and ate the M&S biscuits she normally saved to bribe the Chair of Philosophy with. She said nice things about what she called my 'New Look' and then I asked her what Imogen had been so worked up about.

'Imogen is a very *angry* young woman. She sees favouritism everywhere, I'm afraid. Really, she should be doing the job I gave you. Appointing you was rather unusual, but I felt, with such a sensitive subject, I had to have someone *simpatico*, you understand. No, she feels that I've been helping you unfairly . . . Helping you to "jump the queue" . . .' Laura sketched quote marks in the air and sighed.

I nearly choked on my biscuit, which had suddenly turned to cement in my mouth. 'Jump the queue to what?' I spluttered.

'Your book. Rumour has it you'll be published as soon as you finish it, solely on the grounds that you're Freddy's daughter and because I have "used my influence", whatever that means. Imogen thinks this unfair – not, I will add, that she bothered to check her facts before storming in here.'

'But that's ridiculous! I mean, it's not – I'm not even sure I want it published. It's just my – well, like a hobby, only more so. How did she know about it? I never told anyone, apart from you, obviously, and . . .' The penny dropped with a resounding clatter. Laura saw it on my face and smiled wanly.

'Yes, indeed. Phillip is consolidating his position, I'm afraid. Utterly ruthless. Has he even read any of your work?'

'No. I didn't . . . he never . . . I haven't shown him any of it. He wasn't interested. I *tried* once, but he seemed so *bored*, I gave up. I feel – used to feel – really guilty about it, like I was too tedious and obsessive, but now . . .'

'I see.' Laura sipped her coffee thoughtfully. I seethed.

'God, Laura, it's so unfair. It's bad enough being in Freddy's bloody shadow all your life, without Phillip sticking his neb in, too. Hasn't he done enough already? What does he want?' I filled Laura in on what had happened, the bare bones. Repetition didn't make it easier to tell. It just made me feel stupider and more . . . *humiliated.* My face was burning by the time I'd finished, and not from fever.

Laura looked genuinely distressed. She had cats and knew how much you can love an animal. I wouldn't like to be Phillip the next time he tried to smarm round her.

'Horrible. Absolutely horrible. All I can say is you're better off without him. Without a doubt. You poor . . . Words fail me.'

She turned her thin gold bangles round and round on her wrist as she did if she was upset. I don't know why, but suddenly, I knew what Phillip wanted. Me out of the department. It was no use, I'd have to give the job up. If I stayed, this bollocks about favouritism and the irregularity of hiring me would rebound on Laura. I took a deep breath and saw twinkly spots in front of my eyes.

'Actually, I was thinking of taking time out to . . . to go travelling. Er, you know – see a bit of the world. Yeah, I was going to tell you but then, then this all happened and . . . Well, I might as well get on and do it now.' There, my resignation delivered with my usual flair and aplomb.

Laura knew bullshit when she heard it, but she also knew she had to protect herself. We looked at each other and understood what each of us had to do without speaking.

Laura smiled slightly. 'More coffee? Travelling – how lovely. Have you seen much of Italy? It's fabulous at this time of year. Florence, Rome – *bellissima*! I envy you.' I smiled too. It was like stepping through a surreal minuet when really we wanted to scream with rage. Or at least, I know I did. My teeth were clenched so hard I thought the back ones would shatter.

'Er, no – I haven't been to Italy. I thought . . . somewhere quiet, you know, finish the – the book . . .'

Laura broke in: 'You know, I had an idea the other day – before all this. But it's a good idea, I think. Why not return to university as a mature student and get your Masters and PhD? Then, when your academic record is impeccable, no one could carp if you got your book published. Come on, you'd sail through the academic side of it. And you must finish your book – unfinished projects are a curse and, from what I've read of it, it's rather better than you think. Please, give it some thought. It's such a waste of your potential otherwise. You know I'll help you any way I can . . .'

I sat still as a statue, my mind exploding like sprung clockworks. I was flattered Laura liked my stuff, but *go back to Uni?* No – I'd given up on all that, it was over. Finished. I was too old, too . . . I couldn't . . .

But it tickled in my head. I could . . . I might even enjoy it . . .

A spasm of coughing doubled me up and left me purple and gasping, my glasses misty.

'Are you all right, Al? My God, you're not well. Look, you get off ho–, er, to where you're staying, and we'll sort any details out later. You need to rest. That sounds nasty.'

Why was everyone telling me to rest all the time? Didn't they think I would if I could? OK, OK, they were right, I needed to get well before . . . doing whatever it was I was going to do with the rest of my life. I stuttered through a goodbye, feeling as if I should say more, and left.

It had turned humid as I wandered down the hill into Town. I felt light-headed and sweat was rolling off me. I wished fervently it would break. A big thunderstorm, lightning, the works. Something grand and operatic to mark the way my old life was slipping away like a skiff trailing its moorings. The tower on City Hall yawed alarmingly as I craned my neck to take in the crazed mass of statues and gargoyles that crusted every possible surface of the huge building. I liked Bradford, I really did. No, strike that – I loved it. Sure, it was crap; backwards and barmy, not smart, clever and smug like London or Leeds. But it was beautiful in its crazed, surly, don't-give-a-fuck way; full of character, even if it wasn't a very agreeable character sometimes. Like a great stone crag rearing out of the moors, weather-beaten, fretted into fantastic shapes by the wind, it was solid, real, indomitable. It was home. I didn't want to leave. But Laura was right. I had to make a life-plan and stick to it, not flip-flop around aimlessly, hoping it'd all come right by magic.

The fever boiled in my blood like poison. I felt like shit. I'd think about it all tomorrow. Aw, fuck it – make that a four-taxi day . . .

9

I spent the next four days in bed. Really in bed, I could hardly move. Millie wanted me to see a doctor but I knew there wasn't any point. Me and URTIs – upper respiratory tract infections, to the uninitiated – were old buddies. All the doc would give me were antibiotics that would fuck up my system and give me thrush. More drugs to feed the bugs and make them immune. Ta, but no ta.

So I lay and sweated and drank black tea. No dairy, it makes phlegm. I read a lot, books I'd meant to read but hadn't had time for. When I couldn't read any more, I got up and sat wrapped in a quilt on the sofa watching late-night, true-life B-movies on Channel 5. I *longed* to go swimming, to slide into the cool, forgiving blue as only a habitual swimmer can desire that chlorine soup. I felt like a hot, greasy, fat slug.

Mills was great. She came home at lunch-times to check on me. She changed my bed linen and made tempting little dinners. Maz came and ordered me to get better, on the grounds that I was being slack (playing nurses never was her strong point). Then she said I was the same colour as my hair, and laughed like a drain.

By the following Thursday I was well enough to go and see Matty, though I felt ghastly and looked worse. He talked to me in his cool, calm way about the divorce and said that it would be OK, provided I didn't want maintenance, a settlement or anything else along those lines. I definitely did not. I'd got what I wanted out of the cottage and the bank. I never, ever wanted to see or speak to Phillip again. If he played sticky, Matty could threaten him with anything, as far as I was concerned, to keep him away from me. Matty said he'd do his utmost and smiled his rare, beautiful smile from behind his steepled fingers. He didn't mention how much his lawyering would cost – and, to be honest, I never thought about asking. He made the whole visit seem like a nice chat with an old friend. Then he drove me home in his new silver BMW, saying he had some business out that way. Really I think he thought I was going to peg out in front of him, the way I kept coughing.

After thanking him profusely, I staggered up to the flat and collapsed on the sofa. It was a weight off my mind, knowing Matty was handling the legals, but I was getting more and more worried. I had to *do* something.

Frankie phoned again and after a long chat reminded me I ought to tell the Parents. I mooched about the flat in that not-quite-better way, plugging in my laptop on the kitchen table and staring moodily at my book, now code-named 'The Great Project'. I cleaned up, washed the dishes, washed my bed linen, washed my hair, painted my nails . . . Yeah, you got it: avoidance tactics. It was no good. I phoned Spain.

Now, I realize that if you've had a happy childhood and love your parents dearly, this may seem a trifle melodramatic. If, on the other hand, you always felt that sneaky, nagging worry that you weren't good enough for Mummy and Daddy, that on the whole – no offence and all that – they'd rather not have you around, and that you were a dreadful *disappointment* to them in every possible way, you'll understand I wasn't looking forward to informing them I'd fucked up yet again. You see, despite being an 'adult', it still got to me, the whole family thing. It still stuck in my side like a wound that wouldn't quite heal. I knew they'd never wanted me, never planned to have more than the one, golden child that was Frankie. They'd said as much – hastily adding that, of course, they'd been thrilled when I came along . . . Not hastily enough, though, for a worried kid. It had coloured my whole life, this feeling that I wasn't really wanted. Tolerated, but not *wanted*. So, you can imagine how I felt as I dialled Spain. My hands were shaking and my mouth was cottony, like I'd been sucking a hankie.

It rang twice and Vi picked up. 'Yes?' Her voice sounded slightly irritated, and I could imagine her wiping her paint-smeared hands crossly on her artist's smock – a real one – and leaving rose madder on the handset. It drove Freddy bonkers, her leaving paint everywhere.

'Er, hi, it's me . . .'

'I'm sorry?'

'Me, Mum – Al, Alma . . .'

'Oh, *Alma* – why didn't you say so? Goodness, it's been *ages*. How are you?'

I leant on edge of the work surface, twiddled one foot around and pushed my specs back up my nose with one finger while I tried to phrase it in a way that would cause the least trouble. I wished I'd got my inhaler.

'Alma – are you there?'

'Yes, er, sorry, Mum. Look, um, Phillip and I are getting divorced. We've separated and I'm staying with Millie just for the minute.' There, it was out.

I heard her sigh heavily and I knew she was rolling her eyes. 'I see. Well, I'm sure you have your reasons. Your father will be . . .' She was searching for the right word. She couldn't say 'upset' because Freddy had never particularly *liked* Phillip. What word could describe the state of mind of an academic rudely disturbed from his studies by what he would consider completely irrelevant news?

'Your father *will* be disappointed.' There, that word again. Like 'despite'. My least favourite words. I felt unreasonable anger welling up in me. Couldn't she be a bit more . . . *motherly*? Couldn't she take my side unquestioningly for once? I tried to breathe deeply. I was a grown woman. This should not bother me so much.

I felt a whine creep into my voice as I said, 'He never got on with Phillip, Mum, neither did you. If you must know, he's been a complete bastard, and . . .'

'Try and calm down, Alma, you're overwrought. Getting so upset won't solve anything. You know your father and I accept whatever you decide to do. It's just that you don't seem to have given this marriage much of a chance . . .'

I told her, calmly, what had happened. About Wells. About being chucked out on my ear. About my bloody chest infection, even. There was a silence at the other end.

'Ah. I see . . . I don't know what to say, I'm . . . Um, your father's in Ronda at the supermarket. I'll . . . I'll tell him when he gets back. Have you seen a doctor? You know your chest . . .'

I felt the anger drain out of me. This was pointless. I'd done my duty. I don't know what I'd expected. This was how it had always been.

'Well, erm, look, I just thought you should know. So, OK then – love to Dad. Er, bye . . .' I put the phone down.

Then I went back to bed and refused to cry.

When Millie got home I'd pretty much recovered. I told her about the call and offered to pay but she waved me away and said we'd sort money out sometime in the future. She looked tired, so I offered to cook my legendary Spaghetti Surprise. I laid the table, made a sauce that would have made the angels weep (probably from the garlic fumes) and listened to Millie describing her latest crisis at the office and taking off the arty types she worked with. She was a great mimic in her quiet way, with a wicked sense of humour, and soon we were giggling like loons.

Halfway through dinner, the phone rang.

Millie struggled up from the table, still laughing, her round cheeks red, tears in her crescent-moon eyes, and answered it. She turned to me, her hand over the mouth-piece, her face suddenly solemn.

'It's your *mum* . . .' she said, her face now registering incredulity.

I got up and took the phone while Millie tactfully retired to the sitting room with the remains of her food.

'Hi, Mum, what's the matter?'

'Oh, nothing's *wrong*. It's just that – well, I talked to your father about this divorce business and, Alma, we're both agreed, it's outrageous. Your father's quite upset by it all, really – and, yes, so am I.' She sounded slightly amazed.

'Oh,' I managed lamely. This was highly unusual. Normally, it would all have been firmly under the rug by now. I was dumbstruck, my usual responses off kilter.

'Alma, I – *we,* your father and I, we've had a lot of time to think now we live here permanently. It's . . . I've been meaning to ring you for some time, but now this – I feel we've drifted apart, as a family – your father thinks so too. Francis lives so far away, and now we live here – it seems we're scattered all over the globe . . . We're not getting any younger and, well, we'd like it if you'd come out here, for a visit. Perhaps we could . . . talk. Daddy says he'll have the swimming pool sorted out for you, if you'd like. I must say it *would* be nice, but you know what your father's like about those things normally. We'd be happy – more than happy – to pay for a plane ticket, and we could pick you up at Malaga . . . The sun would do you good, do your chest good. You could rest – convalesce, as it were.'

I was so shocked I forgot to breathe. What the fuck was this? Talk? Fix up the old swimming pool? Convalesce? Bloody *hell*. The World Turned Upside Down.

'Alma? Alma? Are you there?' Vi sounded anxious, also very unlike her. She sounded – old. Unexpectedly, a small pain jabbed my heart.

'Uh, yeah, yeah – I'm here.' I coughed, clearing my tight throat.

'Dear, please think about it. You don't have to stay a long time – or you can stay as long as you like. This is a big house for two old fogies . . .'

That was another first: Vi admitting age. What next, I wondered, rains of frogs? I know I sound flippant, but I can't help it. It was as if my whole life and everything I'd bumbled along taking for granted was undergoing some sort of *shift*. I'd grown used to having a totally crap non-relationship with my parents. I made jokes about it, I used it – if I'm honest – as an excuse for everything from taking drugs to dyeing my hair puke green, as I did one memorable Christmas . . . I had all the excuses off by heart. That familial fuck-up rode my back like a wizened, immortal monkey digging its bony fingers deep into my heart. The sheer crapness of my parents and me was a steady point in my universe. It couldn't possibly change. How could something like that change? What would I do if it changed? No. I didn't get on with my parents and that, let me say once and for all, was that. Graven in stone. And now my mother was being *nice*. Uh-oh, this does not compute.

'Um, well, yeah – er, thank you. I'll think about it . . . I mean, I don't know what I'm going to do, really . . . I thought I might go back to university, you know . . .' Now, *that* fell out of my mouth by accident, let me tell you.

'Oh, Alma, that would be wonderful! Your father will be thrilled – I'm *so* glad . . .'

'I haven't decided yet, you know . . .'

'No, no, of course. But it would be tremendous. Just wait till I tell your father. He'll be so thrilled. Now, Alma, you will seriously think about coming, won't you? Your father would really like to see you.'

The Daddy Card – that's what Frankie called it. *Oh no! She's playing The Daddy Card,* he'd stage-whisper during a ticking off, or if Vi wanted us to do something we didn't want to do. It usually worked; it was like the High Priestess invoking the god.

I wound up the conversation as quickly as I could, promising to let them know my decision. That in itself was bizarre. In my whole life I couldn't remember being in anything other than the supplicant's position.

Mills was as gobsmacked as I was when I recounted the conversation, but she was all for it. She zipped it all through her brain and flipped everything into place like a card sharp doing the one-hand shuffle. Go to Spain and get myself together, mend relationship with Aged Parents, come back, sort out a suitable course and the necessary funding. Then, get a place to live – she'd make tentative enquiries while I was away – and bingo! They all lived happily ever after. Millie glowed with satisfaction. At last, a cure for my personal chaos. Nothing Mills hates worse than *chaos.*

It did all sound foolproof. And at the very least it was a plan. When Maz rang later, Millie had it all sorted out, like it was a double-done deal. Then Millie phoned Frankie – her buddy. He adored the whole thing, thought it was a *d*-ream, honey. *Everyone* thought it was a great idea.

Fact was, it scared me shitless. University – or rather, the possibility of failure it contained in its desiccated ivory towers; the Parents; *being on my own . . .* Soz, but it frightened me to death. I wasn't stupid, I knew what it was. The world, Fate, call it what you like, was unwrapping the neat cocoon of depression and gosh-aren't-I-witty-in-a-self-deprecating-sort-of-way I'd carefully made to hide in since Jack died. The light was flooding in and it blinded me. It was flight or fight. My heart was thudding like a jackhammer.

But at the same time, I wanted it. I wanted to . . . to *be real.* You know, move on, grow up, get a life. If I crawled along doing nothing, I'd be as good as dead. Like one of those nuns they used to brick up alive in the convent walls for luck. Walled up in Bradford, hearing life go on outside my windows but never being part of it . . . No, even *Spain* was preferable, even *academia.*

So, that was me, all stitched up like a kipper, good stylee.

10

I made lists. Then I made lists of the lists I'd made. I started packing. Then I realized I had no suitable clothing at all. Anything that was not actually full-on Arctic-wear was black, which was not a great idea for Andalucia in spring.

I needed cheap and cheerful light-coloured kit so I wouldn't broil. I found Top Man, just when I needed him, and stocked up on some sale-price XL drawstring combat baggies and T-shirts in 'natural' and 'sesame' – i.e. beige. An oversized linen-mix bloke's shirt ('stone'), and a pair of Velcro-fastened walking sandals ('light tan') from ASDA, *et voilà*! Madame's Spring Wardrobe, dirt cheap. At least it wasn't *black*.

I stocked up my sponge bag and bought some of those big old electric hair clippers with number four and number six guards. I didn't want the bother of hair things so I decided to keep it clipped for the meantime, and anyways, buzzed hair feels so nice and velvety. I could rub my own head even if no one else would.

The whole going-away thing had its own momentum. Like a swaying juggernaut getting faster and faster as it's pulled along by its ecstatic devotees. A client of Maz's ran a travel agency so she got me an incredibly cheap ticket departing on the first of June, just under two weeks away. I phoned the Parents and they – well, Vi sounded quite tearful.

The next day, Mills staggered home from work bearing a big box that Frankie had FedExed over. It was fantastic, like Aladdin's Cave, only in a box, if you see what I mean. There was a slot-in modem and a tiny printer for my computer, a mad bottle of factor-20 sunblock in the form of shocking pink gel with glitter in it called 'Sungirl Velvet Sheen' and a gorgeous silver pendant shaped like the outline of a heart, really heavy and smoothly rounded, threaded on a leather thong and worn choker style. It was engraved with the word 'Corazon', which means 'heart' in Spanish. It's an endearment as well, like, '*mi corazon*' – 'my heart'. So sweet. I was made up. And there were chocolates, boxes of pot-pourri, shells and crystals, packets of sequins in the shapes of cats, stars and daisies to put in letters – loads of *stuff*. Plus a really lovely suede-covered designer notebook and matching pen in soft rose for Millie and a transparent plastic pouch full of 'Beauty Components' by Armani for Maz that made her hiss with pleasure. What a thoughtful brother; or brother's partner . . .

When we rang Frankie, shrieking with the sugar high from the sweets, he was totally cool about it, but we could hear Thom laughing in the background. The modem and printer were freebies, he said, and the printer was a Euro version, no good for USA voltage systems. I told him, very quietly while the girls were giggling, that he was *OK*. He understood – it was our personal slang for 'excellent' and beyond the call of duty.

I felt so much better. I mean, I still missed Wells – I'd carry that around for ever – but in myself, healthwise and in my head, I felt better. Instead of moping around, being drippy, I felt energized and happy. Especially that night, the parcel night. It was like being a kid at Christmas again. It was *family*.

What with making arrangements, trying to learn the bloody Internet and sorting things out, the fortnight flew past. The day dawned when I was to catch the four thirty flight from Manchester to Malaga and all my stuff was in Freddy's rucksack tied up with extra luggage straps and mini-locks to satisfy Millie's travel paranoias. My daysack and computer would go as hand luggage – I'd bundled up my winter clothes and my Virgins and stowed them away in Mills' spare-room wardrobe. I mean, I'd only be gone for six weeks at the outside, so it wouldn't matter; I'd sort it all out when I got back and found a place of my own.

We got in Millie's purple Ka – she'd got the day off, saying mysteriously that they owed her it after the Halifax thing. Maz had said goodbye the night before as she couldn't really leave Le Salon. She was in a funny mood, too, very jumpy and irritable. We thought she must be under a lot of strain with work and with Tatum, who had a heavy cold; Millie suspected she was having trouble with Rom, too. Maz being as she was, you couldn't make her tell you anything, you just had to wait for her to come to you. She's such a self-contained person, it's like she's living inside a suit of armour, or an exoskeleton – opaque, chitinous, like an insect. You can see her roiling about inside it, but you can't get to her. I felt bad, skipping off on what was really a holiday when she wasn't OK, but I knew she'd think I was soft if I put it off on her account.

The little toy-like car smelt of synthetic vanilla from the air freshener hanging from the mirror; I watched it sway around, bouncing and jumping over Bradford's notoriously potholed roads until it settled as we got on to the motorway. Streams of traffic flowed past us like mercury as we talked and drove through the slanting rain. The soft, dove-coloured clouds soaked through with silvery light spread out above the line of the road; it was like driving into the clouds themselves, the rain, the road, the light all merging into one watery, grey wash. Millie said how much she wished she was coming with me and how tired she was of the weather. Spain, the sun, the colours, the heat – it seemed like a wholly alien idea, to both of us.

Then, all of a sudden, we were in Manchester at the airport. We checked in my pitiful raggy old rucksack and sat drinking a coffee in the café. Millie, bless her, was quite tearful. She always got weepy at sentimental moments, like soppy adverts on the telly or goodbyes in airports. I promised to send lots of lurid postcards including the ones featuring Flamenco dancers with real net skirts stuck on the card, and I'd e-mail and everything. Still she seemed quite upset at me going, which I found really touching. I hadn't thought she'd be so bothered.

Finally it was time to go through. I gave Mills a big hug and kiss and turned to leave, feeling a bit weepy myself, to be honest. Just as I got to the barrier, Millie ran round and grabbed my hand – she seemed genuinely anxious. I stepped out of the line and asked her what was wrong.

'I don't know, I don't know . . . Al, I feel funny about your going – I mean . . . oh, I don't know *what* I mean . . . Al, *promise* you'll take care of yourself, won't you? I've had *such* a funny feeling about all this, ever since I saw you in the doorway. You looked so . . . so *alone*. God, I'm sorry. Don't pay any attention to me, I'm just being silly . . . But you will *take care*, won't you? Extra care. Try and pay attention to what's going on around you – you're so *absent-minded* about things sometimes. Promise?' She hung on to my hand in a very un-Ems-like way.

Of course I swore on my honour as a scholar and a gentleman to be very careful about absolutely everything. I mean, she looked so woebegone; her round ivory face strained and tense, the wispy flicks of black hair floating loose as ever from her ponytail. I bent down and kissed her smooth forehead – another unusual move for us – but I could see she was really concerned. We hugged again and I got back in line. I turned as I went through and there she was, my friend, smiling gamely and waving her pale little starfish hand. I waved back madly, and then – I was through the gate.

BOOK II

'Gutta cavat lapidem non vi sed saepe cadendo' Proverb

11

The sun filtered through the dark, old shutters of the deep-set little window, each ray full of glittering dust motes dancing in the light. It was cool in here, mostly because the walls of the house are about two-foot thick and all the floors are laid with big, ancient, crumbling terracotta tiles. I lay on the saggy double bed stark bollock naked, contemplating getting up. It felt like I'd been here for three years, not coming up for three weeks. Time was so elastic here, so unlike Northern time, I could hardly remember the chilly, pallid spring I'd left behind.

I lay still and drifted in a state of bliss. If I listened hard I could I could hear the faint burble of the river flowing past the bottom courtyard. It was so familiar and unchanged I could see it perfectly in my mind's eye: a brown, shining ribbon, shallow, pocked with stones and edged with thick, scented swathes of water mint. Further downstream it joined a deeper stretch that was seriously polluted with effluent from the industrial zone in Ronda – but here, our branch of it was still sweet and clear. We had our own well, too, with good, flinty-tasting water which made us the envy of our neighbours. Having a source of water meant a house was alive; the ones that didn't littered the mountain fields with their dead brown shells. It was dry, dry, dry here – and this was the region they called 'wet' Andalucia. 'Dry' Andalucia was where they filmed all those Spaghetti Westerns with Clint and co. Real desert, that. Here we had greenery: palms, orange and lemon trees brilliant with clustered, jewel-like fruit, cactus, poppies, eucalyptus trees, and everywhere great falls of bougainvillaea spilling its livid pinky-purple blossoms over every available wall like the ruffled skirts of flamenco dresses.

Still, couldn't slug in bed for ever. I'd had to for the first few days after the flight; the recycled air and all that had about ripped my chest to bits again and when I staggered down the fancy tiled hallway and out into the terminal at Malaga I nearly fainted, I felt so ill. Mind you, the Parents fairly passed out with shock at the sight of me too, so a right set we were. The drive up to Ronda and out to La Morena was like a dream sequence designed by Dali – all looming mountains and tortuous roads winding past bizarre new developments nestling like bright white cuckoos in the dusty hillsides; strange faux Spanish villages for foreign tourists who wanted a Spain that had all the 'advantages' of Cologne, or London.

Still, I felt fine now. The sun, fresh fruit, lots of sleep, going for walks, swimming in the newly restored pool. It's not bad for a house pool; you can do nearly six strokes before bashing your head on the opposite wall. Lots of houses round here have pools – in this heat it's a necessity, not a luxury. Same principle as all those elaborate water features in the old Moorish villas and gardens. Just the *sound* of water . . .

Every day, memories of my childhood summers here came flooding back – things I'd forgotten entirely as I trolled grimly through homey old Bradford of an afternoon. Bradford . . . I'd really have to think about getting back there soon and sorting myself out, course-and-home-wise. Still, I couldn't say the idea appealed that much.

I got up and pulled on an old stripy fawn djellaba of Mum's. It was a bit gone under the arms and raggy round the hem, but still serviceable. The house was full of their souvenirs from trips to North Africa – backless slippers, curly metal teapots and gold-painted tea glasses, rugs, throws, cushions – the place was like a Moroccan jumble sale. Smelt like it, too, a mixture of strong coffee, proper turpentine and the bowls of dried roses Vi used as pot-pourri. I looked at the clock, it was eight fifteen. It would still be fresh and bearable out; time to get myself together and think about what to do today before siesta. Hmm, how about a nice, long brekkie on the little veranda, check my e-mails, do some clothes washing, saunter round a bit, plod on with the book. Heavy stuff, I know, but, hey, someone's gotta do it. Did I feel guilty about my new-found slackness? Would you? OK, well, a bit then . . .

There was no sign of the Parents when I climbed the stairs to the kitchen. The house is split-level, built sometime in the fourteenth century as a farmhouse. The 'new' annexe where my room, two other bedrooms and the second bathroom was had been made out of the old cellars when the house was a full-time summer rental. For years it had generated a nice little income for the Barlows, who had owned it from the fifties, when La Morena had really taken off as the belly-button of the Andalusian ex-pat artists' colonies. Everyone who was anyone came here: Hemingway, Laurie Lee, about ten million painters lusting after the pure, savage light and the abundance of *vino tinto*. The valley was still peppered with arty drop-outs like my parents; it still had the wild, gypsy siren song that they couldn't resist.

I toddled into the living room, carefully stepping over a crusted palette and squished tubes of paint laid on a colour-splattered old rug beside Vi's indoor easel. I don't know why she had to paint all over the house, she had her own studio. No sign of the artist, though. Must have gone into Ronda, shopping. Only old Ishmael, the ill-made mongrel hound Vi had 'rescued' from a life of piracy and free-ranging rape and pillage on the streets of Ronda snuffled his grey muzzle at me from the sofa in the living room and thumped his whippy tail feebly on the dusty velvet, raising a cloud of dog fluff.

'Mornin', Ishymo. *¿Qué pasa, hombre*?' I walked over and rubbed the grizzled belly he offered me so obligingly. He dribbled happily and let off an evil fart, as was his wont. A martyr to flatulence, that dog. Ishy and I got on very well, both of us feeling like reformed old lags doing trusty time in the Guvnor's house. I knelt beside him and laid my cheek on the narrow dome of his chest, smelling his warm fur and hearing the fast trot of his heart. He licked my ear and sighed, like only an old dog can, then closed his rheumy, amber eyes and went back to sleep.

The French windows at the far end of the living room were open, the long muslin curtains swelling in the slight breeze. Freddy must still be in, then; probably 'thinking', i.e. dozing, in his tiny study at the other end of the house. This level housed said study and living room, the Parents' bedroom and the other bathroom, Vi's huge barn-studio and the kitchen. A tatterdemalion, scruffy old hotch-potch this place was, stuffed full of paintings, books, big knackered sofas covered with old feria shawls, some *rather* nice Virgin Marys – now including the severed head of my first VM, laid to rest on the mantelshelf – and the antique junk of several generations. Not exactly your House Beautiful, more your House Lived-In.

I shuffled through the clouds of fabric and out on to the small top-of-the-porch veranda. I settled by the blue tiled table and under the pergola that was draped in some weedy creeper that lay there like an exhausted green snake and frazzled in the heat. A big pot of rosemary sizzled pungently in a patch of sun and some scarlet geraniums managed to look ten times as interesting as their English cousins. Eating my bread and honey, sipping my coffee, I gazed out dopily at the craggy hills and down the rutted track to the river. The Germans who lived in the pink house across the river had tethered their horse there and it cropped mindlessly at the weedy scrub grass. I knew how it felt, frankly.

As I ate, I thought. Nearly three weeks I'd been here, and the whole 'Let's talk it all out and be a family' thing seemed further away than ever. I'd slipped back into the role of the Invisible Daughter like a goldfish into the bowl. Being poorly hadn't helped. Vi, like Maz, hated illness and became very bustling and overly-practical to compensate. I didn't believe Freddy ever had any interest in the whole project. He was struggling with his interpretation of Lorca's bizarre sexuality and its effects on his writing – Lorca's, that is, not Freddy's – and barely surfaced unless strictly necessary. We went our separate ways all day and ate dinner together. I did the same chores I'd always done when I lived with them: tending to my own washing and doing the dishes. It was like the intervening years between me leaving home and now hadn't happened.

Did it make me angry? Yeah, I suppose it did in a faint, wishy-washy way. I mean, I had come here intending to heal the breach, to sort everything out, and all I got was 'Pass the mustard,' and 'What's on the TV tonight?' They watched more TV than I'd ever known them to, as well. The satellite dish enabled them to veg out after they finished their work and watch films, or, in Freddy's case, indulge his sad addiction to cheap Yankee serials like *Renegade*. If I tried to start a conversation, I got shushed.

So I'd given up, I suppose. I counted it a victory that we'd at least suspended hostilities. We could chat about

Art and Literature and any family things from before Frankie reached puberty and found boys – you know, holidays here in La Morena, visits to Granna and Grandad at Polwenna, trips to see Nana and Auntie Audrey in York, that sort of thing. But if I tried to steer it towards what Vi called *unpleasantness,* they froze. Nada. Rien. Fuck all. It was intensely frustrating. I poured it all out to Frankie and Mills via cyber space and they both said just have patience. But believe me, that is a virtue I don't have. At all. No, I reckoned I'd drift here in the sun for a little bit longer then head home. At least I'd tried.

I sighed and munched some bread and honey. Actually, all this stupid family stuff aside, tonight was going to be a bit exciting. We'd been invited to a party – a real party – over at the Taylors'. David Taylor was *very* high up at the Beeb, a veritable Grandee, but in his early, formative, menial years had worked on that bloody *Sol y Sombre* with Freddy. He'd fallen for Ronda at that time, and who wouldn't? You can't say it ain't picture-skew, perched on top of its vertiginous gorge like a white dove nesting on a sheer cliff. Having acquired his fortune, Davey-boy bought his dream house; one of the new villas built where the old Morales farm used to be. Locals didn't buy them, they couldn't afford to. Only wealthy foreigners had that kind of cash. Fab location, darling, looming mountain behind, fields of sunflowers and corn all around – so *authentic.* And such *artistic* neighbours. Gossip – and a filched prospectus from the builder – had it that the villas were all huge up-chucked low-level ranch-style bungalows, all cod-Moorish arches, elaborate tilework and white stucco, with proper, big pools and landscaped walled gardens with security gates. I was dying to nosy around inside one. The word was Jilly Taylor had furnished theirs *exclusively* from the really posh antique shops in town. *Mucho dinero, amigos.* She called it her 'little Spanish hideaway'. Apparently, when it was finally finished, and before it was too lived-in, *Homes and Gardens* was going to do a piece on it. You know, amphorae, painted tiles, paella. I couldn't wait to get a glimpse of how the really, really rich lived. It was going to be catered, too, by the head chef from the Hotel Parador. *Blimey.*

Freddy normally ignored what he called 'the summer crowd' – like he'd never been one. But dear David was dangling the TV carrot in front of him and Fred, well, no matter how he pooh-poohed fame and media attention, secretly loved it. Strange really, you wouldn't think someone like Freddy would need an ego boost, but he couldn't resist and offers had been very few and far between since he retired. This was a juicy morsel worth nosing out of his den for. And anyway, Vi loved an excuse to dress up and large it. The Taylors insisted Freddy and Vi would be the guests of honour, the pieces of resistance and all that. Really tweaked The Big Fred's self-image. There was mention of a Lorca documentary and a whole crew of summering arty types – no ragged bohemians, these, but solid-gold media whores – would be there. Schmooze time a go-go.

All right, that was a bit snobby, but it would be a larff – and a change. I was a tad bored, I have to admit it. I did get out and about, scootering aimlessly all over Ronda on the battered old Piaggio 125 that came with the house and had belonged to the Barlows' son. I called it 'the Banshee' because it screamed like the legendary faery-woman you supposedly heard before someone died. As I wound the throttle back and the engine made that hideous eldrich shriek, death certainly seemed an option, if only for peace and quiet.

In the evenings, I sometimes had my coffee and a nice bit of *tarte manzana* at La Jionenca, my favourite café. I'd sit under the red-and-white umbrellas and sup *café solo*s while watching all Ronda do the big evening promenade, the *paseo*, up and down the main drag, Carrera Espinel. I marvelled at the beauty of the young Andalucian blokes, all of whom knocked Antonio Banderas into a cocked hat and wouldn't look at the likes of me twice – especially when the pretty señoritas wriggled down town in their skin-tight micro-frocks. My God, but the Spanish knew how to dress. They were all so well turned out, so rightly proud of themselves, so polished. What did Laurie Lee say about Spain? Oh yeah, its *'anarchic indifference, asking no discipline but the discipline of manners.'* Those evenings, gazing at the slow-moving parade of Ronda, I knew what he meant. I wished I could be part of it, but that indifference shut me out. I was a tourist, after all. A sort of ghost that they tolerated, but didn't really see. Perhaps if my Spanish had been better . . .

So, a party would be a nice change. I could eat the food and drink the plonk while observing the mêlée from some dim corner. Even if I hated it, or got arseholed, I could easily stagger back under my own steam; it was only ten minutes' walk back to ours.

I finished my coffee, breathing in its bitter incense which mingled with the rosemary and the spicy, dusty scent of the eucalyptus logs Freddy had piled up in the corner, ready for a fire if it ever got cold enough. The sky was a cloudless cerulean blue and the sun was just starting to heat up. It was going to be a scorcher, again. The breeze danced the dry rose leaves by the front door with a faint desiccated rustle and swung the pomegranates in the tree that drooped in the tumbled front garden. I really fancied a swim, and the pool winked flirtatiously, a turquoise dropped in the ochre dust of the back field, but Juan the odd-job bloke was coming to do something to it so I couldn't. I turned back into the house and sat down at my laptop which I'd set up in a corner.

I had two messages. One invited me to check out a

porn site featuring college girls dying to make my acquaintance, and the other was from Mills.

dear al

not much to tell you, weather quite nice, stopped raining – but bet it's not as nice as you're having, you lucky thing! everyone says hello and sends their love. how is your chest now? don't overdo it you are supposed to be resting. i e-mailed laura and gave her your address so you will be hearing from her i should think. maz is a bit miserable these days. it's rom – she thinks he's seeing someone else plus tatum has an ear infection so is in a real state poor little lamb. bradford is the same. matthew says hi and don't worry everything is fine.

love millie xxxx

I could picture her typing this, a phone wedged in her neck, people asking her important questions. Poor Maz, though. This was the story of her life with Rom. He couldn't keep it in his trousers for two seconds. I got a postcard out of my stock of lurid views and wrote her a note. I didn't mention anything Mills had said because Maz hated being 'personal'. She'd know Mills had told me, but as long as I waited for her to tell me herself it would be OK. God, people were complicated. Life was complicated. I looked at Ishy, snoring like a train, laid on his back with his legs at all angles. At least animals weren't complicated.

12

I plugged in the hair clippers and gave myself my first No. 4 once-over. Bleached bits fell to the floor like a rain of bluey-white lint. My head felt light and velvety, but rather bald. Then I showered and got dressed in my beige baggy ensemble, with Maz's 'Le Salon' glitter-print strappy Tee on under my shirt. Well, gotta make an effort at glam for a do, haven't you? I had the necklace Frankie sent me which I never took off, my piercing jewellery but no make-up – I hadn't brought any, not even a lippie. Well, less is more – more or less. At least I looked *clean*.

Freddy had gone so far as to don a pale pink shirt with his usual voluminous white linen suit and huaraches. He did look pretty distinguished: tall, thin, brown, his bright blue eyes positively twinkling from his beaky-bony face. His hair was prematurely white – all his side of the family went white early – and he'd let it grow ever-so-slightly long, swept back from his forehead. A gift for TV . . .

Vi had outdone herself with her trademark BoHo finery: a thickly embroidered Mexican smock dress trailing to sequinned Chinese slippers, the magnificent antique feria shawl in rose silk with cream-coloured flower embroidery and fringing, the painted fan, the beaded purse, the turquoise and silver Navajo jewellery – a vision of Haute Hippie. It suited her voluptuous, Earth-Mothery figure and her broad, strong-featured face – the face I got bits of and the body I knew would eventually be mine, like it or not. Mind you, she didn't consider her style fashionable; this was the required costume of her arty youth and she'd never changed it. See, wait long enough and fashion catches up with you again. I should never have thrown my Goth frocks out . . .

They certainly made a handsome pair. I was proud of them, and said so. They seemed startled, then Vi suddenly enfolded me in a big, scented hug. I nearly choked with the perfume and the shock. Freddy was smiling like a fond paterfamilias. God, we were the very picture of a Happy Family. Maybe Frankie and Mills had been right after all – patience, patience . . .

The party invite said eight thirty for nine. We got there at ten, because nothing in Spain happens until after ten thirty. Us arriving so 'early' was a concession to the Brits who never understood the siesta system and insisted on behaving as if they were at home – and suffered the consequences.

We negotiated the security gates and strolled up to the antique double doors where we were greeted with squeals from our hostess, who was so sun-baked she looked like a salami dressed in emerald raw silk and a straw wig. When her voice came down a few tones from bat-squeak, I gathered she'd been *sure* we'd decided not to come. This would have been a *disaster* – Davey would have been *heartbroken*. People had come *especially* to meet Freddy – oh, and Vi, of *course*, what was a genius without his *muse*? Tinkle of crystalline laughter. I stood back instinctively after a brief intro and she swept the Parents off into the house. The place wasn't small, believe me, but it was absolutely stuffed to the rafters with people. I couldn't believe how many had turned up. A sound system was blaring Latino pop music in the enormous living room and red-faced English people were gyrating insanely to a techno-mambo. I turned away from this fascinating spectacle to snoop unashamedly around the house.

It was everything I'd expected – and more, much more. There wasn't a nook or cranny that wasn't rag-washed, antique'd, rustic'd or made of terracotta. There were niches rotten with baroque Madonnas and gigantic sofas swathed in cream damask. The wrought-iron chandelier in the huge, open-plan living room alone must have cost a fortune and it was nothing in comparison to the ancient carved oak sideboard that a skinny youth with big Jarvis-style specs and a lavender pimp shirt was stubbing his fag out on.

I decided, that despite my normal sobriety, drink had to be taken in order to cope. I headed for the bar and got a glass of a rather nice *tinto*. I smiled winningly at the handsome Spanish barman. He ignored me – in fact, he almost sneered. Oh, never mind, this crowd would put anyone's back up. I didn't take it too personally.

I studied the party-goers. They were a pretty samey bunch; 90 per cent Brit, as far as I could see, with a sprinkle of other nationalities. Some young, some middle-aged, some firmly entrenched in middle-youth. All middle-class. There was a definite patina of designer clothes and funky accessories – they weren't a scruffy lot. I felt out of place in my Top Man ensemble, but what the hell, I didn't think anyone would notice me as they all seemed to know each other. They were so busy air-kissing and wiping coke off their noses they probably wouldn't have noticed an earthquake unless it scattered a line. It was, by my current standards, a pretty druggie crowd. There was some spliff about, I could smell it, and everyone was downing a great deal of booze – but the keynote was coke: brittle, high-pitched, shiny.

After forty-five minutes I'd about covered the interior and not spoken a word to anyone. I tried to find the

Parents, but they were seriously ensconced in the library with some superior fino, Davey, and his in-crowd.

Feeling a bit at a loose end, and itching to cop a glimpse of the fabled pool, I weaved through the squawking, heaving scrum to the patio. The patio itself was very big and exquisitely floored in a terracotta and blue herring-bone pattern. There were statues of vaguely classical women with bits missing and enormous pottery amphorae filled with fuchsias and geraniums. The trees and bushes were strung through with masses of tiny white lights and big citronella candles burned everywhere – dozens of them, the four-wick kind. As for the pool – it made ours look like a kiddie's splashabout. God, was I jealous. It was fabulous, almost Olympic. A swimmer's wet dream, so to speak; Maxfield Parrish blue, luminous, enticing, empty . . . Why, you could just slide into that illuminated water and . . .

Someone tugged wildly at my sleeve. Blinking, I half turned to see an appallingly thin girl of about eighteen or so staring at me fixedly, her eyes heavily circled with shiny black eyeshadow, her square little face dead white. She licked her fat cupid's bow lips with a dry-looking pointed tongue and fiddled nervously with her short, scrubby thatch of expensively hacked ebony hair which sparkled with diamanté hair-jewels. Her perfume was pungently modern, mixing with a strange, almost sour under-scent . . . She smelt odd, if you know what I mean, not right, somehow. She was saying something urgently, but I couldn't hear her over the raucous thud of the Ibiza-sounds CD that had replaced the pop comp.

'Sorry? What? I can't hear – this music. What's the matter . . . ?' I turned towards her and bent my head to her mouth.

All I caught was, '. . . when are you going to Solly's Dad? Please, *please* let me come . . .'

'What?' I shook my head to indicate I didn't understand. Then I realized she was staring fixedly at my glittery 'Le Salon' vest. An expression of utter disgust crawled over her face and she dropped my sleeve as if it were a cobra.

'Fuck, Fuck – *fuck.*' Shooting me a white-hot look of pure hatred, she clumped off, nearly twisting her primrose-stem ankle in the process.

Drugs are a terrible thing, really. What's the expression? Cocaine is God's way of telling you you have too much money. And she was so young – or was I getting old? Christ, silly little bitch. What *had* she been going on about? Who knows, and who the fuck cares? Not me.

But I did, actually. It made me feel uncomfortable. Old, out of it and uncomfortable. I walked around the pool, avoiding the snogging couples, the knots of earnest drinkers and dopers and the inevitable topless party girl threatening to jump in the water. I slumped gracelessly on to a smart wooden lounger thing on the furthest side from the house and gazed at the pool. It was almost quiet, and the stars looked like little chips of diamond in the navy velvet sky. I willed myself to relax, inwardly chanting soothing thoughts I remembered from one of the demented relaxation tapes Mills had lent me. *You are in a beautiful palace in the sky, walking down a broad marble staircase; with each step you become more and more relaxed* . . . I was practically dozing off when I felt someone sit on the lounger next to mine.

'Well, well, well – what have we here? Jack Collier's Muse – am I right? Yes, I rather think I *am*. Don't you remember me, darling? It's dear old Leo, Leo Brindle, your *favourite* journalist . . . What was it you called me last time we met . . . Ah, yes, I have it: "A slavering fuck-wit." But hey! Forgive and forget is what I *always* say. So here I am, holidaying at the Pendles' *dire* little hovel with their *poisonous* crowd, when they tell me simply everyone who's *anyone* this summer is going to be at this party. And lo and behold, who do I find but the very girl I want to see . . . It's fate, darling, simply fate . . .'

I froze in horror. Leo Brindle? *Leonard fucking Brindle?* God Almighty, it wasn't possible. I sneaked a sideways glance and, sure enough, there was the 'young' man in the lavender fitted shirt and aviator specs. Not so youthful at close quarters; more a chemically thin forty-odd. My nemesis, Leo B – the Addison De Witt of the London set.

He smiled like a chimp preparing to bite. Then busied himself lighting a cigarette with his silver Tiffany lighter. He dragged deeply and exhaled a double stream of smoke through his narrow nose. That surprised me; I wouldn't have thought he had a septum left.

'Now, darling, shall we talk?' he oozed. 'I must confess when I heard dear Freddy was guest of honour at this little shindig I *rather* hoped – I don't know why, perhaps I'm *psychic* – but I rather hoped my *dear* old chum Alma would be here. Gosh – and here you *are* – still quite the Roaring Girl we knew and loved, eh?'

Behind the graduated tint of his lenses, his wicked, simian eyes twinkled malevolently. I felt a knot of tension hunch through my neck and shoulders. What the fuck did he expect? I'd told him I wasn't playing his literary kiss-and-tell game before Jack died – and after. Surely, he couldn't, after all this time . . . I wanted to get up and leave, but I felt strangely paralysed, as if the past had risen up from some abyss and seized me in a clammy embrace. Like one of those old horror movies where no matter how fast you run, and no matter how slowly the Mummy walks, it always get you in the end. You can never, ever escape.

He tapped his ash on to the tiles and stretched out one arm, twisting his skeletal hand around as if he had a cramp. 'Oh, this dammed repetitive strain thing – we writers, what we have to put up with! Ghastly. Now, do pay attention, dear. I think it's time we got together. A nice publisher has commissioned me to write the definitive volume on Modern *Lit* – *Britlit*, you understand. None of your desperate old fogeys. Damian is doing the cover for us, Will is penning an intro, and it's going to be very, very glossy. And very, very expensive. The Germans are *salivating* already and, as for the Americans – *need* I say more? Fabulous funding, natch. I can tell you in confidence, the PM is right behind us – positively *fucking* our collective arses, as it were.'

He giggled. I felt nauseous. I knew where this was going and I didn't like it one bit, but I seemed to be in slow motion. I could see his big, flabby Mick Jaggery mouth working, and hear the words he was speaking, but they were out of sync, a badly dubbed film. The night seemed to close in on us and the party receded like a wave sucking back off the shore.

'Oh, I can see from your expression, you've guessed! You clever little thing – but you always were *clever*, weren't you, dear? Clever enough to hold out for the best offer. Well, this is it – you won't get another like this. So tell me everything – *everything*, mind you – about our beautiful Jacky-boy and I'll see you get simply *astonishing* amounts of cash. I do mean *all*, by the way – the sex, the drugs, the suicide. It *was* suicide, wasn't it, Alma? That was no *accident*. I've talked to those two morons who were with him that night and they've *sworn* on their mothers' graves – and for a fat fee – that he was smashed out of his brain and deliberately . . .'

I unfroze and got up. He sprang up too and, throwing his cig away in an arc of red, seized my wrist. His breath was foul with fags and cocaine.

'Come on, dear, don't hold out on me. The publisher will only take this book if it's *sexy*, if it's *hot* – and it will be. He wants Jack – he's a big, big fan – and I *promised* him Jack . . .'

It was like he'd jabbed me with a tazer; an electric shock ran through me and I felt my temper ignite. I wrenched my wrist away and felt a surge of adrenaline pour through my body.

'Get the *fuck* away from me. What the fuck d'you think you're playin' at?' I hissed. 'Fuck *off* and leave me alone. I've got friends here, blokes – if you come near me they'll . . . *Fuck right off.* God, you sick *fuck.* You're not fit to kiss Jack's foot, alive or dead. I don't care what anyone else – it was an accident, an *accident.* Christ, d'you seriously think I'd tell you *anything* about Jack? Are you fuckin' mental? If you write anything – *anything* – I'll, I'll fuckin' sue you, I *will* . . .'

He fell back a step, a look of actual fear on his wizened face. I kicked the lounger out of the way and strode back into the house. I was shaking like a leaf and I felt the wheeze clutch my lungs. Stepping into a vacant corner, I pulled my inhaler out and had a shot. I saw Leo stumble in after me and start jabbering at a skinny woman in a black trouser suit and deep fuchsia lipstick. She beckoned another, similarly dressed woman with a viciously sharp aubergine Louise Brooks bob over and I could see he was recounting the tale. They began to scan the crowd – hoping to find me, I suppose – and I shrank back into my hidey-hole. Oh, why didn't I have a bloke here for real? In desperation I cast around for a friendly face I could persuade to walk me home.

My eye fell on a tall, long-haired, Spanish-looking chap in his late twenties. He didn't look like the rest of the crowd and he seemed to be alone. More usefully, he seemed faintly bored. What had I got to lose? Taking a deep, wheezy breath I marched up to him.

'Hola, Señor. ¿Habla inglés?' God, God, please, please, *please* let him speak English . . .

He studied me for a long moment and then said, 'Well, yes, I do. Or at least, I try. And you?' He had a strong Scottish accent. My mouth fell open.

'I . . . er . . . God . . . sorry, I thought you were local . . . I, er, look, I know this sounds mad, but could you do me a *huge* favour, could you pretend you know me, like we were long-lost buddies? I'll explain to your wife or whatever, only I'm in a – I've got myself into a bit of hassle and . . .' I gazed pleadingly at him.

He looked at me calmly, as if women often besieged him with strange demands. I hopped from one foot to the other in an agonized way.

'Hmmm, these things happen in the best-regulated parties, I suppose. Who's upset you so much, if you don't mind me asking?' He was smiling slightly now, which I took to be a good sign.

'You – I – See over there? That skinny wan-, er, person in the purple shirt and big glasses? God, he's not your best mate or anything, is he?'

'Leo? No. I only just met him myself. He's staying with the same folks I am, unfortunately. He turned up last night – came over specially for this party. Loads of folk did. London people, you know.'

'Oh, right – weird. Could you walk out the door with me – you know, make like we're mates? Our house isn't far; I can get myself home after that. It's just, I don't want him nabbing me again and causing a scene. We had a right ding-dong.' I sighed heavily, feeling suddenly wobbly.

There was silence. Then he nodded. 'No problem. Always a sucker for a damsel in distress. I know, look, play along, right? My name's Cam, by the way. Diego Cameron. Mum's Spanish, Dad's Scottish, hence the name. Pleased to meet you, by the way.' He was definitely smiling now. I grinned back in relief.

'Al –Alma Greer, but everyone calls me Al. Pleased to

meet you too. And thanks. I really mean that, thanks a million.'

I was still grinning when I looked across the room and saw that Leo and his harpies had spotted me and were on a collision course. Cam saw it too. He grabbed me into a hug, nearly suffocating me, then kissed me smackingly on both cheeks.

'My God! How long is it? You're looking wonderful! I can't believe you're here! What a fantastic coincidence!' He sounded like we'd known each other for years. I increased my grin.

'Wow, yeah. And, er, Cam – you – you don't look a day older than . . . than when we last met!'

Leo shimmied into position in front of us, fixing us with a baleful glare only partly filtered by his shades. The harpies simmered like boiling oil, their sharp, painted faces intent.

Cam smiled beatifically at Leo. I waited.

'Well, well. Cam. Our own Reformed Character. I didn't know you and *dear* Alma were acquainted. What a *small* world,' Leo hissed. The harpies seethed.

'Indeed it is, Leo. Hello, Corinthia, Phoebe. But, er, Al and I were just leaving, I'm afraid. Parties aren't my scene and we've a lot to catch up on. See you back at the villa, eh?'

Leo was absolutely livid. His complexion went the colour of dried liver and his flabby mouth was slick with spittle.

I tried to appear innocent. Cam took my arm and, with a brief nod at the unholy triumvirate, walked me briskly out of the front door and down the drive.

13

Outside, on the track leading to our house, I stopped and turned to Cam, who was gazing up at the stars, a worried look on his face. I looked up too, but couldn't see, like, an alien spaceship or anything.

I squinted. 'What is it?'

'God damn it, I *cannot* find Cassiopeia.'

'Ah. Well. Soz, but I'm not exactly an astrologer . . .'

'Astronomer – astrologer is the zodiac. Mystic Meg, that sort of caper. I used to be dead keen, you know – as a wee boy – dead keen on the stars . . .' He shrugged regretfully. 'It's terrible what you lose, isn't it?'

'Christ – not me. I can't seem to bloody lose anything. Look, thanks. That was great of you. I'm fine now, honestly. You can go back in, if you like – tell Leo I dumped you or something. He thinks I'm barmy anyway. *I* think I'm barmy, God alone knows. Seriously, though, really decent of you.'

'I'd like to walk a bit with you, if you don't mind. I don't think that –' he jerked his head indicating the party – 'well, it's not really my scene any more. Can I see you home? I'm perfectly harmless, I assure you, nothing freaky. It's just that I'd like some . . . How can I put it? Sensible company. I get a wee bit pissed off with that sort of folk, if you see what I mean.' He looked mournful, like a Labrador puppy waiting for his dinner. How could

I refuse? A bloke after my own heart and all that. And he wasn't *that* bad looking . . .

I nodded and we ambled down the track as if we really were the mates we'd made out to be. I stole a glance at Cam, who was humming some tune I thought I recognized but couldn't place. I felt relaxed and safe with him; he seemed a quiet, funny, restful sort of fella. I imagined people always prefixed his name with 'that nice . . .' Careful, I thought, don't jump the gun, he was just being kind to an obviously bonkers woman in trouble. Nothing romantic there. Men don't exactly fall over themselves to sweet-talk baldy-headed birds in beige baggy outfits – unless things really *had* changed . . .

I coughed. 'Er, what did Leo mean, "Our Reformed Character"? I thought you said you two didn't know each other very well . . . Sorry, you don't have to answer that if it's personal or anything. Soz, dead nosey . . .'

'No, it's OK. I'm just out of de-tox. My therapist thought it would be the best thing if I had a complete change of scene. My mum's from this part of Spain, so when Toby and Sara invited me over I thought it would be a good idea – I speak the lingo an' all that, I love the country, it'd be restful . . . I shouldn't really have gone to the party, though. Dr Elias would be very disappointed. Still, you know . . .'

I made suitable noises; those noncommittal noises the English are so good at. It seemed to encourage him and he went on.

'I was a pretty heavy user. It was all going down the tubes, I don't have to tell you . . .' Didn't he? Did I look like a junkie or something? Thanks a billion, mate. Still, I was sure he didn't mean it nastily, so I kept schtum and looked encouraging.

He sighed. 'In my business, well, there's gear everywhere. The whole thing runs on gear, in fact. Coke, smoke, skag – you name it. Coke, mostly. But then I heard about Dr Elias and The Shambhala Institute and I thought, what have I got to lose? She's a great, great healer, you know? Saved my life, really. I'm totally clean now, don't even use caffeine, and – well, I'm just not going down that road again.'

Yeah, right. And make mine an organic carrot juice with a wheatgrass shot chaser. I took a deep breath and tried to be a nicer person. *Shambhala*. OK.

'So, what business were you – are you in? I mean, if you're still . . .' What did I mean? What was the correct etiquette with an ex-user?

'Oh, don't worry – I can talk about it. Dr Elias thinks talking about things gets them out in the open, disempowers them . . .' He paused, scuffing the stony track with his hiking sandals. 'I was – well, I am – a session man – musician. Acoustic guitar, mostly, but I play a bit of lead, plus I'm fair on keyboards and a few other bits and pieces. It's a living, you know.'

A musician, wow. Rock'n'roll. A *guitar player*. God, I always wanted to sing in a band, as well. Pity I had the voice of a strangled pig and couldn't carry a tune to save my life. Apart from that, I had it down perfect. At least, I did in front of my mirror, miming to the Red Hot Chilli Peppers with a hairbrush for a mic.

'Have you made any records, then? What band are you in?' Jesus, Teen Fan Mania. Thank God it was too dark for him to see me go red.

He laughed. 'I'm a session player – I don't have a band. I play for whoever pays me. A hired gun, if you like. Say some band or singer wants a bit of Spanish-style guitar on their record – well, they call me, and off I go to the studio and lay down the bits they want, collect my wages, and there you are. Done. You don't know my name, I'm not famous, but the music industry depends on the likes of me. Mercenaries. Jeez, most bands can't even play their own fuckin' instruments, never mind do anything *clever*.'

He sounded positively moody about it. Still, it must be a pisser being dead clever at something, then watching some talentless idiot get all the credit.

'Um, have you been on any records I might have heard, then?'

He laughed, and then snorted in a particularly Scottish way. 'Oh, aye – remember 'Sol Y Sombre' by Teena B?'

Did I! It drove Freddy *mental* that some half-dressed, yodelling teeny-popster had 'stolen' the title of his deadly serious Telly opus and frugged her blonde extensions into a frenzy whilst rendering the sacred phrase as, *'Sol-lyeeesom-brer / ooooo, the sun an' shadd-owws / 'ere on my eye-land heav-en / wiv my latt-ine lurve-er / ooooo, ooooo, take mee too-night-I-I-ight . . .'* Thud, thud, boing, boing, thud, thud. *Couldn't* have been more satisfying. I *loved* Teena B all that summer . . . Frankie bought three copies.

'Yeah – I certainly do . . .'

'That bit of imitation Flamenco guitar in the middle? That was me. I nicked the riff off Paco de Lucía.'

'Won't he mind?'

He laughed. 'I don't think old Paco listens much to Teena B, as it goes. I should be safe.'

I told him about our family connection to the lovely Teena B. He laughed so much he had to sit down on our front steps to get his breath.

When we finally stopped giggling, I asked him if he'd like to come in for a coffee – well, a herb tea, or something. It *did* feel a bit strange. I mean, 'coffee' these days – you may as well say 'shag'. I actually started stumbling around the subject trying to explain I just meant – no intention, etc, etc. Like a right bloody ha'porth, as Maz would say.

He got up and stretched. 'No – thanks anyway. I ought to get some sleep. We learn to get up dead early at Shambhala. Bit of a strain for me at first, what with working nights for so long, but now it's OK. D'you wanna go for a coffee, juice or whatever tomorrow? Go round the town a bit? I haven't seen a thing yet – Sara and Toby are pool people, they lie around in the sun all day roasting while the kids run riot. I like to be up an' doing these days. So, how about it?'

Naturally, I agreed like a shot and arranged to meet him at La Jionenca at 9.30 a.m., before it got too hot to breathe.

I had my final cup of tea on the veranda, looking out at the hills, and the deep, still night. Why shouldn't I go out with a man, enjoy myself, even flirt a bit? Even . . . who knows? It wasn't a crime. I mean, no one else, no other woman, would think twice about it. I was free, single. Cam was a nice bloke, if a bit New-Agey with his Shambhala nonsense. But still, beggars can't be choosers and he did seem very keen to see me again.

Maybe it was time to chill a bit, get loose, unscrew my screwed-up self. Yeah, why not?

14

The next morning I was up bright and early. I had planned a nice little lie-in after my torrid socializing, but I just couldn't sleep. I kept having these weird dreams. You know that horrible thing where you dream you've woken up but you haven't, you're still dreaming and mad stuff happens and you think, 'Christ, this is *real*!' Sweaty, horrible panic, that sort of palaver. OK, it sounds stupid, but it was really scary and when I finally *did* wake up I felt really odd.

When I took my coffee out to my favourite haunt, it got odder still. Freddy was sitting there in his grotty old dressing gown and pyjamas having his brekkie, as if that was what he always did, when I knew full well he usually squirrelled it away into his study.

'Ah, Alma. Good morning.'

'Mornin', Pa. Er, enjoy the party?'

He tipped his head back slightly and closed his eyes, then opened them and looked at me through his half-specs. Typical Freddy pose.

'Mmm, yes. To a point. Yes. I might be making another television programme – Lorca, you know. But that's not why I wanted to speak to you. Have you been enjoying yourself, resting, that sort of thing?'

He didn't wait for a reply and, anyway, I knew better than to offer one.

'Your mother thinks I should mention something to

you, Alma. You see, at that affair last night, after you left apparently, some chap – odd sort of fella, wearing a purple shirt – accosted us. Quite belligerent. In fact, downright offensive . . .'

My heart sank. OK, here we go, the Phantom Leo strikes again and I get my marching orders. Disturbing the peace, that sort of thing.

'Don't worry, Pa, I was planning to go soon anyway, I –'

'What? Nonsense. Do be quiet. Take after your mother – never quiet. Now, as I was saying, this chap came out with some rigmarole about Jack Collier and some blasted book he was writing. Now, your mother told him to sling his hook – and I agree with her. I know what he was on about – I may be old, but I'm not entirely dim. That type always want to make money, and they don't care how they do it.'

He leant forward, his blue eyes piercing under his white spiky eyebrows, looking like a sort of English University Leonardo da Vinci. 'Alma, I'm aware you haven't been happy. You were an unhappy child. All that Cornish blood – damn Celts. Dark, very dark. Now, your mother says it's all off with Phillip and I can't say I'm surprised. Bloody cold fish, in my opinion. But this purple fella, it's Jack Collier he wants and I gather you wouldn't play his game. Quite right, too. I won't say Collier was my type of chap – no, I can't say that – but I do know you loved him. Yes, I know that. Whole thing was bloody tragic. I want you to know, Alma, your mother and I, we're glad you came. We've talked a lot lately about you children, and we feel . . . well, we feel we may have made a few mistakes. Expected too much, or the wrong things of you both. And I'd be the first to admit I didn't spend as much time with you as I should – the work, you see. Always came first. Drove your mother mad as well, if that helps. What I'm getting at is . . . well, the family – it's not easy, you've got to give us time. You're damn prickly yourself, I will say – that's the Cornish again, I don't doubt. But what I'm trying to say – and making a pretty hash of it is, don't go running off on account of this purple chap, or anything else. Stay here a while longer. Give the family a chance, hmm?'

He looked away. I looked at my feet. If we hadn't been *English* we'd have cried and hugged each other. But we were, so I said, 'OK. I'll . . . I'll stop a bit longer – get some rest.'

He coughed and cleared his throat. 'That's the spirit. Good. Excellent. Got to take care of your health. Well, I'll take your mother a cup of tea, then. She'll be pleased. Yes.'

He got up and shuffled past me in his old Moroccan slippers – then paused and laid his long, bony hand on my head. 'Terrific – just like fur. I had a dog once, felt like this. Hmm.'

My gob was smacked in a way that defies description. *Wait* 'til I told Frankie: Freddy *spoke*!

I didn't cry or anything, but I felt like someone had punched me in the throat.

Still, by the time I met Cam, that had all worn off and I was bursting with love and goodwill to all men. So, naturally I had *un gran café solo* and, with my adrenaline rush turbo-assisted by massive amounts of caffeine, I dragged Cam all over tourist Ronda at double speed talking like an express train. Cocaine – who needs it? Give me manic depression any day. Cheaper, too.

We ate lunch in El Verdad, my favourite bar, down by the bullring. Cam and I talked about everything under the sun. His career, his experiences, the wonderfulness of Dr Elias; my book (briefly, he didn't seem the literary type), my divorce, my friends, Bradford. The usual kind of thing. I asked him if he'd seen Leo, but he said no, the London contingent hadn't even *woken* by the time he set off to meet me. Then he said he had to catch up on writing his 'life-journal', whatever that was, then finish some letters, do his meditation and get an early night – doctor's orders. So we trundled off back to La Morena in his cheapo rented Twingo. He dropped me off at the end of the track. I hoped he'd . . . Oh, well, he didn't. But hey, I'm not a first-date kinda gal anyhow.

We arranged to meet the next day and go for a drive, maybe visit some of the other White Towns. He seemed to want to go everywhere, see everything, which was fine with me. Scootering about on your own all the time is a drag.

I fuzzed up Ishy, who was lying comatose on my chair dribbling, dragged him on to my lap and booted up my 'puter. 'You have two messages' – oo-er. Cyber-chick.

dear al,

maz has finally split up with rom. she found him at it with a girl in their bed at his flat and the girl was even wearing her nightie. god alone knows what happened but I can tell you maz is livid, really livid. she is working like a devil all hours, totally re-styling the salon, setting up a proper nail area, new outfits for the girls – everything. she will wear herself out but she won't listen to reason, you know her. i am fine, matthew says everything is in hand so don't worry. is your chest better? lief says a big hello and get well soon. he is off again in a few days so we haven't had long together this time – but he's so nice, he bought me a lovely ring. not engagement or anything but really lovely. we all miss you very much but we know this is the best thing for you. don't forget to contact laura about a course.

best love millie

ps the girl in the little flatlet in our attic says she's thinking of moving. it's a tiny tiny place but fine for one. shall I tell her you're interested? it would be great to have you living in the building. xxxxxxxxxxx

Was I interested! The perfect solution. I replied pronto saying how interested I was and briefly mentioning that I'd made a new friend . . . I didn't know what to say about Maz. This Rom business had been going on so long that another split was nothing new. Unfortunately, Maz really loved him, always had. I was worried now, that she'd work herself into a state and get ill or something. I wrote her another postcard – bland, friendly, not mentioning anything – and prayed she'd ring me or write so I could talk to her properly. Maz, Mills; I missed them so much, they seemed a million miles away. *Bradford* seemed a million miles away. God. I scratched Ishy's ragged ears and we sighed in unison. Then I looked at the other message.

Hello darling [] [] :* :*

:-Y how's it going in Parentland??????? %-(I). Progress??? I hope so. %-I @I@ so am totally %-). Buzz buzz buzz. OK, just checking in – love you to bits – & pieces!!!!!!!!!

@>–>— @>–>— by the dozen

lurrrrrrve, F&T

OK, fine – Frankie's messages took a week to translate, but I managed to work out that he was knackered, had been up all night at the computer and was sending me a bouquet of cyber-roses (@>–->—). How nice. I bashed out a suitably cryptic reply and, dislodging Ish, went and put the kettle on.

That night, my life did a full-on turnaround. Vi breezed in with bags of food and said we were having a special dinner. She kept patting me and smiling. Obviously Freddy had filled her in on our little chat. Good, I thought. I'm glad. I did my special salad dressing – yes, tons of garlic – and set the table. I didn't expect what happened next. My parents and I talked properly for the first time in years.

All right, it wasn't easy, or perfect, but in the flickering of the candles, and with a glass of wine, we really talked. Especially about Frankie. I suppose I'd never truly understood how hurt and bewildered they'd been when it all happened. I was so used to joking about it with Frank that I'd never really stopped to consider that they hadn't even known he was *gay*, until the headlines screamed out *'Top Prof's Son in S&M Slaying Scandal'*. They'd had absolutely no idea that Frankie had been a big-time leather guy since for ever, and was a long-serving habitué of some of the more *interesting* London clubs. I knew. Had known for years. To be honest, it was just one more thing the Parents didn't twig, as far as I was concerned. Them and Us. It had been our secret, all a big giggle. I'd covered up for him and his boyfriends without a second thought. A true-blue fag-hag. But to my folks, Frank had been their beautiful, innocent, studious son; the first-born, the accredited genius with a fabulous future ahead.

Then the scandal broke. It hadn't mattered that 'golden boy' Frankie had just been a witness at the trial of the so-called Leatherman Killer. The way the papers went on, you'd have thought he'd been the murderer. Not that I'm saying it wasn't bad enough, being the last person to talk to (or have sex with, as it happened) that poor, poor sod they fished out of the Thames. God knows, it took Frankie years to get over the feelings of guilt. He was in therapy for ages – still is, on and off. No, it was the fact he actually *knew* the killer, Evan Hewlitt, and had been with him, like all the leather boys had. Hewlitt had come up North and *been to our house* when the rest of us were on holiday, and he and Frankie had organized an orgy with a load of 'bad' lads from our area, during which Hewlitt had nearly strangled Frank then laughed it off as 'foreplay'. All that was what almost destroyed Frankie. He knew – he'd *sensed* that Hewlitt was dangerous; but he hadn't said anything because, well, because he got a kick out of fucking someone that wicked. Right on the edge. Pushing the limit.

Hewlitt had killed eight leather boys by the time they got him, and he hanged himself in his cell before the trial ended. But the damage to our family was complete. Our house was besieged by journalists wanting the *'snob boffin's genius son is weirdo bondage pervert'* story – as if we'd sob into our hankies, pocket the cash and tell all. They did it to the victims' families too, and Hewlitt's poor, destroyed mother. It wasn't just us or anything. But it was bad enough. I was sent to Polwenna for the summer to get me out of the way, and when I got back Frankie had gone to America. My parents and I never talked about it, or anything really, again.

Until now, that is.

I'd never realized how near to splitting up they'd been. How the strain and the horror of it had worn them down. All their dreams for Frankie, smashed. I found out things I'd never thought about, like the fact Vi hadn't *left* that prestigious teaching post at Arncliffe School to concentrate on her painting like she'd given out. No, they sacked her because of the scandal; didn't want the school's good name sullied by association. Even Freddy's work suffered. He'd nearly had a breakdown – another thing I hadn't realized. I'd assumed they hated me because I wasn't a genius like Frankie, when, in fact, they were struggling too hard to survive to stroke a troubled adolescent's irritable ego. So many things became clear, so much stuff I'd thought was aimed specifically at me, personally, was just them lashing out in pain. It got to me, big style. *How* stupid had I been? How bloody childish and self-centred? God. What a whingeing little toe-rag, always grinding on about how misunderstood I was. Urgh – cringe.

I tried to say I was sorry, but they shushed me. I'd been a child, caught up in the difficult teenage years. They were sorry now they had excluded me, that so many years had gone past while they buried themselves in their work, refusing to take the initiative and face up to the gradual disintegration of the family. Vi, especially, felt terrible. She felt she'd been a dreadful mother. Well, be fair, some people shouldn't have kids. Vi was an artist first and foremost; motherhood ran second to that. Not, of course, that I actually *said* that out loud. There are times when silence, and a sympathetic expression, are the better part of valour. Anyway, according to her lights, she'd done her best . . . Or tried.

It was hard, and it wouldn't be like some blinding flash, movie-style, but I felt we'd really started on the road to reconciliation. Whatever. It was only now, after buying the house here and leaving the rat-race, that the Parents felt they'd found some kind of small redemption. They'd come to terms with Frankie's sexuality and were positively *fond* of Thom – such a courteous, thoughtful boy . . . And just when they'd given up any thoughts of more TV work, recognition or fame, up pops Davey-boy with this fabulous offer for Freddy. *Plus* an American collector friend of the lovely Thom (whom they really did consider one of the family, practically a son-in-law, you could say – how I *wished* I'd had a tape-recorder at this point) was very, very interested in a whole slew of Vi's paintings, which he considered on a par with Georgia

O'Keeffe's. Oh yeah, things were looking up for the Greers, all right.

It was only me who needed sorting out, and now I'd split with the odious Phillip and decided to return to Uni, the future was assured. Freddy even offered to take a look at my book, but I wriggled out of that one. I remembered what he'd been like with that first Sylvia Plath essay; no nit left unpicked, you might say.

We had our coffee in the living room, cosy and content. It was just how I'd always imagined a family would be.

Nothing could go wrong now, everything was perfect. I couldn't wait to e-mail Millie and Frankie and share it all with them. They'd gloat, but never mind. They'd been right. 'Be patient, stay calm and . . .' Well, fair enough, fair enough.

I was happy that night – you know? Really happy.

15

The whole of the following week was like an excerpt from someone else's life. Someone who laughed all the time, got on with everyone, was having a great holiday. I was with Cam nearly every minute of the day, we went everywhere together. Everything we did was cool, everywhere we went was beautiful. The sun shone like a smile and polished everything to a golden sheen. Even the oranges hanging from the trees looked – more orange.

I told Cam everything. All about Jack, Phillip, my reconciliation with Freddy and Vi – oh, everything. We talked for *hours*. He told me all about growing up in Scotland, his dad who died of lung cancer when he was only ten; how his mum re-married disastrously, forcing him to leave home at sixteen. He talked about his music, his addictions, and his cure. Everything.

OK, he wasn't my ideal man. For a start, he was bloody obsessed with Dr Elias and her holistic claptrap, and his sense of humour deserted him where that was concerned. But he was sweet, you know, and we got on in an easy, comfortable way. He was always calm about things, 'walking Valium', I called him jokingly. Nothing I told him fazed him, and he was so used to working with celebrities in the big, bad rock'n'roll world that Jack and Freddy's niche-market literary fame didn't interest him much at all except in a general way. It was such a relief to be around someone who didn't want to use me to get to either Jack or my family.

We even had a laugh about Leo Brindle, who managed to fuck absolutely everyone at the Pendles' villa off so much that no one would run him down to Malaga to get his flight and he had to shell out for a taxi. Served the wanker right. I hoped he wet himself on that terrifying mountain road down to the coast.

Then one day we decided to visit the famous Cueva de la Pileta, the stupendous series of caverns decorated with magic – literally magic – paintings of animals dating from prehistoric times. Now, I'm a bit squeamish about caves. I took a hissy fit in Stump Cross Caverns on a school trip once, so I wasn't that keen at first. But in line with our go-everywhere-and-see-stuff policy, I agreed to do it. The road to the caves snaked through little villages and along mountainsides until we got to the steps leading up to the caves themselves. An oldish bloke was the guide; he seemed a really nice chap when he spoke to the other queuing tourists but when he saw me he made a face, and crossed himself. I was used to this sort of thing by now; like I said, I'd had a pretty frosty reception in Ronda and roundabouts from the locals. Still, this was a bit extreme. I was a tad peeved but I just shrugged; maybe he wasn't into piercing or shaved heads.

Cam spoke to him in Spanish – it always surprised me when he spoke Spanish, probably because otherwise he was so *Scottish*. Anyhow, the guide and Cam talked for a minute, then the guide smiled at me and nodded vigorously. Weird. Still nodding and smiling, he led us into the caves, which were lit only by the white flare of the gas lanterns some of the party were given.

'What was all that about?' I hissed as we stumbled through huge echoing caverns, along narrow passages where the stone was rippled like water and up slippery hand-cut steps into the dark.

'He thought you were a . . . member, disciple, whatever it is, of this bizarre cult that's got its HQ round here. In fact, d'you remember seeing that big white house on the hill – like, right on top of the biggest hill opposite the road as we drove in?'

'Yeah,' I said, falling over an American fella who was wowing at a big painting of a fish. 'Sorry, mate. Yeah, fantastic, isn't it? Soz, Cam – the house?'

'Well, that's the cult HQ, Casa Soledad. And get this, hen, they all shave their heads, have loads of piercings and wear the same sort of clothes you do. Man, you'd fit right in! The guide was convinced you were one of them, and they hate 'em round here. Well, Catholic country and all that, they wouldn't like a bunch of foreigners getting up to God knows what – Black Masses, naked goats, orgies . . . Stands to reason. That's the priest's prerogative, eh?' He snorted with laughter and I hushed him while the American party tutted. 'Wanna go up there and say hiya?'

'Yeah, right. Fab idea. Shush now, we're spoiling the atmosphere. You Jocks, honestly – savages. Still, that would account for why everyone's been so stand-offish with me. The barman at that party nearly spat in my drink – remember, I told you . . . God, look at that! Isn't it brilliant?'

We went the rest of the way in silence, broken only by whispered ohhs and ahhs. It did freak me out, being underground like that, but the guide was extra nice to me now he knew I wasn't a dyed-in-the-wool Satanist; he even showed me a little picture of a horse people normally didn't see.

It was a great day. When Cam held my hand as we staggered out into the light, I was so sure he felt the same feelings I did. I mean, he was so kind, so attentive, so willing to fill up every moment of his day with me, I just knew we were starting something good. Now, don't get me wrong, I'm not talking like, deathless, passionate *love*, or anything – but a, let's say, a nice little holiday romance?

That evening, we ate dinner at El Verdad in Ronda. It was perfect. I had a glass of wine to celebrate how great I felt, and it was so delicious, I had another. Nothing seemed to matter except this fantastic feeling of freedom and happiness. This was how a person should live. Not crushed by worries and scoured by the Northern cold, bundled up in English reticence and always being frightened of *feeling* things. Spain, God. How wrong I'd been all those years, hating it reflexively because my parents loved it so much. Never even bothering to learn the language, never seeing how fantastically beautiful it was. Well, I could admit I was wrong, I thought expansively. I'd been wrong about so much, but it was OK, it wasn't too late to change myself, to grow up.

We walked along the edge of the big municipal park that edged the terrible drop of El Tajo, the cliffs that form the gorge, our feet coated in the luminous powdery yellow dust from the pathway, swallows skimming like tiny jets around our heads. I loved the park, with its broad cool, marble paths and ratty, endearing flowerbeds. All around us, lovers held hands in the hazy blue veil of the twilight. We leant on the wall by the old bandstand and looked out over the spread of the farmlands below, the lights of distant farmhouses twinkling in the dusk. On the road way, way beneath us, a rider paced his horse, trotting along the dusty track like an illustration from an old story book.

I turned, leaning against the low stone wall, and smiled at Cam who smiled back quietly. He looked almost handsome in this light; very Spanish with his thick, curly black hair in a ponytail, and a loose white shirt glowing against his tan. I thought, He's got beautiful eyes, he really has.

So I kissed him. Full on that smiling mouth.

It was like kissing one of the bronze statues of famous bullfighters that stand outside the bullring. *That* cold and rigid. I knew instantly I'd made a big mistake.

I pulled back, a cold sweat of embarrassment trickling down my back. Suddenly, the hideous drop of the cliff looked really inviting.

'Sorry – um, I, er . . .' I spread my trembling hands out in a sorry-gesture. 'God – I don't – the wine – stupid of me – Cam, I . . .'

He seemed to unfreeze himself with an effort of will and shook his head.

'No, no. It's fine – no, honestly. It's me that should be sorry . . . Look, I ought to get going, if that's OK – I've got my meditation and stuff . . . Er, shall we?' And he walked off towards the car.

We drove home in virtual silence. I felt like a complete idiot. What had possessed me? It was obvious the guy simply considered us mates, and now I'd pounced on him like a sex-starved nympho.

I got out of the car at the usual place and bent down to the window. Play it dead normal, I thought; maybe he'll want to forget it, too. It wasn't *that* bad, we could go on like we had. It was only a kiss, for God's sake . . .

'Wanna go check out the Roman ruins tomorrow, like you said? Or we could –'

He cut in. 'Uh, well, no, I can't, sorry. Toby's off to Seville for the day and – I thought I'd go with him. You know, tourist stuff, while I'm here and all that . . .'

Yeah, I knew all right. He couldn't even look me in the face.

I never saw him again.

Oh, I waited for a couple of days before scootering up to the Pendles' – I had some pride. I found Toby, Sara and the two bratty kids by the pool, where they told me with false nonchalance that Cam had gone back to Blighty. He'd left a note for me. Gosh, Toby *had* meant to drop it in, but . . . here it was.

I pocketed it and screamed the Banshee off in a cloud of dust, scattering stones and sparrows as I tore round the rutted backroads. Fortunately, when I got home no one was in except Ish. I tore open the envelope. It contained some flimsy pages printed with the letterhead of the Shambhala Institute, Bucks. I read the scrawly handwriting while Ishy struggled up on to my lap – animals, they always know.

Dear Al

Firstly, I'm crap at writing letters so sorry if this is a bit useless. As you may gather, I have decided to return to England and go back to Shambhala for a while. Rather short notice, I know, but it had to be. When I got back after our day at the caves, I found Sara had collected a letter from the PO for me. It was from Jemma, a friend of mine at the Institute. I don't know if I mentioned her at all, we are kind of seeing each other. Dr Elias thinks that's OK as long as we don't transfer dependence from drugs to each other, which is one of the reasons why I came away for a while, to make sure we weren't doing that. Anyhow, Jem is having a bit of a crisis with her treatment and really needs my help. She isn't a strong person like you. She is very fragile and vulnerable. It's so hard for her, she knows she's a very creative person but she just hasn't found her medium yet, though she's tried most things. That's how she got into such a mess in the first place, it was so frustrating for her.

I want you to know how much I enjoyed our time together though. You really helped me fill up my days. Never a dull moment with you, hen! You're so full of life. I'm very, very sorry if you were upset at all that night. Sorry for any misunderstanding. You've been a real mate, though, and a really good person. I shall always be grateful and remember you with lots of affection. You made my trip special.

Yours,

Diego Cameron, 'Cam'

I don't think I have to tell you how I felt. Apart, obviously, from being a big, carthorsey blabbermouth who steamrollered through life without a care in the world.

Jemma. Hmm. Yes, Cam, you *did* neglect to mention poor, frail Jemma, as it goes. You let me 'fill up your days' as the good doctor prescribed.

I should have known. Fuck it, I did know. I just hadn't wanted to admit it. I was so caught up in my vision of a new, perfect life. Cam was a weak, spineless boy, a man who'd never grown up, who was looking for a distraction, a reason not to think for a while. And there I was, on a silver platter, with a fucking apple stuffed in my *enormous* mouth.

Urrgh. Yuck. Shite and double shite. With fucking knobs on.

In a fit of childishness I tore the letter into tiny pieces and chucked them in the compost bin.

I wasn't, like, heartbroken or anything. I wasn't, honest. I was embarrassed, which was worse. I felt all hot and squirmy, as if I'd gotten pissed and taken all my clothes off in public.

I was angry, too, with that slow-burning fury that comes when you think you've made a dick of yourself. The kind of anger that squats in your chest like a fat little demon and lashes out at anyone near. In fact, I was so moody, my new-found rapport with Freddy and Vi started to show signs of strain. So putting aside years of conditioning, I confided – somewhat – in Vi. Told her I'd thought Cam and I were getting along famously and then he'd done a bunk. Left out the attempted-snog bit, mind you; there's a limit. Played it as a holiday romance gone sour. She was very sympathetic, and told me Gran had always told her never to trust a musician or a man who wore white socks.

Well, she could have told me that *before* . . .

It was very strange having sympathetic parents. Even Freddy murmured, *'Bad luck, old girl,'* as we passed in the hall. I couldn't really get used to it. As I wrote to Frankie, it was positively unnatural.

But that cross little goblin in my heart muttered over and over, *'It's all your fault, you silly bitch. It's all your fault – stupid, stupid – fucked up again, haven't we?'* I couldn't shake the deep, fibrous idea that I had fucked it up from start to finish. From importuning the sap at that idiot party right up to manufacturing a dreamboy out of such poor clay.

I told Millie, of course. She e-mailed back one of her 'Oh, Al, you always jump in at the deep end' messages and I knew she was right. I had. Fully clothed and without a second thought. At least I hadn't *shagged* Cam. As Frankie said so rightly, I didn't even know his HIV/Hep status, his age, his home address or anything real. It could have been a whole lot worse, in his view.

Not that any of this improved my mood. I felt intensely restless and, when I wasn't dragging Ishy out for walks – or carrys, actually, since I usually had to carry him home – I scootered off using Freddy's tattered old map to navigate the hideous twisty roads. I took trails up mountains to watch the sunrise from impossibly high look-out points, the air as clear as spring water and scented with the resinous tang of the pines. I watched the great motley herds of goats being driven out to graze on the mulberry-coloured hillsides every morning and saw them fetched back in the evening, the bells round their scrawny necks sounding like jangling rivers of metal. I went down to the shores of the eerie turquoise reservoir that hides a drowned village; water so cursed and sterile that no one would swim in it, even in this desert place. I sat brooding amongst the twisted, dying yucca plants that lined its shores, their huge leathery spear-shaped leaves desiccated and stripped to their filigree of veins. I saw eagles soaring in the deep-blue skies and a family of albino mules stampeding through a blond-tasselled cornfield. I stared at the rumpled, dusty velvet patchwork of the immense landscape as if it contained some answer to the questions I could barely frame, and I lay on my back on hilltops feeling so diminished by the vast skies I felt I could almost melt back into the earth. The sun, hanging like a blazing wheel in the midday heat, seemed like a great door through which I could pass if *only* I knew the way . . .

Some days, I bounced the Banshee over rutted tracks and past great villas hidden behind huge security fences topped with barbed wire, and wondered who lived in them. Crazed reclusive old ladies, perhaps, like Spanish Miss Havershams trailing their tattered black mantillas through the moonlit courtyards, tittering madly behind their painted fans. Drug barons, more likely; hot from the Balearics and stinking with cash and corruption. And then there were the desolate ruins I sometimes discovered in odd, out of the way corners, their pot-bellied collapsing walls still brilliant with broken swathes of Moorish tiles and strangled by obscenely luminous pink ruffles of flowers. Who owned them? Who'd lived and died and borne children in those decaying rooms now open to the boiling sky like spread-eagled skeletons beyond shame or consolation? Dry, dead houses. Stones and dust and no hearts left.

What was wrong with me? Why did I fuck it up with every man I met? I hadn't had sex for years, really, *years*. It had gotten so bad I didn't even wank any more; what was the point? Who could I fantasize about? Film stars? Pop stars? The fumbling idiots of my youth? Or a dead poet and two wash-out tossers. *Great.* Oh, I didn't really mean that – not about Jack, at any rate. Only, sometimes, I couldn't bear to think about him. It was as if I resented him for ruining other men for me. Like, how could anyone ever measure up to Jack? Who was that passionate, that intense? No one. Other men were poor substitutes. God, if a bloke made a pass at me now, I'd probably scream and faint like some wan Victorian spinster. I felt as if my insides had shrivelled like the dying plants at the lake; desiccated, deformed, dead. Maybe that's what men sensed, me being dead inside. Hollow, not a real woman any more like I'd been with Jack. All my so-called cleverness, all that privileged education, the endless fucking *talk* – it all meant nothing. What good was it without Jack? Without someone to hold my hand and kiss me and tell me I was beautiful, and that he loved me. *He loved me.*

Oh, I know there are any amount of people who'd say it was pathetic, me wanting to be in love. 'A strong woman needs no one but herself.' Well, yeah – but only tossers like Cam thought I was *strong*. I knew I was utterly pathetic. I *wished* I was strong; strong, single-minded, dedicated and *pure*. But I wasn't. I was lonely, furious and confused.

I didn't know what I wanted to do. Go home, back to Bradford, I suppose. Yeah, go home. Bradford awaited with its grey, no-nonsense winter, its freezing rain, its sightless, ruined saints gazing blindly from their niches on the City Hall. Go home to my friends, my box-fresh new life. Because, what else was there?

16

The next afternoon, I forced the complaining Banshee up the stony, rutted track to home and saw a spanking new hired Ford Scorpio in a tasteful shade of metallic burgundy parked outside the house.

Bunging the filthy old scooter in the shed, I went in to find Freddy and Vi having a tea party with David and Jilly Taylor. Well, I say *party*, but in fact Jilly was sobbing into a Kleenex and Davey-boy was looking cheese-white under his brick-red tan.

I started to back out of the room, suddenly aware of my dirty clothes and grubby face.

'Ah. Alma.' Freddy's voice sounded strained, and at the sight of me Jilly burst into a fresh torrent of sobs. Freddy visibly took a deep breath. 'Alma, sit down, won't you? No, don't worry about your clothes – I'm sure David and Jilly will excuse you, under the circumstances.'

Oh, would they? Fab. I perched on the edge of a rickety old chair and cleaned my specs ineptly on a fold of my T-shirt while Vi poured me a cuppa. Jilly struggled and finally got herself under control, eyeing me from behind a soggy mass of tissues. Davey-boy cleared his throat and, nodding at Freddy – who waved at him in a go-ahead-old-chap sort of way – inched forward a smidgen on the dog-hairy sofa, his expensive Ralph Lauren casual strides already felted with Ishy fluff.

'Alma, lovely to see you. In fact, we . . . we were very much hoping to catch you.'

Me? What on earth did they want with me? Serialize my book? Maybe Leonardo DiCaprio could play Bramwell. Like, yeah, right. I tried to look composed and interested.

'Jilly and I are . . . having a bit of a problem. Our youngest daughter, Dido, appears to have run off to join some bloody *cult* that's got a place round here. I asked your parents – well, they know the country and so forth – about the advisability of contacting the local police vis-à-vis their going up there and getting her back, but . . .'

Freddy shook his head. 'Not a lot of point, old man. The Guardia Civil are certainly not advisable, and even if you could get the Policía Municipal interested . . . well, it's not as if the girl's *dead*, is it?' He looked sympathetic. Honestly, talk about Mr Tactless. Even Vi winced, and Jilly erupted in a new storm of tears. David looked visibly shaken.

'My God, how many types of police do these people have? I want my child back. Is it too much to ask . . .' He was turning the colour of his car. I thought I'd better say something before his head exploded.

'Er, three sorts of coppers, actually.' I ticked them off on my fingers: 'Guardia Civil, Policía Municipal and the Policía Nacional – though you hardly ever see *them*. They're all armed, and they all hate being dragged into domestics with foreigners. Look, if your lass has gone off, why not go and get her yourselves? It'd be easier.'

Jilly blew her nose loudly and snuffled. 'But that's the point: she *won't* talk to us. She says we're too materialistic to understand her spirituality – which is *rubbish!* I've been going to yoga for *years!* It's just –we can't get *through* to her these days. It's all so *awful*. And now this . . .' Renewed sobbing. I passed the tissues silently.

Davey-boy gritted his jaw and cast a look at Jilly she fortunately didn't see.

'Dido met some chap on holiday last year in Ibiza; calls himself Rain. He's one of them. Dido's besotted with him. When she learnt their HQ was near here and we'd got the villa, she flew out immediately. Usually, we couldn't *drag* her on holiday with us. I thought perhaps we'd made some progress with her, but obviously it was all a ruse to be near this bloody Rain chap. They've been e-mailing each other constantly, and now she's run off. These *bloody* people – Moonie types – they brainwash youngsters, you know, turn them against their families. A girl from a good home, with parents who have a decent income, must be gold dust to them. They'll try and milk us for every penny if we go up there to get her back, that's why we need a go-between, someone who can speak to them in their own language. I know what they're like – we commissioned a docu-drama on the very subject last year. Little did I think it would be me – us – in that position one day . . .' He started forward and clenched his jaw tighter still. Talk about apoplexy.

Jilly turned her watery oyster eyes to me, her pointy little nose raw with crying and sunburn, and pushed her stiff hair behind her ear with a limp paw. 'You talked to her at our party, Alma. I saw you. You look so much like Rain, same clothes and hair, that sort of thing, I thought you were one of them too, until I realized you were Freddy's daughter . . . Oh, did she *say* anything, give you any hint what she might be thinking?'

'Did I talk to her? I'm sorry, I . . .'

'Yes, yes, you did . . .' Jilly fumbled in her bag and passed me a snapshot. It was the anorexic girl from the party, only younger looking and wearing a jumper. But it was her, all right. The same furious, sulky expression; the same bitten-off designer hair. My God, that was their precious Dido – the coke-kiddie!

'Er, right – yeah, I didn't realize she was your . . . She asked was I going to see someone called Solly, or his dad, and would I take her with me. I didn't get it, to be honest. Then she stormed off. She did seem upset, yeah . . .'

David looked blank for a second and then practically jumped off the sofa. 'Solly – no, it was Soledad! That's their HQ: Soledad. My God, she was planning this all along, I . . .'

I twigged. *Casa Soledad,* the big white house on the hill near the Cueva di la Pileta – the place Cam had *said* was a cult's house. The name means 'Solitude', and you couldn't get more isolated than that place.

'I know the place you mean. It's up near the show caves.' I nodded at Freddy who was looking faintly bored. Vi made English noises and re-filled the cups.

'You *know* it – d'you mean . . . ?'

'Oh, no – I've seen it, that's all. It's not that far, why don't you pop up there and . . .'

They both looked sheepish. 'Well, we rather thought it would be better if a go-between – someone neutral, who could *relate* to younger people . . .' David looked at Jilly for support and she took his hand. 'I was going to ask your parents if perhaps . . . You're nearer her age and you look so much like a . . . Maybe you could *reach* her, in a way we couldn't . . .'

Freddy stirred into action. 'Now look here, David. I really don't think –'

Jilly gazed at me beseechingly. Davey turned his attention to Freddy, his plump face suddenly hard. You could see how he'd gotten so far up the corporate ladder: that bluff, decent-chap style draped like a slice of ham over a frame of solid iron.

'Freddy, old man, in view of our joint commitments, I do think we should help each other, don't you? Bearing in mind your family's knowledge of local customs, the area, the *language* . . . I really don't want Jilly to have to endure any more distressing scenes; she's worn out as it is. You *do* see my point?'

I wasn't sure Big Fred did, but Vi and I certainly got the message. I could see Vi swelling up with outrage and I was disgusted. Either I go get their stupid brat, or Freddy doesn't get his TV thing. Bish bash bosh.

I could have refused, of course. The Parents wouldn't have blamed me in the least. They'd have been disappointed to lose the gig, but . . .

I felt that old, familiar heat of anger creep through me, mixed this time with loathing. What sort of people went on like this? Who cared if their skinny kid got religion and fucked off to a convent, or the modern equivalent? *I'd* join a fucking cult if Davey and Jilly were *my* mummy and daddy.

But Davey had me stitched up like the proverbial kipper. Do it, or watch him carve up Freddy. He must have worked it all out before they came.

'We could take you up there in the car, Alma. You could see Dido while we wait outside. Maybe she would come with you straight away and . . .'

I drank some tea to make him wait. Fuck him.

'No. I'll go on the scooter. If she wants to get out of there, she can ride down on the back of me. If she doesn't fancy that, you can go get her. Whatever. I'll go tomorrow, early. Now, sorry, but I need to grab a shower and I think everyone's pretty tired . . .'

They got the hint. With much thanking and air-kissing, generously laced with tears and manly handshakes, they were gone.

Vi said in a tight voice, 'I'll start dinner, then, shall I?' As she bustled out furiously to the kitchen and started throwing the crockery about, Freddy regarded me from the depths of his old wing armchair, Ishy wheezing at his feet.

He steepled his bony fingers. 'That was very decent of you, Alma. Very kind.'

I burbled something about my getting a wash before tea and stood up.

'I want you to know how much I appreciate this, my dear.' He touched the tips of his fingers to his lips thoughtfully.

I smiled a very small smile at him. We both knew the score, all right. I suddenly thought: this is my father. This is where I come from. He'd fought all his life, for acceptance, for fame, for his work. He hadn't had a privileged background; his people had been genteelly poor, and he'd had to fight hard for his education. Now, with his looks and his carefully constructed manner it was so easy to see him as the typical absent-minded Prof; but that was a mistake people only made once. Under his scatty exterior there was a soldier: tough, seasoned, pragmatic. People – they were never exactly what you thought they were. Just when you had it sorted, off they slid out of your grasp like eels back through the grass to the river.

I got an early night. Tomorrow was going to be a long, long day.

BOOK III

'Corruptio optimi pessima' Proverb

17

I stopped by the roadside in Benaoján village and consulted my map. I had a pretty good idea of where I was going as far as Santa Rita, but after that . . . Well, I'd just have to ask.

It was still early, even by Spanish standards. The sun was lighting the pink clouds from behind, edging them in silvery-grey and white. They reflected on to the limestone cliffs across the valley, turning them a sort of matte pinky-blue. The colours were so intensely pastel that, if you saw them in a painting, you'd think the artist was having you on. But clouds, hmmm. They were the first I'd seen for a while. Not that it meant rain – they'd burn off as the day hotted up. Still, it was the first little hint that summer was starting to fade.

I took a swig from my water bottle and then set off again. It didn't take long to reach Santa Rita, a nowhere sort of burg with a railway line cutting through it and one bar. I parked up in front of the village shop and went in to ask for directions to Casa Soledad in my execrable Spanish. Even allowing for my difficulty with the language, it got me nowhere, *squared*. Oh, sorr-*ree* – hang up the garlic and make a cross out of lolly-sticks. It was like that bit in *Dracula* when the hapless hero goes to the inn and asks the way to Chez Drac. The silence was deafening. I'd never realized I had two heads until then. I left.

I stared moodily at the Banshee and studied the map again. There weren't any obvious roads leading up to the Casa, and I couldn't see any tracks. Bollocks. OK – Plan B. I would ask in the bar, and if I got the same go-round I'd head for home and say I tried, got hopelessly lost, they'd have to go themselves, etc. Right.

The bar was tiny, dark and inhabited by three old gimmers, a scrawny yellow mongrel and a fat barman polishing a glass and whistling through his straggly moustache. Great; out of a vampire film and into a Spaghetti Western. I walked up to the counter manfully.

'Perdóneme Señor. ¿Cómo puedo llegar a la Casa Soledad?'

The three old blokes and the barman stopped what they were doing and stared at me. The dog coughed. I could feel myself getting hot under the collar. Pushing my specs back up my shiny nose defiantly, I started again. I didn't get past 'Perd–'

'What you wanna go up there for?' the barman said in a thick Manchester–Andalucian accent.

'I –er – I know it's . . . There's a little lass up there – her parents want her back. I said I'd . . . Look, I'm not one of *them*. I just want to get the girl and go. A rescue mission sort of thing.'

He polished the glass reflectively. 'Relation, is she? Well, you do right – but I'm bloody glad it's you an' not me. Bloody freaks, that lot.'

'Are you from Manchester, by any chance?'

'No, Salford. I were born here, like, but I worked in Manchester for nearly fifteen year. Can y'tell?' He bridled pleasurably. 'Retired, you might say, an' come 'ome. This is my place – nice, innit? Look, y'go back out the way you come, then just before the railway bridge there's a little cut – go up there a bit an' it turns into a road. That leads up to the old English Lord's House – your Casa Soledad. Oh aye.'

'Er, thanks.'

'Don't thank me, lovie. Fetch your lass an' get the hell outta there right off, like. Come back here after an' I'll get you a Coke or summat. But I wouldn't stop up there long. They get up to stuff.' He nodded sagely and tapped the side of his bulbous nose with his forefinger. 'Where you from, then?'

'Bradford,' I said, edging towards the door.

'Oh 'eck. All them bloody Pakis – not my cuppa tea.'

'Fuck off, you stupid racist fucker,' I muttered under my breath as I scootered off furiously. Christ almighty, even here. It certainly put a fine edge on my crossness as I wanged the Banshee up what appeared to be precipitous goat-track lined with smoky Retama bushes, their sulphurous tassels almost brushing my elbows.

Then suddenly, the track became a tarmac road: smooth, well-tended and curving upwards. The Banshee gave a wild shriek and shot off alarmingly with me practically flapping in the wind behind like Superman's cloak.

I had just about managed to get my machine under control, when I realized it wasn't a road as such, but a sort of drive. Looming in front of me was a high, white crenellated wall topped with a roofette of terracotta tiles done in the old way. A huge pair of antique iron-studded oak doors was set in it. In the doors was a smaller, human-sized door, and on the wall, an intercom. The whole thing looked super-neat, well-kept, freshly painted – and very forbidding.

The walls seemed to stretch away forever: this was a serious house. I wrestled the Banshee on to her centre stand, chain-locked her and walked to the doors. A small brass plaque under the intercom said 'CDS Foundation'. I took a moment to pull myself together, then pressed the buzzer. As I did so, I saw there was a CCTV camera attached to the wall above the doors, trained on anyone who approached. Those things give me the creeps. In fact the whole thing – the house, the plaque with its stupid 'Foundation' bullshit, the huge doors – it was all creepy. Suddenly I felt very nervous and then cross with myself for being nervous, and then nervous again. What if the villagers were right and this lot really were a bunch of freaky weirdoes who 'did stuff'? I didn't even have a mobile phone. Oh, *shit.*

I nearly jumped out of my skin when a disembodied voice said, in a strong American accent, *'Sí? ¿Qué quiere?'*

'I've come to speak to Dido – Dido Taylor. She's here with someone called Rain.'

There was a pause. Then the voice said, 'Uh, I'm sorry, but . . .'

I saw red. I wasn't going through all this to have some Yank halfwit 'uh' at me. 'Listen, mate, you just get hold of your boss right now – d'you hear me? *Right now!* I am not, repeat, *not,* leaving until I've spoken to Dido Taylor. If you fuck me about I'll go straight to the Policía, and you know what *that* means.' I bridled self-righteously.

There was another, longer pause while I scuffed my foot crossly in the dust and stared furiously up at the camera. Then there was a burble and the voice said, 'Uh, like, uh, right. OK. You have clearance. Welcome to the CDS Foundation.'

The small door clicked open.

I resisted putting two fingers up at the camera and stepped inside.

18

It was beautiful. More beautiful than I could have thought possible. I don't know exactly what I'd expected; something grim and barracks-like, I suppose. Certainly not this exquisite old garden. I was standing on an immaculate gravel path which meandered gently up through the greenery to the house itself, which I could just see, perched breathtakingly on the edge of the high cliffs. There were flowers everywhere and the air was thick with the droning of bees. Butterflies floated past like scraps of torn silk and the faint sound of running water freshened the air.

As I stood bemused, a young man hurried towards me down the path. He was very tall and thin, with a shaved head and . . . you got it – baggy beige clothes. A long-sleeved tunic and flappy drawstringy trousers, a pair of flip-flops and a bag; what we used to call a disco-bag, meaning a smallish shoulder bag slung across his body. Except this one wasn't in puce glitter, it was unbleached calico to match his outfit. The perfect hippie. Only, he was *covered* in piercings. I had never seen anyone so heavily pierced except in body-art mags. One eyebrow was done with a row of steel ball closure rings, at least six of them. The other had one ring and it looked like it was set to go the way of its twin. Two rings in each nostril; a bridge-of-the-nose bar closed at each end with a ball; a similar bar, only vertical, pinched through the flesh of his forehead above his eyes; four steel studs in his upper lip and four corresponding under his lower lip. I didn't need to see his tongue to be pretty sure it was done too. He had studs, like dimples, in each cheek. His ears were almost obscured by metal. A series of rings stepped down his throat, and the web of skin between the thumb and forefinger of the hand he extended to me had a ring through it.

He smiled broadly. I was right about the tongue; at least four studs. And a ring in that bit of skin that attaches your upper lip to your gum. I felt positively naked.

'Uh . . .'

Great. It was the 'uh' guy. I shook his hand – I mean, what else could I do? He was grinning like an *American*, for fuck's sake – it would have been mean not to.

'Uh, welcome! I'm Brother Sierra and I'm here to escort you to the house. If you'll follow me . . .'

'Look here, er, Sierra – I'm here to see Dido Taylor, so maybe we can just do that and then I'll be on my way . . .'

'Uhhh, well, OK. I hear you, I do, but hey, uh, Mama Jay said for me to bring you to the house and Do, uh, *Dido* will meet you there. You know, civilized, kinda? Mama Jay thinks it's, like, rude not to at least speak with you, being as you're a guest and all.'

All this was said as we walked up the terraced path through the profusion of flowers to an ornamental arch leading to what I assumed would be the courtyard of the main building. I'm no architect, but I tell you – what greeted me then was the most fantastic bit of design I ever saw. As you walked through the arch, you turned a slight corner and, suddenly, there before you was a huge, oblong reflecting pool tiled in pale cerulean blue that extended to the very edge of the cliff and was the size of a proper swimming pool. It was as if it joined the sky itself; water and air fusing in a perfectly smooth mirror reflection of each other; no beginning, no end. It was hypnotic, extreme. Completely pure. Exquisite.

I stood gawping like a fool at the grand optical illusion. Sierra smiled even more, if that was possible.

'Cool, huh? It, like, totally blew me away the first time I saw it, too. Awesome, really.'

It was. Awesome. Somebody's dream made real; so big, and so completely without distractions that it could only have sprung from a mind used to obedience; there was not a shred of doubt in it.

I was still gazing when I felt Sierra gently tap my arm. 'Uh, we gotta go. Sorry. Maybe you can come back and, like, meditate some more later.'

I followed him through another arch, part of what I now saw were cool, shadowy colonnaded cloisters running either side of the pool, but far enough back not to interfere with the reflective quality.

There didn't seem to be anyone about, though I thought I could hear voices and laughter in the distance. As we walked through a door in the back of the right-hand cloister and entered the main house, I asked Sierra where everyone was. He slowed his frantic flip-flopping pace slightly and bobbed his head from side to side.

'OK, well, uh, I guess some people are painting the dorm block and there's gardening and . . .'

Before he could finish his sentence, a door off the corridor we were walking down burst open and a man thrust himself out. He brought such a wave of anger and aggression with him, I stepped back involuntarily. He stopped, quivering, in front of us and levelled a finger at Sierra's chest. Now, I know it's all subjective, beauty is only skin-deep, you shouldn't judge a book by its cover and all that, but believe me, this was one fella who'd had a right fucking smack with the ugly stick. He was about five foot six, heavily built with a curving barrel chest and thick, mottled flabby arms. Since he was wearing the regulation baggies with a grubby, food-stained white singlet, I could see his body was covered with patchy black hair and his shaved head showed blue-black stubble. He had numerous piercings, natch, and most of them were septic and crusty. Whoever had made him hadn't progressed beyond doing thumb-pots. His eyes were really weird, like they'd been slit out of the soggy skin of his face, the eyelashes growing at angles, the muddy brown of his irises barely visible. If all that wasn't enough he had acne, too, poor bastard, and the best crop of blackheads I'd seen in ages.

But however shit he looked, it wasn't as shit as the temper he was in. I felt my whole body tense with adrenaline and I prepared myself for a ding-dong row. Sierra backed away from the pointy finger and spread his big, square hands out in front of himself placatingly.

'Uh – uh – uh, God, man, like . . .'

'You. Stupid. Wanker.' He had a thick, gloopy London–Estuary accent. Each mini-sentence was punctuated with a finger stab.

Sierra looked crushed. 'Hey, hey, Wolf, I thought . . .'

Wolf? *Wolf?* Oh, pul-lease. I started to speak but he cut in, ignoring me.

'Listen, you thick Septic, who is the Head of Security round 'ere? Who? Do you fuckin' well know? Eh?'

'Well, like, you are, Brother Wolf, yeah, but . . .'

'Don't "but" me, you tosser. Haven't we had enough fuckin' bother recently wiv *intruders*? *Strangers*? An' now here we are again. You lot never learn, do yer? You cannot bring your fuckin' totty up here willy-fuckin'-nilly . . .'

I was about to have a go at him when a phone rang in the room he'd shot out of. He glared at us and said, 'Not a fuckin' inch, right? You do not move a fuckin' inch.' Then he went back in, muttering, and answered it.

Sierra looked at me like a whipped puppy. 'Uh, sorry, man. Brother Wolf, you know, he's a genius, really, but, like, he can be pretty *intense*. Sorry.'

Yeah, OK, whatever – just get this over with, I prayed silently, *and let me go home.*

Wolf came out again like a malevolent weatherman in a cuckoo clock. 'Right. That was Mama Jay – she's in the control room. She says she authorized you to bring this – person – to the North Room.'

He didn't look any happier and he cast me a glance of pure dislike.

'Thank you *so* much,' I said sweetly.

He backstepped into his room. In the second before the door slammed shut behind him, I saw shelves crammed with computer gear. Screens, printers, stacks of disks, mysterious boxes with cables coming out of them, heaps of stuff.

Sierra now looked visibly shaken and he hurried me through the house. I barely had time to take in the priceless antique tilework, carved wood and tantalizing paintings before he opened a big old ornate door and said, 'Uh, if you'll wait here, Mama Jay will be, like, uh, with you in a moment.'

Then he shut me in and I was alone in a room full of wonders.

The first thing was the view out of the huge ceiling-to-floor windows. You looked out over miles and miles of folded hills – sage green, olive–silver, faded mulberry, lavender, dusty ochre – and very faintly, in the distance, the road leading to the Cueva de la Pileta. The vast French windows opened on to a filigree ironwork balcony that was buttressed directly on to the sheer rock face. I peeked out; it seemed to hang into nothing. I didn't stand on it. Vertigo, claustrophobia – two sides of the same coin, as far as I'm concerned.

The rest of the room – and it wasn't small, let me tell

you – was a solid mass of carved wood panels, intricate William Morris-type murals of some medieval goings on I couldn't place; big, comfy-looking inlaid sofas heaped with scatter cushions and chairs squashily upholstered in old-gold raw silk. There were more whatnots, bibelots, statuettes, thingummys and bijouterie than you could shake a stick at. A big fireplace with some logs laid for a fire stood in one corner and on an old rose velvet chaise longue lay a massive black Persian cat, staring at me with luminous amber eyes the size of car headlights.

I went over to it, trying not to scuff the priceless rug or knock anything over with my daysack. I sat on the chaise and gave the cat my fingers to sniff – which it did. Then it started purring like a freight train and pushed its head under my fingers, demanding to be rubbed behind the ears.

'Ooo, you're sohhh cute. Aren't you a bab, eh, hmmm?' I cooed, having been deprived of cat company for so long. Then I shut up, embarrassed, in case the room was bugged. The cat's flat pug face was nearly the size of a dinner plate, but it looked very well groomed. I knew these cats had to be brushed every single day or else they got dreadlocks, but this one was a fluffy marvel of night-black fur. At least they cared for their pets, that was something.

I was beginning to get antsy, despite the cat-fuzzing, when the door opened, and a small woman came in.

'Hello,' she said, smiling. 'I'm Jane.'

Jane. God. How can I describe Jane? If Wolf had been made by an apprentice on a Friday afternoon, then Jane had been created by a master craftsman at the height of his powers on a fine summer's day. She was the most beautiful person I have ever seen. Genuinely. Like, you don't see that many really *beautiful* people, do you? Oh, pretty, nice-looking, not-arf-bad types – sure. World's full of 'em, and we take that as the standard. But truly, amazingly beautiful – no. It's a rare and unsettling thing; it puts the mundane old world off kilter.

And here was Jane, a little masterpiece. Like a Persian miniature, or a pocket ikon. Her skin was a flawless cream, like finest porcelain. I looked for wrinkles, imperfections, but there weren't any. She wasn't young, though; in her mid-to-late fifties at a guess, but the years seemed to have laid a silvered patina to her, as if she had been polished and polished until she was without flaw and glowed with a warm light from within. Her face was a composition of graceful curves that led gently from one to another. A small, elegant nose, fine black calligraphic eyebrows, high sculptured cheekbones, a roseate recurved bow of smiling lips. Perfect little white teeth; very short, close-cropped hair obviously once thick and black, now like a gleaming dark silver cap. Tiny, pale hands like flying doves that gestured me to the sofa where she sat and patted the seat next to her. The room was filled with the subtle, warm citrus of her perfume. Her large eyes were a clear, guileless cornflower blue. In fact, she was like a flower in her absolute perfection; not a statue, not classical and cold – but warm, natural, *of nature*.

'Now,' she said, 'would you like some tea? I hear you came on a scooter – golly, how brave!' Her voice was musical, gentle. I was fascinated, as if I were sitting next to a famous painting, or a film star. It was too strange for words. I just wanted to look at her; she was so magical, so unearthly. I felt confused and at a loss – where were the evil freaks? Where was the demonic cult leader? OK, Wolf was a fuckwit, but no worse than your typical aggressive computer nerd, the sort I always avoided on campus. A little tyrant with a power complex. But Jane – she seemed to have stepped out of an Edith Wharton novel, only English. Or rather, Welsh, from the faint trace of that melodious sing-song in her accent. Yeah,

Welsh, definitely. No doubt about it, nothing was what I'd expected *at all.* I was feeling decidedly wobbly in the brain area.

Then I remembered I was here for a purpose. 'I'm, er, here to see Dido Taylor. Her parents want her back and they'll – they'll make trouble if she doesn't . . . Look, they're wealthy people, influential. I need to . . . Who's the boss, or whatever you call it? Is it this Mama Jay they keep talking about? I really must speak . . .'

She laughed, and put her hand to her throat. 'Gosh, I'm rather afraid that's me – Jane – Mama Jay, d'you see? It's the Chelas nickname for me, bless them. Well, I'm so old, and they're so young – I suppose I am like a sort of mother to them!'

'The Chelas?'

'The students who are studying here at the Foundation. You met our Brother Sierra, didn't you? *Such* a sweet boy, and so brilliant. Quite exceptional. I do think Americans have that special quality of youthfulness and innocence, don't you? So charming . . .'

'Er, yes, very nice. Unfortunately, *Wolf* didn't seem too impressed at receiving visitors.' Let's see how she fields that one; she can't be all sweetness and light.

Her blue eyes looked wistful and she sighed, as if the cares of the world were on her delicate shoulders. 'Oh dear. Yes, poor, poor Wolf – so troubled. The penalties of genius in many ways; his social skills are not all they might be. I hope you aren't too upset?'

I realized that, somehow, she knew what had happened. Maybe Sierra had briefed her. But then I remembered the CCTV camera, probably one of many. 'No, not really. Look, Jane – Mama Jay, I really *must* see Dido.'

'Yes, yes indeed. How remiss of me. Would you excuse me a moment.' She slipped off the sofa and went across to a phone. I couldn't quite make out what she was saying, but I did catch the words 'Dido' and 'tea'. *OK, OK, we'll do the bloody tea thing if it makes her happy,* I thought. *Just as long as I get this done with.* If nothing else, I'd have some gossip to tell the troops when I got home.

She sat back down as I was clucking at the cat in an attempt to appear casual and confident.

'I see you've met Gwydion. Do you like cats? I love them, and all animals, really. Ah – I'm so sorry, I didn't catch your name, dear.'

You wouldn't have, I thought, *since I haven't told it to anyone.*

'He certainly is tremendous, isn't he?' I could do the small-talk thing if I had to, and I didn't want this strange little person to know my name, however nicey-nicey she seemed. This was a cult headquarters, after all. Mind control, that sort of malarkey. You couldn't be too careful.

Mama Jay leant across slightly and patted my hand. 'You needn't worry, dear. This isn't some sort of cult, you know. We are a study centre, that's all. Rather dull, really. We are completely aware of what the villagers think and I can't tell you how we've tried to persuade them otherwise, but it's no use. I suspect they rather enjoy thinking we're crazy; it gives them something to gossip about!' She laughed as if it were a grand joke, everyone thinking she was Satan in a bleached linen palazzo ensemble.

I was foxed. Was she telepathic? 'So what *are* you then?' I sounded rude, even to myself. But what the hell – I wasn't on a social call.

'Why, the Foundation is really a kind of retreat – for students. The Chelas come here to study various esoteric subjects, to benefit from our extensive library, our resources. Most Universities pooh-pooh research in the more spiritual subjects; the world is a very materialistic place these days. Here at the Foundation, the Chelas are encouraged to pursue the paths to enlightenment, to spiritual awareness, that interest them most. They do some work around the place – grow vegetables, that sort of thing. It's all communal. We help each other in whatever ways we can. And of course, the Chelas come to benefit from the wisdom of our great teacher; our prophet, if you will. Such a marvellous man. I wish you could meet him, I really do, but unfortunately, he's unwell at the moment. Oh yes, we live a very secluded, peaceful life here. Perhaps that's why we're so . . .'

At that moment the door opened and Dido stomped in, followed by a short, plump girl pushing a tea trolley, and a tall man. Dido looked like – to use a Mazism – a bulldog chewing a wasp. Talk about livid. The plump girl bobbed a little bow towards Jane and left. I couldn't make out the features of the tall fella as he was turned slightly away from me helping with the trolley.

'Ah! Tea! How lovely. So kind of Marigold, but then she's our little treasure. Isn't that right, Donner?' Jane smiled happily, seemingly unaware of the black thunder cloud that was Dido. The man turned to face us.

It was Jack.

My heart nearly leapt out of my chest, then it seemed to be beating all over my body. My blood felt as if it were bubbling in my veins and my legs went shaky. Jack – no! It was – it was impossible – how – God, what the fuck was going on? I felt the instant constriction of my lungs; everything seemed to blur and go very far away. Jack! Jack – fuck! *Jack.* I must have looked dreadful, because the man turned to me and looked concerned. Then he said *in a German accent*:

'Are you OK, miss? You look unwell. Are you an asthmatic?'

I looked again. I stared into that face so nearly, so very *nearly* Jack's, and felt my heart squeeze; but this time, in excruciating disappointment.

'I, er . . . yes, I am. My inhaler – ' And I fumbled it out of my bag and sucked. Everyone except Dido looked deeply sympathetic. Not embarrassed, as most people were if you did the inhaler thing. You know, *'Oh God, not a sickie – what if she does something physical and I have to deal with it – yuck.'* No, they just looked as if they cared, or were interested and slightly worried.

Jane poured me a cup of tea and I sipped it gratefully. Dido had flounced off to the window and was staring out as if she might commit suicide just to spite us.

'Oh, Donner, you dear man, so thoughtful. Donner is a proper, medical doctor you know. We all feel so secure, knowing he's here to help us if we need it.' Jane beamed at the man who shrugged his shoulders and smiled.

'Well, you know, a doctor – there are thousands of doctors. It's not so great . . . Do you feel a little better now, miss?'

'Yes, I . . . the – the heat – it's hot today, and . . . On the scooter . . .' Burble, burble, rabbit, rabbit. *Shit.*

When the first shock had worn off and I looked more closely, Donner didn't look that much like Jack. Well, he did, but not *identical.* He was taller, more slender and much blonder. He had the crop, the piercings – not many – the outfit and the smiley attitude of the Foundation. It was those prominent cheekbones, those slanty green eyes, that *Nordic* thing. And his colouring: old ivory, faintly tanned to a beautiful paper-brown. All that was Jack. But Jack was dead. Yeah, Jack was . . .

I was so lost in this wheezy reverie I didn't realize at first that darling Dido was winding up to the mother of all hissy-fits.

She turned on me with her eyes blazing, her square face greeney white except where a splotch of red burned in her cheeks. She'd cropped her hair nearly to the scalp and it seemed to bristle and crawl on her head.

'I don't know – *I don't know* what you think you're

doing here, I really *don't.* It's no good her sending you. I know she has. She hates me, she's so jealous of Daddy and me . . . God, I won't – you can't make me go back, you know. Oh, no. Rain and I love each other. Not like her, dragging Daddy into her stupid, fat, disgusting life, and her stupid, *stupid* parties and her stupid, stupid, horrible . . .'

Jane raised her hand. For someone so tiny and fey, she suddenly exuded an air of solid platinum authority. She didn't raise her voice or look any different; no scowls, no frowns. Just that implacable sweetness and those huge blue eyes, full of what appeared to be genuine sadness.

'Dido . . . Dido, my dear. We have gone over this many times since you came to Casa Soledad. You know – no, please don't interrupt me – you know you cannot stay here. It is not possible. Rain knows this and he fully acknowledges that his affection for you blinded him to the realities of our life here. Dido . . .'

Dido began to cry with a loud, forced, raw, howling. Her excruciatingly thin frame convulsed with the effort. She clutched her head in her hands, pressing her fingertips deep into her cheeks and dragging them down her face. Donner went over to her and gently pulled her fingers away, sighing as he saw the red weals she'd left on her skin. As he put his hand up, I noticed he'd lost the first joint of the little finger of his left hand; it gave his hands a lopsided look.

'Dido, please . . .' he said unhappily.

'I AM NOT DIDO!' she screamed at full volume. 'I – am – not – Dido! I'm Dove now. *Dove,* not Dido . . .' The rest was lost in a full-on roaring, choking temper tantrum. She crouched on the rug rocking and carrying on like a two-year-old.

My first impulse was to slap her. OK, she was upset about leaving her boyfriend. She didn't like her parents (and who could blame her?) and she wanted to stay in the lovely Foundation – until the craze wore off and she ran away to play somewhere else. But this was way, way over the top. If she'd been in Bradford, I would have smacked her into sense or chucked a bucket of water over her because she was hysterical; proper, old-fashioned hysterical. But here . . . I just sat like a lemon, feeling embarrassed.

No one else moved, either. Jane sat looking terribly concerned and Donner stood where he could reach her if necessary, saying nothing. It was perfect. Dido thrashed herself into a gulping heap and her sobs trickled off into snotty bubbling. If no one reacted, what was the point of her carrying on? In about three seconds, I witnessed a turnabout that would have done an Oscar-winner proud. She sat up and wiped her face on her sleeve, then glared at us all defiantly. You could see her daddy in her, then.

'OK, that's *it*. Have it your own way. I'll go – oh, I'll go all right – but my daddy's going to *sue* you when he hears what you've done to me here. Just wait 'til I tell him how you made me work an' do horrible cooking, treating me like some fucking slave. All because Rain loves me more than he loves you – you horrible old *bitch.*'

This last was fairly spat at Jane, who just shook her head sorrowfully. Donner, behind Dido, looked bloody furious, mind you. He obviously thought the world of Jane and 'bitch' didn't go down too well.

I decided to put my oar in and try and wind this whole thing up before it got *stupid* – to use a Dido word. 'Come on, Dido. Your mum and dad are very worried . . .'

'She's not my mother! She's my step-mother, my *step*-mother. I hate her! I hate her! She *made* Daddy leave Mummy. *Made* him leave us and live with her and her brats. She's like a fucking *witch*. I wish she was *dead!'*

'OK, OK – I didn't know that. I'm sorry. Look, your

dad, then – he asked specially if I'd come and talk to you . . .'

Her eyes narrowed and a twisted little smile distorted her swollen mouth. 'Oh, sure. You mean she *nagged* Daddy until he got round that old has-been of a father of yours and *made* him send you. God, God, *God* – I am so sick of Daddy ranting on about Mr oh-so-fucking-marvellous Freddy *bloody* Greer! That's why they got that crappy house in this crappy, *skanky* country instead of Ibiza, like I wanted. It was all to impress *him*. I mean, who cares? Who cares about some tedious old *wanker* . . .'

Jane dropped her teacup. We all stared at her – me, Dido with her mouth still open, and Donner with a look of deep concern.

She turned to me and laid a trembling hand on my arm. 'Freddy Greer? You're *Freddy Greer's daughter*?'

Christ, not another *Sol y Sombre* fan. Well, I wasn't getting her his autograph, if that's what she had in mind.

'Yes, Freddy's my father. He and Davey – er, Dido's father – are friends; they work together. Her family thought . . .'

'And your mother – your mother is Violet Trelannon? The artist?'

Weirder and weirder. 'Uh, yes, as a matter of fact. Why?'

'Oh my dear! My dear! How – oh, I can hardly – Donner, this is the child of The Prophet's saviour! Oh, to think – *his child* is here among us! Frederick Greer's child! Oh, I don't – why, I don't even know your name . . .'

Dido looked like she was going to throw up. I was *totally* confused. The Prophet's saviour? What the *fuck* was this all about?

'Alma. My name's Alma – Al,' I blurted, without really knowing why.

'*Alma!* How perfect! It means "soul" in Spanish, Donner. Isn't that marvellous? Why, I can hardly – oh, the joy of it! I must tell The Prophet!'

Dido got up and dusted herself off. 'That's it. I'm not staying here – you're all headcases. God, your crappy old Prophet and her crappy old dad – yuck. I'm going to see Rain . . .'

Jane swung her gaze to Dido and, astonishingly, Dido shut up.

In a quiet voice, Jane suggested to Dido that she collect her things and Donner would drive her to her parents. Dido (formerly Dove) stuck her angular jaw out attractively and stomped off, slamming the door. Donner turned to me, a look of reverence on his face.

'I cannot tell you . . . This is such an honour. I will treasure this moment for always.'

He looked as if he was going to *cry*, for God's sake. I just wanted to get out and Banshee off pronto-pronto. This was *bizarre*.

I turned to Jane, who was gazing at me, her big blues filled with tears. God Almighty. 'Look, it's been . . . I mean, I'm glad Dido's sorted out, but I have to . . .'

Jane wiped a crystal tear from her long lashes and said, 'Has your dear father never told you? Oh, but then he always was so modest, so unselfish.'

Freddy – modest? *Unselfish*? I felt that old cat-killing curiosity creeping over me. It wouldn't hurt to get the story; it certainly would ping them back at home. Then I'd definitely fuck off and leave these barmy hippies to their navel-gazing.

'Uh, no, he hasn't . . .'

'That's so like him! Never one to make a fuss! I suppose Huw and I are too emotional in many ways – it's the Welsh heritage. We *feel* so much . . .'

She looked all far away and misty-eyed.

'Who's *Huw?* And, for that matter, who's The Prophet,

and what's all this about my dad? Really, I can't stay long, my parents are expecting me and . . .'

'*They're here?* Here in Spain? Truly?' She looked fit to pass out with bliss. I sighed.

'Yeah. They live . . .' I thought better of saying where they lived. Jane and her bloody Prophet and this Huw character might turn out to be the spiritual equivalent of those people you meet on holiday who really believe you mean it when you say, *'Drop in any time you're passing, won't you?'* I coughed diplomatically. 'They live out Ronda way. You know, retired, and all that.'

I had to do a double-take, but I was pretty sure Jane was *praying*. Like, right there, on the sofa. I coughed again.

Her eyes flew open and she looked somewhat calmer. 'I'm so sorry, my dear. I got a bit carried away with myself.' She laughed merrily. I smiled, like I was totally *au fait* with religious lunatics having fits of ecstasy and praying in public. Happens all the time in Bradford. Well, actually, come to think of it, it does, what with the Mosques doing calls to prayer and the bloody loony evangelists honking out their blather on Saturday afternoons in the precinct. I kept smiling and poured myself some more tea. I hoped they had a toilet; my bladder wouldn't stand two litres of cha and any more shocks.

'Let me start properly, my dear, at the beginning. I suppose it *is* a little bit complicated if you aren't used to us. Now, my name isn't actually Jane, it's Blodeuedd – Blodeuedd Griffiths. Terrible mouthful, isn't it? So everyone except our father called me Jane!' She laughed again. 'Huw is my brother; my twin.'

She paused as if I should know the name. I didn't. No bells rang, not a tinkle. She saw my blank expression and sighed.

'Huw is The Prophet, our teacher – our leader here at Soledad. Our father, Math Griffiths . . .' Again she paused to see if I recognized the name and seemed disappointed when I sorry-smiled.

'Well, never mind. Father built this house as a wedding present to our mother, Maria. Her people had Spanish blood, you see. He was fascinated with the old legends of our people and hers. You see the murals? The Mabinogion – the legend of Blodeuedd, my namesake. Oh, no expense spared – Father was terribly wealthy even by the standards of his day, terribly. But it didn't make him happy – oh no. He was always searching; got involved in the Welsh Spiritual Revival, before the First World War. Even though he was very young, he was a great friend of the prophet Evan Roberts, poor chap. They liked young people in the movement . . . Everyone prophesied then, even babies. Huw and I grew up in a very spiritual atmosphere – oh yes, very. We lived in this big old house way out in Anglesey – lovely, wild country, but terribly isolated.'

She paused to sip her cold tea and gazed dreamily at the room with its wall-to-wall family heirlooms.

'So, you see, Huw and I are very close – growing up like that, the only children. Mother died quite young and we were left pretty much on our own. Our Auntie Gwyneth looked after us, but she passed away too when we were seventeen. Then . . . well, Huw had a tutor and crammed terribly and went up to Oxford – and that's where he met your father! He was a year below Freddy. So dashing and handsome, your father, dear. We girls all had dreadful crushes on him. Huw had rooms near his. It all went swimmingly, until Huw began to be disappointed with the course he'd chosen; he thought it was too old-fashioned and stuffy. So he started exploring other subjects – things more to do with Father's interests. He realized he had a Calling, you see. It came to him in a vision, that he should give himself body and soul to the study of the Old Truths. Even then it was quite clear to him – well, to us all – that he was destined for great things. But with the amount of studying, he became quite exhausted. Huw wouldn't consider taking it easy like the other students – oh, not meaning your father, of course, he was exceptional. Huw, though, he's very . . . well, you'll understand when you meet him. An extraordinary brain – a mind like no other. He simply wouldn't rest; he studied day and night until he *collapsed* – it was simply awful. But your wonderful father *saved his life* – saved our Prophet, our Beloved Teacher's life so he could carry on his Work, his vision. Oh, Alma, I can't *tell* you how we love and respect your father! If Freddy Greer hadn't found Huw and made all the arrangements for his care – contacted the family, dealt with the college people – I *dread* to think what would have happened, I really do! Your father is a perfect *hero*.'

She beamed at me, her little white hands clasped passionately. She looked like a Raphael Virgin, her face illuminated with love.

I was absolutely speechless. I managed to nod and look questioningly at her, but a comment was beyond me.

'But, dear, hasn't he ever said anything to you about this? No? How strange . . . Perhaps he's too selfless, too reserved. Yes, I'm sure that's it. Well, I know you are very busy and you must be tired after being so brave and wonderful about poor little Dido, so let me scribble a note to your parents inviting them for tea and you can be off. Yes?'

So that was how I found myself scootering back towards La Morena with an invitation for my parents to take tea with The Prophet of Soledad and his devoted handmaiden. Blood-ee *hell*.

19

'Huw and Jane Griffiths? How very odd . . .' Freddy looked like someone had invited him to do *This is Your Life* on pain of torture. Vi put his after-dinner coffee on the table and plumped down on the sofa.

'I remember *Jane.* My God!' Vi smiled wickedly, raising her eyebrows. 'All the boys were *mad* about her – absolutely potty. The beautiful Welsh witch. She had some bloody awful Welsh name, too: Blodwen, or Bronwen, or something – not Jane at all, that was a nickname. Your father had a tremendous crush on her, didn't you, darling?' She took a sip of coffee to hide her laughter.

'I think that's a bit strong, my dear. Hardly a *crush* . . . And it was Blodeuedd, the flower woman of Welsh mythology. Now, Alma, your mother finds this very amusing, as you can see; but really . . . The Griffiths twins. How very strange. And you say they live up there? With lots of students?'

'Well, I don't know about "lots", but it's a huge place. Jane said their dad had built it years ago, so I suppose they inherited it and turned it into a sort of shrine to Huw's enormous brain.'

'Don't be mistaken – Huw was, as I recall, very gifted. But very unstable – very. Jane, now, she was a great beauty, tremendously charming and quite devoted to Huw. Utterly under his spell. In fact, it was all rather peculiar. The father was one of your great blow-hard

Welshmen. Incredibly wealthy, involved with that strange Welsh Spiritual Revival business when he was a young man; all that speaking in tongues and housewives turning prophet . . . *Celts,* you see.'

This last was directed at Vi, who was pink with suppressed laughter.

'Oh dear me.' Vi paused for breath and wiped her eyes. 'And we're invited for tea – wonderful! What shall I wear to meet a prophet? Do you think my blue dress would be suitable?'

'I shan't go,' Freddy said crossly. 'Damned nonsense.'

'But you must!' Vi and I chorused.

'Anyway, Dad, what's all this business about your saving Huw's life? They think you're a positive saint up there. You've got to go. Jane would be so disappointed – *heartbroken,* even.'

Freddy knew when he was outnumbered. 'Oh, very well. But it's a waste of my time, I tell you. As to saving Huw – well, to cut a long story short, the silly young fool overworked himself into a nervous breakdown. He'd started studying some pretty obscure anthropological texts in the library, and had become obsessed with various tribal rituals in Africa, South America – voodoo and what have you. His tutor, Old Pennyworth, tried to have it out with him – I mean, it was hardly Classics – but the young idiot laughed in his face. Gave him some rigmarole about hidden secrets, the forgotten magics, all that cod-spiritual nonsense. I blame the father; Math Griffiths was a damn fool about things like that. Anyway, the inevitable collapse came. I got home one night to find a crowd outside Huw's room and a filthy stink of burning and incense. Bunch of fools were jabbering on about a woman being in there and Huw setting the place alight and the police. Lot of nonsense, and I told 'em so. Well, the upshot was, I banged on the door, got no answer; just this droning, chanting noise coming from inside. So

I got Paddy O'Keefe, the fullback, and we broke the door down.'

Freddy paused and drank some coffee. Vi and I waited with bated breath. We unbated long enough to beg him to go on. I rather think he was enjoying himself, secretly.

'Terrible sight inside. O'Keefe was off like a hare. There was Huw, stark naked and covered in black writing of some sort – runes or somesuch – all over his body. He looked insane, quite insane. His eyes kept rolling up to show the whites and he was drooling like an animal. There was a naked woman – a local tart, as it turned out, that he'd paid – spread-eagled on the bed, bound and gagged with a red cloth. She was covered with the same damned writing. Place was full of stinking incense smoke and stuff burning on a brazier. Boiling hot, it was. And Huw was standing there with a bloody great knife in his hand. I grabbed it from him and he fainted. End of story. The tart wanted to press charges, but the college hushed it up. I had Jane fetched, then I rang Math. I put Huw in my room, cleaned him up, got a doctor who said a rest cure was in order – or the asylum. Next morning Math turned up in his old Roller and spirited the twins away . . . And that was it. Never saw them again.'

'Wow!' I breathed. 'Fab.'

'*Fab*, eh? Hmm. Huw went on to write a couple of books – all nonsense, of course – about his travels amongst the tribes. Neither good anthropology nor good research, and certainly not good literature. Barely readable, most of it. Gibberish. I tried one called – now, what was it? – *The Rose and the* . . . No, that's not right . . . Oh, yes: *The Mystic Rose*. Utter tosh. Tragic. He *was* very bright. Jane followed him around or kept the home fires burning, as far as I know. Lost track of them after that. Bill Foreshaw from Cardiff University – you remember him, Vi; decent little fella – told me Math had died, but I never gave it a second thought, to be honest.'

He scowled at Vi, who was rolling about on the sofa clutching Ishy and chortling.

'Oh, *how* I look forward to it! I shall ring tomorrow and arrange a time. Alma, dear, isn't this funny? And the girl – Dido – all sorted out?'

'Yeah. Nothing much to sort – bit of a spoilt-brat thing. You know, boyfriend trouble. One of the student chaps ran her home.'

Freddy cast me a look, but I just smiled placidly. 'I'll take Ishy out, shall I?'

Outside, the night was breathlessly still, the scent of the water mint by the river was fresh and reviving. I watched as Ishy routed various imaginary enemies and pissed over anything stationary.

I must e-mail Frank, he'd die laughing. And The Ems. Life – stranger than fiction, or what?

20

I'd just crawled out of the pool and had a shower when the Parents returned from their tea with the Griffiths twins.

Vi had phoned and managed to get Jane to calm down long enough to set a date for the Friday and off they trotted; Vi in her nice blue dress and Freddy rather dandified in his usual white linen suit. His jaws were shaved to baby pinkness and he smelt strongly of Wright's Coal Tar soap. I suspected he was making an effort to impress.

He needn't have bothered. He was welcomed as a sort of minor godling; people positively fainting with joy at his arrival. Vi was bursting with excitement and dying to tell all. I made them a couple of gin and tonics and got myself a ginger beer out of the fridge – alcohol and I were still not on speaking terms. I'd barely sat down before Vi started.

'My dear, I wouldn't have believed it! Jane Griffiths! That house! Those people! Quite, quite mad, of course. But your father, my God, they absolutely *worship* him! It was *so* funny!'

'Don't exaggerate, Violet. They're simply rather grateful for whatever service I rendered Huw. They're a bit, shall we say, *eccentric,* but quite harmless. It's some kind of finishing school for New Agers, from what I can gather. A lot of airy-fairy rubbish connected with Huw's books, of course. Still, the students are a pretty high-powered lot. All graduates of good universities: Berkeley, The Sorbonne, Trinity, Florence, Berlin – top notch. It's a damn shame they've got embroiled with this silly religious nonsense. I wish I'd had them at Leeds, and no mistake. Oh yes, very attentive, very courteous . . .'

'They hung on your father's every word, darling! Asked him all sorts of *searching* questions about his books – homework done there, I rather think!' Vi broke in excitedly. 'And my paintings – they all knew my stuff. Very gratifying. When I told Jane how well Francis was doing, and that you were writing a book about the Brontës, she was *most* impressed; said we were a "superb bloodline"!'

'Oh, Mum, you *didn't* tell her about my *book* . . .' I realized I sounded about twelve years old and quickly shut up again.

'Well, why not? Your father and I are very proud of you. I do wish you'd let us read it, Alma.'

She saw my face and swiftly went on. 'But really, that place! It was decorated as if it were a fiesta: flowers, a buffet, music, all by that fantastic reflecting pool – my God, the cost of that alone! And the water! They must have a spring or perhaps an underground river. Jane, I must say, looked marvellous. All the students had on that beige hippie outfit – Jane says it's so no one stands out above anyone else – but please! The linen version *she* had on was gorgeous. I think we know who's Queen there, thank you!'

'Did you see Huw?'

Freddy looked concerned, and suddenly even Vi was quiet. 'Well, a glimpse. I don't think he's at all well. Never took care of himself, and now . . . Jane took us to his room. It's a kind of cavern, under the house. He's got to have a constant temperature, no fluctuations. Strange place, completely silent except for the hissing of the damned machinery. Like a Frankenstein film. Tremendous set-up they've got for him, top medical stuff, lots of equipment – breathing apparatus, heart monitors – that sort of thing. We just put our heads round the door and said hello, really. He wasn't up to talking, but he managed a wave. The bed was draped in some sort of tent, for the oxygen I suppose, so we couldn't see him that well . . . He's not long for this world, poor chap. Your mother said the same. Terrible waste. There's a young German doctor looking after him. Donner . . . odd name for a chap, but of course in German it means "Thunder". I thought it was "Donna", but he explained. Nice chap; very conscientious. Reminded me of –'

'The food was *wonderful!*' Vi cut in with a warning glance at the Big Fred, who was oblivious to having his foot firmly in his mouth. 'And we saw everything. The paintings must be worth millions. A genuine Goya engraving, a Lopez Madonna . . . I'm sure I spied a gorgeous little Garcia-Albarez seascape. Oh, wonderful things, wonderful. And the library! Freddy!'

'Tremendous library. Math collected anything that took his fancy, y'know: Dickens first editions, letters from Dylan Thomas to his various chums, handwritten drafts by Owen and Sassoon, an edition of Wordsworth given by Coleridge to his fancy woman . . . Terribly efficient French girl looking after it all, name of Souris – "Mouse", don't you know. Looked rather like one too. Sorbonne graduate, certainly knew her stuff. They all choose a name when they go there apparently . . .'

'Yes, there was Donner, and Souris; the American boys Sierra, Sage and . . . Sundance, that's it – like the film. A charming girl called Marigold; an Irish girl called Rose; and the infamous Rain – very sweet boy but rather subdued. Now who was that very thin girl? Topaz, that's it! A chap called Spirit, another called Estrela, from Brazil I think; River, Leaf, and, oh yes, Azul – a sweet little Spanish boy from Seville. I can't remember them all;

they were all so *samey*. Ah, except there was a rather odd chap called Wolf who knew all about Francis and said he was a big fan of his work. Anyway, I think they're rather sweet names, myself – all to do with nature. If *only* they wouldn't cover themselves with that *metalwork* they'd be so much nicer to look at. I can't help feeling it's a sort of mutilation. Earrings, even a nose thing, perhaps – but really, darling, some of those youngsters were walking *ironmongery* shops . . . Don't laugh at me, Alma.'

'Are you seeing Jane again?' I asked.

'No, shouldn't think so. Oh, it was interesting – but not my cup of tea. Your mother asked her here, but she never leaves the place, apparently. Worried about Huw, I shouldn't wonder. Shame – but there you are.' Freddy pursed his mouth and sighed heavily.

Well, that was that then. My brush with a devil-worshipping, brainwashing cult all done with. Back to reality. I felt slightly cheated. I mean, they were a bit dull, really. All smiley-smiley and happy thoughts. Mind you, all those culty-type things were probably boring on closer examination. Just a lot of spiritual train-spotters.

Two days later, as I was about to go into Ronda for a coffee, the phone rang. It was Jane.

'Hello? It's Jane Griffiths here . . .'

'Hello, Jane – it's Al. Shall I fetch . . .'

'Oh, Alma! No, no, dear – you're the one I was wanting to speak to. How lovely to hear your voice! We did miss you at the tea, such a shame you couldn't come. Still, writing is such a vocation, isn't it? Violet told me you were busy on your wonderful book about those *poor* Brontë Sisters! In fact, that's why I'm ringing you. After your parents left, it niggled at me – I'm sure Father had some Brontë material, documents actually written by them. Why don't you just pop up and have a chat with Sister Souris? I'm sure she'd love to help you further.

And we'd love to see you. Huw is quite desperate to meet you – he was so thrilled to see Freddy and Violet. Shall we say tomorrow, about half past ten? Oh, *do* say yes . . .'

They had original material from one of the Sisters? What had Freddy said? Treasures in the library? If it was true . . .

'Er, well, OK then, tomorrow it is . . . Looking forward to it . . .' I tried to sound cool and casual.

There was a slight pause – she wasn't praying again, was she? I hated that creepy bollocks. 'Oh, lovely – we'll have a nice lunch and you can explore the library to your heart's content! I know you intellectuals, never happier than when you've got your noses in a book! Just like Huw. Well, bye-bye, then, until tomorrow!'

'Intellectuals', for God's sake. Still, she meant well, poor barmy cow. Hippies – you couldn't invent anything that crap, could you? I tried not to actually salivate at the thought of what was contained in that house. Half of me was going, *It'll be nothing, don't get your hopes up,* and the other half was screaming, *Yes! Yes! Yes!*

You see, the problem with the book was not that I couldn't write. I can, that sort of stuff, anyhow. I don't think I could do a novel – you know, make things up – but I can make academic things sound interesting. A bit more up there than the usual professorial tosh. And the Bronts (as I called them) had fascinated me since Uni. Like Haworth, the village way out on the windswept moors where they lived. Oh, it's dead nice *now,* very chi-chi, homespun, cute, picturesque, etc. But way back in the nineteenth century – quite another matter, believe me. It was fucking ghastly; the arse-end of nowhere, a huddle of houses on the steep hill, and the vicarage. All the Bront-kids and Auntie and Daddy Bront and the Faithful Serving Woman creeping round that hideous slab-sided box of a house built bang up against the cemetery like a punishment, with the icy keening wind slicing off the moors . . . And that was *summer*.

Of course, the kids weren't supposed to fraternize with anyone in the village because they were gentry and the villagers were, well, villagers; peasants. So they wandered about the moors, or sat in the house going gently crackers and dying like flies of TB. Every time one of those poor bitches wrote a book, one of the family fucking *died*. Anyone else would have lost it good stylee. Bramwell, the brother, certainly did. Went right off the rails. Drugs, drink, thieving, illicit affairs with married women, public scenes – you name it, Bramwell did it. Total fuck-up. But not the Sisters, oh no. Hung on like grim death to respectability, but wrote those fantastic books. I mean, *Wuthering Heights* – pul-*lease*! Heathcliffe? Talk about erotica. That bit where he locks himself in the bedroom and begs Cathy's ghost to come in! It makes the hair stand up on the back of my neck every time I read it.

What a family – what a story. Fantastic stuff. I knew I could make it come alive for people, make them see it all how I saw it. And I could put the lie to the tourist industry version of the Sisters' lives – all dainty crinolines and bouncing ringlets. OK, maybe I'm a lone voice, but I hate all that rubbish. Brontë tea-shops. Brontë bijou boutiques. Brontë knitwear outlets. The Brontë Heritage Walks. Coach trips, charabancs, the car parks are all full up, sorry.

The way I see it, if you don't admit those Sisters suffered horribly, if you make them into acceptable, appropriate little girly-dollies who wrote a few rather racy romances, then what happened to them, their pain, was for *nothing*. Because who *reads* those books any more? Most people just watch the BBC costume dramatization, or film versions with drippy French birds playing Cathy. Or – oh, my good God – *Heathcliffe, The Musical*. Drives me batty. But if old Math Griffiths really had got hold of the goods, actual Bront stuff no one had ever seen before, well, Bob's yer auntie! I'd write a book no one could ignore! If only . . .

Yeah, I'd visit the hippies, no probs. They might have something I needed. OK, they might not. Might be fuck-all in a bottle . . . *but it might not.*

I was beside myself with excitement; it would have taken an elephant tranquillizer to get me to sleep that night. I could see it all: the rave reviews, the long, searching, reverential interviews. Then the celebrity lectures, the TV, Radio Four . . . At last, I'd be *visible.* I wouldn't be in anyone's – not *anyone's* – shadow any more. I'd be *real.*

If you've never lived with someone famous, or even a little bit famous, you don't know what it does to you. The only way I can put it is, it's like *you* don't exist; you're a non-person, invisible. Let's say you're at a party. The smiling person coming towards you both isn't wanting to shake *your* hand, smile at *you* – oh, no. You're not there. It's the famous person they see; that's *all* they see. And they don't care, no one cares. They aren't ashamed of the way they treat you to get to the famous person. It's like, fame is the biggest drug there is and if you can't be famous yourself, then kiss the arse of someone who is. You might get a second-hand buzz. Don't bogart that celeb, my friend, pass it over to me . . .

Oh, I don't mean to sound bitter. But when you've lived with it all your life . . . It's like the famous person is in a cone of light, illuminated, glowing, fascinating. They can't see out of it, either, it dazzles them. They don't understand why you get upset; I mean, so-and-so seemed like a really nice guy/gal to *them,* so interested, so attentive . . . Yeah, right.

In this celeb-obsessed world, everything the famous person does is good, everything they make, say or touch is brilliant. And you're outside of that brilliance; way, way outside. Doesn't matter that you love them, that you help them, that they love you and couldn't do what they do without you. The shadow they cast is dark and deep and it swallows you up . . . It swallowed me up.

All my life I've never been as good as the rest of my family. Or Jack. My beautiful Jack. Tell the truth, it was just the same. That's what made it so hard. I loved him, but I knew that excoriating light, the light I knew so well and he couldn't see, was wrapping him up in its blinding glow. I knew I was slipping further and further into the dark. Maybe you could say I was repeating old, familiar patterns with him; psychs are always harping on about how you repeat your childhood all your adult life . . . I don't fucking know. Ask *Phillip*.

But if I could do this book I would be famous myself. *I* would be in the light, I'd be free. OK, I wouldn't be, like, a rock star or anything, but I'd be literary-famous, arty-famous and that's the life I knew. Nothing else would cut it, see. Not with my lot. Not even if I was a global-celeb like Madonna. *Very nice,* they'd say. *But, not really worth anything, not valid. Popular culture. Oh yes. Fascinating.*

But a brilliant, controversial book, that was quite a different kettle of haddock, matey. And my book would do it. It would. For me *and* the poor old Bronts.

All this ran through my brain like electricity, sparking and firing. I'm sure, in a way, I was driven a bit . . . well, a bit potty. It was just that the book got blown up into something so important that I sort of lost control of my . . . nerves? Moods? Whatever. And I'd been feeling so down; the stupid Cam episode had been like the bitter icing on a spoiled cake. The last straw. Inside, I felt that old familiar sense of utter failure, that I wasn't good enough, bright enough – not even fanciable enough. That I was nobody, nothing. I know, I know, I had lovely friends, a good life by most people's standards . . . But it had nothing to do with logic, with rationality. I'd convinced myself that this book was the only answer.

That night, I thrashed and twisted in my bed totally unable to rest or get comfortable, willing it all to be as I wanted it to be. Willing it with every cell in my body. Like casting a spell.

Or like making a bargain with the Devil: *Give me what I want, Mr Lucifer sir, give me the thing I want, and fuck the consequences. Fuck them. Just give it to me now . . .*

I did sleep eventually, but I felt breathless and hot, and kept waking up and having to go for a piss.

I had a really weird dream, too. It was like, my nose was dead blocked up, really swollen, and my sinuses were painfully stuffed and sore. I felt as if the little seams of my skull were being forced apart. And it was dawn, the lurid red of the rising sun casting a bloody transparent glow over everything. Time was fucked up, too. Everything kept jerking and then fast-forwarding, then stopping dead. I felt cold but feverish, shivery and weak with this pain and blockage, so I started to try and snort the stuff out of my nose, closing one nostril off and snorting. At first nothing budged, but then a little stringy bit of membrane, a sort of fibrous, twisted thing, came out and I nipped it in my fingers and started tugging.

I pulled at it, and started to feel as if something huge in my head was turning, being pulled down out of my nose. I wanted to stop – it was agony, squeezing and ripping away in my skull – but I couldn't. Then it seemed to pull free with a sickening, tearing feeling, and I yanked – against my will because I was mortally afraid – and this enormous clot of stuff came out of my nose, out from my head.

It was a dead baby. It stank of clammy, cold rot. The stringy thing was the umbilical cord. It was my baby, but it had been in the wrong place and it was dead. Deformed by the pressure, crushed, bluish and bruised in the mad, flickering light. My baby . . .

I woke up drenched in sweat, with a fierce headache, nearly falling out of bed in panic. I scrabbled for my specs then sat up in the sour tangled knots of bed linen, trying to make my heart stop racing. Bloody hell, this is what came of getting ahead of yourself; building air castles and getting in a state about summat and nowt. Sod, sod and buggery.

When I lurched into the kitchen I found one of the Parents had collected the mail and there was a letter for me. A real, honest-to-God paper letter, with real handwriting on the envelope. I was positively excited.

It was from – you'd never credit it – Maz. Yepedy-do-dah, Maz had actually set pen to paper and written to me. I felt suddenly happy; all the clinging shreds of my horrible night washed away with the thought that Maz had bothered to *write* to me. I took the letter out on to the veranda and settled down to read it.

> Dear Al,
>
> Well I bet your surprised and shocked at me writing but here we are and I have. Tatum and Mum and Dad are well and they sent their best love and Tatum said where's Auntie Al the other day so your honoured all right.
>
> I am writing because I dont know if Bruce said anything but me and Rom have split up for good now after I caught him at it with some little slag in my bed the bastard. I know hes no good. Well I always did but you know how nice he can be and I loved him but I dont now not any more.
>
> Im useless at this writing busness so I won't go on but I wanted you to know that we do miss you lots and maybe we will be able to come on a holiday to Marbella because Mrs Fowler one of my ladies has a big apartment there and she says me and Bruce can stay there

for free because I am such a good hairdresser. Well you should have seen her before I got her and youd know why shes grateful. Bruce will let you know with the email if we come. I need a break and so does Bruce. We are fine dont worry but tired and the weather here is shit your missing nothing.

You take care now dont get into trouble and don't worry about that scotch tosser he is nothing just another wanker you are worth a million of him.

Love Maz XXXXXXX

My gob was smacked. A letter from Maz; it was like getting a letter from God, only rarer. Marbella, eh? That would be brilliant, we could have such a laugh.

I set off to Soledad in a terrific frame of mind. Everything was going to be great. Really, really *great*.

21

'Souris? Souris, where's that other box? The one you thought might have that fragment in it?'

'I put him on the table. You don't look when you look, you. There! See?'

'OK, soz, mate – I got it.'

'Alma, you must be careful. This is the one I am not finished checking, I don't know what's in him. Please, there is so much work and . . .'

'Yeah, I promise – don't look at me like that. I promise; cross my heart.' I crossed my heart, but she didn't look convinced.

I pulled the box over to the big table under the drop-light and started sorting through it. It was one of hundreds that Math Griffiths had filled with odds and ends of papers he'd bought, swapped and 'acquired' over the years, then shoved away in this labyrinthine library. Some of the papers were definitely dodgy, obviously stolen and then sold to Math on the QT. I don't think he cared a bit how he got stuff, as long as he got what he wanted and had the quick hit of possession. Then he obviously lost interest, shoving his prize any old how into one of these long, narrow wooden boxes.

Souris was trying to sort it all out, but it was a mammoth task. She'd been at Soledad for ages and still despaired of getting it all in any kind of order. She'd done wonders with the books – including, I may add, a full set of Freddy's, in the posh hardback editions no less – but the papers! I mean, you could faff through six boxes of old receipts and bills and come up with nothing; or you could turn up a scrap of illuminated manuscript from Durrow folded into a letter from Disraeli to one of his mistresses like a bibliomaniac's sandwich. You never knew what you'd find. It was amazing.

I could hear Souris breathing heavily as she pulled down another box to go through. I was pretty sure she wasn't well. A heart condition or something? She was always short of breath and tired, her black eyes dull with fatigue. Her long nose seemed almost greenish sometimes and there was an unhealthy, drained pallor to her complexion. She was a bit different from the others, it seemed to me, partly because of her being poorly and partly because she had hardly any piercings. Just a nose ring and a few pairs of earrings. I kept meaning to ask her why she didn't have more, but the opportunity never came up, what with her squirrelling away in the stacks morning, noon and night. Though she took part in the daily meditation sessions, 'group discussions' and that bloody cod-shamanic drumming and chanting nonsense they all did after their dinner – and before the nightly piercing parties – I couldn't see her summoning up any enthusiasm for it all. She was so *French*, if you see what I mean. I supposed she must be missing her friend, Topaz, the other French lass. This was the skinny girl Vi had mentioned, but she'd gone home shortly before I started coming up to the house. They'd had some kind of big leaving do for her. They always did, apparently, when someone left; graduated, you could say. Some of the Foundation's 'sponsors', the rich types who funded the place, would come out for a long weekend. Golly gosh, I bet they had such fun. All-night chanting and largeing it on a glass of the local plonk. *Fab*-ulous. Poor old Souris, though. Topaz had been her total best mate. Well, maybe they could write to each other or have class reunions in some chic intellectuals' café on the Rive Gauche.

I was about to start on the box when Marigold came panting in, her round, plump face red with exertion, her ample bosom boinging around under her tunic.

'Oh, Alma – Mama Jay wants to know if you'd have tea with her?'

'I can't really, love. Tell her I'm very sorry and all that, but I'm right in the middle of something.' I gestured to the box and shrugged.

Marigold's face fell and she looked panic-stricken. I did feel sorry for her but I'd had to make a decision regarding Jane. Don't think for a minute I wasn't grateful for the use of the library, I was, but Jane – God – all she wanted to do was sit drinking tea and chatting about the 'good old days'. I think she was lonely, what with Huw – who I still hadn't seen, due to a relapse – out of the way. It must be that weird twinny thing where they can't bear to be parted for a second. They probably finished each other's sentences, too.

'OK, Marigold, tell her I'll pop up before I go, if she likes. But I really have to get on. The book, you know?' I'd found mentioning the book usually did the trick with the Chelas, as they were all in awe of anything to do with creativity, especially writing. Considering they were all pretty high-powered brains I thought it was odd; but there you are, that's academic types for you. All brain, no nous.

Marigold nodded so hard her piercings rattled. 'Oh, yes, of course, *the book,*' she breathed reverentially. 'I'll tell Mama Jay – she'll understand. Good luck, Alma. You know, we're all, um, rooting for you.'

She trotted off while Souris glared after her crossly. I grinned at her and she frowned.

'Why don't you like poor old Marigold, Sou?'

'Oh, I don't not like her, you know. I like everyone,

of course. We are all brothers and sisters 'ere, Alma. But she is so . . . she make a mess everywhere she go, that one. She is a disturbance, she has no discipline. Look how she eats all the time – a little pig.'

Ooooh, Miss Kitty. The tyranny of the skinny. I felt sorry for chubby little Marigold, a lost butterball in the land of the gaunt. 'But Donner told me she's got a brilliant mind – bang-up First with honours in Maths at Cambridge . . .'

I was teasing Souris now. I knew she couldn't bear not to be top brain; she only tolerated me on the grounds I was 'creative' rather than purely academic. And because she'd had her orders direct (via Jane, natch) from The Prophet himself. I was allowed full access. I don't think she liked it, but she had to put up with it. She wasn't a bad lass, really, underneath all the snorting and tutting. Generally we left each other alone and got on with our work, which suited us both. But get her on to Marigold and, phew-ee, let battle commence.

'Marigold, huh. Mathematic – oh, yes, superb. Naturally, I love her completely.'

Yeah, naturally.

'But the mess she is, she make – no. Is better she do her cooking and sewing with Sister Rose and leave my library alone, eh?'

I couldn't resist. 'But Donner . . .'

'Brother Donner, Brother Donner – he thinks he is Jesus Christ, that man. Well, he is not. He is no better than the rest of us. We are all here to learn; but him – oh no. He knows everything. Topaz, she . . .' Her face darkened alarmingly and I could hear her labouring for breath. Suddenly, I felt terrible for egging her on, but the smileyness of everyone else made Souris' fits of temperament appealing. Not if it made her ill, though – God, she looked awful.

I got up and went towards her. As I did so, her eyes

rolled up showing the whites and she slid to the floor. Christ! Talk about a dead faint! I rushed to her and put my arms round her waist to lift her up . . .

And let go with a scream I couldn't control. There was nothing there, nothing where her waist should be but a tiny *stalk*. It was horrible, she was obviously deformed, the problem hidden by her voluminous tunic. It wasn't the fact she was disabled that bothered me, just that it was so unexpected. Scolding myself for being silly, I reached under her arms and sat her up. She was breathing far too rapidly and her heart was thudding so hard I could see it lifting her top.

Propping her up against a cabinet, I ran out, shouting for help. In what seemed like a second, Sage, Rose and Donner belted in and Donner snapped a pungent-smelling capsule under Souris' nose. With a moan, she came to and he and Sage carried her out, ignoring me. I felt the goosebumps prickling my arms and I was rubbing them as I turned to Rose.

Rose gazed at me narrowly, her brilliant grey eyes snapping. A faint smile curved her small red mouth and she cocked her head, hands on hips. I liked Rose a lot, she was a no-bullshit colleen from Donegal who was yet another honours grad, this time from Trinity. She was a literature freak, so we had that in common. She'd even read Jack's work, but regarded him as 'too modern' for her taste, and not a patch on John Donne. She was one of those naturally witty types, you know, it was just the way she said things . . . And, unlike some of them, she had very tastefully done piercings, all nicely aligned and spaced, a real testament to her faith . . . Christ, listen to me! I was beginning to sound like one of *them*. I shivered again, feeling the unnatural shape of Souris body in my arms.

'So, she passed out, then?'

'Yeah . . . Uh, Rose, is there something . . . *wrong* with Souris?'

'In what way?'

'Well, when I went to pick her up – I – she – God, Rose, she hadn't got a waist, like she was cut in half. It was awful . . .'

'Oh, she tight-laces. So did Topaz. She must have tightened her corset again; that'll be why she fainted – it takes her a while to get used to it.' She sounded as if wearing a corset was the most normal thing in the world.

'She does *what*?'

'She tight-laces. You know, like Fakir Mustafa. She's aiming for a fourteen-inch waist, but . . . well, she might, I suppose. She's very small-boned . . .'

'God Almighty, Rose! What the fuck would she want to do that to herself for? I thought she was pretty norm – I mean, she's hardly got any piercings and . . .'

Rose looked amused. 'Oh, hasn't she? You should see her in the showers – she's got about twice as many as *I* have, has our little Mouse.'

I gawked at Rose, who had about twenty rings in each ear, never mind the septum, labrets and finger-webs. Where on earth could Souris have hers . . . ? Oh. Rose saw I'd twigged.

'You got it. Big on genital stuff is Souris. I'm not a terrific fan of that end of things, myself, but there you are. Each to their own.'

I sat down heavily in one of the library chairs and Rose plonked down opposite me, leaning on the table, her pointed chin cupped in her hands. Even though I was used to the Chelas and their passion for 'bodywork', this was something else.

'But why, Rose? I don't get it, I really don't. She could do herself some damage – cut her liver in half or something, it's . . .'

'Weird? Yeah, that's what I thought before I *understood.* Look, people have been using pain and bodily restriction for centuries – for ever – to reach spiritual heights. Look at tribal people – they know stuff we've forgotten about using your own body to understand the true feeling of being alive. Of what it means to really *be* alive, to understand life and death and the higher consciousness. The Prophet says we're all just dwellers in our bodies, you know? We can use the sensations of the physical to transcend the life of the flesh. The only time you really, individually feel who you are is that moment the needle goes through your flesh or – whatever. You ride the pain, the boundaries of what you are– it's a little victory over your crap everyday self. You're in control. With enough training, you can transcend the prison of the flesh, be at one with the universal. That's why we do it. It's an old, old religious practice that, unfortunately, the West has turned into a trivial fashion thing.'

'Bullshit! You don't honestly think that, do you, Rose? How can Souris wearing a fucking corset make her more religious . . . ?'

Rose smiled patiently while I spluttered. 'It doesn't. It just reminds her *she's* in control of her physical self, not anyone else. The discipline comforts her, makes her feel strong. But it's difficult for someone with a temper like hers. Some part of her – the shadow part – fights it. Fortunately, she's not a big foodie like me and Marigold. We like our dinners too much. Talking of which . . .'

She got up as if to leave but I grabbed her wrist. 'Rose, wait. I . . . I don't get it. Well, I do in my head, but not . . .'

She sighed, as if I was being deliberately dense. 'See that labret you've got? Didn't you get a big rush when you had it done? Yeah, I thought so. But you didn't channel that feeling, did you? You just got off on it like a typical Western sensation junkie – like it was one more roller-coaster ride, a quick thrill. Not that it's your fault. How could you possibly know any different?' she added quickly. 'But we *use* that feeling. We train ourselves to become conscious of our lives. Like The Prophet says, even *animals* have a higher state of consciousness than most of those people out there – and that includes the ones who think they're so spiritual because they bought a fucking *dreamcatcher.* Oh, The Prophet knows, all right. Didn't he go through the ancient rituals, push himself beyond the limits so we could go there safely knowing he'd Opened The Way?'

'If you say so, but . . .'

'No – let me tell you, I was so fucked up before I found Huw Griffiths' books. I was on the edge of something desperate. But I read his stuff and I knew – I just *knew* he'd found the Truth. Look, you're special, you're The Prophet's guest – the rest of us had to work our arses off to get a chance of coming here. We had to serve our time in the world and present a major piece of work – a thesis if you like – to The Prophet that showed we weren't time-wasters, novelty-seekers like that silly cow Dido. We had to show we'd studied The Prophet's writings in depth and that we *understood.* It wasn't easy. If a Chela's not one hundred per cent committed to the Foundation, there's no point them being here, see? They might as well be out there, in the fucking world, living a half-life like the rest of 'em.'

'I'm sorry, Rose – I didn't mean to be rude . . .'

'No problem, don't worry about it. Look, you're really in tune with The Prophet – we all sensed that straight off. You were just searching, out there – look how you got started with the piercings, your tattoo. I mean, what's that if it isn't a sign? The *Rose*? It's a fate thing. You even shaved your head, dressed like us – dressed to show people you weren't falling into their sad little fashion traps. Even that necklace. Oh, we all knew you were special from the first time . . .'

'What about my necklace?'

Rose laughed out loud. 'You mean you don't know? Oh man! The heart, Alma; the CDS Foundation – Corazon Di Sangre . . . Honestly, you are terrible! Of course you knew . . .' She went out laughing and I sat back, totally bemused.

Corazon – 'heart' . . . So CDS stood for 'Heart of . . .' *Sangre* . . . Santa Sangre: 'Holy Blood'. Blood! The Heart of Blood Foundation! God, no wonder they initialized it. Another result of Huw's cod-mystic twaddle, I suppose. Still, oo-er – I obviously had been *tuned in*. Cue *Twilight Zone* music. Frankie too – yeah, right. As if.

I sighed. That's how people got sucked into this kind of thing; finding coincidences and calling them fate. Messages from the fucking beyond. Fortunately, I was a bit more clued up than *that*. Rose might think their flappy beige hippie ensembles were anti-fashion, but that just proved she hadn't been to Top Man recently. As for the head shave – hey, even my *hairdresser* sussed that one out. Nothing remotely freaky about any of it. But it obviously impressed the Chelas, and who was I to destroy their illusions? I didn't mind accommodating them if it rang their bells and got me into the library. They were just poor sweet saps who'd gotten caught up in Huw and Jane's misguided dippy-hippie shit. Not me, though. Definitely not my thing.

My high evaporated quickly in a chilly thunk as I remembered poor old Souris. I didn't think I could ever look at her straight again, knowing that under her tunic was the deformed body of a Victorian pin-up. Biz-*arre*. Mingled with my sympathy, though, was a dreadful curiosity; not nice of me, I know, but there you are. I should never have gone to the old freak-show at Scarborough as a child; marked me for life with a morbid imagination. I must get her to show me her 'waistline' sometime. Purely scientific interest, you understand.

I sat back and pulled the file box towards me, picking

through the contents in a desultory way. I unfolded a wad of Spanish receipts for various household items dating from the fifties and put them to one side. It was no good, I couldn't stop thinking about what Rose had said, and about Souris . . . Sure, it was codswallop, but I understood what she meant. I had felt that rush, that elation, and I agreed with her that everything interesting, everything even vaguely spiritual had been dirtied by the voracious appetite for sensation that ruled the Western nations. I could see how you'd get totally pissed off with everything being *used* by corporate concerns to sell a Boy Band, or a tub of marge, or a deodorant. 'Spiritual', 'zen', 'inner peace', 'purifying', 'uplifting', 'harmony', 'awakening' – all ad slogans, the original meaning lost and forgotten. Religion in a bubble-bath. God, there was even a mountain bike called a Guru. What sacred knowledge would it impart, eh? How to do a horrendous downhill in a state of blissed-out relaxation?

Me, I'd long since given up fighting against the immovable system. After Jack died, I didn't seem to care any more, the oomph went out of me. No matter what you did, the corporations won with their buy-it-now-and-be-happy philosophy. Nothing you did to fight it seemed to work. If you won a battle and patted yourself on the back, they'd won the war while you were celebrating. I understood why the Chelas turned their backs on it all and thought Soledad was heaven on earth.

It still wasn't my scene, though. Oh, the piercing and body stuff didn't bother me – it was the constant smiley-smiley thing. I'm from Yorkshire, after all. Smiling's all right for them as likes it, I suppose, but try smiling willy-nilly in Bradford – they'd lock you up.

I got up, stretched, and rubbed my scalp. Taking my specs off, I gave them a quick polish. It was no use; I was too confused to work properly. I felt a twitchy little worry that perhaps I'd become cynical because I'd given up. It was a way of justifying myself, and it had become a habit I couldn't shake. But come on, all that twee bollocks about 'higher consciousness' – nothing more than New Age codswallop.

Grabbing my daysack, I wandered out through the house to the courtyard. There were a few clouds in the sky and I sat on a tiled bench and gazed at them in the huge reflecting pool. The shimmering water, faintly rippled by a breeze, with the misty grey and purple hills layering into the distance made a scene of almost unearthly beauty. A faint scent of lavender growing in the great urns by the colonnades drifted across, mingled with the spicy dust of the land itself. I felt the weirdness and tension slowly uncoil from my stomach and the air slide easily into my poor old lungs. I sighed with relief and pleasure, totally relaxed, my eyes closing. What a beautiful idea it was to build this fantastic place. Really, whoever designed it deserved a –

'When will you be goin' exactly?'

I started with an audible gasp. It was Wolf, clipboard in hand, peering at me truculently. I could smell the sour odour of him overpowering the lavender. His big, hairy shoulders were lobster red with sunburn; as he shifted about I could see the clammy white marks where his vest had been.

'Well? I have to be informed, for security purposes. You can't just wander about 'ere, it's . . .'

'Yes I can, and you know it.' I was so cross I didn't care how I spoke to him. He was always on my case, snooping around, making 'notes' on his clipboard or entries in his Psion. He knew perfectly well I was allowed to come and go as I pleased, as long as I didn't interrupt the meditation sessions. I'd been there when Jane had told him. Head of Security, my bum; a sop for his ego, more like.

'You can't talk to me like that. I'm the Head –'

'Yeah, yeah, yeah, I know: Head of Sweet FA. Look, mate, give it a rest, right? I won't be here that long. As soon as I find the stuff I'm after in the library, I'll be off – so have a bit of patience, right?'

He glowered at me, his whole body tense. I did the same – a stand-off. Then he took a step back, a sneer twisting his slack lips, his crusty labret rings distorting his mouth even further.

'Yeah, get your precious "stuff" and off you fuck, eh? Well, you may 'ave fooled Mama Jay an' The Prophet, 'cos they ain't worldly people, but you don't fool me. I know your type. You're another fuckin' user, like all the other fuckers who try it on. I'm 'ere to protect The Prophet an' Mama Jay, just you remember that. I protect 'em against the likes of you. You think you're so fuckin' clever, don't you? With your high-an'-mighty mum an' dad an' Mr Frankie-Whizz-Kid Greer for a brother – well, it don't fuckin' wash with me. I'm better than your poncey brother any day, only *I* didn't get born with a silver fuckin' spoon in *my* mouth, I had to –'

I was on my feet in a flash, all the uncomfortable, mixed-up feelings that had been brewing in me since Souris' collapse quickening into anger. 'Shut your fucking mouth, you hear? Don't you *dare* say owt about my family, *you*. Not *ever*.' The Bradford accent thickened in my mouth like it always did when I was pissed off.

A brief look of alarm crossed his face and I could feel my heart pounding with rage. How dare he? What a twat, sucking up to Vi about how great he thought Frankie was, then giving me all this shit about him. Two-faced bastard. I turned on my heel – and walked straight into Donner.

'What is this? Alma, Wolf . . .' He sighed heavily. 'Wolf, I think you are wanted in the control room. Perhaps you should go there straight away, yes?'

Wolf was stark white with fury, his sunburnt nose glowing like a light bulb. 'How long do we 'ave to put up with this *crap*?' He gestured at me with his clipboard.

Donner stiffened and a spot of colour appeared on his prominent cheekbones, but he replied in a calm, steady voice. 'That is enough, Wolf. As I said, you are wanted elsewhere. If you have anything to complain of, talk about it at tonight's meeting. Now, I think you should go, yes?'

Wolf made a disgusted sound and stomped off towards the house. Donner turned to me, smiling slightly as usual. Apart from the rapidly fading red on his cheekbones, he seemed totally unruffled. I, however, was shaking like a leaf, the air whistling in my lungs.

'Do you need your inhaler, Alma?'

God, he was so fucking *doctory*. 'No, no. I'm fine, really. I just – Wolf – he hates me – and . . .' Sod it, I sounded like an eight-year-old after a playground spat.

He shook his head and sat on the bench, gesturing me to join him, which I did, clutching my bag to my bosom like a comforter.

'Alma, Wolf does not hate you – it is more that he loves Mama Jay and The Prophet very much and he wishes to protect them.' He paused a moment, tapping his knuckle against his lip thoughtfully, then continued: 'OK, normally I would not discuss a person's medical problems, but in this case . . . I know you will be discreet. Wolf suffers from Grant-Folkind Syndrome; a genetic condition. You note the slight deformation of his eyes and the shape of his physique – the over-developed upper body, barrel chest and somewhat wasted hips and legs? Yes? Also, there is a tendency to suppressed immune responses which is why his piercings take so long to heal. I have suggested to him that he might forgo the Offering, but he wishes to demonstrate his loyalty to The Prophet – which leads me to the other part of the condition, the one that affects you. As you've seen, he is quite unstable in his emotions. Erratic, even. Persons with this syndrome have difficulty controlling their moods. Emotionally, Wolf has never progressed beyond adolescence. He is jealous of you, Alma, as a child might be.' He sighed, gazing out across the pool. Again, I felt that shiver when I saw his resemblance to Jack and I looked away, a quick little pang nipping my heart.

'The other side of this condition is what you might call the *gift* it brings of extreme intelligence, particularly for intricate, mathematical work, or as with Wolf, in computer technology. Mozart is now thought to have suffered with this syndrome. The same uncontrolled behaviour, emotional immaturity, brilliance . . .

'You see, Alma, Wolf worships The Prophet and Mama Jay – I do not think it is too strong to say that. His devotion is absolute, obsessive. He was so ill when he came here, exhausted, no longer able to care for himself – what do you call it? Oh yes – burn-out. He had worked for his father's company for many, many years – since he was a child almost – creating computer programs, running the whole thing. It grew bigger and bigger, more and more success, but Wolf's father . . . All the work Wolf did could not make his father love him. Wolf was never good enough. The older brother, who escaped the syndrome and is quite normal, got all the praise. Wolf got nothing. From what I am told, he spent all his free time on the Internet, with all the pornography, the strangeness. His physical appearance is something he finds very hard to cope with, Alma. He knows people judge him by his – well, by what the world sees as ugliness. Pornography allowed him to fantasize that he was a normal youth, that he could be desired. It was tearing him apart; he owed thousands of pounds to the persons who run these sex websites; he had used the company's credit cards to pay for his addiction. Then he found something written on the Internet about the Foundation and so he came. We found him lying on the ground outside the gates, like someone dead. Mama Jay nursed him with her own hands. She and The Prophet agreed we could not turn him away, it would be too cruel. Now he is happy, he runs our computers, our website, our security. OK, he is not good with people, but he has a purpose in his life, yes? A good purpose: he helps people. He does not *hate* you, Alma.'

I felt horribly deflated. It had been easy to loathe Wolf with his lardy, scabby sulkiness and his whining Estuary accent. Just another tedious computer nerd with zero social skills. I still didn't exactly *love* him, but I did feel sorry for him, poor sod. It wasn't his fault he'd got Wotsit-Thingy Syndrome and God, I knew how it felt not to measure up. At least I'd got it halfway sorted with my family, but him? Not a hope, by the sound of it. OK, Cow of the Century Award goes to me, *again*.

'Soz, Donner . . .'

He smiled, his slanty eyes crinkling up. 'What is "soz"? Something from your home area?'

'Oh, it means "sorry". It's stupid, really. Kids say it – it's like saying sorry, only you don't have to actually *say* it, if you know what I mean. It's sort of a private joke with me and my friends, a stupid habit. I shouldn't do it.'

'You understand a lot, don't you, Alma? The way we use language to cover what we really feel. To say this "soz", you know, is to say you cannot really say you are sorry. It saves your pride, but the other person must accept you have apologized even when they suspect you are not sorry at all. Words . . . I don't know, sometimes they mean nothing.'

He gazed off again at the middle distance, looking thoughtful. I was acutely aware of his nearness; I could feel the warmth of his body and, if I squinted sideways, I could glimpse the neat sculpture of his ear with its perfectly placed earrings. I liked being near him, talking to him – I liked . . . Jesus! Was I getting a crush on him because he looked like Jack? Well, he wasn't Jack, not even a bit, and certainly not in his character. No. It was just that Donner was so . . . comforting. He made me feel at ease, safe. Not like Cam had, but deep-down safe, as if he was protecting me . . . I suddenly realized he was asking me a question.

'. . . so you see, it would be most useful, don't you think?'

'So–, I mean, sorry, I was miles away, what did you say?'

He laughed and rubbed his head, then stretched his arms out and interlaced his fingers; his poor, shortened pinkie sticking out slightly. I felt a stab of pity for him – he must have had some kind of accident. 'I was saying, some of the Chelas feel that you are in a privileged position, and perhaps you take a little for granted what they have worked so hard for. This, I think, is the basis of Wolf's problems. So I was asking if you would like to stay over some night in one of the guest rooms, come to our evening meal, eat with us, stay for the evening discussion . . . get to know us a bit better.'

Hoist by my own petard. What could I say? *Oh, no ta, I think you're a bunch of hippie dipshits and I just want to get the Bronts info and leg it?* I felt that particularly English thing creeping over me, that don't-be-awful-don't-be-rude thing.

'Er, yeah, OK, sure . . .'

'Tomorrow? That would be good. I know Mama Jay and Sister Rose and our little Marigold will be very pleased. They are so fond of you. And The Prophet, too. Such a shame he can no longer eat with us.' He looked very sad and I felt double-crap.

'Sure – fine. Tomorrow, then. Um, Donner, what's wrong with Huw?'

'Ah, he is very ill. I cannot say that he will recover. I am only a typical medical doctor, OK for daily care in such a case, but . . . The Prophet is, in a way, dying for us. After your father saved his life, he left university and travelled the world seeking the truth. He is one of the greatest anthropologists there has ever been. It was not enough for him, being the observer; he participated in the rituals and life of the tribes he lived with. Not many have such courage. But it has broken his health. In other cultures, a person such as The Prophet is seen as a valuable gift to the world, not a crazy man. They expect such a person will give *everything* of themselves to attain enlightenment. It is the old way. For example, in these other cultures The Prophet's so-called breakdown at the university would be seen as only natural, a temporary imbalance in a gifted mind struck by the force of realizing there is more to life than appears, that things are more deeply interfused, sacred . . . Only the truly sensitive can fully realize this, and so often, such people are not physically strong. But this sensitivity, this intuition – you have this too, Alma. Your rational mind fights it. We can see it is there, though. You have suffered, and you have found no rest, no true understanding yet. Perhaps, in a small way, we can help you by supporting you in your work. A repayment for your father's goodness to our Prophet, also. But I talk too much – such a bad habit. Maybe it is your fault, Alma, you are so easy to talk to!'

I was? Obviously I was a hippie magnet. Still, I felt pleased that he could relax with me and chat away like we'd known each other for years. Poor old Donner. He had a lot on his plate, caring for all the Chelas and nursing Huw who it seemed was not long for this world. Poor old Jane, for that matter! What would she do without her precious twinny? I felt guilty for not having tea with her. Never mind, I'd make a real effort to be more sociable – and not so judgmental – tomorrow at the sleep-over.

22

Vi stood at the sink, tears pouring down her face. I got up and passed her a clean dishcloth and she wiped her eyes and nose, then came over and sat down at the table.

'Have you tried putting a spoon in your mouth when you cut onions?' I asked as she squinted and snuffled.

'Oh darling – such rubbish. Really, don't change the subject, Alma. Your father and I aren't happy about your spending so much time up at the Griffiths'. Every time I see you you've got more and more bits of metal through your ears. And those outfits –'

'I thought you liked linen.'

'I do. That's got nothing to do with it. You look like one of those bloody students – as you know full well. We thought you'd just pop up to their library now and again, not *move in* . . .'

I sighed and smiled at her. 'Come on, Ma. Let's face it, with that dealer fella coming over from America, you'll need my room anyway. Don't *worry,* everything's all right. I get treated like royalty up there – my own en-suite guest room, food, clothes . . . I mean, look at this –' I showed her the bag Marigold had made for me as a present, rather wonkily embroidered with my name and a heart.

'Yes, it's lovely. I'm sure they're all very nice people. Still, a *cult* . . .'

'Not cult, Ma – study centre, that's all. A sort of study commune.'

'But your father thinks Huw's work is . . .'

'I know what Freddy thinks of Huw, but he's too harsh. You know he is, Ma. Huw may be a bit different, not academic as such, but the books are really interesting. He did things no one else would have dared. When he was with the Ikkfaala people he –'

'Yes, yes, you've told me.' She shuddered. 'It still seems unbalanced to me. Surely he could have just observed the – whatever it was?'

'The Sun Placation Ritual – *Lo Kinfaala Hebbe,*' I said patiently. 'Well, he *could* have, of course – but he didn't. He became one of their shamans, actually went through it. No other European . . .'

'Yes, yes – quite.' Vi sighed and tucked a loose strand of hair behind her ear. 'Oh, Alma, I realize Mr Glassman coming here is a bit awkward, but please don't run off to the Griffiths and not come home. I *am* worried. I'm your mother, after all. At least this break with your friends will be nice. Marbella is very *modern,* these days, I believe. Nightclubs, that sort of thing. You will enjoy yourself, won't you?'

I went round the table and gave her a big hug. It was hard for Vi, suddenly trying to be Mumsie. But like The Prophet wrote: *Even in dying, some may see the Truth and still be Redeemed, their last seconds of perfection more valuable than all the life of blindness they lived.* At least Vi was far from dying. In fact, with this big exhibition planned, she was positively *blooming*.

Honestly, everything was fab. Freddy was off ferreting round Lorca sites with the researchers from the telly, and me – I'd never felt so happy.

I flung my stuff into the big frame ruckie and, pausing only to give Vi a kiss, ran out to the bottom of the track to wait for the Foundation Jeep. Rain had stuff to buy in Malaga and had offered me a lift to the airport where I was to meet The Ems. I was looking forward to seeing them so much I could have squeaked out loud. Wait until I told them everything – oh, they'd be so pleased for me, I knew it.

As I sat hung around for the Jeep, I ran over in my head the events of the past few weeks. Funny how things change. I thought I knew it all, my mind totally made up. God, how pathetic I'd been; so resentful, so fucking *stubborn*. That first night when I stayed over to please Donner! Man, I'd been so *embarrassed*. After dinner in the Great Hall had been cleared away, everyone had clustered round the dais and Huw's enormous carved wooden 'throne', now sadly empty, his Prophet's Staff propped against it. Jane's smaller, matching chair was set alongside, draped in a cream-coloured throw. The dying rays of the sun through the glass wall at one end drenched the huge, cross-beamed space in garnet and citrine, casting weird shadows from the huge, ugly steel Shamanic Tree of Immortality sculpture. The shadows looked like nasty, fingery shapes reaching out for the ashy black cavern of the big old fireplace on the long side wall. As if the shadows were being sucked up the chimney. Very *Grimm's Fairy Tales*. Personally, I hated the sculpture; I thought it was a nasty ten-foot bit of fake abstract Modernism. But it was a gift from a 'sponsor' and they all thought it was fantastic. Always giving it a once-over with a damp rag and some polish. No accounting for taste, is there? I wouldn't have put in a Retail Park.

Anyway, first off it was OK, everyone discussing the day's events and practical bits of business. Then Donner asked if anyone needed, or wanted to share something they'd remembered from their past or thought about in general. *That* opened the floodgates. Talk about 'Get it all out you'll feel better'! You'd get locked up for going on like that in Bradford. People cried and rocked themselves and told *everything*. Everyone kissed and hugged them, told them how wonderful they were and how much everyone loved them and thought they were great. Everyone except *me*, of course. I hadn't wanted to know. To me, their openness seemed a sort of emotional exhibitionism. And the stories; the Chelas must have heard at least some of them before, but they behaved as if it was all brand new. When Souris cried, I *cringed.* I mean, Souris; the icy Parisienne, the Marianne of the Stacks, sobbing her squashed little heart out and going on about how she was an orphan and her foster-parents had treated her as an unpaid skivvie who was only there to wait hand and foot on their real daughter while they took the fostering fees and lied to the authorities; how they'd tried to stop her going to Uni and her foster father had . . . you know. How she'd eventually got her degree but nearly starved doing it, then her foster-parents demanded that she came back to slave for them but instead she'd escaped with her true love, Topaz, and they'd roamed the streets, little better than prostitutes, selling sex for food, heroin and a place to crash – until they'd met a Chela and been saved! Amen! Halle-lu-ja! I remember thinking: *What's it got to do with me*?

All right, to be brutally honest, I'd felt a bit jealous, too. *I'd* had my fair share of troubles, and no one had hugged me and wiped my tears and told me how brave I was and . . . all the stuff the Chelas did for Sou that night. It wasn't fair. I couldn't handle it, so I'd sloped off to the glass wall and stared moodily out at the last ashy crimson light washing the hills out beyond the valley. Faint twinkles from car headlights had flickered once or twice on the far lonely road to the Caves of Pileta, but staring out at that vast emptiness from high up here on the cliff I'd felt so totally alone I could have wept. I'd had to bite my lip when Rose came up and said Donner was worried about me – they all were. Her husky Irish voice with its quirky, half-laughing lilt had made me pull myself together and wander back with her as she explained that now there'd be chanting and drumming in the shamanic way that Huw had taught them, then someone would offer up their pain by being pierced and try to reach a higher state. That had set us off arguing, as usual, and made me at least feel more *real.* A Chela I didn't know called Ocean had his septum pierced, but he'd just looked agonized to me, not blissed out. Afterwards, he insisted he'd seen a vision of a fiery door opening . . . Well, who was *I* to disagree? At least the piercing was extremely hygienic with a stainless steel mobile dressing station, professional sterilizers, and Dr Donner in latex gloves.

In the end, I'd stayed another night. I'd felt so . . . unsettled, I worked like a nutter in the library the next day in a sort of furious reaction, totally exhausting myself. Also, I stayed because the beautiful little guest suite, with its white roughcast walls, iron bedstead and fresh white linen was so gorgeous. They'd put a tiny bunch of flowers on the bedside table, and the miniature shower-and-loo cubicle was outfitted with everything you could want, including toiletries scented with Jane's favourite Acqua di Parma. So I stayed. Then I went home. Then I came back. This went on for nearly a month until one day I asked myself, what was I afraid of? I'd realized by this time I wasn't going to be brainwashed or kidnapped, so why not stay for a few days at a time? I was sick to death of transcribing scrawled notes when I got home and picking up huge wads of e-mail instead of answering it as it came in. That sounds like I got loads, but you know what I mean. If Frankie or Mills went to the trouble of contacting me, it seemed rude to keep them waiting. Besides, I wanted to share all my news with them, tell them about my progress. Eventually, I left the Banshee up at Soledad and went home in the

Jeep with Donner to fetch my computer for a long weekend – and stayed for a week. Then another, and another, popping back now and again to check on the Parents so they wouldn't worry.

One of Wolf's assistants (not *Wolf*, of course; he was too busy protecting and serving), the skinny Spanish boy called Azul, set up my modem for me in my room, so I didn't feel even a bit isolated. He was so heavily pierced I could hardly make out his features and he had holes in his earlobes stretched to the size of bottle-bottoms by huge steel flesh-tunnels. I could see daylight, and more, through them. Funny kid, Azul, he thanked *me* for 'letting' him help me and when I put my hand out to shake, he kissed it before scurrying off like a mouse. That's the Spanish for you, beautiful manners. Sigh. But that's what all the Chelas were like: super-courteous, nothing too much trouble. Barmy New-Agers they might be, but they made you feel welcome. Straight people could certainly do with learning *that* skill.

I still dreaded the after-dinner sessions, though. I felt quite guilty that I couldn't 'fess up something and be part of the gang. But I couldn't. It just wasn't me. The shamanism didn't bother me; it seemed like those tribal things you see on TV documentaries – a bit silly, but it was their choice. And if they wanted to turn piercing into some sort of religious experience, well, again, their choice. To me it was still an alternative fashion-type thing, despite what they said.

But it niggled me. Why couldn't I share my troubles easily and honestly like them? They seemed so happy, so comforted by the support of their Chela-buddies and dear old dippy Jane. When she – or rather, Techno-Wizard Wolf – played a tape of Huw croaking out some Thought for the Day on the top-of-the-line sound system they had in the Great Hall, they were besides themselves with joy. Was I so fucking cynical and narrow-minded, so addicted to being miserable that I no longer wanted to be happy?

One night I couldn't get to sleep, so in desperation I read one of Huw's books that had been left in my room: *The Mystic Rose*. It was a bit weird, but after a while I could see what he was getting at and that he'd certainly put his money where his mouth was concerning his research. What a life story! I began to understand his reasoning, despite the arcane language. He wanted a return to a simpler life, more in touch with the basic human spirituality; to revive the ancient mythic themes and rituals, promote a reverence for the Earth and the unbroken rhythm of the generations. He thought that was a kind of immortality, and the Chelas were a sort of priesthood – with him as High Priest, of course. It was all very Jungian in parts, sure, but very appealing. The whole thing was full of a yearning for a sense of family, love and kindness; a world where the 'different' weren't treated as freaks but as valued bridges between this world and the sacred world of dreams and visions. It was beautiful; poetic, even. Pity his writing was so convoluted. Still, it meant you had to work a tad harder than the Western mind was used to, what with the telly and such. I could do that. I'd spent my life doing *that.*

I read two of his other books in quick succession – *The Immanent Dream* and *Blood Mothers of the Tribes*. Fascinating, really. I stopped dreading the evening discussions now I knew a bit more about what they were trying to achieve, but I still couldn't get *into* it like the Chelas.

Then it just – happened. Honestly, I didn't plan it – nothing had been further from my thoughts. One minute I was sitting there *observing,* the next minute I found myself telling them everything. Yeah, everything. Even the secret that had tormented me all these years, that I was so ashamed of, that had crucified me. It poured out of me like a river, washing all the debris and shit along with it. I could hardly believe it was happening, but I couldn't stop. And when I cried, the sobs seeming to rack my bones apart, Donner held me in his arms while the others patted me and cried too. Mama Jay held my hand and told me over and over how special I was, how blessed.

I was exhausted, my brain whirling, but when they began the ceremony, I joined in the chanting this time and felt myself float away on the drumming, just float and be free, as though I'd set my burden down at last. It was such a relief. I had forgotten what it was like to be without that secret weight of guilt and fear. I felt like I had as a child on holiday in Polwenna: happy, tired and *safe*. The next night, I offered up my pain as Donner pierced my eyebrow and everyone was so proud of me. Mama Jay played a message on the sound system from The Prophet which singled me out by name as a 'Daughter of Truth' and everyone was thrilled. I felt like Queen for a Day.

Oh, don't get me wrong. I wasn't some sort of *convert*. It was just that I'd found being so set in my ways wasn't worth it any more. I was still the same – ratty and obsessive and cranky and always being flip – but I felt I could let the past go now, and get on. It had been great therapy for me. Though I didn't have the blind faith of the Chelas – and never would; that wasn't in my nature – I did believe that the life at Soledad was a bloody sight better than anything else I'd known. I felt at peace there, like at last I *belonged*.

The only difficult thing would be telling The Ems I wasn't coming back to Bradford for the winter after all. Or going to university for the foreseeable future. Because I'd struck lucky. So lucky, I couldn't quite believe it. I'd found a letter from a young woman called Letty Gates to – Charlotte Brontë. Apparently, Letty had been a school friend of Charlotte's at the crap boarding school they'd both been sent to. I can't tell you how excited I was when I realized what I'd found. I actually shouted for joy, nearly causing Souris to fall off her moveable ladder. I'd be the death of that poor lass if I wasn't careful. But she was as thrilled giddy as I was. She insisted we tell Mama Jay, who immediately had Rose and Marigold whip up a celebratory tea party with almond cake and the works. I felt like an explorer who'd sighted El Dorado. We all got hysterically giggly, and when Donner came in to see what we were up to we shoo'ed him away laughing and saying it was a women-only party. He smiled and shook his finger at us, then Rose threw a cushion at him which set us all off again. It was good to see Mama Jay laughing, and the others. I felt I'd given them something back for their kindness to me.

You see, that letter was utterly and totally unique. No one had ever mentioned Letty Gates before. No biographer, no critic, no reference in other correspondence – nothing. But that letter had been so warm in tone, it was the kind of thing you'd only write to a dear friend:

> From Miss Laeticia Gates, Thorn Cottage, Downley, to Miss Charlotte Brontë, The Parsonage, Haworth.
>
> My dearest, dearest Lotte,
>
> What a good and true friend you are! Your letters mean so very much to me . . .

OK, it wasn't exactly earth-shattering. How she went on a walk with her mother. The dogs, the garden, her new shawl. But it was so relaxed and intimate it could only be the letter of someone writing to a friend she was used to exchanging confidences with. And who knew what other secrets they'd written to each other, this unknown girl and her 'dearest friend' who happened to be one of the greatest writers, from one of the strangest and most brilliant families in the history of the English language, in my humble opinion. I began to think that perhaps, just *perhaps,* Letty was Charlotte's 'secret' friend. The friend she told no one about and the bulk of whose letters she herself must have destroyed. But why? Why keep a friend so secret? A thousand theories chased around in my head . . .

Rain pulled up in a cloud of dust and I jumped in the Jeep.

We didn't talk much at first. Rain was pretty depressed at first because he was being sent out into the world again as a *Malakh* – a messenger. I liked Rain; he was tall and rangy with a long, pleasant, open face. I did feel slightly awkward with him, though, on account of being the person who broke up his idyll with Dido–Dove. He didn't seem to hold it against me, mind. He was a big piercing nut and was reputed to have more metal in his dick than you could shake a stick at. Anyway, that's what Rose said – but she was terrible, honestly. He certainly hadn't stinted on the facial and ear-'ole stuff either. Whacking big flesh tunnels, rings all over and one of those bars that run through the ear from the top to the tragus, on both sides.

I asked him if he knew where he was being sent, just to make conversation, and he said he was to go to the Amsterdam house first then on to the other houses one by one, raising morale and telling them the happenings at Soledad, which was a Malakh's job. There were Foundation houses dotted all over the world, each housing a few Chelas or Malakhs who worked for the sponsors and counselled prospective new followers. They kept in touch with each other and Soledad by letter, phone, and via e-mail and the website. The Malakhs were the living link of faith and so considered very important – not that that impressed Rain right then. He didn't want to leave Soledad.

I asked him about how they recruited new members, but he told me they had to be very careful about who they let study for the Foundation 'entrance exam'. In fact, the Malakhs did as much as they could to put people *off*. So many worldly types wanted to hook up with the Foundation as a sort of quick New Age thrill. Cam's type, all jargon and no backbone, I thought. Or Dido's – though I didn't say that to poor old heartbroken Rain.

This was his third trip as a Malakh. Although he was a clever lad with a slew of degrees from New Zealand, his homeland, he was a big, soft-hearted boy who couldn't stop letting his love-life interfere with his duties to the Foundation. But he was resigned to the Malakh role, and the Amsterdam house was considered a pretty cool location by the Chelas because the sponsor was very generous. I didn't fully understand the sponsor thing, but from what I'd gathered they were wealthy types who believed in The Prophet and contributed to the Foundation's upkeep but didn't want to live there full time. They'd visit Soledad occasionally, for events like the gathering I'd missed – the big send-off for Topaz – or for weekend retreats. Fair enough, each to their own and all that; better than them spending their spare thousands on whatever millionaires spend their pocket change on. Baths full of Bovril and nights out at the dog track. Whatever.

'Do you know how she is?'

I jumped a mile. 'What?'

'Dido – Dove – d'you know how she is? I really miss her, y'know.'

'Er, no, I don't. I'm sorry, Rain – you must miss her.' I didn't suppose she'd given him a second thought, but I couldn't say that, he looked so pathetic. 'Last I heard she went off back to London – but that's all I know.'

'Yis. Oh well. S'pose I could go over and see her when I get to Amsterdam. She's a great kid, y'know, underneath it all. She's just got a lotta problems. I hoped a spell at Soledad would sort her out – I mean, it worked for me. Christ, you wouldn't have recognized me five years ago. I was one more drop-out bumming round the beaches surfing and wasting my life . . .'

I drifted off slightly as he recounted what had become a familiar story. The brilliant misfit, disastrous family, abuse, drugs, crap sex, rejection, a feeling of being lost in a world that didn't care if he/she lived or died. Then finding a Chela, or the Foundation website, or one of The Prophet's books and – bingo! Somewhere to *belong*. Family. Tribe. The blessed relief of being loved and wanted. Of being useful and needed. All the Chelas told similar tales and the joy of their salvation shone in their eyes like a beacon.

'. . . Not like you, of course. It's different for you, what with your father saving The Prophet's life an' you being so close to Mama Jay, an' all . . .'

'Yeah, maybe. But I didn't intend any of this, you know.'

He looked puzzled, his faded-denim-blue eyes squinting at me in bafflement. 'You must be real pleased, though, eh? To be so special? Being a Daughter of Truth, an' all – God, you're so lucky. I mean, The Prophet *name-checked* you. Man, I'd die for that, we all would. Mama Jay told us after the first time you came that we were all to look after you extra, because you were Freddy Greer's blood and The Prophet owed His life to your dad. You must be so happy, coming from such a special family, and you *being* so special and everything. Me, I just do numbers like Sister Marigold. She's a great girl, don't you think? I really like her, and Sister Rose. They're a real laugh . . .'

Special. I suppose I was feeling a bit special these days. Mama Jay had talked at length to me about how important my genealogy was – my bloodline, as she put it. OK, it didn't mean much to me, but she and The Prophet obviously put a lot of store by these things. Ancestors, lineage, that kind of thing. Like tribal people's reverence for their forebears. A spiritual family tree, almost. Well, why not feel good about it? It was no worse than doing that self-help stuff Millie was always on about. Those bloody tapes that droned on about being good to yourself and *Every day in every way, I am getting better.*

I relaxed as Rain wittered on. When would I let all the suspicion, the fear, out of my system? After the first flush of enthusiasm, it had seemed an impossible task. I was too fucked-up and repressed. But Donner especially had spent hours talking with me, explaining that these things take time. Instead of beating myself up because I wasn't perfect, I should accept myself and not be afraid of thinking good things about myself. Running yourself down all the time led to spiritual death, he said. Well, I wouldn't go *that* far, but I got what he meant. Donner – what a kind, decent man he was. It made me shudder to think of the silly, hysterical way I'd thrown myself at Cam. What had I been thinking of? Donner had explained that such behaviour was another form of self-destructive addiction. As The Prophet says: *Real love is the breath of the God in your heart, the precious gift of the Universal, not the storm of lust in your flesh.*

I knew I loved Donner, I'd known it for some time. It had just sort of crept up on me, until one day I saw him walking by himself in the garden looking so careworn, so melancholy and – well, I just *knew*. It unfolded in my heart in an instant. I wasn't ashamed or upset or even ecstatic; it seemed natural. I loved him for his kindness, his intelligence, his strength of character. Sure, you could say it was because he looked a little like Jack, and I admit that did have something to do with it. He was attractive. Handsome. My type, if you like. Pointless to deny it. But it was more than that. Donner was wholly his own person.

Did he love me? As a sister, of course. As anything else . . . I'd wait and see. I thought sometimes – maybe. But it wasn't important. *A true marriage is the Wedding of Bliss, the Male And Female in each nature calling to its Opposite, creating Universal balance, the Sun and Moon locked in the eternal Dance.* I could wait. For the first time in my life I had the patience to wait – until he felt he was ready to speak.

'. . . an' I always wanted to know where you got your tat. It's really cool you got the Mystic Rose without even knowing about it. Donner says some people are lucky, they just *know* stuff, like they were *born* to it. Same as your necklace – freaky, eh? You even looked like one of us. We all thought that was *awesome*, like you knew we were out there in the world somewhere waiting for you. Like, *fate*.' He smiled ruefully and shook his head, his earrings jangling. 'Not me, though, I *never* git it right. So who did it?'

'What? Oh, my tattoo – Van Burgess.'

'Wow, Van Burgess! I've seen his stuff in the mags. It's brilliant! I'm definitely going to make a trip to England if I can get hooked up with *him*!' He laughed and bounced the Jeep into the airport car park.

'Well, here we are! A bit early, but . . . Look, I probably won't see you again for like, ages – I'll be gone by the time you get back.' He looked suddenly solemn, his open surfer's face losing the boyish veneer, and an older, more serious man looking out of those sea–sky eyes. 'It's been an honour to meet you, Sister Alma, a real honour. You're a really decent person – not stuck-up or snobby, like you could be. I mean, you're so straight up and everything. We – I think you're . . . well, we're real glad you found us. Y'know, it's hard with The Prophet suffering so much, but we know how happy you've made Him and Mama Jay.'

He stuck his hand out and we shook. Then he was

gone in a cloud of dust and dancing bits of rubbish. The Chelas were all a bit over the top about the honoured-to-meet-you thing, but how sweet was Rain? What a pet lamb. I felt faintly bad about not having really listened to him on the drive, but it was washed away in a wave of excitement – The Ems! My Ems! I couldn't *wait*!

23

'Ooohhh! *Yorkshire Tea!* Mills, you little diamond! *Totally* fab – I missed it *so* much . . .'

'I'll set kettle on then, eh?' Maz stalked off in her white high-heeled knee-length boots into the enormous fitted kitchen. Millie beamed at me from the depths of the midnight-blue embossed Dralon sofa, her eyes vanishing into her round pink cheeks.

'I thought you'd like some, I know you and your tea. Oh, and I got you this – for your collection.' She handed me a tissue-wrapped object that I immediately ravaged to reveal a Virgin Mary key-ring that lit up if you pressed a little button on the bottom. It was – what would Rain say? *Awesome.*

'*Wow!* Where did you get it? I love it – thank you so much.'

'There's a place in Leeds that sells weird stuff; it was in there. I thought you'd like it. What I can't work out is whether it's a serious item – you know, if real Catholics would buy it seriously – or just a kitsch thing . . . I mean, it's so mad. There were other things too, like a Virgin lamp and a . . .'

Maz came in with the tea on a tray and a fag in the corner of her mouth. 'Cha time. 'Ere, get this down yer, it'll put hairs on yer chest. An' what's wi't head shave, by the by? I thought I told yer, no more than a number six wi' them clippers.'

I smiled and rubbed my head ruefully then reached for the tea. Maz seemed very edgy, but I put that down to all this business with Rom. Like her outfit; I'd been a bit taken aback when, behind Millie in her Liberty-print sunfrock, pink beaded cardi and matching power-bead bracelet loomed Maz in the boots, a white micro side-slit slip, shorty silver hologram jean-jacket and her hair in a spiky platinum crop. She'd always loved fashion, but this outfit veered towards tarty, something she'd never been. She was wearing much more make-up than usual, too. I didn't think I was being prudish, but it looked like she was trying too hard. Plus she was smoking a lot more, and Millie kept glancing at her with an expression I couldn't quite read.

Still, we were together again – what did anything else matter? Maz was probably over-tired and stressed, she'd relax. The apartment was vast and apparently furnished by a blind person on acid. Maz had immediately bagged the peach-and-lime master bedroom with its king-sized gilt bed, leaving Millie and me the other room (egg-yolk yellow) which contained two doubles and enough room to quarter an army. I didn't mind sharing and neither did Millie, so after much squealing at the avocado kitchen and black bathroom suite featuring a circular bath, we unpacked, then settled down to talk.

The French windows on to the veranda were open and the sound of the waves was hypnotic; I'd forgotten how much I loved the sea. We were in one of the sea-view apartments – very not-cheap. The Apartamentos del Playa Oro were certainly not for the poor or the package crowd. It was a huge complex, totally self-contained and brand spanking new. Maz's lady had come up trumps. I particularly admired the Louis Quinze-esque crystal chandeliers; they would make to-die-for earrings – miniaturized.

Maz stretched out on the tan leather recliner and gave me the once-over.

'You've lost weight. An' what's wi' all the fuckin' metalwork? Bruce says you've got religion or summat daft, eh?'

'*Maz* – I didn't say that! Honestly, Al, I didn't. I just said you'd said you were staying at that commune or whatever it is. I think you look wonderful – really healthy. I mean, you looked dreadful when I put you on the plane, I was really worr–'

Maz snorted and lit a ciggie from the butt of her last one. 'Bollocks. That outfit makes y'look like a fuckin' nun.'

I was puzzled by her tone. She was always brusque, but there was an altogether sharper edge to her voice than I remembered.

'Don't be soft, Maz. It's just that we all wear the same so no one sticks out; we don't believe in all that fashion crap . . .' I stopped suddenly, aware of Maz' raised eyebrow and her outfit. 'I mean, er, The Prophet says all should be equal in the flesh, and . . .'

Maz snorted so hard she nearly spilt her tea. 'The *what*? Yer kiddin' me – The Prophet? Prophet of what? Don't tell me y've turned fuckin' Moonie?'

'You don't understand, Maz. I've been through a lot of changes, I –'

'Been brainwashed, more like!'

'Maz, Al – please.' Millie looked concerned. 'Please don't argue. Let's all relax and have a nice holiday. I'm sure it's nothing like the – Moonies or whatever, is it, Al?'

'Of *course* it isn't. It's like a – oh, a place where you study spiritual things. The Prophet is a teacher. Freddy knows him and his twin sister; he used to be at university with The P–, with the bloke. There's nothing weird going on, just a different way of seeing things. As The Prophet says . . .'

'Christ! Spare me the bullshit, *please*. OK, OK . . . sorry,

Al. Each to their own, like, eh? You allus were off wi't pixies, weren't yer? Don't mind me, I'm a bit knackered, like. I don't mean owt by it, do I, Bruce?'

Millie shook her head and brushed an imaginary speck off the sofa. 'Of course you don't, Maz. I expect we're all a bit tired. Especially after that flight – talk about sardines! I don't know where you put your legs, Maz; even *I* was squashed . . .'

After a long dissection of the evils of package flights, we decided to go for a late stroll on the beach. As we walked slowly along, Maz stumbling on the sand and cursing her boots, Millie filled me in on Bradford gossip, Leif, and the latest scandals at work. I felt the old comradeship return. I suppose it was bound to be a bit awkward at first; we'd never been apart for so long before and I had changed a bit. They'd see it was for the better, though. I just had to be patient. God! I was turning into the Queen of Patience, me! But that was OK, too. *Learn from errors, do not repeat them or your Life will close in upon you as the Serpent takes its tail into its own mouth and becomes a Circle looking ever inwards.* Yeah. I'd learnt all right and I'd been rewarded. It was cool.

'Is that a fuckin' bar? Ovver there, where it says "Lucky's"?' Maz limped up to catch us. 'Fancy a nightcap?'

She pointed to a neon sign flashing alternately pink and blue that did indeed spell 'Lucky's English Pub'. I looked doubtfully at Mills, but she nudged me and said in a meaningful voice that it might be fun. Fun? A dive like that? Oh well, maybe I *was* being a bit offish. Maybe it'd be like old times in the dreaded Brandy's.

We walked into the bar behind Maz, who seemed oblivious to the stares of every bloke – attached and unattached – in the place. She ordered a Piña Colada (retro cocktails were *in*, apparently). I had a mineral water and Millie decided on a glass of red wine. We looked around, then sat at a little table next to the hankie-sized dance floor. The DJ clocked Maz, who was glowing eerily in the UV light, and cranked up the volume for an extended re-mix of the summer hit 'Phantasie' by Blookreeme Inc. The beat banged away and Maz seemed content to eyeball the DJ and down her cocktail. I begged a taste, like we always used to do, and nearly choked it was so disgusting, but she just laughed and shouted in my ear that she didn't 'alf fancy a dance.

She didn't have to wait long for a partner. When she shed her sparkly jacket, it was obvious she was wearing nothing but a thong under her tiny frock. A tall, fair Australian-looking bloke said something to her, his eyes never leaving her face. She uncoiled herself and slinked on to the dance floor with him. Millie and I watched as she frugged expertly round the floor, the Strine fella practically drooling as he lumbered after her.

OK, I confess. It made me feel uncomfortable. I mean, Maz was often headstrong and she could be downright bloody awkward, but she always stuck with us. This time we seemed superfluous, she didn't even glance our way as she wriggled and gyrated and gulped cocktail after cocktail, bought by a series of dick-led blokes who obviously thought they were on to a winner.

Eventually I shouted to Mills that I was going to sit out on the terrace and she nodded, miming she'd come with me. We picked up Maz' bag and coat and, after signalling to her what we were up to, went outside.

It was slightly quieter out there, and an enormous, gravid full moon hung like an opal in the dark blue velvet sky, a few stars floating round it like a tiara. The moon-path, that tempting silver ribbon that the moon lays in the night-sea, wavered like an omen. Nana always told me if you succumbed to that shining lure and swam out along it, you got magically stuck, unable to turn back, swimming and swimming until you drowned.

It made me remember one night Donner and I had walked in the garden, ending up as usual by the reflecting pool that had also mirrored that silver path, and I'd told him the old superstition. That was the night he'd told me about his life as a medical student, the golden boy tipped for the highest possible honours – and the pressures that brought with it. He'd lowered his head, his voice full of pain, as he described his wealthy father's brutal bullying, the constant aggression that had cowed his mother into a trembling shadow and finally driven his younger brother Lutz to hang himself. I'd cried when he'd told me how he'd left Med School and wandered the world alone, full of despair and self-destruction, hating his father, despising his mother for being so weak, and mourning his beloved little brother. There'd been something else, too, I could sense he was holding something back, but I hadn't wanted to push it. He would tell me if he wanted to, in time. He'd had tears in his eyes and I'd gently reached up and wiped them away. We'd gazed at each other for a long, long moment, then he'd put his arm round me and said everything was all right now, he'd found The Prophet and his healing way, and that I was a very spiritual, empathic woman to share his grief. If anyone had said that to me in the past, I'd have laughed in their face and thought it a corny New Agey chat-up line. But it wasn't like that; he'd really meant it. We'd sat for a long time in silence, my head resting against his shoulder, then he'd kissed me on the forehead and I'd gone to bed dreaming of . . .

'Al – Al, do you want another drink?'

'Oh, soz – sorry, Mills. No, not really. I could murder a cuppa, to be honest, but . . .'

Mills gazed miserably back at the bar and sighed heavily, slumping against the metal chair while she nervously twiddled with a paper napkin from the table dispenser. 'I know, I know – Maz. She's been like this since she caught Rom with that – that girl. It's like she doesn't *care* about anything any more. I know she's out nearly every night and taking . . .' she lowered her voice and glanced around: '*cocaine* – tons of it. And Ecstasy.' Mills never had been big into the drug thing. I think it scared her. Loss of control, making a fool of yourself – very non-Mills. A glass of wine, a bit of draw maybe, to relax. Apart from that she was a chemical virgin.

'Not *tons,* Mills . . .'

'Don't laugh at me – you know what I mean. And the salon's suffering too. One day last week she didn't open until *twelve thirty* because she'd been out all night and ended up at some bloke's flat in *Leeds.* There were cancellations and *everything.* It's not like her, it really isn't.'

Mills was right, it wasn't. The only time I'd ever seen Maz off the rails was after Olga died, but even then she'd still been clockwork at college and never let her social life interfere with business.

'Is it the Rom thing?'

'I think so. I reckon she feels she's wasted her life on him – her youth, that is. We're none of us getting any younger; it's the big three-oh soon and she sees me and Lief so settled and . . .'

'But age doesn't matter. Yeah, OK, it's thirty, but that doesn't mean you're *dead* or anything – I *hope.*'

'Well, that's how I feel too. But Maz, she's always been a big socializer, going to raves, concerts, then all this clubbing business. She said the other day the girls at these clubs make her feel like a granny out on the pull. And she hasn't *got* anything but that; she doesn't read, she won't go to the pictures, she isn't even interested in the TV really. It's nightlife or no life where she's concerned.'

I did – and it wasn't a pretty picture. I remembered how at sixteen we all used to snigger at the old Goths – the thirty-something vamps, greying hair still dyed purple or blue, their paint cracking in the heat of the Alternative Night disco, their sagging figures trussed up into skin-tight black, as if they could be the shape they'd been at twenty by sheer force of will. How we laughed at the boys who snogged them – or worse, shagged them. 'Granny-grabbers', we called them. The women we thought of as tacky, undignified, whorish. *We'd* never be like that; desperate, ridiculous.

It wasn't possible that Maz – young, stylish Maz – could . . . No, she was . . . Oh, poor Maz. I could see Mills was thinking the same way I was. It was awful.

'Look, I'll go get her and we'll pick up a pizza from that takeaway down the road – it'll be like old times. How about it? Oh, Millie, she'll be all right. The Rom thing's been a terrible shock for her, but she'll get over it. This place will do her good – sun, sea, and it's still quite warm –'

'*Quite* warm! God, what's it like in August?'

'Don't ask. Believe me, you don't want to know. Now, you wait here and I'll fetch Little Miss Flirtypants.'

But she wouldn't come. At first, I couldn't find her, then I spotted her sitting astride the knees of the Aussie bloke while they sucked each other's faces and he groped her partly exposed bum. I stood there like a wart for a bit then tapped her on the shoulder. She looked up, her pale blue pearl lippie smeared over her chin like a nacreous slug trail. Her eyes were huge and dark and her nose red round the nostrils. You didn't need to be Dickwad of the Yard to work out what she'd been doing. The Aussie grinned brainlessly, his flies unzipped and his *equipment* bulging through his Calvins.

'Er, Maz, me an' Mills are off for a pizza – coming?'

She laughed harshly and wriggled on her captive's lap. 'Not yet, lass – not yet, eh? Oh, off you go an' get yer dinner like good little girlies. I'm . . . *busy*. Leave us me bag, and take me coat 'ome with yer. Bruce has the other key.'

And she went back to her *business* with a vengeance. I wanted to slap her, I was so cross. Showing herself up like that in public with some surfie fuckbrain. And that off-colour comment; that wasn't like her at all. Swearing, sure. But crude jokes? Never. That was common, and Maz hated anything common. Or she had done. Now it seemed *common* was the plat du jour.

We hung her bag on the chair-back as we passed. She just glanced up and grunted. I could see Mills was rigid with anger and we walked to the takeaway in silence.

We waited up for her. Flipping channels on the satellite TV and not saying much. About two thirty Millie crawled off to kip, a look of dumb misery on her face. I waited another hour, reading a copy of The Prophet's last book, *Keeper of the Gate*. The sentiments seemed doubly poignant here, and I felt myself missing the quiet, happy life of Soledad more than I'd thought possible. I even found myself missing the meditation and the chanting, all of us together like a family, bound in the rise and fall of the voices and drumming. I wondered if they missed me . . . If Donner missed me. I could hardly credit that, less than a year ago, I'd have given an arm and a leg to be out giving it some big-stylee in a club. Now, it all seemed sordid and shallow.

I wasn't giving up on Maz, though. I was sure she just needed to relax in the sun, go on a few trips to beautiful places, and she'd be her old self again – acerbic, funny, sharp as a pin. We'd get the old team back, no probs. Patience, I reminded myself, patience. *The road to bliss lies in the Heart's Blood, not in the desert of worldly desire; listen to the sound of your heart beating and be still. Wait calmly. You will see your path.* Maz would be all right, when she finally heard the voice of her heart.

Yeah, you guessed it – I couldn't have been more wrong if I'd tried.

That first night set the tone for the days that followed.

She woke me up at around six in the morning, crashing and cursing round the kitchen, and when I stumbled out to see what was going on she laughed groggily and said she'd 'gone for a walk'. Yeah – through a briar patch. Her flimsy dress was filthy with sand, one strap nearly torn off, and as she bent to open the fridge, I saw she'd lost her knickers somewhere along the way, too.

I made some tea, but by the time I brought it to her she was fast asleep, snoring on the big sofa, one boot on, one off. I took the remaining boot off and covered her with the blanket from her room. My heart ached to see her in that state. I was reminded of Rain's belief that Dido would have benefited from the peaceful atmosphere at Soledad. Maybe Maz . . .

She woke at about ten a.m. and crawled into the shower. Mills had been out shopping and made us a big fried breakfast; you could get everything you needed for that sort of scran at the complex's mini-supermarket. This was a Brit area. Maz ate virtually nothing, her who normally ate everyone out of house and home. In the afternoon she slept on a plastic lounger by the pool, covered in Factor 2 sun lotion and wearing a gold lamé dental-floss bikini. That night it was a different bar, and then Planeta Platino, a big new club. Different venues, same result.

After three nights like this, me and Mills stopped going with her. All right, maybe we shouldn't have, maybe we should have stuck with her; but she didn't care. For the first time, we weren't the Three Stooges, we were Two Stooges and a woman I didn't seem to know.

We sat in front of the telly in the evenings, waiting for her. Sad, eh? We talked about old times and I told Mills all about the Foundation and how well I was doing with the book. We gossiped in a stilted way about Bradford, now languishing under the bituminous clouds of autumn. A London film company was making a TV movie about the Night Creeper murders with Sean Bean as the Creeper and some skinny Southern actresses playing those women he held hostage. Town was in an uproar about it, saying it had been bad enough with the Ripper; but that's the media for you – money, money, money and never mind who you hurt and exploit. I told her how I was getting on with the Parents, and their news. I discussed Frankie with her. She filled me in on how Lief and her family were keeping. We didn't talk about Maz. It was *shit.*

Don't get me wrong. I was well aware that what Maz was doing was exactly what the majority of tourists coming to the beaches of Spain wanted to do: sun, sex, clubs and drugs. The British dream-come-true. I knew Millie and I were the odd ones out, wandering round cathedrals and eating ice-cream in the shade while the end-of-season die-hards partied till they dropped, their sunburn and love-bites the uniform of the fun generation, just like their wonky navel piercings and their 'cheeky' buttock tattoos. Crap, crap, *crap.*

Maz felt old – what the fuck did she think *we* felt like?

The day before they were to fly home, Mills and I took the little hire car that came with the fly-and-drive deal they'd got, and went up into the Parque de las Nieves National Park. As we picnicked under the aromatic canopy of the ancient pines, I told her that I wouldn't be coming back to Bradford for a while. She sighed and said she'd thought as much. I felt very sad, but at the same time, it seemed almost *natural,* as if I were getting on with my life, and our childhood friendship was changing, evolving. I still believed Maz was just going through a phase, and Mills agreed. Still, it was a shame their holiday had been such a disaster – well, for Mills, at least. She wasn't totally pissed off, though, as Lief was currently in New York and was going to pay for her to visit him, which she was very excited about.

Then I told her I was in love. Well, that I loved someone, someone serious and gentle and good through and through, and we hugged in our lumpy, unphysical Bradfordian way. We promised each other we'd always be mates and that we wouldn't abandon Maz, no matter what she did. We'd be OK, it was just a matter of time.

The drive back was beautiful, and Mills and I were tired but happy as we dragged ourselves laughing up the stairs and into the apartment.

What we hadn't expected was to find Maz, white as a sheet, her eyes huge, dark and shadowed, sitting bundled up on the sofa, smoking like a woman on a mission to lung cancer.

'Well, 'appy now you've dished t'dirt on me, are you?'

'Maz . . .'

'Don't fuckin' "Maz" me, you. I know what you've bin up to – goin' off on your little *outin's*, getting t'knife stuck in.'

It was the coke talking. She was a brittle shell, her chemically fuelled rage and paranoia jittering through her empty insides like electricity shorting. I could *smell* the wrongness of her body; sour and metallic.

She ran a reddened, knuckley hand through the sticky-up brush of her bleached hair, then rubbed her raw nostrilled nose, sniffing loudly. Her complexion looked drained and sick, the pink sunburn laying a stain over the pallid white beneath like a cheap red chiffon scarf draped on a corpse.

I walked towards her, my hands outspread. 'Maz, come on – you're tired, this isn't . . .'

'Oh yes, I'm fuckin' tired, all right. Dead fuckin' tired. I am *so fuckin' tired*. What the *fuck* would you know, eh? Eh? Got up like some sorta skanky fuckin' *Harry Krishna* . . .' She was trembling all over, and she laid her head back, eyes closed, on the cushions; the tendons of her neck standing out like cables.

I sat on the chair opposite her and made the 'T' sign with my fingers to Mills, who put her bag down and went into the kitchen. A tear trickled out from under Maz's eyelid, running down her cheek into her ear. She scrubbed at it irritably and lifted her head, staring moodily past me into nothing.

'Look, love, I know you're upset . . .'

She skinned her lips back and grinned at me mirthlessly. 'Upset? Upset? What the fuck would you know? You've never 'ad to work for owt in yer whole fuckin' life – you wi' yer nose stuck in a fuckin' book all the time.' She glared at me, the pale blue-grey of her 'real' eyes startling against her sunburnt cheeks. 'Go on, why don't yer? Give us some o' that fuckin' wank yer allus spouting these days? Give it some o' that god-botherin' bullshit!'

'Maz, it's not like that. *I'm* not like that, you know I'm not. It's just I've chosen a different way of life now. Can't you be pleased for me? I'm happy, I really am . . .'

She laughed, the sound catching in her throat and turning into a phlegmy smoker's hack. 'Oh, right. Sorry for breathin', I'm sure. Y'know, some of us in the fuckin' *real* world have fuckin' problems, y'know, not just toss about what fuckin' flowers to pick or whatever you fuckin' lot get up to.'

Millie came in, and put the teapot down with a trembling hand. Maz cast her a sullen look and lit another cigarette. I poured the tea, but Maz made a chopping gesture with her hand in dismissal when I offered her a cup.

'Maz, I know you're not right, love. I know you're unhappy. But a trouble shared . . .' I took a deep breath. I'd wanted to tell The Ems about that night at Soledad when I'd let go of my terrible secret. For years I'd carried it inside me, worrying what people would think. Even my two best friends. I'd been wrong not to let them help me, but somehow the moment hadn't presented itself – because I was afraid they wouldn't understand. Well, that was plain daft. As if The Ems would *judge* me. I had to be brave now, and share it with them so Maz could see that she was wasn't alone. Maybe if I told Maz how I'd felt the weight lift from my heart that night, she could . . . you know. I had to do it.

'Maz, see – up at The Foundation – no, hang on, let me finish – up there, we all believe that if you share your problems with your friends, you let the family, the sort of family you and your mates have together, help you sort things out. Oh, I'm not being very clear. It's like . . . in the evenings they have a sort of discussion group, to let people share stuff. I thought it was bollocks at first, but then one night . . . I told them something, and after I felt, oh, tons better. It was something I'd kept secret for ages, and it was hard to, you know, carry it. So I told. Then, after, I could see it hadn't been *my* fault, and I . . . well, I felt so much better . . .'

I looked at them, my heart thudding and a trickle of sweat running down my back. Mills was staring at the rug, her hair fanning down like silk across her face. Maz was half smiling, her eyes narrowed and glittering. I felt *wrong* – but I couldn't stop now I'd started. I ran my forefinger shakily over my upper lip and stumbled on.

'You see, er – God, this is really hard – Jack . . . Jack used to beat me – when we had a row. He used to hit me and then he'd be really, really sorry, but he always did it again. That night – the night he died – we'd rowed and he went crazy. I thought he'd kill me. I . . .'

The deathly silence was broken by Maz' laughter. Harsh, choking laughter. She was almost doubled over, her arm across her belly, the hand holding her cigarette waving a nauseating counterpoint to the dragging in-drawn breaths. I couldn't understand – I felt a freezing chill ice the sweat on my body.

'Well, fuck me! D'yer hear that, Bruce? Loverboy used to knock her around. Oh, for fuck's sake – every bugger knew *that.* D'you seriously think anyone fuckin' believed all that crap about you walking into doors and fallin' down the fuckin' steps? D'you think you're the only lass who's had all that? Christ Almighty! Is that your big fuckin' secret?'

Millie looked up now, and through the dull, roaring haze that seemed to be enveloping me, I could see she was on the point of tears, her hands bunching the fabric of her dress convulsively.

'Maz, don't – please – we . . .' Mills was almost sobbing now.

'Aw, fer fuck's sake, Bruce. I've fuckin' had enough of *secrets* – 'aven't you? Eh? Time to tell a few secrets of me own – let's see if sharin' and fuckin' carin' works both ways, eh? You make me poorly sometimes, A, you wi't silver fuckin' spoon in yer gob, wanderin' about playin' the wounded fuckin' Bambi. Well, you don't know the 'alf of it. *Christ,* am I *sick* of you goin' on about that fucker Jack Collier like he were some sort of fuckin' saint – just because he wrote poetry. *Poetry,* for fuck's sake! Who gives a flyin' toss about *poetry*? Only arty fuckin' idiots like you an' your lot. It's not like he were Robbie fuckin' Williams, is it? Not like he were *worth* owt . . .'

A terrible feeling of dread ran through me. I wanted that rasping, dreadful voice to stop; I wanted to put my hands over my ears and shout like we did in school when we didn't want to hear. But I couldn't, my arms and legs were trembling uncontrollably and I couldn't move while that voice ground on, crushing everything in its path.

'Let me tell you about your precious Jacky Boy – no, it's been long enough, Bruce, an' I've got my reasons. I *fucked* your sainted bloody poet, Al-*ma.* I fucked him up against the wall out the back of Brandy's. He shagged owt that moved, he did – everyone knew it. He told me – *me* – that he'd been havin' an affair wi some bird from London ever since he got that fuckin' book out. Said he went to see her all the time and she were beggin' him to go an' live wi her, but he were scared you'd top yerself. Oh, he said he loved yer, but y' dragged 'im down, clingin' to 'im, goin' on about how ugly an' stupid you were an' how yer mam an' dad dint love yer an' 'ow he mustn't *ever* leave yer. An' I didn't give a fuck that night. My sister died in that shitehole, by hersel, like a fuckin' dog chokin' on her own puke . . . An' nothing made sense any more – nothin'. Only the drinkin' took the edge off it – only the gear. But I int makin' no excuses for it. It just 'appened. I couldn't fuckin' believe it when he come on to me. I told 'im to fuck right off, but he laughed an' said he liked a fightin' woman – liked a *challenge*. So I said, "You want it, yer bastard? Outside now, then." An' he follered me, laughin', and I fucked him like a whore up against that dirty old wall; standin' up, his cum runnin' down my legs after. Christ . . .'

I could hear Mills crying and begging her to stop but she just spat and rubbed her mouth. I felt a pulse in my ears like blood and my lungs closing down, shutting off, but I didn't care, I didn't care – if only she'd *stop* . . .

'Problems, missy? You want to know about fuckin' *problems*, eh? I'll tell you something. Tatum's not Rom's kiddie – she's your precious fuckin' Jack's babby. D'you hear me? *Jack's babby*. Rom can't 'ave kids, he's sterile. He had mumps real bad, now he's firin' blanks. That's why he whores around; thinks it meks him more of a man. Oh, he dint mind lettin' on he'd fathered a kid, but he knew she weren't his. That's why he never bothered with 'er. *Tatum's Jack's babby.*'

I slid off the chair on to my knees, the room turning round me in a cold white fog of poison. Jack's child? No, no, please . . . it wasn't . . .

Maz's voice ground on, as if now she'd started, she couldn't stop:

'Yeah, I'm sick of fuckin' secrets, Al. That's why I'm gonna tek this fuckin' writer bloke's money. He's writin' a book about your Jacky-Boy. He's bin snoopin' around Town askin' all sorts of questions. Mike an' Terry give me 'is number – they knew Jack'd bin wi' me. They were there that night, eggin' 'im on, havin' a right laugh. This bloke's gonna give me loads of money to tell the tale – an' I'm tekkin' it. Your darlin' Jack's nowt ter me – nowt but a fuckin' sperm-donor. I don't give a flyin' fuck what this fella writes about Jack Collier, as long as I get the money. I've got *expenses* –'

Millie's voice rose in a wavering shriek. 'Maz – no! It's for drugs, isn't it? You can't, please . . .'

'*Drugs*! Don't be fuckin' daft! It's the business, if yer must know. I've overstretched meself, pushed the boat out a bit too far – all the new salon stuff, the basins, the floors, new windows, wages . . . I've been stupid wi't accounts. Now the fuckin' taxman wants an enormous wedge off me. An' I lent Rom five grand towards startin' up a club in Town – I'll never see that again. Don't start, Bruce. He won't pay me back – I know 'im. It's ovver with us; he'll fuck off to Ibiza or Ayia Napa, and I'll never find 'im if he don't want findin'. Christ, can't you understand? I *need* this money, an' I'm 'avin' it – so that's an' end of it. I need the salon, my family need the money. *My* mam an' dad aren't fuckin' loaded like *hers* . . .'

I crouched on the floor, numb, my mouth working but no sound coming out. My lungs heaved and laboured in my chest, the wheezing whistle ringing in my ears. I felt Millie bend over me and push my inhaler into my hand but I didn't want it. I wanted to squat there like that forever, to *not exist*.

'God, Maz, look at the state of her! *Al,* please – your inhaler. Please, I'll have to get an ambulance if you don't

. . . please, Al. *God,* I hope you're satisfied Maz, I *really* hope you're satisfied. I can't believe – it was wrong, Maz, what you've done. It's ruined everything, *everything.*'

I fumbled with my Ventolin, my hand shaking wildly, and felt the chemical, gassy taste in my mouth and my lungs releasing slightly. There was something I had to ask Mills, something I had to know.

'Millie?' My voice was a reedy, pathetic whisper. I coughed, spasming double, then tried again: 'Millie – *did you know?*'

She flopped down on the floor beside me as if someone had cut her tendons. Her face was luminously pale; even her lips were colourless. I noticed that outside, in one of the other flats, someone was listening to a Flamenco CD, the eerie, savage voice of the singer howling like a fallen angel. I wanted to listen to its rending beauty, to lose myself in it and make all this – horror disappear. Then, suddenly, the sound stopped. I heard Maz grunt, 'Thank Christ fer that – fuckin' racket!' and I turned back to Millie.

'Yes,' she said. 'I knew. We all knew – he was a horrible man, a bastard. I knew . . . about Tatum. Oh, Al, we just wanted to protect you. You loved him so much, you wouldn't hear a word against him. We – we tried. No one wanted to hurt you. I mean, we thought Jack would go off to London, that you'd be upset for a while but then you'd get on with your life. But he went and killed himself. And we thought, "What good will her knowing do? It won't make it right. It won't make it better." We love you, Al – we do, don't we, Maz? Oh, *Maz* . . . She does, Al, it's just . . .'

'Jack didn't kill himself, it was an –'

'Oh, Al, *stop it.* He walked into the road on purpose. That poor lorry driver – he had a nervous breakdown, you know. Terry said Jack was laughing; he'd said he was sick of everything, sick of people expecting things of him all the time and he . . . You know he did, Al. Don't you?'

Yes, I knew. I'd always known. In my heart, the shrine toppled, breaking up into a million glittering, tawdry pieces, floating away on the cruel, deadly laughter that had rolled from Jack's mouth that night like a curse.

And now Maz was going to sell this to Leo Brindle. How happy he'd be with his secrets and his brilliant coup. How he'd smile, and flourish like a rank, stinking weed. How they'd all laugh at me: poor Alma, who thought she was so good, so perfect, the fucking handmaiden to a false god, the stupid, self-important *girlfriend* – the patsy. The groupie. The *fool.*

I staggered to my feet, shoved past the chair and into the bedroom like an automaton. Picking up my bag, I stuffed my things into it. Nothing mattered and I felt *nothing.*

I didn't look at Maz as I walked out of the door.

24

I crossed to the central piazza, by the pool that was sheeny with an iridescent film of sun oil heaving and gleaming in the artificial light. My lungs were still sore and tight, and the coarse stink of chlorine, sweat and synthetic perfumes clung to the air and made me sneeze. I sat down bonelessly on a lounger and took off my glasses, rubbing my eyes. What should I do? Where could I go?

Nothing made any sense. I'd thought I was suffering when Phillip had Wellington killed and made me homeless, but it was nothing compared to this. I couldn't really grasp it. They'd kept it a secret all this time . . . How could they? But I knew how. The same way I'd kept Jack's violence a secret. First you make the decision not to tell – out of fear, or love, or pride – and for a while it scrapes like a badly fitting shoe; sore, blistering, constant. Then a sort of callus forms, thickening over your heart, layering skin on skin, opaque and heavy. You refuse to think about it, so the pain of the secret becomes a dull, far-away thing you hardly feel. It's always there yet not there, at the same time. It just *is.* It sits there in you, dense and clotted, unmoving. Then you make up some cover story, some lie, and you repeat it so often, so very often, that it becomes a kind of truth you almost believe in yourself. You believe, because it's easier to live with than the reality.

I knew that's what Maz – and Millie – had done. I knew how it was. I'd done it myself. God, though – Jack's child. The image of Tatum hovered before me. Why hadn't I known? I pictured her all bundled up for the winter, her face with its Slavic bones, her eyes . . . I'd assumed she looked like Maz. Oh, come on, she *did* look like Maz; I was kidding myself if I thought otherwise. I hadn't known even subconsciously. Tatum was all Maz'. Like she said, Jack had been nothing more than a sperm-donor. Christ, how he'd have hated that! What a blow to his ego! Well, tough fucking titty, Jack. Tough fucking luck.

A hot wave of blood flooded my cheeks and I groaned out loud. What a fucking idiot I'd been. All those nights I'd thought Jack was ladding about with his mates. Of course he'd been shagging around. What had I thought? That he'd been having a few pints and playing dominoes? It all fell into place now. The way people treated me, the way conversation would stop when I came in the room. God, Mike had once tried to tell me, but I'd accused him of being jealous of Jack's success. Poor bastard, he'd been trying to do the right thing but I was too obsessed to hear it.

I couldn't go back to Bradford – to England – now. Not once Leo's book came out. I felt nauseous with humiliation. How could I live with this? But it was a done deal; there was no going back. Oh God . . .

I had to get away. I stumbled off to the mini-mart and changed a note for coins. The guy behind the till didn't bat an eyelid at the state of me; I suppose he was used to much worse. I found a payphone and rang the Parents; my 'wealthy' parents who'd given me this oh-so-privileged existence. I listened to the ringing tone for what seemed like hours until I gave up; they were probably out with the TV people or Vi's art dealer. How was I going to get home now? I could get a bus to the railway station, but probably not until morning . . .

I leaned my forehead against the cool plastic and steel of the phone unit. Who was I kidding? How could I tell the Parents? God, it was so, so humiliating, so sordid and disgusting. I couldn't tell them. I just *couldn't.*

There was only one person I could turn to. I fumbled in my bag for my notebook and looked up the number. Then I rang Soledad. Donner would help me. He wouldn't let me down; he cared too much about me. I was glad we weren't lovers, then. Because his friendship was totally pure with no 'relationship' baggage attached to it.

'CDS Foundation – how may I help you?'

'Rose? Is that you? It's – God, Rose, it's Alma . . .'

'Alma? What's the matter? Are you in trouble?'

'Oh, Rose, Rose – it's awful. I don't know what to do . . . Is Donner there?'

'Donner? Of course – wait, OK? Hang on and I'll get him. Don't go off, right?'

I clung to the receiver, my eyes shut, praying he'd come quickly. Please don't let this all be another lie. Let it all be OK. Please, please . . .

'Alma? It's Donner. What is the matter?'

His voice was full of concern. I could hear the love in it. It wasn't a lie; he really cared. I told him everything. It was such a relief, such a blessed relief not to be alone.

'OK, Alma. Wait in front of the building, and I will send Rose and some others to fetch you. It is the place you told me about, yes? The big place, Apartamentos del Playa Oro? Yes – all is clear. It will take maybe one hour, or at most two. You must wait and be calm. We are coming for you. Remember that we love you, Alma; you are part of us, we want you to come home. OK? Can you do that? You must be brave – I know you can do it. I have to remain here with The Prophet because he is not so well tonight, but your brothers and sisters are coming for you, yes? OK?'

'OK. Thank you. There's a kind of ornamental bench thing, I'll wait there – oh, Donner . . .'

'I know, I know. These people – they are so cruel. But you will be safe soon. They cannot hurt you any more, I promise. Go now and wait. The van is setting off straight away. Soon this will be nothing more than a bad dream. I will see you soon, Alma.'

Godbotherers? Weirdoes? *Freaks?* Yeah – sure. At least they didn't let people down, humiliate them, sell them for money. At least they told the truth. Cared about each other. Tried to make sense of an insane world, slavering for money and crawling with *lies.* Better to be a fucking freak, if straight people behaved like my so-called *best mates.*

I walked across the piazza towards the exit, planning to sit on the bench and try to get myself together. It was fairly warm, and even the ruined stink of Marbella couldn't totally overcome the salt whisper of the sea. I kept up a kind of running commentary to myself: *It'll be fine, I'm fine, everything's going to be – fine.* The sound of my flip-flops slapping the tiles seemed incredibly loud and I could hear everything that was going on around me. I could smell cooking and cigarettes, the decaying sweetness of lilies and the sharp resinous pines, but I felt as if I was alone on a high, cold mountain. The air seemed to congeal into ice around me as I walked. Cold, cold, cold. Despite the warmth of the night, I felt cold inside and out. Oh, why wasn't Donner here?

Millie stepped out of the shadows.

'Al – thank God. Oh, love, I thought you'd run off. Look, come back upstairs and we'll sort all this out. Maz doesn't mean it; she's just upset, worried about money and things. We can sort it all out – we always do, don't we? Come back now, please . . .'

I looked at her as she stood twisting her stubby little hands together anxiously. She really thought she could 'organize' this all away. Somehow, her betrayal hurt more than Maz'. Maybe it was because she was so steady, so bloody normal. If Millie could lie like this, what hope was there? Her eyes were shining with tears. I felt I *ought* to be furious. Be dramatic, yell at her. But I just felt empty. I knew all this would really hurt her, and I didn't want that. I still loved her. There was no way I could be with her, though. Not now, not ever.

'Look, Millie, I don't hate you or anything, right? But it's over. I'm going to Soledad – the Chelas are coming to fetch me. It's over, Millie. You should have told me. How could you not? How could you? Jack's baby – all those secrets. I thought you were my friends, but you've fucked up my whole life . . .'

She bowed her head and I saw the glint as a tear fell to the floor. 'Al, don't. *Please* try to understand. Everything's been so hard for Maz, and she thinks it's all been so easy for you. I *know* that's not true, but it's what she thinks sometimes. She loves you really, we both do. We didn't want to hurt you – nobody did. Please, come back with me, talk to her . . .'

Poor Millie – desperate to keep everything *civilized*. But I knew Maz wouldn't see it that way. Telling me about Jack and Tatum had cost her too much, she'd ripped it out of herself like an animal tearing its own paw off to get out of a trap. She wouldn't want me in front of her eyes ever again. I was a living reproach to her and she wouldn't be able to stick it. She'd just cut me out like I was a dead woman walking; she wasn't troubled by Millie's middle-class sensibilities. Somehow, I could understand Maz better than Millie in that way; there was a kind of pride in it, a sort of brutal honesty after all the falseness. But Millie . . . I knew this was killing her. Part of me wanted to reach out to her and say it was all all right, but the other half was frozen, dead. I believed her when she said she'd meant well. But it was no good. It was all fucked up.

'No, Millie. Go back now. I can't – it's – there's nothing to say. Some things can't be mended. Look, go on. Have a good life, whatever. Don't cry – I know you didn't mean any harm. I don't hate you, Millie, and I'm not angry. I – I feel sorry for you. It's just . . . that – I can't come back home, not now, maybe not ever . . . I've got to sort this out in my head. Please, go *away*, Millie, please – *go*.'

Her face was livid with misery. I kept thinking, *This is Mills – Mills, your friend. Don't let her go* . . . But I couldn't move, my throat, my voice seemed paralysed and she stepped back into the dark of the entrance. In the second before the auto-light came on, her round, ivory face seemed to hang suspended like a mask, her narrow, folded eyes darker than the shadows that wrapped her.

I turned away. I didn't look back; Lot's wife made that error, but not me, I was salt and ice and dead already.

25

I sat in bed, picking through an old copy of Marcus Aurelius, aching with fatigue. Someone had put a statuette of the Virgin, a beautiful, baroque thing, on my side table and the pure, patinated curve of Mary's face was lit by the reading lamp. 'Mary' – I'd read somewhere it meant 'bitter', the name given to unwanted daughters. I had looked at the statue for a long time in a kind of waking stupor when I got in; the journey up from Marbella in the Jeep had been an exhausting blur of precipitous roads and looming mountains. Azul had sat in the back with me, totally wired, his pupils like pinpoints. He was on a Vision Quest and so not sleeping or eating. His little face had screwed up into a wrinkled point of concentration as he strained to understand what I was telling Sierra and Rose. When he understood, he cried. Poor little bugger. I didn't cry. I didn't think I'd ever cry again. I felt like someone had stuck a blunt knife in my chest leaving a thudding, bruise-edged wound in my heart.

I guessed it was Marigold who had made my bed up and put the statuette there. As I had unpacked my bits and pieces, I'd found Millie's post-modern ironic Virgin keyring stuffed in with my underwear. It seemed suddenly trivial next to the lovely old statue, so I shoved it in a drawer. I knew Millie had meant well, but it showed yet again how no one had ever really understood my fondness for the Virgin. I don't think I did myself. The very idea of her seemed to satisfy something in my heart, to make me feel better, somehow. It was more than the ever-so amusing pigs/frogs/sick-bags collecting-type thing – you know, *This is my mate, she collects Madonnas . . . Oh, I collect beer towels, myself. Haven't we got a lot in common?* No, actually. Fuck all in common, as it goes.

I let the book drop on to my lap and stared at that face, that oval of passionate, tender love. Between the two of them, Mary and Marcus, I felt I was with friends. *On Pain: what we cannot bear removes us from life; what lasts can be borne.* Good old Marcus, never one to mince his words. Absolute anathema to the counselling generation, with their endless excuses and feverish searches for someone to solve their problems for them. I sighed heavily and thought about trying to sleep.

There was a knock on the door. *Donner*? 'Come in –'

Rose backed in, carrying a tray. 'Oh – I thought I'd lost it then! Look, I brought you some tea – the good stuff, eh? And – see this? You're not wrong – you can believe it, it's really happening . . . Dairy Milk! I've been saving it for a special occasion, but – ah, fuck it – let's pig out. Don't tell Souris, or the boys, OK? I gave Marigold a Twix I had stashed as hush money, so she's on our side – sends her best love, by the way, the little bless, but she's worn out and gone beddy-bye-byes.'

She sat on the end of the bed and I chucked her a pillow to put between her back and the knobbly old iron frame.

There was a short silence, broken only by the squelchy sound of chocolate being chewed.

Rose sighed heavily and a faint chocolately exhalation wafted my way. 'I swear I'd go completely barmy if I didn't have a bit of a munchie moment now and then. Y'know, much as I *adore* everyone, the skinny-is-pure thing gets me down sometimes. I've argued meself blue in the face at meetings about it – I even wrote a paper on it, I got so pissed off – but it does no good. They're stuck in that impurity-of-the-flesh bag . . . Mind you, you never see a fat holy woman, do you? You never see a fat saint. Ah, spare me! Bloody holy anorexics, the lot of 'em. Want this last bit . . . ? No? Good.'

She ate the last square slowly, looking like that famous statue of Saint Theresa and the angel – pure ecstasy.

'Drink up now, that's Mama Jay's best Assam. She sent it – along with that Madonna. Thought it might make you feel better, you being so fond of the Holy Mother an' all that. Oh, the nightie fits all right, then? I made that for you – had to guess the size, but I think it's OK. Is it long enough?'

'Yeah, it's beautiful. *You* made it? All the pin-tucking and everything? How did you learn to sew like this?'

'Nuns,' she said gloomily, rolling her big grey eyes. Rose wasn't pretty, really; she had a vaguely neotenous look, her face tapering from a broad white brow to a small pointed chin and rosebud mouth. Her coarse black hair threatened to sprout from her crop into the sort of springy mad curls that were described as 'unmanageable' in beauty mags. She was hairy, too. A shadow draped her upper lip and her eyebrows met in the middle, Frida Kahlo style. But she had those beautiful eyes – almost lilac-grey, like the sky when snow's coming – fringed with double-thick black lashes. She smiled, her piercings gleaming in the lamplight. I remembered how everyone thought Rose was the bravest of all the Chelas when it came to the pain offerings. She never made a sound or breathed hard but seemed to light up when the rush hit. Her insights afterwards were always clear and brilliant, too. Not like me, babbling on about how freaky it made me feel.

Rose smiled at me and raised her eyebrow; half of it, at any rate, bless. 'Donner's in a terrible state over you, missy. I've never seen him so worked up – I mean, he's not exactly the *madcap* type, now is he?'

I nearly snorted my tea up my nose. *That* came out of the blue.

'Oh, don't worry – it'll do him good, stir him up a bit. We can all do with a bit of that sometimes, don't you think?'

Maybe. I thought back to Marbella; there again, maybe not. Rose read my mind – or my face.

'God – sorry. Me an' my big mouth. I didn't mean like what happened to you – that's just plain cruel, to my mind. What were they thinking of? Why do straight people insist upon keeping their bloody stupid secrets like they were in the fucking CIA? Jesus, Mary and Joseph, it makes you sick the way they go on. You must be devastated. And the baby – you must be thinking it should have been yours, you being so motherly and all . . .'

What?

I could hear Rose's voice as she rambled on about how glad she was not to be in the outside world any more – but a great, biting *thing* had uncoiled in my brain. Tatum should have been mine – mine and Jack's. *Our* child. In the beginning, we'd talked about having a baby; picked names, even. Hester, Alexander, Storm, Asa. Oh yes, we were going to be the perfect arty family. Until it all started going wrong. Until he started hitting me. After that, the baby-name game stopped sharpish. I hadn't thought about it before. I hadn't thought about a lot of things. Motherly? Me? No, I was too moody, too immature, too . . . Tatum's oblique green eyes – *Jack's eyes* – seemed to gaze at me from out of nowhere. My child. She could have been mine . . . ours . . .

Something twisted sickeningly in my belly. *What we cannot bear removes us from life; what lasts can be borne . . . What we cannot bear* . . . Oh, Christ.

'Here, drink up. You want a paracetamol? I know

we're not supposed to, but in the circumstances . . . Or I can get you something homeopathic, if you'd prefer . . . Have you a headache? God, and there's me wittering on at you. You sure? Look, I'm going to let you get some sleep now. Have a rest and then just, you know, help Souris and do your work. Mama Jay says can you come to tea with her tomorrow? She needs a little talk. OK . . . oh, you poor thing, you look dreadful. Get your head down now . . . And, Alma, we're all really, really pleased to have you back. Some people were a bit worried you'd . . . you know, go off with those people. But I knew you'd come home; you belong here, with us. We love you, and we're so proud of you . . . Ah, enough with the soppiness, you'll have me blubbing. Nighty-night, sweet dreams.'

And she was gone. I was alone. I turned out the light and lay with my arms behind my head. Faintly, I could hear drumming and the distant thread of chanting; the lads' Vision Quest, I supposed. I thought about getting up to join them; there was no way I was going to sleep. It felt as if someone had drawn out my veins and filled the spaces with barbed wire. My skin itched, my lungs laboured like furnace bellows. Tatum, Jack, Maz, Millie – oh, fuck it, fuck them all, fuck everything, everything . . .

Sleep hit me like a concussing blow. It wasn't really sleep; I think I fell unconscious; fell into the Deep, no dreams, no nothing.

The next morning the hard blue dome of the sky was striated with cloud; a breeze stirred the soft dust and clattered the dry fronds of the old palm tree outside my door in a parched minuet.

I didn't feel very hungry but I ate with the others and did the morning meditation. The theme was 'Inner Stillness and the Voice of the Spirit'. Everyone seemed very into it, really putting some extra depth into it, especially the Vision Quest boys. I felt like an impostor as I chanted mechanically while my thoughts returned to my own problems, ragging and worrying at them as if that would do any good. I glanced around and caught sight of Wolf, his face blank and ecstatic as he mouthed the chant. Even he was more into it than I was. Could ever be, if I were honest. I tried meditating again, feeling the waves of sound swelling around me, trying to let go, feel the stillness inside . . . Bollocks. It was no good. I murmured an apology and slipped outside, where I sat by the great pool and watched Gwydion hunting through the colonnades, his night-black fur on end with excitement. He came purring and snaking round my ankles and I rubbed his favourite ear-massage spot, glad of his company. His body vibrated like miniature thunder under my hand for a moment, then, spying something by the colonnades, he streaked off. I wished heartily, and not for the first time, that I was a cat.

I sat awhile longer, then sloped off to the library. I couldn't settle, though, and Sou cast me more than one severe Gallic look from her obsidian eyes. Making my excuses, I went to the office and phoned the Parents. Vi answered and I told her that Maz and Millie had gone home a bit early. I didn't say anything about what had happened. She hardly heard me anyway, she was so full of the visit from the American bloke – he was besotted with her work, apparently. Freddy was with the tellyfolk, doing walking shots round Seville. All was hunky-dory. It was like the old days; I felt like an outsider again. Still, my fault, really. If I'd wanted to, I could have made a fuss, got her attention. But it seemed pointless – wrong, even; she was so happy. And I had grown used to *not* talking to them . . . Oh, I don't know, it was just easier to let things drift. It made me realize how mistaken I'd been to think we could heal our differences in a few weeks. Now all this, too – not a hope. I picked up my e-mail. There was only a note from Frankie:

darling :* [] – vi says u are involved with some cult freaks please be careful thom says he nearly got dragged into something like that at college and those people are very sneaky and prey on your mind. don't believe a word they say, y'hear? how was yr reunion – do tell soonest. 0☺!!!!!!! we are fine here and the parents are planning a big visit to coincide with vi's exhibition – you *R* coming too?????? of *course* you r. love u 2 bitz & pieces, 0-Z-<
Frankie-boy @>–>— xxxxxxxxxxxxxxxxx

I think I'd hoped for something from Millie. Something that would explain everything, make it all all right . . . I felt my heart contract into a tight knot again. Fuck 'em, then. But it hurt. Maybe I should . . . No. It was their fault, not mine. I wasn't going crawling back to them.

I shook myself and in a spat of crossness started to reply to Frankie. Then a weird thing happened. For no good reason, I suddenly felt – and I really can't explain why – that someone had been using the computer. Someone other than me. Not that it mattered; I had no secrets. The text of my book as it stood was hardly worth nicking, and I've never kept journals or diaries because if you write a secret down it's not a secret any more, is it? Still, it was a creepy feeling all the same. I tried being reasonable about it but I couldn't shake the impression someone had been, well, *spying* on me. Talk about paranoia. I got up and went through my things. Of course, everything was as I'd left it – as far as a clutter-freak like myself could tell, that is. No missing pants or anything. It was just nerves – overtiredness. I gave up on replying to Frankie and tried to read instead, but couldn't, so I dozed and brooded.

I was positively grateful when tea-time arrived and I sloped glumly off to my appointment with Mama Jay.

She was in the painted room, as usual; the tea trolley

was set out with vanilla cakes and biscuits – chocolate Hobnobs. Around the walls the fantastic figures of Lleu Llaw Gyffes and Blodeuedd acted out their mythic romance in stiff, medieval-type attitudes. The light from the huge balcony window was beginning to turn gold; it made Mama Jay's hair into a cap of silver-gilt. She patted the seat next to her on the sofa with her familiar gesture.

'Oh, sit here next to me, dear. You poor, poor girl – how you've suffered! I can't tell you how sorry I am you should have been put through such awfulness. Donner told us everything. Dreadful, really. The Prophet was most upset, He feels so much for you and your family, you know.'

'God, Mama Jay, you shouldn't have bothered him. I know he's not well . . .'

'No, no, He likes to know everything – especially whatever concerns you, my dear. Donner is with Him almost constantly at present . . .' She sighed and laid her shell-white hand on her breast. Her soft blue eyes glistened with unshed tears. I immediately felt a right cow for intruding my petty troubles into her worries about The Prophet. She took a hankie out of her pocket and dabbed her eyes, smiling. 'Donner thinks a great deal of you, dear, did you know? You young ones – well, it's only natural. You'd make a lovely couple, perfect – oh, listen to me, matchmaking! Ignore me; you don't need an old woman interfering with your lives!'

Funny how hard it was to ignore Mama Jay. She was like a titanium fist in a lace mitten. I don't mean that bitchily, either. I admired it, that willpower. With someone like The Prophet to look after and the Foundation to run it would have been no good being a girlie little fuzzbunny. No, not daft, Mama Jay, not daft at all. I didn't mind her knowing my business, either. I would have, with some people, but not anyone at Soledad. They were so much on my side. OK, maybe that was a childish way of looking at it, but they made me feel as if someone cared about me. Anyway, Mama Jay poured tea and we munched Hobnobs in companionable silence for a while. Then she suddenly jumped up and clapped her hands. I nearly had a fucking coronary.

'Oh! I nearly forgot! I *am* silly! I've been meaning to share this with you for ages, but –' She scampered over to a big mahogany cabinet on castors and began wheeling it awkwardly towards the sofa. I got up and helped her, mystified. There were cables trailing out of a port in the base of the thing, plugged in the wall socket. She opened the front panels and – lo and behold: a whacking big telly and video set-up! A *telly* in Soledad! What was she up to, the old pixie? Secret all-night satellite orgies? I felt myself smiling despite my miserableness at her obvious excitement with her toy.

'See? Isn't it all clever! Dear Wolf did it for me – the good, kind boy! Oh, it's not for television programmes, just video cassettes. You see, I had lots and lots of film of our travels, of The Prophet's Work – and Wolf put a selection on to video! Eventually he'll do all of it, he says. Isn't that amazing! Why, it's like science fiction come true, don't you think!' She beamed at me. Video – science fiction! Bless.

We sat back on the sofa as she fiddled with the remote, a frown of concentration wrinkling her smooth forehead. Finally, a caption appeared: 'Travels with The Prophet'. Mama Jay clapped again, like a child.

The next hour was extraordinary. She must have filmed everything they did together, for years; these were just edited highlights. There was the young Huw – easily recognizable from his author photo – at home in Wales wearing a shirt and Fair Isle tanktop, pretending to scold Jane as she wonkily filmed him studying. There were shots of the crumbling old mansion house and Math

Griffiths: stout, paternal, pipe in mouth and looking not unlike a sort of industrial-strength Harry Secombe. Then – and at first I couldn't believe it – a tea party at university; all the young turks and their girls gathered round a table piled high with cakes and sandwiches . . . And who was that handsome, bony-faced dude in the natty waistcoat pouring tea? *Freddy*! Mama Jay grabbed my arm and giggled.

'Isn't he good-looking!' She was like a teenage girl with a crush.

It was weird, seeing my father like this, caught on jerky black-and-white film, being young. You don't really imagine your parents as young people. I mean, you do intellectually, but emotionally, well . . . They're your mam and dad. Grown-ups. Adults. Yet here was Freddy, hooking his thumbs in his waistcoat armholes, grinning for the camera, a thick lock of hair falling over his forehead, just as it did now. Only in the film, it was black. Now it was white. And there was Huw, seated next to him, his dark, hawk's face curiously watchful and aware. A secret face, like a wild creature's; as different from the hearty, happy types around him, as a kestrel from a flock of canaries . . . Then Freddy nudged him and whispered an aside – about Jane, I suspect – and Huw looked at Freddy with such an expression of hero-worship in his great liquid eyes it was painful to witness. But then the moment was gone as some wag in corduroys started clowning around with a teacup and the scene was over.

It was jungle next; South America, probably. Huw lying in a hammock, the people surrounding him naked and smooth, their hair in thickly painted bowl-cuts, their gleaming skins patterned in white clay. Their earlobes were distended with wooden plugs, their septums pierced with great bone hoops and stiff black filaments like cats' whiskers protruding from the sides of their nostrils. They were handsome, strong; the children fat and robust. Huw lay as if unconscious, a stick man in the swaying hammock, his eyes rolled back to the whites, his eyelids fluttering.

'The Ikkfaala,' Mama Jay whispered, her face serious and reverential. 'They recognized The Prophet first. Look, here's Xangu, the shaman – he's going to administer the Sacred Gift . . .'

An incredibly thin, leathery old bloke, his hair a wild mass stuck full of leaves and feathers, his naked body almost obscured by paint and tattooing, popped up from behind the hammock and laid his hand on Huw's forehead, for all the world as if he was checking his temperature. Then suddenly, he looked directly into the lens. I felt the hairs rise up on my arms at that gaze, even diluted as it was by the camera and time. His stare held such power – an unshakeable, calculated self-belief burning in his pupil-filled eyes – that you knew immediately he was not, repeat *not*, pissing about. This was the real deal. Here was a man who *knew* things. Not a 'good' man, as the West would like its shamans to be; not the gentle, calm, *caring* spiritual leader of Western New Age fantasies but a human shape filled with power, his skin barely containing its savage fire. He held the stare for a tad longer then broke it off as if he were bored. After fiddling around in his ditty-bag for a bit, he produced a thick wooden tube and packed some dry herby stuff into one end. I could hear Mama Jay's intake of breath as Xangu roughly forced the end of the tube up Huw's nostril and, inflating his cheeks like Louis Armstrong, blew the lot up poor old Huw's nose with some considerable force.

The effect was electrifying. I mean, OK, no one would enjoy having Sainsbury's Dried Mixed Herbs shot up their conk by an old nutter – but Huw immediately arced into a rigid spasm while Xangu stood back, a malevolent smirk on his face. Two women manhandled Huw to the floor, where he spasmed again and again, his body nearly a half-moon, head to heels, foam bubbling from his writhing lips, his eyes right back in his head. I felt Mama Jay grip my hand and saw her face was livid with fear.

Xangu moved over to the fire, casting a knowing glance at the camera – and Jane, presumably. He seemed immeasurably wicked and ancient. He threw some more herbs on the flames, producing a thick smoke, then he swayed rhythmically, his lips moving. Though there was no sound with the film, you could see he was chanting the same phrase over and over, as we did during meditation. I looked at Mama Jay questioningly.

She nodded, her face intense. 'I thought you'd notice. It's the same chant we meditate with now. *Ikk Maalu Halu Bhai*, the sun-returning chant. It's old, so old – from the very beginnings of everything. Look! Look at The Prophet!'

Through the thick smoke, I could just make out Huw, now crouching, saliva dripping in thick glutinous strings from his slack mouth, all the muscles in his body rigid and roped with tension. It seemed – it seemed, for a split second – God – I – it *seemed* as if he changed into a big cat, a jaguar. Then the illusion or whatever it was vanished and there was Huw, collapsed in a shivering heap, with the women tending him and Xangu leaning against the hut-pole, a look of cocky satisfaction on his seamed old face.

Mama Jay pressed pause. Xangu's face fuzzed into a malevolent blur.

'There!' Mama Jay's voice was triumphant. 'Did you see it? The Spirit Possession? The Jaguar? I know you did – I know it! You, of all people . . . Oh, I shared with Him the ultimate moment, as I shared everything on our Journey. But to have you here, my dear, dear Alma, to have you Witness it as I did . . .'

I didn't know what I'd seen. I didn't want to have

seen anything; certainly not something that fucking impossible – and I definitely didn't want to talk about it. It was too – shocking. I wanted to think it was a camera trick; that if you freeze-framed it you'd see the deception. But something in my head refused to let me think that; it had been too – too *strange*. Maybe there are lots of things that happen in the world that we simply don't – won't – see. Strange things to do with the spirit. We pretend it's all fakery because that's more comfortable for us in our secular, materialistic paradise. But that doesn't mean we're right. In fact, perhaps we're horribly, stupidly *wrong*. Unaccountable things did happen, and I'd just seen one. It scared me shitless. I coughed nervously and saw Mama Jay was doing the bloody praying thing again. Only this time, I wanted to join her. Not that I did, you understand. But I wanted to. Oh yes. Let there please be a God – because if there was and this sort of thing was possible then God might protect me. If there wasn't a God and this sort of thing still happened – I was fucked. We all were.

I poured myself some tea with a shaky hand. Mama Jay returned from Planet Prayer and smiled at me beatifically.

'Now – here are some scenes from Benin and The Prophet's examination of the Vodoun religion there. Look, there's The Prophet, and the priest, Dajalé . . .'

The camera was being manned by someone else. There was Huw, all right, and a tall, white-robed black man with aristocratic features and a serious expression, his snowy head-wrap and multicoloured, many-stranded bead necklaces giving him an other-worldly look. And there was Jane, her thick hair in a chin-length bob, her safari jacket and culottes blending into the dusty tones of the compound . . . *and a baby in her arms*. A European baby, in European clothes. I glanced quickly at Mama Jay. Tears were pouring down her face and her hands lay loosely in her lap. She looked at me and smiled wanly, wiping her eyes with her hankie.

'That's Tammuz, my son. He was not long with us here; he only had two earthly years with me. Tammuz is a very old name, The Prophet chose it himself. It's the name of the resurrected god, you know, the Son of the Abyss Who Rises; the Gatekeeper. Mesopotamian. A very powerful name, very . . . He was a beautiful child, quite perfect – but not strong. He was too pure for this world. Not a day goes by that I don't pray for him, talk to him. Foolish of me, I suppose, but – oh, Alma, I loved him so very much.'

'God, Mama Jay – Jane – I'm sorry . . .' I sounded like a clod. Poor little Mama Jay, no wonder she liked to play mother to us. The child probably died of some tropical bug while Huw dragged them round the world and back. And who was the father? The mystery camera-operator? Some chap she met on their travels? I couldn't see Huw tolerating a 'boyfriend'. I wanted to ask, but it seemed totally rude to pry so I just tried to look sympathetic.

She sighed, and didn't say any more. I could barely pay attention as we watched the priest conduct a long, complex ritual in a dark hut lit by hundreds of candles and almost filled by the shapeless image of a god that had been smoothed into a lump over the centuries by layer after layer of thick, coagulating sacrificial blood. The worshippers howled soundlessly on the shaky film and writhed on the dirt floor as the loa – the spirits – possessed and rode their bodies.

'Who's filming?' I asked quietly. Jane's face was suffused with a terrible longing as she watched herself carrying her dead child.

'Oh, that's Safaa, The Prophet's great friend and helper. An Egyptian, you know. Tremendously brilliant. A prince among his people, from an ancient family – wonderful man. We travelled together for some years, but he went home shortly after my Tammuz left us. Dear Safaa – so good, so kind. A true disciple, a dedicated Believer. See, there he is . . .'

Huw and Safaa sat together on a rock, looking out at a long, empty beach fringed with palms, the surf breaking in broad loops of foam on the ashen, volcanic sands. They sat very close. Safaa smiled, and waved at the camera, his black curls ruffled by the breeze, his oval face and huge, black eyes full of intelligence and good spirits. He was certainly very handsome and I could see Mama Jay had thought a lot of him – Tammuz' daddy? I was pretty certain; you know, the way she said his name . . . Still, it wasn't really my business, if she wanted to tell me, she would.

It was pretty obvious Huw thought a lot of the Egyptian, too. Again, the camera caught that moment his grave, melancholic glance fell on his laughing companion. It was the same look of worshipful adoration he'd given Freddy, and it didn't take a genius to read his body-language as the two young men sat together. As my nana would say – each to their own . . . It was pretty obvious why *Huw* had never married. It must have been so difficult for men of Huw's generation, being gay; they had none of the freedoms Frankie and Thom enjoyed. Mind you, saying that, maybe Huw had never come out of the closet even to himself. That inner conflict alone would be enough to turn you to the more spiritual side of things as a kind of comfort, or perhaps a search for answers. Unlucky for Huw, but lucky for us since we got the benefits of that long, painful search. The Prophet – so brilliant, so tragic. Life was cruel and kind by turns, you know what I mean?

I was pondering all this while the film flickered on. There were images of The Prophet among the Native Americans, being initiated into the Sundance, hanging from a tree by ropes tied to thick bars piercing his chest muscles, blood running down his body, that same tranced, ecstatic expression suffusing his face I'd seen when he was with Xangu. How hard it must have been for Mama Jay to film his pain, to nurse him – especially after losing her child. She really was an exceptional person. I felt bad about calling her a dippy hippie; OK, she was, but that was just her outer shell. Inside, she was practically a saint, really.

The film stuttered to a close and for a long moment we sat in silence, then Mama Jay turned to me and laid her hand on mine. Her skin was cool and smooth, like marble.

'Do you see now, my dear, how very important The Prophet's Work is to all the lost young souls who strive so hard and find nothing but materialism and decadence? He has suffered and come through the Fire, He truly knows what pain and faith are – unlike those great frauds in the worldly religions. And I wanted you to see my darling boy, because I know you must feel that your beloved's child should have been yours by rights. It's as if you too have lost a child. I sensed from the beginning that you were a mother, a True Mother; there was something so loving in you, so beautiful in your devotion to the Virgin. I was immensely touched by that, you know; that's why I sent the little Mother to your room, I knew She would comfort you . . .'

I started to say I only collected those Madonnas, it wasn't a religious thing – but then I stopped. Perhaps, subconsciously . . . I had never felt maternal, or broody as such, but . . . I did love kids – who doesn't? Like I said, I'd always assumed Jack and I would have children. Maybe . . . It was all too much, my head felt stuffed with images and ideas. It was all so – *unsettling*. The Prophet had written: *Our souls have lives we sometimes cannot fathom; in their Truth, when it is revealed, we see our own Reality.* Maybe I hadn't listened to my own self, trusted my instincts enough. Perhaps I had been so brainwashed by the hypocritical society I was raised in, I couldn't admit my true spiritual self. It wasn't very *English*, was it? In fact, a bit barmy. Fuck the world, please yourself, that was the new faith.

Blind yourself, more like. Thank God I was out of it for a while. I suddenly felt exhausted. I needed to think – and I wanted to talk to Donner. He could help me make sense of it all.

I said I was tired and Mama Jay kissed me and told me to go and rest. As I went out, I looked back. Mama Jay had rewound the video to the part where she was holding her boy in her arms. I couldn't see her face, but I knew she was weeping. I crept out and closed the door. No human comfort could help her with her long agony. The Prophet wasn't the only one who knew about pain.

26

The next few days I threw myself headlong into work. I was totally disturbed by what I'd seen, or thought I'd seen on the video. And the whole thing about Tatum. I couldn't seem to rest, so I worked until my eyes blurred and my neck and spine ached from crouching over and sorting the bloody file boxes. I found treasures – sure. Scraps of ancient hieroglyphs on crumbling papyrus; illuminated vellum fragments thick with red-robed angels, lapis and gold leaf. Part of a letter from Byron to Lady Caroline, and a thing in crabbed French which turned out to be a spell from Haiti for revenge on an unfaithful spouse. Too late, that one, I rather felt. I found wonders, all right, and Souris was ecstatic – but it wasn't what I needed. Not even a sniff of a Bront.

Autumn was definitely here.

In Bradford, the streets would be pewter from rain, the air iron-cold and the light a permanent dusky grey; I'd be bundled up in sweaters and fleeces with a permanently snotty nose and frozen feet. Still, without Phillip, at least I wouldn't have had to suffer his minimalist anti-glitter Christmas. Perhaps I would have been having a spinster's Yuletide in front of the telly with a turkey-breast sandwich and a packet of mince pies? Bradford. I could feel the wet, tearing wind howling round Centenary Square and pulling my brolly inside out for spite as I struggled into Cha-Cha's. It might be autumn here, but it was still warm by UK standards and the occasional rain was like comfy bath-water compared to West Yorkshire's penetrating icy sleet.

When I wasn't burrowing through old papers or crouched over my computer, straining to get some life into my less-than-immortal prose, I spent a lot of time with Rose. I grew more and more fond of her. She was so matter-of-fact about the life at Soledad, so reasonable and practical, able to have a laugh about things. We talked for hours, walking in the garden, or sitting out on the cliff after we'd finished our work. She was incredibly bright, with an incisive mind that cut straight through the crap and got to the bottom line immediately. She freely admitted that the Foundation was her family now. Her parents were dead and she had no other relatives to speak of. She told me how being brainy had always made her feel like a freak; her folks had been conservative shopkeepers from Donegal who had definitely not approved of her desire to go to university.

'God,' she sighed as we wandered around the garden one afternoon with a couple of baskets, helping the boys tidy up a bit. 'My Mammy used to take fits about me going to Dublin. Sin City, let me tell you. She thought I'd be white-slaved, turned into a drug fiend – all that. Mind you, she wasn't far wrong, I did go a bit mad in me first year – but, hey, doesn't everyone? You know, drink four pints and throw up on yer duvet, then wonder who the fuck is going to do the laundry. It's a sad awakening when you find out it's yerself. No, I wasn't that bad, it was just – ah, I found the Uni lot so – so – dull. Not like I'd imagined. I wanted more, you know?'

I did know, I knew exactly what she meant and told her so, recalling how I'd imagined people in black polo necks talking about Sartre over espressos.

'Oh, absolutely. And it wasn't, at all. I felt I was looking for something these people could never grasp. Then me daddy had a heart attack and bang! Mammy sort of faded away, lost the will to live. I took a year out to sort things. Gave the shop to Uncle Joseph, the miserable old sod – but what could *I* do with it? I meant to go back and do a Masters and then a PhD. I finished the course; got a First, it should have been easy after that – but I couldn't do it. I bought an old VW camper with the money from the Will and took off. The camper died in Morocco, so I left it; went on travelling. I started to get pretty disorientated; I was doing a lot of drugs, but it doesn't suit me, I can't handle them. I was drinking too – properly, not like at Uni. I'd been travelling with a – well, a friend – and we split up. Two months later I heard he'd died of an overdose in Thailand. The old traveller's grapevine. I kind of lost the plot after that, you know? There's a few weeks I can't even remember, then I ended up in Tenerife, sellin' timeshares. I found one of The Prophet's books in an English bookshop, one of those second-hand places. I didn't go for that kind of stuff usually, but I was desperate for something to read and, well, I was blown away. It made so much sense. Then, to cut a long, boring story short, I met one of the Malakhs – Eagle – a great guy, Australian, really nice. You won't have seen him, he went home last year. Anyways, I lived in the Paris house for a bit, working and stuff, then submitted my paper. I've been here ever since. I can't tell you what The Prophet's meant to me. What a mind! God – what a life! I'd be jealous if I didn't love him so much, you know?'

I smiled at the expression of worship on her face. She caught me doing it and chucked a handful of palm frond bits at me. That's what I liked about her, she was never too serious or intense about things. Sierra and the other boys could get a bit heavy, a bit holier than thou, sometimes. But Rose wasn't at all precious, and her explanations of The Prophet's books were brilliant. No one doubted her faith, or her authority about The Prophet's Work; not even Wolf, who was, I think, a little afraid of her. I liked her a lot, and I think she liked me, too. It almost made up for The Ems . . .

The days passed quickly. The only thing that bugged me, apart from the obvious, was that I so seldom saw Donner, and never alone. Except once. It was strange, and unexpected. I'd had a pretty tiring day, first in the library, then helping unload and stash the monthly food shop; two of the Chelas fetched it in the van from one of the hypermarkets in Seville. It was easier and more anonymous that way; no one from Soledad was particularly welcome in Ronda and surrounds, seeing as we were supposed to be a crazed Satanic cult and all. I'd had a quick wash and wandered out to my favourite spot on the cliff-edge, where Rose and I often went to relax and have a quiet think. I was watching the sun set and considering going to get my regulation sponsor-donated hoodie fleece, when suddenly he was there. He looked so tired; his summer tan had faded and there were plum-blue shadows under his eyes. He seemed to move awkwardly, as if he had pulled a leg muscle, or hurt his lower back. Lifting The Prophet, probably. He hadn't been away from the sick room for weeks, except for meetings and offering nights – and not always then. He never complained, even though he was doctor *and* nurse to The Prophet. How many blokes can you picture doing that? Oh, rushing around being manly and heroic, sure, but wiping arses? No. Not many examples spring to mind. It's not a *guy* thing, ya dig?

Everyone thought Donner was wonderful, and so did I. Rose said he was like one of those medieval angels in the illuminated manuscripts in the library – strong and fierce, with an inner light of pure certainty. Not a wishy-washy, trendy, babe-type angel. A proper angel. Don't get me wrong, he could be moody, but that just made him more real. He was the serious type – a warrior monk. God's militia. Michael, Gabriel, Raphael, Uriel, Chamuel, Jophiel, Zadkiel – that lot. And Donner. Our own guardian angel.

But anyhow, there we were on the rocks at the lip of the cliff, the ochre sunset filtering everything into a gilded haze, the descending falls of stone tangerine and rose madder, carved by the weather into fluted folds like the stiff draperies of those medieval angels. The hills across the valley looked like cutouts placed one in front of the other; lavender, plum, grey. The air was brilliantly clear, flavoured with the scent of mountain thyme and woodsmoke. It was so completely beautiful it made my heart ache. Donner sat silently beside me. Then, to my surprise, he lay down and put his head in my lap. His eyes closed and I gently stroked his forehead. He sighed. We didn't speak a word – we didn't need to. We stayed like that for, oh, it must have been nearly half an hour. I could see the little bristly bit next to his ear that he'd missed when he shaved that morning, and feel the faint, irregular contours of his skull as I stroked his forehead; he smelt slightly of antiseptic. His eyes moved flickeringly under his lids as he rested, and despite the growing chill, his skin was hot, feverish. I was about to ask if he was OK, or whether I could help him with anything, maybe get him a jumper or something, when he struggled up to a sitting position and, taking my hands, kissed them gently. The expression of love and gratitude in his eyes really got to me. How he suffered, how hard he worked for The Prophet, for Mama Jay, for all of us. He was such a good man. I was glad to have comforted him a bit and, as he walked away, I thought: this is what love really is – calm, gentle, giving. Not the brutal savagery of Jack, or the calculating coldness of Phillip. Just this loving kindness, devoid of the grasping urgency of passion, the greed of bodies and the heat of sex. I suppose we could have done it if we'd wanted to; celibacy wasn't enforced – nothing was *enforced* – but like fasting and working extra hard, it was part of the way of life. If you wanted sex, or to be lazy, you went back out into the world, got it out of your system. At Soledad, you were with the elite, the chosen. No one wanted to be less than perfect. Sometimes it was a bit of a holiness contest, like being in the spiritual Brownies; you wanted to get all your ascetic badges. Rose said convents could be like that, too. Human nature, after all. Born competitors.

But the thought of that moment with Donner was like a talisman for me in the days that followed, as I struggled in the library, and fought against the waves of depression that threatened to engulf me. The nights were the worst; I would wake sweating and trembling, reaching for my inhaler and my specs with shaking hands. Nightmare after nightmare, about blood, and everything falling apart as I touched it – gelid, stinking, decayed. The dead-baby-in-my-head dream. Ugh, gives me the creeps just thinking about it.

There was a definite change in the atmosphere at Soledad, too. Everyone was worried about The Prophet and rumours abounded, which made Rose furious. She hated sloppy thinking or gossip, and when Sage asked whether she thought the Foundation was going to close, she nearly bit his head off then had to apologize because he burst into tears, poor sap.

'Uh, God,' he blubbered, 'I don't know what I'd *do*, man – if this all went, you know . . . I don't wanna go back to LA. It sucks, like, *toadally*. Uh, don't be mad, Sister Rose. Hey, Alma, you're real close to Mama Jay an' all – like, what do you think . . .'

'Sage, don't be bothering Alma with this stuff. She's got a lot on her mind, in her position, hmm? Nothing's going to happen that isn't meant to happen and everything will be for the best, I promise you. Now, go on with you, haven't you work to do? I thought you boys were preparing for the Sundance?'

He sloped off miserably. I turned to Rose. 'Are they really going to do the Sundance?'

'Yeah, seems so. At least, Azul, Sierra, Sage and Sundance will. Well, he would, wouldn't he, with that name?'

'But it's so dangerous . . .' I hated the wimpy tone in my voice, but I couldn't help it. I'd seen The Prophet's Sundance, I knew what it entailed.

'No, not if you know what you're doing. And they want to, it's a sort of exorcism, get rid of their doubts and fears – the 'bad spirits', if you like. They should be ready at the full moon.'

'But Rose – I've seen The P–, er, someone do the Sundance. I know . . .'

She looked at me sharply. 'You've seen! Where?'

I told her about the video. About what I'd seen, or thought I'd seen. When I finished, I saw her head was down and her eyes full of tears.

'I can't believe it.' Her voice, usually so wick and vibrant, was a subdued whisper. 'It's everything I ever wanted: to be a Witness, to see what you've seen. Thank you, Alma, thank you. I had my doubts – oh yeah, I know what everyone thinks: "Good old Rose, so fucking dependable." But I tell you, I've struggled against my upbringing, against Catholicism, against myself. But you've Witnessed it – The Prophet's Passion, His Epiphany, His Re-Birth – with your own eyes. There aren't words to tell you how grateful I am to you for sharing this. It's made everything all right for me. You really are the Daughter of Truth, like The Prophet says.'

'Rose, I'm sorry, I – I wish it had been you, not me. Look, I have to tell you, I thought – I hoped – it was a camera trick: the changing, the Jaguar. I wanted it to be. I'm not like you, I didn't believe, didn't want to. But didn't *Wolf* say anything to you? He must have seen it all himself, he did the video and . . .'

Her face darkened slightly, like the sun moving behind a cloud, chill, shadowed. 'Wolf – no. Wolf wouldn't give me the wipings off his nose. He thinks he *owns* the Holy Twins. Ah, he's a . . . God, forget him! I'm just so glad I heard the Truth from you – from someone who really deserves to be a Witness!'

She grabbed hold of me and gave me a big hug. Normally, I'm not a hugger, as you know, but she was so . . . *thrilled* by what I'd told her. I felt like shit, because I'd tried so hard to rationalize it all away, and there she was, lit up like a Christmas tree with happiness. 'Deserved' to be a Witness – I didn't think so. Out of anyone here, I deserved it least. But there was no telling Rose that; her mind was made up that I was a VIP of some sort. That's how she was: generous-minded to a fault.

She stepped back and grinned at me. 'Oh, Alma, there's so much about yourself you don't realize. The Prophet knows – do you think you'd have been called to Witness if He didn't think you were someone really special? Mama Jay is his voice, his eyes, but He's the Master.'

'You're not – well, you're not jealous?' I would have been livid if I'd been her, I really would. But she just smiled, her silvery eyes lambent.

'Jealous? Don't be foolish. I'm honoured – honoured and privileged. Proud you chose *me* to share your Witnessing with. You have no idea what you've done for me – it's lifted a ton weight off my heart. All my doubts, gone: pouf! Vanished! I could – ooh, I could run a mile!'

We laughed like schoolies. I grabbed her arm and dragged her towards the house. 'How about a cuppa instead?' We ran to the kitchen where Marigold was baking and we all raided the chocolate stash again.

Fuck holy anorexia; Soledad Bad Girls Are Go, Baby! That's one thing I was always good at: being a bad influence.

Rose and I were even closer after that. In fact everyone at the Foundation seemed to be more attentive to one another, as if we were all holding our breaths, if you see what I mean. Like we all had a premonition it was The Prophet's Last Days. We all walked like people on a tight-rope. It was a bit scary, even for me, and I wasn't a dyed-in-the-wool True Believer like the rest of the Chelas. I'd just found a sanctuary, somewhere I could lick my wounds. OK, I loved it: the peace and quiet, the library, the people. It was perfect for me and I honestly thought The Prophet had the right ideas about things, about how you should try and live your life. But I didn't feel as *terrified* as some of the Chelas all too obviously did. Still, if, or rather, when The Prophet died, would this castle come tumbling down? Was Sage right to worry about us all having to leave? The Foundation closing? Rose said it wasn't likely, even if The Prophet did leave us. The sponsors would see we were taken care of materially, like they always did, providing us with everything from washing-up liquid to piercing equipment, and Mama Jay would either succeed to the leadership herself, or, if The Prophet didn't make his choice clear, pick a new leader. It'd be the same, just – different. But like The Prophet said: *Change is the living heart of nature and the Universal.* We had to be brave, that was all.

But it was hard. The messages Mama Jay recorded and played for us from The Prophet stopped. He was too weak, she said. Without His Voice, the Chelas felt cut off from His life-force. It seemed harder for the boys, somehow; perhaps it was more difficult for them to deal with their emotions. On the night of the Sundance, what with the fasting, the sweat-lodge and everything, they were keyed up to breaking point. The mood was electric, like neon; bright and hectic as fever. And the great moon, a vast globe of luminous silver, hung in the inky sky, pregnant with power, pulling at the tide of our sea-water blood.

27

I was late for breakfast that morning, having overslept something chronic, what with my insomnia and those fucking awful dreams. Rose tutted at me as I hurriedly greeted everyone and sat down next to her on the bench in time to scarf down a bit of bread and honey and a cuppa. The boys were noticeably absent; they'd been fasting for the past couple of days. Azul especially seemed to be constantly fasting, his short, stocky body reduced to nothing more than a knobbly frame to hang his skin on. Mama Jay gave me that motherly reproving smile and then led us in a meditation of good energy for the boys, kind of a thinking-good-thoughts type thing. Mercifully, it was short, and as we cleared away the long table and pushed it back against the wall, I whispered to Rose:

'When are they . . . ?

She looked round and mouthed back, 'Sunset, at the Twins.'

The 'Twins' were a pair of huge old eucalyptus trees that had grown close together and each had a big branch growing out backwards (or forwards, depending how you looked at it) at about the seven-foot mark. Very handy. Sometimes we strung a washing line between them, if we'd run out of drying space. Tonight, a scaffold pole wrapped in white cloth would be laid upon those thick branches and bound in place across the gap; it was enough space for the four boys to – hang. God, I couldn't believe they were really going to do it. A nervous jittery feeling filled my belly just thinking about it. I couldn't really believe they'd go through with it.

But they did. As soon as it was dusk, we all wrapped up warm and filed down to the Twins. No one spoke, everyone kept their eyes down. The Chelas set up the drums and bells and started the chant. A great bonfire was already burning and the waves of heat rippled the air, the smoke thick with eucalyptus. I joined in the chant mechanically, sneaking sideways glances at everyone else. Rose's face was as closed and smooth as a shell, blanched in the metallic light of the moon. Marigold and a Brazilian girl called Prata who'd recently arrived from America stood holding hands; they were best friends from way back. Round them clustered some of the other sisters: Daisy, Saffron, Aspen, Souris and little Morningstar. The men – Ocean, Spirit, the Dutch guy called Pure who was so fair as to be nearly albino, Rowan, Sonne, Tierra and all the others I didn't know so well – stood close by looking far too calm, the way blokes do sometimes if they're nervous. Now and again you could see their nostrils dilating like spooked horses and there was that little muscle jumping in their cheeks. Well, all of them except Wolf, who just stared at the floor like shoegazing had never gone out of fashion. Mama Jay was seated in her carved Big Hall chair which had been brought down for her. She raised her hand and the noise stopped. It suddenly seemed unnaturally quiet; over the fire crackling and the rustling leaves, I could hear my own breathing.

'The Prophet is with us. He blesses these Initiates who will perform the Ancient Rite. He who has suffered and borne great agony for our sakes knows well that their Journey will be Terrible and their Sacrifice the Gateway to the Higher Consciousness. I must return to Him now, but may you all be most blessed and know that The Prophet calls you, Sage, Sierra, Sundance and Azul, His most dearly beloved sons.'

She got up and walked to the Twins, and suddenly, there were Azul, Sierra, Sage and Sundance, naked except for Japanese-style loincloths made of twisted white fabric.

Mama Jay laid her hand on their heads one by one, then turned and walked away.

The boys' eyes were like burning coals; in the phosphorescent light their gaunt faces resembled skulls. It was pretty cold, but apart from the white vapour of their breathing, they didn't seem to feel it. They didn't seem to feel anything, or to be in the world with the rest of us. The chanting started again, faster, louder – the sound of the drums like waves crashing on the beach. But the boys were perfectly still; unblinking, waiting.

They didn't have to wait long. Donner and Ocean moved forward, carrying the great flesh hooks, each attached to a length of thick cord weighted at the end. There were two hooks for each lad. Donner and Ocean flung the ends of the cords over the horizontal pole at intervals, where they dangled, the sharp steel points catching the moonlight, balanced by the weighted ends.

I felt a watery, nauseous feeling and my limbs started to tremble. I wished I had gone to the loo one more time before I'd come out here; a cold sweat chilled me suddenly. It still wasn't too late, they could call it off. This wasn't a game, this wasn't getting a piercing and thinking you were the bee's knees for ten minutes; this was – oh God, I didn't think I could handle it. I really . . .

Azul stepped forward and Donner looked at him intently for a moment. Then he murmured something – I couldn't hear what – and, pinching up a thick wedge of flesh on Azul's chest, *he pushed a meat hook right through it.*

He did the same on the other side, and then Ocean and another lad hoisted little Azul into the air, his feet dangling six inches off the floor, the cords over the bar twisting and straining as Ocean secured them to the tree behind the Twins.

I wanted to scream. Like in a cheap film, I felt my hand go to my mouth as I stared in absolute horror while Azul and then the others hung by the flesh of their chests, fine rivulets of blood running black in the moonlight, tracing their bodies like a spider's web. I stumbled backwards, and nearly fell. I wanted to run away, escape this nauseous mixture of revulsion and fear that wrapped me in a clammy fog . . .

Rose's hand gripped my arm. 'Be still, now, Alma and Witness. This is the reality of what you saw on the film – this is The Prophet's Gift. The *O-Kee-Pa*. Look at your Brothers; they are in another place now, they need our strength.'

They hung for over an hour, maybe even two hours; the weight of their bodies on the hooks causing their flesh to stretch like meat. The chanting and drumming dropped in pace to a gentle, murmuring rhythm; I knew I was joining in, yet I seemed wholly detached from it. I couldn't take my eyes off those hanging figures, their chests monstrously distorted, distended loops of skin and muscle speared on the thick hooks. Enduring more brutal agony than I could comprehend. As The Prophet had. They had gone to the edge and leapt into the great emptiness with only faith to save them, believing that they would not be allowed to fall; that the Spirit would bear them up.

And somewhere inside myself, somewhere deep and cellular and ancient, *I wanted that knowledge.* I wanted to feel that perfect bliss; that safety, that *love*.

When they were lowered to the floor and the hooks removed, I fell to my knees with the others and gave thanks that they'd returned to us alive. Then everyone jumped up and started kissing and hugging, and shouting. It was amazing, the air seemed to sparkle with energy. I could feel the adrenaline jolting through my system. A silly smile grew on my numb face, and Rose was grinning like a maniac. It was like a fiesta, everyone was laughing and the sense of triumph was incredible. I wasn't afraid or sickened any more; my mind seemed to have made a sort of quantum leap into some other way of seeing things. I couldn't explain it, just *feel* it. I wanted to talk to Rose about it, she'd understand, she must have felt it too . . .

I was about to suggest we went back to the house when the crowd parted and a silence dropped clean, like a blade. Azul, half supported, half carried by Donner, was dragging himself towards me through the Chelas, who were standing back, making a pathway. Automatically, I looked around and behind me, you know, in case I was in the way and Mama Jay had come back. But she hadn't; it was me he wanted. He fell into a kneeling position at my feet, and raised his poor skinny little paws in supplication, gasping in Spanish, imploring me; but for what? My Spanish didn't cut it. I felt my cheeks burn as everyone stared at me and whispered to their companions.

'I – I don't understand, Azul. I don't understand, what is it you . . . ?' My voice sounded reedy and thin, my gaze riveted by the desperate, hungry expression in his dark eyes.

The Brazilian girl, Prata, darted forward and spoke to Azul, who grabbed her hands gratefully and poured out a torrent of Spanish. He must have forgotten his small store of English because he didn't mix the languages as he usually did, trying to get things across. Prata listened, then straightened up and spoke:

'I have a little Spanish, OK? Is not so different from

Portuguese. He says he wishes you to bless him. He says you are a special . . . No, you have seen – you are a witness. You are the daughter of the truth . . . the favourite of The Prophet and so will you please bless him? He says he is your "devote"? He has seen you in the dark . . . ? I don't know. But he wants you to bless him. Yes. This is what he wants.' She shrugged, her huge green eyes fixed on mine. The dense rows of rings piercing her brows gave her a solemn expression. Everyone was staring at me.

I shook my head and stepped back. What kind of craziness was this? I was about to speak when Rose grabbed my arm. 'He knows, Alma – he knows you are a Witness to The Prophet's Ordeal. Do it – bless him. I'll explain later . . . look at him, poor thing. It can't hurt.' Her voice was breathless with urgency.

So I did it. OK, I know a lot of people would think it was a hypocritical thing to do, considering my all too apparent lack of faith. Perhaps it was. But I did it. Maybe it was the whole, mad thing that had happened, maybe it was a sort of mothering reflex because he needed me to do it so much. The words came automatically out of my mouth, the words I heard every night at Meeting, the words Mama Jay said with such belief and authority. I just changed 'children' to 'brother' – I mean, it seemed the natural thing to do . . .

'In the name of the Spirit, most Ancient, most Pure; by the will of The Prophet and the Faith of our lives, be blessed, Brother, and know you are most beloved.'

As I laid my hand on his head, I heard the collective intake of breath and saw a look of terrible happiness smooth out Azul's withered face. He seized my hand and kissed it, and for the first time in ages I felt the heat of my tears streaming down my face. Then Donner stepped forward and, smiling his grave, beautiful smile at me, he lifted Azul and helped him away.

Everyone immediately surrounded me, hugging me, shaking my hand, patting my back, kissing my cheek. It was like being a rock star; their smiling faces glowed with adoration. I didn't have a clue what I was supposed to say or do.

Rose stepped in and pulled me away, into the shadow of the Twins.

'Thank you for doing that. It meant so much to him.'

Reality began to seep back into my fuzzed-up brain. I mean, what I had felt before about seeing things differently was one thing, but this . . .

'What the fuck is going on, Rose? What the fuck was all that? I can't go around blessing people – I'm not religious. It's stupid, I . . .'

She sighed and leant against the tree, picking absently at its rough, peeling bark. 'OK, OK.' She spread her hands in front of her, the rings in her finger-webs glinting. 'I didn't want to tell you this . . . I wanted to – oh, let you come to it yourself. But now . . . Look, we all know you're special, Alma. We knew from the first. Your family, the signs, then you being called to Witness. You know what we think about your father, don't you? No, hold on, let me finish. What I was going to say is, I don't think you fully realize *exactly* what your pa means to The Prophet and Mama Jay. It's more than just a 'jolly decent chap who helped a chum out of a bit of a bind at college'. Oh, I wish you'd come to us sooner, love, I really do. There's so much to explain, and now, with The Prophet so close to . . . You see, when your father saved The Prophet, we believe – The Prophet believes – he was sent by the Great Universal to prevent him going down the Dark Path and to set his foot on the Road to Truth. The Prophet had studied too fast, too intensely and without guidance. When he tried to re-enact the old Mesopotamian ritual, he was out of control. He admits it himself. The sacrifice wasn't willing, He himself was struggling, groping in ignorance – it would have been a total disaster. The Prophet uses it as a lesson to demonstrate how dangerous picking up fag-ends of arcane knowledge can be. If even He could be drawn into the Dark so easily . . . well. But then your father came – was sent. It bound them together in spirit, like brothers. It's a very strong bond; the strongest. Your father did more than save The Prophet, Alma, *he saved us all.* Without him, none of this would have been possible. It's all interlinked, you see. You were destined to come here – I mean, look how your parents came to live in nearly the exact same place as The Prophet, without "knowing" it.' She made air-quotes and smiled. 'Spooky, eh? Well, not to us, it isn't. It's yet more proof that you and yours are part of The Prophet's life, His Work. And you – you've been sent to us, just like your pa was sent to The Prophet. In our hour of need . . .'

'No way, Rose. No, it's ridiculous –'

'It's not. You're The Prophet's Chosen. He knows your doubts, but he knows your strengths, too. Oh, he knows you, and when he – when he dies . . .'

Like a dead thing rising from the grave, livid in the moonlight, his face contorted with fury, Wolf pushed himself between us. The sour stink of his odour made me gag; I glimpsed the expression of disgust, quickly suppressed, on Rose's face, too.

'Shut up! Shut up! *Shut up*! He won't die! He can't! Shut the fuck up, you fuckin' bitches. Wishin' Him dead – that's what you're doin'. Wishing Him dead so you can get on with all your fuckin' plottin' an' schemin'. Well you can fuckin' well think again, 'cos not everyone's under your fuckin' spell, Miss High-an'-fuckin'-mighty Al-*ma*. I know what's goin' on. Who d'you think runs this place? Who d'you think set up the cameras, the computers, the surveillance systems? Nothing goes on here I don't know about – *nothing*. I've heard all the bollocks about you being something special, you slag. Well, you ain't. You're nothing. I don't care who your fuckin' dad is, I won't let you ruin everythin'. I gave my whole fuckin' life to this place, to Mama Jay an' The Prophet, an' if anyone's *special* round here, it's me – *me*, d'you hear? Not some fuckin' user out to screw us, like you, you –'

Spittle was flying from his mottled lips and he was practically screaming. I shrank back instinctively; he wasn't *right*, like they say in Bradford, not right at all. His whole body was shaking with tension, the muscles of his neck rigid, his Adam's apple sticking out like a tumour.

'That's *enough*.' Rose's voice was thick with anger, her face a white blur. Wolf made a jerky move towards her and I steeled myself to punch him if he touched her.

With a visible effort, she controlled her temper and spoke with steely composure: 'Stop it now, Wolf, just stop it. You know as well as I do that we can't alter what's happening to The Prophet. Look, I know how much you love Him, we all do, but you must try to stay calm. No one wants to take your place; we all know how much the Holy Twins value your work – value *you* . . .'

'You lyin' bitch! He won't leave me, He won't . . . I 'ate you! I don't give a fuck what you say.'

I pulled myself together. 'Leave it, Wolf – just leave it, all right. It's not – I'm not . . . Listen, everything will be all right, I'm sure. Donner will . . .'

He snorted, mucus globbing on his upper lip. 'Donner? *Donner?* Ho yes, your fuckin' boyfriend. Well, you silly cow, I could tell you about *Donner*, all right.' He gurgled with a choking, phlegmy laughter. 'That snobby kraut fucker's no use to you, no use to any –'

'*Wolf!*' Rose cut him off, dead, her eyes blazing. He seemed to shiver all over, his face suddenly going slack and his shoulders drooping, as if someone had cut his wires. It was weird, the way he slumped back into himself, all the anger gone. He gave one last glare and stomped off, pausing only to spit a big gob just short of our feet. I felt my skin crawl. He was seriously unbalanced. What had Donner said . . . 'Erratic'? It was a bit more than that. And what was all that stuff about Donner, and surveillance systems, for fuck's sake? Pure paranoia. Probably brought on by the stress of watching the ceremony or something. Not that I was being, like, empathic or anything – he made me puke. But he wasn't a well boy, by anyone's standards. Not well at all.

I turned to Rose, who was breathing hard and trying to look calm; I didn't even try.

'Christ, Rose, what was all that about? What's any of it about? OK, Wolf's a weirdo, but he's right about one thing – I'm not special. Sure, I agree with lots The Prophet says, I think the world of Mama Jay, and I love being here, living here – I don't want to leave, ever. But, Rose, come *on*. All that stuff about being sent? It's just not true. I don't have the sort of faith you lot do. I wish I did, and maybe one day I will, but right now I don't. All this – the Sundance, Wolf, and me being special – it's not . . . God, Rose, it's not *me*. I'm sorry, but . . .'

She smiled sadly and shook her head. I saw she was shaking like a leaf.

'Come on, Rose. I'll make you a cuppa, we'll look in on the boys, see the others – come on. Forget all this stuff about me. Let it be how it was, eh?'

We never talked about it again. Sometimes when I remember that night, I see her hands, nacreous in the cold moonlight, shaking and shaking, the nails bitten to the quick.

28

I'd meant to talk to her about it. You know, explain that I was honoured they thought so highly of me, etc, etc, but unhappily, blah blah, couldn't accept it, yadda yadda yadda. I would talk to Mama Jay, get it all sorted, and . . . you know, cop out. Well, I couldn't go on letting them think like that, could I? Oh, don't think I wasn't tempted – I was. Really tempted. It's not often you get treated like royalty by people who seem to think you're the bloody Messiah. All I'd have to do was go along with it . . . The ego boost of a lifetime. But I was always crap at lying, and I would've had to lie every single day. I wasn't someone *special*; I was Alma Greer from Bradford. The idea of me being some sort of guru was ludicrous . . .

So that was that sorted. Except for two things. First, I'd have to leave Soledad. I couldn't stay after telling them I thought their ideas about me and my family were bollocks. It wouldn't be possible. That gutted me. I loved Soledad: the library, the house – yeah, and the people. Second, and much, much worse, I'd probably lose Donner for ever. No, I *would* lose him, I knew it. He was totally dedicated to The Prophet; I couldn't see him packing it all in and wandering off with me just because he was . . . I was going to say, 'because he was fond of me'. But I didn't actually know that, did I? I mean, he was always kind and attentive, and that moment on the cliff . . . Maybe I was reading too much into it. He'd never *said* anything, and he was kind and attentive to everyone, even Wolf. OK, he'd kissed my hands, but he was European. Everyone knows they're more demonstrative than the English; it could all be a cultural misunderstanding. And even if he was head over heels for me, there was no point in destroying his life because I was a wash-out *again*. God! Why had fate got it in for me? I find something good and, bingo! Do not pass, *go*, motherfucker. As much as I twisted and turned and rived at it all in my mind, hour after hour, it wouldn't come out how I wanted it to. My escape from reality was over; finito. It was back into the churning sea of shit that was Real Life, and there was nothing I could do about it.

I decided to handle it all in a mature, responsible fashion, like a real grown-up.

I refused to think about it. No, that's not quite accurate. In fact, the words of one of my favourite screen heroines became my mantra: *'I'll think about it tomorrow.'* Thank you, Miss Scarlett. And goodnight.

Mind you, that didn't mean it wasn't all simmering away in the back of my mind. I wandered around like a bear with a sore head. I only hope some of the people I snapped at thought I was menstruating.

The one place I felt all right was the library. Work was something I could get to grips with and it passed the time. Sorting through the papers was mind-numbingly soothing. I didn't even try writing, and I couldn't remember the last time I'd checked for e-mails or even considered phoning home. I mean, imagine trying to tell them about the things I'd seen, or the idea that the people here thought I was some kind of Enlightened One. It made me go hot and cringey just thinking about it. They'd think it was me being funny, fooling around. If I pushed it, tried to make them understand, I'd look a right idiot. Or a freak, if I told them about the Sundance. It made me realize how much of a gap there was between my old life and now. Things I'd have jeered at or been horrified by in the past were now normal for me. I could never go back, be as I was. And so I let the hours, then the weeks slip past.

One day I sloped into the library like a grumpy, squashy-faced pig – my current style statement – to discover Souris had found a locked oak chest, a huge old Spanish Main, pirate-style thing, under a heap of mouldy curtains and rubbish. It looked interesting, so we struggled with it for a while – well, I struggled with it, she just stood by issuing instructions, due to her bloody corset (how convenient) – until I managed to knock the padlock off with a hammer and chisel. It was pretty rusty, I didn't have to play Superwoman or anything. Still, I was red-faced and sweaty by the time I finished.

Sou daintily lifted the lid; it was packed solid with papers and books.

'Ah, the gold mine, perhaps? Maybe we find a treasure in this, maybe shit – who knows? Come along, Alma, stop making so much noise and help me.'

Cheeky cow, that 'noise' was me panting for breath.

We shuffled that stuff around for ages. It was like archaeology. Layer upon compressed layer of documents, paper strata. Some of it was torn or crushed beyond hope. Then there were masses of old bills and family documents which Souris carefully put aside for Mama Jay.

The gold was near the bottom. I nearly missed it. It was sandwiched in between an invoice from a plumber and a newspaper clipping. But I found it. Not Sou, *me*.

OK, it was only a fragment, but it was real, in her own handwriting – it couldn't be a fake. A letter from Charlotte to Letty. An artefact! Something the Brontë freaks would kill for, and I had it in my hand! God, there just had to be more – all I had to do was find it and . . .

To Miss Laeticia Gates, Thorn Cottage, Downley, from Miss Charlotte Brontë, The Parsonage, Haworth.

Dearest Letty

> I hardly know how to tell you, but that which I both feared and wanted has come to pass. A Gentleman – I think you know Who – has asked for my hand! He has done me the honour of asking me to be his Bride . . .

I tell you, I felt like shouting out loud. My skin was rippling with goosebumps and my crop stood on end like I'd been electrified. OK, OK, I know it doesn't sound the most exciting thing in the world, a mouldy old scrap of paper – but to me it was fantastic. Everything would be all right after all, you see. I'd find the rest of the letter – more letters, even – finish the book, publish, dedicate the whole thing to the Foundation and say to them: 'Look, I can't be the special person you think I am, but I can be your voice.' I'd be respected in the world; I could write a life of The Prophet, spread the word. I could be *valuable*. They'd let me stay, but on my terms, not as some kind of Holy Woman.

I slipped the letter into one of Souris' special protective plastic sleeves and put it in my bag. I called for her, but she wasn't there. Glancing at the clock, I saw it was dinner-time and yet again, I was late. I dragged my fleece on and ran to the Big Hall. Wait until I told them what I'd found! I hugged myself with joy as I trotted through the colonnades.

I flung the door open and bounced in, grinning from ear to ear.

It was as if I'd run giggling into a funeral. In a way, I had. Everyone turned to look at me, then turned back to stare hungrily at Mama Jay. She was sitting rigidly in her big chair on the dais opposite the glass wall and the ugly tree sculpture. From the enveloping folds of a white challis wool cloak, her face emerged like a mask of tragedy. She seemed to have aged a hundred years. Every line and wrinkle was etched into her face as if it were wind-graven stone. In her hand, she held the ancient carved wooden staff Xangu had given The Prophet when he became a shaman. That Mama Jay was actually touching it was enough to indicate something was horribly wrong. I froze. She nodded at me stiffly. It was like her whole body was in spasm.

'At last, my beloved Daughter. Sit here next to me, Alma, I have something I must share with the Children.'

She indicated the little stool next to her chair. Mystified, and a bit embarrassed, I went over to it and sat. I glanced at Rose, but her eyes were on the table, her fists clenched. Whatever it was Mama Jay was about to say, I'd have bet my last peseta Rose knew already – and it wasn't good news. Wolf knew, too. He was rocking back and forth, tears glazing his lumpy features. I didn't have to be clairvoyant to guess what it was all about . . .

Mama Jay swayed to her feet, leaning heavily on the staff. 'My dearly beloved Children. The hour we have all dreaded is upon us. My – The Prophet is dying. There is no more that earthly medicine can do for Him. He goes to meet Tammuz at the Gate. Brother Donner has indicated to me our Master has no more than two or three weeks to live, at most. It has been decided that the Great Gathering to mark his passing will be held in ten days . . . Oh, my Children, my Children . . .' Her voice, usually so melodious, broke. She almost fell, but I jumped up and caught her, lowering her back on to her chair where she pulled the hood of her cloak over her face and wept.

Mayhem. The Chelas fell to their knees, weeping and screaming. Some of them scratched their faces until the blood ran, some beat their foreheads on the floor. Others sat stunned, their eyes blank and empty. I saw Sage punching the wall, his knuckles blue and swollen, weeping distorting his face into a grimace. Azul crept up to the dais and, sitting on the floor shivering, put his hand on my foot like a child holding the hem of his mother's skirt for comfort. The high roof of the Big Hall acted like an echo chamber, intensifying the sounds of weeping until they crashed and reverberated like the wild sea.

With my arm round Mama Jay's thin shoulders, I glanced across the room. My eyes met Rose's. She was sitting, head up, gazing at me. We locked stares, it seemed we were all alone; then she nodded slightly and dropped her eyes. At least I could depend on her to keep sane, however distressed she was.

Then Mama Jay struggled to her feet again, leaning on the staff and my arm. I felt quite numb, as if I were watching a play. I could hardly take it in as she begged for silence.

'I know how you are feeling, my Children. Tonight we will hear His last message to us. Then, we will prepare for the Gathering. Sister Rose and our dearly beloved Sister Alma will be your guides in this; I must stay with The Prophet, as must our dear Brother Donner.' She nodded at Wolf, who shambled over to the sound system and with shaking hands fumbled it into life.

The Prophet's voice leapt from the speakers like the grating howl of a wounded beast; hardly human. Harsh and shattered, the Message crashed around the Hall and the Chelas wept again. That *voice*; it was agony in a sound. I only remember fragments:

'. . . The Heart, the Mother's Heart . . . I have seen beyond the Veil that must never be lifted . . . I am the Sacrifice and the Voice of the Dream . . . embrace the pain and share the Dream . . .'

I heard Mama Jay give the Blessing, and then she was gone and our world was falling apart.

And all I could think of was that no one would care about me finding the letter. Everything I was working for, that I wanted so much, was all for nothing. I wished I felt as destroyed as the Chelas, because then I wouldn't care. But I didn't. What I was feeling wasn't grief, pain for the loss of a man I'd never met. No, what I was feeling was *panic.*

29

It was cold now, the winter full on, trees losing their leaves in a ragged, unsure way, occasional rainstorms. Even when the sun shone, it was only hot if you stood directly in its light, because the air itself was icy. The nights were freezing and we all got boots, extra quilts, fleeces, waterproofs and stuff like that from the stores. I had some surfer-type sheepskin boots and I wore them with thick hiking socks, it was that cold. All our kit was from the sponsors; good quality outdoor gear in shades of cream and beige, with the labels cut out. Seconds? Not for the first time, I wondered who these wealthy 'sponsors' were. Well, I'd find out soon; they were all coming to The Prophet's last Gathering.

I kept trying to see Rose, but I could never seem to get hold of her. Either she was busy getting the rooms for the visitors ready, washing linen, cleaning and all that, or she just wasn't around. In the end it was Azul, his English recovered, who told me she was spending all her free time attending The Prophet, helping Donner. Well, OK, but it made me feel a bit cut out, and a tad jealous if I told the truth. Donner and Rose were the most dedicated Chelas, we all knew that, but still . . .

I spent a lot of the time with Azul. I can't say I actively went out of my way to find him, but he certainly knew where to find me at any given time. Utilizing Wolf's precious CCTV setup, no doubt. He had been Wolf's right-hand man, after all, another computer freak. These days he just trailed along with me, his sweet face set in an expression of puzzlement and sorrow. Well, as far as I could tell, under the piercings. I didn't mind him being there; he wasn't a demanding person and he seemed glad of my company.

However, when I tripped over him as I walked out of my room one morning and discovered he'd been dossing down in front of my door on a camping mattress, I felt it was time to try and have a chat with him. I didn't think it was a crush, but . . . let's say it was a little strange.

'What are you doing, Azul? You can't kip – sleep there, you'll freeze to death.'

'No, is OK, I having a bag, very warm.'

'Yeah, I can see that, but it's not – oh, it's – I mean, why are you doing it? *¿Por qué?*'

'Ah! I speak with Donner, so I care for you, the Daughter of Truth. The Witness. You know, in my Sundance, I see you very clear. Yes, I see you after the pain go and I am being in such a warm, good place, all pain gone, and everything clear. You are a good woman, like a good mother. I see you in the light. I hear a voice like my own mother who is dead long time, it say, "Find new mother, she waits for you, my son." Then I see you and her in this light. I am so happy and feel no pain then. You are my light. You are a Witness, our Prophet chooses you from all others. I protect you.' His face suddenly seemed fierce, his voice hard. I suppose because he was smaller than me, and so cute, I hadn't taken him seriously before. My God, he'd been through the Sundance, for fuck's sake! Who was I to disrespect him?

'Well, thank you, Azul. *Muchas gracias, amigo mío*. But, what from? Nothing here will hurt me, we're all family.'

'Yes, all family. But in all family there is bad blood, you see? You must be careful, *Hermana* Alma, there is always reason for that. I will be here, I will stay with you. Is my duty, my devotion. You understand?'

What a sweetheart. I extended my hand to shake with him, but again, he seized it and kissed it. Well, big on hand-kissing, the Continentals. I wish English lads were. It was very touching.

He seldom left my side after that. Actually, I found it comforting, and he told me about his Sundance experience, which was fascinating. The other lads hadn't mentioned it at all, not even in Meeting, but I suppose with the news about The Prophet . . . Yeah, like me finding Charlotte's letter. It all seemed a bit of an anti-climax.

I missed Rose, though, I didn't see her until the evening before the Gathering. Everyone was worn out, sitting at the long table in the Hall or picking at a pot-luck supper. Most people were fasting again, even Marigold. I ate her dinner as well as my own. I hate fasting, it makes me even more bloody manic, which of course is the reason most people do it. To get that high, that clarity. Not me, though; I'm bad enough without any help. Anyway, I like my food too much.

I was staring moodily out of the glass wall at a cloudy, grey sunset when Rose came in through the door behind the dais that led directly – so I'd been told, not having had a reason to go there myself – to The Prophet's rooms. She looked ghastly, big blue shadows under her eyes and a gaunt, drawn look about her. Fasting, I supposed. I waved at her and she headed towards me.

It was odd; everyone tried to shake her hand, or kiss it, or touch her. I watched as she patted people's shoulders, spoke a word to them or smiled wanly. Perhaps it was because she was one of the ones nearest to The Prophet these days. She sat next to me. I was at one end of the table and most of the Chelas had left and were clearing up, or dragging logs in for the great fireplace that was so huge, we didn't usually bother. Apart from the noise and the to-ing and fro-ing, we were practically alone.

'What's all this laying on of hands business, then?' Feeble joke, I know, but she seemed so distant.

She gave me the translucent smile. 'Oh yeah. Well, I've been meaning to tell you, but . . . I'm going home, Alma. I think it's time, and . . . it won't be the same here for me without The Prophet, so . . . I suppose they're just saying goodbye. You know how they are.'

I was dumbstruck. Going home? Leaving Soledad? 'Rose, don't, please. I had something to tell you, too: I found part of a letter – a letter from Charlotte to Letty Gates, in her own handwriting! It's real, there's more, I know it. We'll find it and . . . Don't go – I need your help with the book, I need you to read it and tell me, you know, be my editor, and . . .'

She nodded, but you could see she wasn't taking it in. She smiled the little smile again and, getting up, *patted* me, saying, 'Well, that's great. Good for you. But I'm going home; it's what I want. I know you'll wish me well. Goodbye, Alma. Good luck with everything – the book an' all – I'm sure it'll be wonderful.'

'But, Rose, I'm not . . .'

It was too late, she'd drifted off. Just like that, those grey eyes gone all misty and vague, like we'd never . . . what? Been 'best friends'? Yeah. Well. It made things easier; if Rose had decided to leave, and I had to go because of not being – I could hardly say this, even to myself, it sounded so naff – not being *special* or whatever, maybe we could meet in the world and team up? I reasoned she was exhausted by the vigil and fasting. After the Gathering, we'd sort out a plan. I wouldn't be alone then, with nothing but dreams and bits of memories that I'd begin to doubt if I was by myself. With Rose there, I'd know it had all been true . . . Was Rose her real name? I didn't even know that. I didn't know Donner's real name, either. Suddenly I wanted very much to know their given names. To know *them*, if you like. Well, after the Gathering . . .

30

They came in two helicopters – *helicopters*. God, what a racket. They landed the whirring, chittering black machines on the old threshing circle, and the sponsors ran, dodging the dust storm, into the house. Outside the walls, the road was double-parked with expensive hired four-wheel drives – none of your wannabe trash emblazoned with logos and sporting a spare-wheel cover with a drawing of two rhinos shagging on it.

I'd never seen money like it. It put old Davey-boy and his vulgar little casa to shame. Chelas heaved Hermés luggage up to the guest rooms and, as the weather was unseasonably bright, the sponsors took tea round the reflecting pool, the air thick with the chemical reek of expensive perfume. And that was just the men! Come to that, it's amazing how you can tell real diamonds from fakes when someone raises a hand and a stone the size of a hazelnut refracts the light like a laser. Oh, yes. Money walked in through the gates that day, hand in hand with privilege, arrogance and power. It protected those people like bullet-proof glass.

I didn't like it – or them. They had the bland, plump, over-coiffed look of Euro-aristos and business magnates; all silk suits and tans, cashmere overcoats slung over tailored shoulders. Their smooth, exfoliated faces had the bored but calculating expressions of predators. I couldn't imagine what the fuck they were doing here. What could

The Prophet's Work possibly mean to the likes of them? Perhaps I was being judgmental and under their Diors, St Laurents and Chanels they were all yearning for the spiritual life; but if they were, they hid it pretty damned well.

I suppose, if I'd thought about it at all, I'd known the sponsors were very wealthy. But I'd imagined the old hippie rich – health-food-and-good-causes rich – not this bunch of shark-eyed playboys and their caramel-skinned, chemical-blonde women.

And they were just the first wave. Later – fashionably later – came the ones from the edges. The ones with slack mouths and soft, twisting hands. People who I seemed to recognize – but where from? There was a British MP I'd seen in the papers; dangling from his arm was the stick-thin Brazilian transvestite with enormous breast implants whom he had publicly denied ever having met. There were hatchet-faced women wearing stilettos you could drill a hole in the pavement with, and flabby men who wiped their pallid foreheads with big silk hankies and looked nervous, refusing tea with moist hands raised as if to ward off cameras . . .

Then came the extreme types, like the hugely fat fetish queen, her monstrous bulk encased in form-fitting, horribly expensive black leather, her bloated hands, rings sunk into blubber, grasping two leashes snap-locked to wide, studded collars that choked the slim necks of two exquisitely beautiful girls. One was white-blonde, the other café-au-lait brunette. Those girls had the blank, insectile faces of the insane; their tongues churned ceaselessly in their mouths, their lips glossy with saliva as they squirmed and pouted round their mistress' gargantuan thighs.

And the old rock star, his withered face hidden behind wraparound shades which did nothing to hide his identity. Sam Hellerman, a man who'd done it all: found

Judaism, then discarded it for Christianity, then announced Buddhism was the only way, man. His ex-wives and lovers cringed when they heard his songs about them. What was that famous number? '*You got the body of a saint / The mind of an idiot / Little starfucker not / Value for my money . . .*' I believe the wife that one was about tried to sue . . . Most recently, he'd crashed his Porsche spectacularly and lived to sing about it. His life was one spread after another in *Rolling Stone, Q,* and the gossip columns of the world's press. I'd heard his last album, *Dead Skies and No Return,* the one the critics panned. It was like listening to someone masturbate – revolting and boring by turns. I couldn't believe he was here. Sam the Man, a sponsor? While I was gawking, he caught me staring and whispered an aside to his aide, who then called Marigold over and asked her something. She flushed nervously and gave a reply which was whispered in turn to Hellerman. He took off his shades and stared back at me. His eyes were the colour of dirt, his complexion like a wet chamois leather laid over gristle. Resisting the urge to stick my tongue out at him, I turned on my heel and went to my room.

I felt horrible; I couldn't handle those sort of people any more. Well, not that I'd ever actually *mingled* with that sort of crowd – not in Bradford, believe me. The worldliness of them seemed a desecration of what I'd believed Soledad to be about. If it was their money that kept us afloat, if this was some kind of spiritual tourism to while away a dull hour, I wanted no part of it. I stuck my head out of the door, but no one was around, not even Azul.

I'd about decided not to go to the Gathering, as a protest, when someone knocked on my door. Still fuming, I flung it open. Mama Jay, wrapped in her cloak, leaning on the staff, stood outside. She looked about as bad as someone that beautiful could look; like an unwrapped mummy, dry, friable, her beauty falling away from her like the dead leaves outside on the skeleton trees, leaving her bones, nothing else.

I stepped back, the wind knocked out of my sails. There I'd been, happy to sulk on my own, and now Mama Jay had left The Prophet's deathbed to come and see me.

'May I come in, Alma?' Her voice was hardly more than a breath.

I stumbled inside, feeling really awkward. I pulled the one chair in the room out from the table, quickly put a cushion on the seat, and helped her to sit down. Then I stood there, feeling ashamed. She sighed heavily and looked at me.

'I know you're worried, dear. Marigold said you seemed upset earlier. No, you need not tell me why, I think I know. It's the sponsors, isn't it?'

I didn't reply. I didn't have to, she saw it on my face.

'Yes, yes, I know: they seem so worldly, so unlike us. But, as The Prophet says, *''Each must climb the mountain in their own way; some running, some crawling, some weeping.''* Behind those clothes, that paint, the masks, are those who climb weeping, and in fear. Their disguises are the refuges of terror. They desire the knowledge but are too fearful to give up their wealth, because to them, money is safety. Poor deluded children! I pity them, I cannot turn them away. Could you?'

Well, put like that, what could I say? 'But that terrible leather woman, with the girls, Mama Jay – and Sam Hellerman, he's a sensation-seeker, a thrill addict. It's not right, not here . . .'

She looked at me narrowly. 'So loyal, aren't you, my dear? I see how you want to protect us all, but the people you talk of so harshly are just people like any other. They seek, and they shall, one day, find. I pray for them, The Prophet prays for them. Couldn't you find it in your heart – that fierce heart – to pity them, Alma?'

'But the money . . .'

'Aha – dirty money? I'm not such an old fool as you think, my dear girl. We must live, Soledad must live. The money our father made is long gone and The Prophet had to be cared for, so I allow the sponsors to support us. In return, they attend the Gatherings. Each time they come, I hope they get a little closer to the Truth. Didn't Jesus say the stray lamb is more valuable than the rest? Put away your anger, Alma. Be with us tonight. It means so much to us, to me. I will rest easier, knowing you are fully with us – as you will be, after tonight. Please, humour an old woman. I'm so tired, so very tired . . . I want to share the burden of tonight with you, my daughter . . .'

Stuffed. What could I do? 'Of course. I'm sorry, Mama Jay, it was a bit of a shock, not what I was expecting . . . And everything being so . . .'

She got up and hugged me. She felt like a bundle of dead sticks wrapped in the soft, voluminous folds of her cloak. 'Bless you, child. Such strength, such strong blood in you. I know we can rely on you. I need not have worried, silly of me . . .'

After she'd gone I sat and fidgeted, trying not to feel as if I'd sold out. I twiddled around, tidying up for no good reason, stashing the scrap of Charlotte's letter safely in my bedside table drawer, faffing with my papers. I knew this 'do' would be a bit of an ordeal. I imagined speeches, socializing, explaining The Prophet's Work to those idiots – oh yeah, sorry, those *seekers*. I expected we'd lead them in meditation, show how we were getting on, thank them for their generosity, etc. The usual thing when you owed someone your daily bread. They could go away feeling cleansed, spiritualized; even the leather Thing and her dollies. Maybe her more than anyone. After all, wasn't spirituality the new drug? Rose and I had joked about it. Endorphin highs beat coke any day, and a fuck of a sight cheaper, too.

I'd just got out of the shower and was towelling myself dry – a sponsor-bought towel, I reflected grimly – when another knock came on the door.

'Hold on a mo',' I shouted as I struggled into my top and keks. I opened the door in a fragrant cloud of steam.

It was Marigold, breathless, carrying a bundle. God – Marigold. A big guilty surge made me glad my face was already red from the shower. She'd done all the hard work, her and Prata. Baking, organizing, washing, while I'd wandered around making beds and doing scut-work. As for Rose, well . . . AWOL, really. It was plump, flustered Marigold who'd worked like a trooper.

'Hi, Marigold, I was just thinking about you. God, you've worked so hard, I don't know how we'd all manage without you. And Prata, of course,' I added hastily, knowing how fond they were of each other.

She blushed like a kiddie. That made two of us. 'Gosh, no. Do you think so? I really want to be *useful,* you know. I mean, I'm not like you, not special . . .'

'I'm not *special,*' I sighed. 'I'm not, honestly. And you have worked like a bast–, like crazy, you really have.'

'Oh, it was nothing. But gosh, Alma, you are special. The Witness. The Daughter of Truth . . . Anyway – here are your things for tonight. I hope you like them. I think they're smashing, not that that sort of thing matters, of course . . .'

Before I could get it through to her about all that 'special' stuff, she'd put her bundle on the bed and bolted. She was the only person I'd ever met who actually said 'gosh' and meant it. Poor Marigold.

The bundle was a long tunic and drawstring trousers, rather like the Asian shalwar kameez, in exquisite hand-embroidered linen. Stitched round the trouser hems and tunic bottom were little wildflowers and leaves – yellow broom, oak and meadowsweet. It was beautifully done; as neat on the back as it was on the front. Professional.

There was a huge cream cashmere shawl too, with a corded fringe trim. Worth a bob or two. I supposed it must all belong to Mama Jay. But when I put the outfit on, it fitted perfectly, as if it had been made for me. *Rose . . .*

I was standing there, wrapped in the shawl, feeling its softness, when yet another knock came at the door. Bloody hell, my night for visitors.

It was Donner.

'Hello, my Alma.' He looked at me, his tired face almost transparent with fatigue, his green eyes like milky emeralds. 'May I say how nice you look? Is that OK? I came because Mama Jay told me of your talk together, and to bring you this vitamin drink I made for you specially, for strength. You must drink it all up, you hear? Make sure that you drink it. I'm so happy you will be with us to say goodbye to The Prophet, and to our dear Rose. Also, of course, to help Mama Jay. And . . . for myself, I wish you to know how highly I regard you, Alma – above all others, do you understand?' He looked anxiously at me, stooping a little to peer directly into my face.

Yes!

I was about to speak when he coughed hard, his hand over his mouth, his body shuddering with the effort. It was such a hoarse, racking sound I wondered if he was starting a chest infection. But before I could say something clucky, like, 'Why don't you get more rest?', he turned to leave, putting the glass of juice down on the table. I found my voice at last and reached out, putting my hand on his arm. It was very thin under his fleece top.

'I feel the same. About you, I mean. I think a lot of you, Donner. When tonight's over, maybe we should talk?' Christ, I sounded like a picture story from a teen mag. When would I grow up, or at least *sound* adult?

He smiled. 'Of course. I am at your service, as they say. Always.'

As soon as he shut the door, I bounced up and down on the bed until the springs went boing. After tonight . . . I picked up the drink he'd made me and took a big swig, but it tasted bitter under the fruit flavour. Too much vitamin powder, for my taste. A kind thought, though, so sweet of him to be concerned; but I poured the rest of the drink down the loo. I didn't want to offend him by having him think I'd left it.

Then I sat down on the edge of the bed to pull my boots on, and dress for the Gathering.

31

I woke up about an hour later, feeling like shit, my mouth as dry as if I'd been sucking cotton-wool. At first, I was totally disoriented, my head thick and throbbing. God, it must have been one of those lightning naps your body takes sometimes, like on trains and stuff. My arms and legs felt wobbly and uncoordinated. My vision was all wrong, too. I took off my specs, which I'd slept in – never a good idea – and buffed them up on an edge of the shawl. No good, I still had to keep stretching my eyes and blinking. Everything seemed to yaw a bit and the colours were all wrong. I staggered into the bathroom and splashed my face, rubbing my hair with a wet towel because it was stuck up on one side from where I'd conked out. Freaky-deaky – I must have been more tired than I thought . . .

Then I realized, the Gathering must be in full swing by now. Buggeration! Everyone would think I'd been sulking. I grabbed the shawl, wrapped up against the cold outside, and legged it.

The first thing that hit me as I ran through the colonnades was the *noise*. The drumming and bells seemed louder than usual, and the sound was overlaid with a formless, amplified gabbling of voices, like warped snatches of film soundtracks played at random. I stopped short, puzzled. Still feeling dizzy and out of it, I leant against a column to get my breath, but the pillar seemed to stretch up to nothing in a wavy, peculiar way which was very disconcerting, so I tried walking on.

There were shifting waves of light coming from the Great Hall, pulsing through the windows and the acrid smoke of the fire drifted up past the twisted silver crescent of the moon. The sky was a dark, icy sapphire, but when I looked at it, I lost my balance again. This was too weird – was I coming down with flu? Still, I had to get to the Gathering. I'd only stay a little while, then make my excuses and go back to bed. Rose wouldn't be off straight away; I'd have a talk with her tomorrow about my plan to team up.

I paused again, to steady myself. The noise and the lights were even clearer and louder. This wasn't the hushed, formal atmosphere I'd anticipated. Well, no point in freezing my arse off out here; doubtless it was just me being dense and they'd be watching extracts from The Prophet's travel video or something.

I went in via the kitchen, pausing nervously at the door for a second. I can't *do* parties – I know I'm dead loud and all that, but going to social things does me in. Still, same for everyone, I imagine, if the truth be told. *Grin and bear it,* I thought. *In you go.*

The heat hit me first. It was boiling. A huge log fire, like an indoor bonfire, was raging in the old hearth. The central heating was on as well, full blast. I felt sweat trickle down under my arms and my specs misted up. The noise was incredible, too, really loud. I took off my glasses to wipe them. In the blur of my short-sightedness, the hall appeared to be packed with people, lights flickering from what must have been a hundred enormous church candles and another light source I couldn't place. I strained my eyes. There was something wrong – I couldn't see properly . . . And that rank smell – God, what was it? I put my specs back on.

Nothing could have prepared me for what I saw. It

was as if the normal, everyday world had shifted and some insane parallel dimension had warped into existence without me knowing it. Christ, it makes my insides tremble, just thinking about it. Even now, it's as though I can't be rid of the images filling my mind . . .

Hell would be like that, the things I saw when I went into the hall. Like a Hieronymus Bosch painting. Maybe it was all going on then, too; maybe Bosch knew, and tried to tell us through the paintings and the writing. But ordinary folks like us didn't want to hear about it.

When I crossed the threshold into that obscenity I understood, deep inside myself, that this was the negation of everything good I'd ever believed in. There in the Great Hall, stripped bare of the trappings of society and the façade of decency, I saw what people kept untouchable by the power of money could do. People so scoured out by the endless satisfaction of their darkest, most twisted fantasies that they were no more than the hollow, diseased shapes of men and women, lurching through a savage dance that wove and buckled with the gibbering intensity of the insane.

At first, I couldn't take it in. It was as if my mind was trying to protect me by not letting it all through. I know I saw Mama Jay, seated in The Prophet's Chair, His staff in her hand, her blue eyes blank and opaque, gazing like a statue over the heads of the squirming mass. On the long table, which had been put at the foot of the dais, were the big serving bowls we used for soup, now filled with a blackish liquid that the filthy, naked people were scooping into their hands and gulping down. The fluid ran down their chins and on to their bodies, where others licked it off their flesh like dogs eating their own vomit.

Mama Jay sat there, immobile. She didn't seem to see them fucking each other like brutes in front of her; the slap and gleam of wet flesh. She seemed oblivious; the white-wrapped Seer, the Oracle, blind and deaf, not touched by any of it, not smelling the stink of rut and semen . . . And blood.

Blood everywhere, everyone covered with it. The smell of it nauseating, metallic. I drew back against the wall, feeling behind me for the door, terrified. Every particle of my body screamed in panic, willing me to get away from there. I'd never known fear like that. Never. It was like all the circuits in my brain blew at once and only one thought kept yammering and screeching in my mind: *Get out.*

But my body wouldn't work. I was shaking too much, I couldn't find the door, my hands kept losing their grip. I fumbled along the wall, but there were people in the way now. Doing the vile things they'd travelled so far and paid so much for. Things sanctified for them in the name of an ancient and brutal religion from the dead past of our beginnings.

They were *using* the Chelas, you see. That's what their 'sponsorship' paid for. The Chelas were the Temple prostitutes, holy whores. Sure, the sponsors could get this type of thing in specialized brothels where the addicts and the desperate would do anything to get money for the next hit. But there, they risked disease, exposure, blackmail. Here they were safe. And there was the additional titillating frisson of being part of the Ritual. The thrill of sharing in a secret cult dating back past Christ, past everything. And twitching in your mind as you cut and fucked and drank the blood of the pure, the uncorrupted who gave it all to you so willingly, was the thought, *Maybe, jaded as I am, dead as I am inside, I believe . . .*

What was faith, then? The sad, deluded faith of the Chelas, trained to this obscenity by a world that discarded them and made them fit prey for the monstrous egotism of a crazy Prophet and his handmaiden, bonded in a *folie à deux* that resulted in this horror? Or The Prophet's faith that what the shaman Xangu told him was true; that he wasn't mad or outcast, but the Spirit incarnate? Or was it the perverted, scrabbling faith of the sponsors; the faith they hardly dare acknowledge, the teasing thrill of hell-fire and the secret, cringing hope of redemption? Everyone dying for the spirit world, everyone praying there was something else, something more than this walking bone-cage and its sloshing sack of guts. That we hadn't, finally, killed God.

As I stood trembling uncontrollably, these things spread in my mind like ink on wet paper. I saw how I'd fatally misunderstood the Foundation; misunderstood the very language they spoke. I spoke the language of the world, where words had no other resonance, while they spoke the language of prophecy, every word laden with spiritual meaning. Mama Jay had been right: this was an Ordeal, a Trial through which I was to have passed and, having done so, I'd be bound to their ideals for ever, unable to recant, unable to betray them because I would have been cut by the same knife. And like them, in order to live with what I'd done, I'd have to make it into something else, something beautiful and holy. Having destroyed my conscience, I would have gone mad if I hadn't re-made things in a way I could live with. Like Mama Jay, like The Prophet – like Donner. Oh, Donner, no . . .

I came to with a jolt, ice water filling my guts. I had to get away. I turned frantically to try and find the door again, but a man was leaning on it, masturbating with blood he scooped from cuts on Prata's body. She stood in front of him, inserting needle after needle through her skin, pinching up a piece of flesh and pushing the long needle slowly through; fan patterns of needles snaking down her arms, her legs, her breasts. Needles pushed through her nipples, her labia. Her face was like porcelain, gleaming with sweat, her mouth hanging open, her breath foul and her tongue black with the liquid from the bowls.

I staggered backwards as the man grabbed her and started pawing at her breasts. She let him do it, a vacant smile on her face. She was making a mindless cooing noise and stroking his balding head as he sucked at her wounds. I wanted to vomit. As I turned blindly away, someone gripped my arm and spun me round. It was the rock star, Hellerman, his unnaturally white teeth sharp and false looking, the canines elongated into imitation fangs . . . He hissed at me, his stinking black breath making my stomach heave again.

'Well, well, the Special Girl! Mine now, honey, all mine . . . I paid a bundle for their blood, but yours – I'll pay anything you want. Oh, yeah, I can feel it now, feel you in my mouth . . .'

He scrabbled at my clothes, leaving bloody handprints on the white linen. I screamed and pushed him off, bile in my throat. I ran towards Mama Jay, still yelling, shoving through the writhing mêlée, my boots slipping in the viscous mess of blood and fluids on the floor. I knew Hellerman was behind me, like a child knows the boogieman is behind her on the stairs . . .

I ran round the side of the table and grabbed the hem of Mama Jay's robe, yanking it and yelling her name. She didn't move. I looked at the cloth in my hand. It was embroidered with the same flowers as my clothes. Suddenly, it clicked in my head. Flowers – Blodeuedd: the woman made out of flowers. The mural in her sitting room, the story from the Mabinogion. Huw and Blodeuedd – Math Griffiths named his twins from the old legend. The magicians Gwydion and Math made a wife for Lleu out of flowers from the hillside and they named her Blodeuedd, 'Flower Face'. But she wasn't right. Created by man, not the gods, she was an empty vessel waiting to be filled, like a child without a soul. Finally, she betrayed Lleu and Gwydion turned her into an owl. For ever after called 'flower face' in the old language, the fanned feathers like petals round its great staring eyes. Blodeuedd, the great white owl; *tylluan wen*. The silent, beating white wings. Beautiful, cold, without mercy or pity. The razor-sharp beak slashing, the flower face unmoved. She *would* not see this – the filth, the blood, the horror – because she was protecting Huw even as she betrayed him. Her wings outspread, hiding him, saving him as she had since they were children in that strange old house in Wales. The twins. One blood.

I screamed at her. She didn't blink. Blodeuedd. Untouched. Insane.

I shut my eyes, the noise of the drums and the shrieking filled my mind. Everywhere the old rituals were being used and perverted by this army of devourers who paid to keep us like slaves for their use. It had all been a lie, one lie after another . . .

I looked again and saw Azul, his cheeks pierced by a steel spike thicker than my thumb that was garlanded with white blossoms. His gaze was fixed and ecstatic. The raw edges of the wounds in his face turned back like lips round the metal. I screamed his name and started clawing my way to him, but then Hellerman was in my path again, his sneering face lit like a gargoyle by the firelight.

I spat at him, but he just laughed. Hands grasped my tunic. The smell and the noise were confusing me. I hit out at the person who grabbed me, shoving them back – only to see it was Marigold, her round face witless and numb, a rough wooden cup in her hand.

Saliva dribbled from her mouth in ropy strands. 'Drink it, Sister Alma, drink it. It's the Opener of the Way; we are borne into the next world with it. Xangu gave it to The Prophet –'

I knocked it out of her hand, the cup bouncing on the

floor, the black, sticky fluid, clotted with vegetal lumps, spewing on to the tiles. So, this mess was the liquid form of the herbs I saw Xangu administer to Huw on the film. Yeah, easier that way. Easier for the sponsors. Easier to make the huge quantities needed. The sacred drug. The Portal to the Spirit World. Jane had even betrayed that secret, sold it for a few extra years of life for her beloved . . .

Marigold knelt down and licked the drug from the filthy floor, bliss on her empty face. I couldn't look at her. I tried to tell myself it wasn't her but some devil riding the shell of her body. *Be safe, somewhere, Marigold, love,* I prayed. *Don't remember this, don't remember.* I started crying then, watching her licking the floor, twitching like a poisoned animal. I felt the anger swell my heart to bursting. I'd do something to make sure this would never happen again.

I had to find the door by the glass wall and get out, down the mountain path to the village. Get the Police, get help . . .

Outlined against the ashen orange of the sunset was the black, jagged outline of the Tree sculpture. A heaving mass of people surrounded the base, like maggots. They were dipping their hands in the depression at the bottom of the trunk and scooping out a dark liquid. More of the drug? It was black in the shadows, black and . . .

Oh God, Oh God . . . Someone was hanging from the steel branches, blood running down the metal trunk into the bowl at its foot. They were drinking blood.

I staggered towards the Tree, kicking people out of the way, slipping and crying and sobbing until I stood at its foot. The sponsors were whispering. I could hear the sound like the susurration of leaves: *'Don't touch her, don't touch her, she's ours, ours . . .'*

I looked up, my whole body aching, my mind howling in my skull.

It was Rose.

I screamed so loud I thought I'd faint. I screamed her name as I saw her hanging from the great flesh hooks that pierced through the gap between her shoulders and her chest, and through the flesh and muscle of her back. The hooks were attached to the 'branches' of the Tree. It had been specially made for this purpose, I saw that now. Curved needles laced through the skin of Rose's forehead and round her shaved skull like the Crown of Thorns; diagonal cuts in her elbows and wrists opened her veins. I cried as I saw her body was a lumpy network of old scars, self-inflicted for years; she was a cutter, exorcizing her demons with a razorblade. The scars were all over her: the old ones white, some purplish-pink, and the new, red-raw slashes that netted her shrunken thighs. Oh, Rose . . . my poor, sad and savage girl.

All I could think was, *No, no, get her down, get her down you bastards, get her down*! I scrabbled to get to her while those monsters lapped her blood and kissed the hem of my tunic leaving bloody prints, muttering that they knew who I was and that this would never end, they'd have this for ever, they were safe . . .

I punched and kicked, sobbing and shouting, clawing them away. But it was no use, no use. I couldn't get her down off that crucifying Tree, I couldn't get to her, I wasn't strong enough.

I reached up and touched her foot, my hand swollen and bruised from fighting. In the blood-laced mask of her face, her eyes opened, the pale grey like moonlight against the gleaming, congealed black.

'Rose, Rose . . . Oh God, Rose, please – this isn't – Rose, no, no . . .'

I heard her voice. Thin as a reed, barely audible, but it threaded softly, gently, through that unholy Babel.

'I'm Going Home, Alma. Tammuz waits. The Others wait. I'm Going Home . . .'

'No, no – you can't!'

She looked at me, her dove-coloured eyes full of tears, a smile touching her white lips.

'Oh, Alma, I'm so happy, so happy . . .'

32

I must have fainted. I just remember seeing Rose, her eyes rolling back in her head, and knowing, even though I'd never seen anyone die before, that it was over. She was dead.

I came to lying on a couch in a big room I'd never seen before. I fumbled for my glasses with the scrabbling panic short-sighted people have when they're distressed and can't see. Donner handed them to me; he'd been sitting by the couch, watching me. I felt a shiver of disgust as his hand touched mine. The sight of his face, so familiar, so concerned-looking, made me want to scream. It took a moment for me to control myself. I knew that losing it wouldn't be a good idea, not at all.

I could feel my mind folding away the terrible things I'd seen into a box in my head labelled 'Not Yet'. I was still woozy and felt sluggish, distanced from everything. Perhaps that was why I felt so unnaturally calm. Or was it shock? I didn't feel as if I had shock, but how would I know? Nothing like this had ever happened to me before; this sort of thing *didn't* happen to everyday folk from Bradford. But then, look at what had happened to Frankie – I bet he'd thought the same.

I heard Donner's voice through this daydream. At the same time, I became more aware of where I was. I saw ranks of gleaming white medical equipment, connected by tangled leads and wires to blipping monitors, and in the centre, a huge old carved bed draped with ragged hangings. Someone was lying in that bed and Mama – no, fuck all that – *Jane*, was sitting beside them, holding their hand, whispering. Huw! It had to be Huw. I was in Huw's room – or chamber, more like; it was partially carved out of the rock the house stood on. I must be underground. There was a dreadful stench as well, that not even the big air-cleaning extractor fan could cope with. It smelt like spoiled pork; rotten, clinging, nauseating. I wiped my mouth instinctively.

'Alma, how are you?' Donner's gentle voice brought me back to myself. 'You fainted, so I brought you here and gave you a small sedative. You have slept for a few hours. Do you feel all right, now?'

The thing that bugged me the most was that he sounded so fucking ordinary. Like nothing had happened; like I'd just had a hysterical girlie fainting fit. I half expected him to ask me if I was having my period – oh *yeah*, that would account for it.

'Yes, yes, I'm all right. Look, I want to go home now, OK?'

'I don't understand; you are home.'

'Come on, you know what I mean. I want to go back to La Morena. I want to go *now*, Donner.'

He looked at me blankly, as if he didn't know what on earth I was on about. I don't know why, but that frightened me, it really did. It was as if nothing I could ever say could get through to him. Sort of . . . you know when you have an argument with your boyfriend or girlfriend and afterwards they describe what you said and it's absolutely nothing like what you think you said and the whole thing starts all over again? Donner looked at me like that. Only this wasn't a crappy little argument about which film you should go and see, or where to go on your annual holidays. It was about me getting out of a place where murdering someone for a bloody *philosophy* was OK. I swallowed hard; my mouth suddenly dry and my body tense as a tightrope.

I struggled up, and found that Donner – or someone – had changed my clothes. The bloodstained tunic and trousers had been replaced by a clean outfit and fleece jacket. A brand-new pair of sheepskin boots stood by the couch, my ditty-bag, the one Marigold had made for me, leaning against them. I'd been washed, too; at least, my face and hands had. That was a creepy thought, someone touching me while I was asleep. I pulled the boots on, my brain whirling. Had I imagined it all? Was I going mad? Then I saw my hands. Under the nails, short though they were, a black rim showed. Not dirt – blood. Rose's blood.

I walked unsteadily to the door, panic fluttering on the edges of my consciousness like a trapped bird. I had to be cool, mustn't let them see me unravel . . .

It was locked. I yanked at the handle, but it was useless. I tried again, in case the heavy door was just stuck. It wasn't. I was locked in. I lost it then; the fluttering in my head turned to a storm of unreason. I started kicking the door, banging on it with my fists. I could hear myself shouting. I knew I was hurting myself, but nothing mattered, nothing – I had to get out. I hated it in this windowless fucking cave, this stinking fucking hole in the ground. *Let me out, let . . .*

I felt Donner take hold of me round the waist, pulling me away from the door. I twisted in his arms, trying to hit him, trying to scratch and bite him. He held me to him pinning my arms. I kicked hard backwards, catching him on the shin, but he didn't let go. Eventually, I just slumped, the strength draining out of me. He felt it and led me back to the couch.

'You must try to be quiet, Alma, or you will hurt yourself.'

What the fuck was I going to do? I had to get away

from here; I had to think, plan. I concentrated on breathing evenly, not too deeply, steady and slow. It wouldn't help if I got wheezy.

I sat up. Jane was looking at me from where she sat by Huw's side; a faint Mona Lisa smile on her collapsed mouth. Her eyes china blue in their new nest of fine wrinkles.

'Alma, dear, come and greet The Prophet. He is so anxious to speak to you – aren't you, my darling?'

As if nothing was wrong; as if I hadn't just thrown an eppy and tried to break down the door. I felt like Alice in bloody Wonderland. OK, easy does it. Play it their way, they'd let me go in the end, they'd have to. I walked to the foot of the bed. I could feel Donner's eyes on my back.

Huw lay propped up on pillows. I'd never had to deal with serious illness – hospitals did that; nurses, professionals. The sight of Huw Griffiths, the man I'd known as The Prophet, turned my stomach. It was all I could do not to retch. He lay there, his twisted, swollen hands twitching on the immaculate white sheet that covered his lower body, his breath coming in heaving, ragged gulps. He was no more than a lump of rotting meat barely clinging to whatever life still kept those disintegrating lungs moving. Huge, weeping, open sores disfigured his face, eating away at the collapsed bridge of his nose. Pus leaked from under his closed eyelids. His scalp showed raw and crusty through the thin strands of long, white hair that draggled down on to his pillow. Eroded skin stretched over the deformed, gnarled remains of his bones, the joint of one knee hugely distended under the sheet. Sores bubbled all over him, waiting to erupt, and big white blisters like drops of milk splattered his body. The stench of his illness lay like a pall over the bed. How could Jane bear it? How could she bear to kiss that knotted hand, the cuticles so eaten away you could nearly see the bone?

I put my hand over my mouth and nose. Jane was whispering to Huw, but I couldn't take my eyes off the human wreck in the bed. Something niggled in the back of my mind . . .

It hit me like a sledgehammer. Dear God – it was *syphilis*; the final, terrible stages of syphilis. All those gross pictures I'd found for Laura, all those detailed medical texts I'd laboured over – it was all there in front of me. The sores – *gumma*; the milky blisters – *lata*. His leg under the sheet: the classic deformity of Charcot's Knee. Christ, how had he come to be like this? It was a treatable disease, for fuck's sake! It should never have been allowed to get this far.

I spun round to see Donner gazing sadly at Huw. 'It's syphilis, isn't it? *Syphilis*, for fuck's sake!' I spat at him, furious and horrified.

He didn't look at me. 'Yes. Tertiary syphilis. The final stage. His spine, His brain, all destroyed. The greatest Sacrifice. He is truly The Prophet. The pain has been terrible, but He has endured, and for that endurance has been granted His Visions – quite undiminished, until now.' He shook his head. 'How great He is, how unworthy I am –'

'Never mind all that crap! God Almighty, you're a fucking *doctor*, why didn't you treat him instead of letting him suffer like this? It's disgusting, you should be ashamed . . .'

Jane looked up. 'The Prophet willed it to be so, dear. The Holy Scourge came to him in Africa, after a Blood Ritual . . . He knew its ancient power to give Visions and He embraced it. It has been the greatest Ordeal possible, but the rewards have been great, truly.' Her voice was as light and perky as ever; she could have been commenting on the weather.

All his great insights; his prophecies, his wonderful, fantastical, mind-expanding ideas – all grown from the dungheap of the disease. Laura had been right, in many ways. The reward the disease graciously bestowed on its host. Despite everything, I felt a wave of pity for him. His work was brilliant, but how horribly he must have suffered. It didn't bear thinking about. The others, though – how could they have let it happen? What sort of person could sit and watch someone in such hideous pain and do nothing . . . Yeah, well – exactly. I shook my head, clearing my thoughts. It was no use worrying about Huw – or the others. Not now. It was too late. Jane still smiled that fixed little smile at me. I had to make her understand.

'Jane, listen to me. I have to go home now, you have to let me go home.' I would repeat this calmly, rationally, until it got through that blind mask and she saw the impossibility of keeping me there against my will. This wasn't Jonestown, or Waco, for fuck's sake! Jane knew my bloody *parents* – she'd see reason eventually.

'Go Home? Oh no, not yet, not for many years. You have to carry on. I know it's hard, but you must serve The Prophet's will in this, as do we all. You can't Go Home yet, you poor, brave girl.'

Language again. I stifled the desire to yell at her. 'No, I mean, I have to go and see my parents – Freddy and Violet. They miss me, you must see that. I'll come back, but you have to let me go . . .'

She didn't hear a fucking word.

'Many have Gone Home, oh yes. Tammuz waits, my Son waits, guarding the Portal. He is the Light in the Abyss. Donner wants to Go Home, don't you, Donner? But he knows he must stay, with you. How many are now Purified? Oh, those beautiful Children: Topaz, Harmonie, Eagle, Luz, and Sky – such a sweet boy, he reminded me of Tammuz in many ways. And Immacolata, and Sunrise; Joy and Crystal; Clay – oh, I forget, I forget, I'm so old now. The first was my dear Safaa, such a devoted Believer. He followed Tammuz, it gave me such comfort knowing my boy was not alone . . .'

'You let Safaa – Jane, you let Safaa, the father of your child . . . ? God, how could you?'

She looked at me, those great eyes blank as stone. 'Safaa? The Father of Tammuz? Oh dear, Alma, no. The Prophet is the Father of Tammuz, as was proper. The Blood cannot be mingled. I was the Vessel of the Chosen One. How strange! Why did you think Safaa was . . . I'm surprised at you, Alma, thinking I would sully my Heritage. I was The Bride.'

She seemed genuinely affronted, as if I'd committed a tasteless faux pas. Well, to her, no doubt I had. I wasn't shocked by what she told me; there was an awful logic to it. Of course Huw had fathered a child on his twin – who else? He wouldn't have to confront his sexuality if he did it with Jane. It'd be safe, like fucking yourself, not like doing it with a real woman. Just the two of them, same as it always had been in that hermetically sealed little world of the twins. A dynasty, for fuck's sake, like the Ancient Egyptians and the brother–sister marriages that kept the bloodlines pure. Did Safaa put that in their minds? Who knows . . . Jane was still talking, I pulled myself together and concentrated.

'. . . as you will be, my child. And dear, dear Donner will be with you, to look after you always. Mind you, I'm still cross with him for trying to prevent your Ordeal. But he has apologized' – she wagged her finger at Donner, as if he'd been a naughty boy – 'and I forgive him. Love is a beautiful thing, even when it causes us to misbehave. You young things! Never mind. He knows the next Gathering will be extra special, don't you, dear? I do so hope I will be there to Witness, but . . .' She sighed and stroked Huw's hand lovingly.

Donner seemed to be on the verge of tears. For some reason, his resemblance to Jack rose up and overlaid his face. Jack would look like that, after he'd hit me, when he'd cried and begged me to forgive him . . .

'It's true, Alma. I'm so sorry. I put a sedative in your drink, not vitamins. I thought you would sleep through . . . I couldn't bear the idea of your being touched by others. I was wrong, of course. I let my personal feelings . . . You know why . . . it was too painful for me to think of you . . . I failed you. I'm sorry, so very sorry.' Tears rolled down his cheeks.

Jane laughed, a broken, crystalline giggle. 'Well, no harm done. She was too much for you, you bad boy! The Old Blood is so strong in her. I saw it the first time I laid eyes on her!' She turned to me confidentially. 'You must forgive him, dear. He has such a struggle with his feelings – but he'll be the perfect Consort, under the circumstances. Won't you, Donner?'

His face was stark white. He spoke like an automaton. 'Yes, Mama Jay. I will care for The Bride and I will not sully her Purity.'

'What are you going on about?' I was confused, I felt sure I was missing something important.

He nodded again, miserably. 'You see, when I was a student, after Lutz – died . . . I was ill for some time. When I recovered, I thought many things about the world . . . how humanity behaves, this kind of thing. I was at that time in love with a girl, but she did not love me and became pregnant by another man. This upset me very much and I thought how I would never bring a child into such a filthy, evil world as ours. This idea filled my mind. I could think of nothing else. So, I decided to have a vasectomy, to make sure, even by accident, this would never happen. But because I was young, no one would perform this procedure on me.' He paused, swallowing hard. I could see he was shaking, his hands trembling. He caught me looking and locked his fingers together, covering them with his sleeves.

Jane, her lips pursed into a thin, lipless nothing, nodded vigorously. 'Go on, dear. She has a right to know she'll be safe with you. Go on.'

'You don't have to, Donner – it doesn't matter. Look, Jane, I really must go . . .' I tried the rational approach again, but she was having none of it. She gestured at Donner to continue. I was rigid with frustration and the passionate desire to be out of there, but I forced myself to be still, my nails grinding into the palms of my clenched fists.

Donner cleared his throat. 'So, in the end, I asked another student, a brilliant person, much admired by us all, to do it. He said, sure, why not? But it went wrong. There was much infection, scarring inside; I was very ill again but, this time, physically. The student came to the hospital and begged me not to tell. I said I would not, and I haven't. Now he is a famous surgeon, highly thought of in my country and abroad. But the illness . . . it left me damaged. I cannot – I am impotent. I have never functioned properly again. I tried to – with a girl, but she became angry when I could not – you know – and she said terrible things to me. It broke something in my heart. I thought all the time of ending my life as my brother had done. Then, by chance, I found The Prophet's Work, and the Foundation. I was overjoyed to discover a place where this would not matter, I would not be humiliated . . . where it would even be useful not to have such distractions of the body in my studies of The Prophet's Work. But then you came to us and I – I regretted what had happened to me . . .'

Jane interrupted him with a wave of her hand. 'Yes, yes – but you see, Alma, he will make a fine Consort. You will be The Bride, as I was. You will carry on The Prophet's Work, lead the Children to the Truth and you need never worry about unwanted attentions. Donner will protect you from anything unpleasant. Yes, it's all worked out very nicely, hasn't it, dear?'

I glanced, horrified, at Donner, who nodded his agreement with Jane. They had to be joking. This was some kind of mad practical joke, surely. I felt like laughing, it was so barmy. Hysterical giggles tightened my throat and I gripped the foot of the bed to steady myself. The world had gone insane.

'Don't be stupid – this is insane! I'm not anyone's bloody *bride*, whatever the fuck that means. I'm not . . . Don't be like this, Jane. Stop it now – let me go, please. Please . . .'

Donner went to Jane and put his arm round her shoulder. She looked up at him and touched her fingers to his.

'It is true, Alma,' he said. 'We have waited for you for so long, we were frightened you would not come in time; but you are with us now. Soon you will be united with our beloved Prophet in the Blood Wedding. You are the Bride of The Prophet and I am unworthy of the honour of being your Consort.' He bowed his head again.

The thing on the bed mewled in its drugged sleep.

Jane smiled happily. 'You are indeed The Bride, Alma, and The Prophet is your Bridegroom; you will be united for ever in the Mystic Rose. You are the Vessel that will carry the Truth into the future, a link in the unbroken chain. The Great Universal Spirit sent you to us as It sent your father to The Prophet. We're all so pleased for you, we really are.'

'Don't be mad!' I screamed at them, shaking the bed. 'Donner, for fuck's sake! Blood? A blood wedding? What the fuck is that? Stop all this crap now, just stop it and let me *go*!'

He never raised his voice. It was as if we were having a tea-time conversation on the pros and fucking cons of milk or lemon with your Assam.

'The Blood Wedding is the oldest form of marriage, Alma. Your blood and that of The Prophet will be mingled, and it will be as though you are One. Our only sadness is that you cannot now bear His child, as His First Bride did – but it is enough to know you are with us, His Life in Yours for ever.'

I screamed at him, terrified. 'Blood? Are you . . . My God, Donner, I'll be infected! I'll get – Donner, you can't –'

Jane piped up, her face dreamy, her hand covering Huw's gently. 'Oh yes, you will be honoured with the Scourge – but just think, you will see as my darling has seen, you will carry on His Vision . . . I wasn't worthy, you see.' She tapped the side of her head with her free hand. 'Not bright enough. Oh, I wanted to – especially in the First Days, but The Prophet said no. "No, my love," he said. "You must remain in the world, be my Witness, care for me as the Ordeal progresses. Another will come . . ." And here you are! Don't be afraid of the Wedding, it's just a small cut and then . . .'

'Great – like some fucking mad blood brotherhood crap . . .'

Donner looked up. 'Yes. You are correct. This is the ritual which that debased form sprang from. You see, you understand so much . . .'

It was hopeless. They were insane. I turned and flung myself on the couch, choking with sobs that racked me from head to foot. Fuck, fuck – what had I done to deserve this? I couldn't bear it . . . I wasn't . . . Oh God, *God*, get me *out* of here, get me out . . . Dad, Mum, please – anyone, please, please, help me . . .

I didn't feel the needle until it was too late. He'd grabbed my arm, pushed up my sleeve before I understood what he was doing, and I slid down into the dark.

33

I woke on and off, drifting in and out of consciousness. I think I remember Donner coming in and injecting me again, but I couldn't fight him; it all seemed like a dream. Eventually, I woke properly, to find I was locked in one of the guest rooms, the small one with the little round window high up. A barred window, in that Spanish style, with a round boss of black ironwork bulging from the outer wall. Very pretty. It was one of the rooms I'd helped clean for the Gathering. *En suite,* as they say; all the conveniences. Just no fucking way out.

I also had a neat dressing on my right wrist, covering a two-inch incision closed with steri-strips. I screamed out loud, then ran into the bathroom and scrubbed at the wound until it bled into the basin, the blood swirling in the water and spiralling away. I scrubbed and scrubbed until they came in and stopped me – Donner and Sierra. It took two of them to get me back on to the bed. I tried to bite them, I tried to . . . It was no use. I felt the sharp sting of the injection again and . . .

I had no idea how long I'd stayed unconscious. Lost time, I suppose, lost and gone. I cried a lot, I know that. When Donner brought me some food, I threw it at him, but he just cleaned it up and brought some more. I ate it, in the end, because I was hungry. Some hunger-striker I'd make.

I nosed around the room, investigating every nook and cranny, every possible means to get out. There was nothing. Nothing. Nada. I considered suicide, like I used to – but still somehow I hoped they'd see reason. Anyway, how would I do it? Drown myself in the bog? Bite my veins open? Swallow my tongue? Or make a noose out of the bedlinen and hang myself? I thought sometimes I could feel the infection boiling in my blood, crawling in my veins; it made me crazy with panic. Dying seemed the best escape . . . But in the end, I thought, *Save it, save it. Things might get worse.*

I didn't want for anything. I had books – all Huw's – and it was warm. The tiny bathroom was stocked with fluffy towels and Jane's Acqua di Parma; the smell of it made me feel ill, now. I wasn't allowed any of my own stuff, though, like my computer, or the fragment of Charlotte's letter. But it was all very comfy – for a prison cell. I remember pushing the dresser over to the wall under the window and going up on tiptoe to look out. It opened, so I could smell the world outside: the mountain thyme, the lavender – the rich, green scent of vegetation and the flinty smell of the greedy earth after the rain.

One time I saw Marigold, and another girl I didn't recognize. I screamed her name and waved and waved. She looked round surprised, and I kept yelling, '*Help! Help me, Marigold! Get the police, they're . . .*' She saw me at last. Then she smiled broadly, nudged the girl with her and they both waved like mad and smiled. She gave me the thumbs up. Then they walked off across the threshing ground, still grinning like idiots.

I cried for hours.

Donner came and spoke to me, but I wouldn't talk to him – what was the point? He went on about how much everyone loved me and how proud they were of me. I was too low to even hate him; I just wished he'd fuck off and leave me alone. You could tell he really didn't understand why I was being horrible to him. That made it all much worse, so frustrating.

Huw was hanging on. I don't know how, the state of him. Donner said soon I'd feel better about things and accept my good fortune. He went away quite quickly that time, after seeing my expression.

Mostly I brooded about how I'd come to this. I fantasized about Freddy and Vi getting worried and coming to get me; but then I'd imagine the Chelas all smiling and saying, *Oh, she's popped over to Amsterdam and she'll be sure to get in touch as soon as we tell her you came. Tea? Super.*

I also wondered if I was being watched; you know, one of Wolf's famous surveillance devices. I searched, but I couldn't find anything so I contented myself with saying, very loudly, 'If you're watching, Wolf, you little bastard, I still think you're a fucking wanker.' Nothing happened, and it made me feel like I was going crackers, talking to myself.

I couldn't sleep at night, either. I just lay there, looking at the dark, feeling dreadful. I'd get palpitations and wheezes from the stress of it all and wonder whether I'd peg out before I had a chance to escape. At dusk I could hear the high, thin squeaking of the bats that flew round the eaves, like pinpricks in my ears. I'd strain my eyes into the darkness of the room trying to see – I don't know what, really. Sometimes my whole body felt as if it was threaded with burning wires, or my feet would become red hot for no reason. One time I woke up crouched in the shower cubicle, crying my eyes out.

Some nights I'd fall into a heavy sleep and dream weird, clotted dreams that left me drenched in sweat. I dreamed of Maz and Millie, and home – Bradford home. It made me weep pathetically knowing no one would even notice I'd gone missing. I dreamed of Jack, too; often. One time it was so real. I felt him beside my bed, then I saw him, his ivory face gleaming in the darkness, his green eyes shining, and he was kissing me, his mouth opening on mine, his breath beautifully sweet and musky. I was so happy, so incredibly happy and relieved that he'd come back to me. I remember stretching out my arms to him in the dark, crying with happiness. He got in the bed with me, I could feel the warmth and weight of his body against mine and we made love – but it was all wrong. I tried to cry out to him I was infected, it was dangerous, but my tongue was thick in my mouth and I couldn't speak. Then, when he finally entered me he was icy cold. I struggled and struggled against that killing cold . . . But the night swallowed me up again and he was gone.

I don't know exactly how long I was there. At least ten days, I think; the time vanished as if it had never been, or as if it flowed backwards and forwards; knotted, arrhythmic, surreal.

Then one night, I woke with a start. Someone was in the room with me. A real person, not a dream. I lay bolt rigid, terrified, my heart banging so loudly I thought I could hear it.

'So, I'm a fuckin' wanker, am I, *Al*-ma? A little bastard, eh?'

It was Wolf. I could smell his sweet-sour body odour. I scrunched up against the bed-head, wishing I could get to my specs.

'Yes, you were right, as it goes. I do have this room under surveillance. See that bit of carving above the door? Never thought you could get a camera behind that, did yer? Well, y'can; nifty little item, an' all. Very tasty. Peeks out nicely from that flowery bit. Oh yes, Mama Jay and the Squarehead want to know what's up with their precious girlie. Wouldn't do for you to go 'urting yerself, would it?'

'What the fuck d'you want? If you do anything . . .'

'You'll what?' I could see him in the moonlight now my eyes had adjusted a bit. A pallid, blurred blob, his eyes black smears. 'What will you do, eh? Fuck all, missie, as it goes. Fuck all you can do. But I can do somethin', I can. I can get you out of here – if I want.' He laughed softly, a gloopy, liquid sound.

'What? Please, Wolf – I'll do anything you want – my parents –' I hated begging him, but what could I do? I really would do anything if I had to. He knew it, too, I could tell by his voice. He must know I didn't trust him, either, not as far as I could chuck him. But he didn't seem to care.

'Hmm, anythin', eh? Oh, don't fuckin' panic, I don't want nothin' like that, I wouldn't touch you with someone else's – Women, you all think you can get whatever you want that way. Pussy, pussy, pussy. Who gives a fuck?' He paused and spat on the floor. 'Na, I want you gone for me own reasons, see? I got me own reasons. I know you don't trust me, but that don't matter now. See, wiv you gone, I'll have Them back again. It'll be like old times, jus' me an' Them. I'll be the important one again – not you, you fuckin' slag. You fuckin' bitch slag. You cunt . . .' He was reciting the insults like a long-rehearsed chant; savouring them, his slitted eyes with their wonky eyelashes half closed. He seemed almost mesmerized by the words, as if he'd drifted off into some other place in his mind. I had to get him back on track – he was my only hope of escape.

'Wolf, Wolf – OK, OK. Look, you can have it all, I don't want it, I never wanted it, never, honestly. You're right, if I'm gone, they'll see how much they need you again. It'll be like you said, you'll be –'

'Shut the fuck up. You don't know fuck all. *Fuck all.* Before you fuckin' come, it was all great. I ran all this – me. It was mine. I give it everythin'. My whole life, one 'undred per cent. I was The Prophet's favourite . . .'

I doubted that. But Wolf was convinced. Oh, who cared? As long as he got me out.

He carried on ranting about how I'd spoiled it all for him, how he'd expected to be the next leader because of his brilliance, his cleverness with computers, how it was him, not me, who'd take the Foundation into the future, how much Jane and Huw had loved him, etc. On and on. I could smell his breath, he was so close to me. I shivered with revulsion, but he didn't notice; he was off on a trip of his own. I sat there, willing him to return to the idea of getting me out, but I dared not speak.

'Mama Jay loved me like a son, her own son – like Tammuz had been. She depended on me. She needed me, for everythin'. She'd talk to me for hours while I fixed up her telly an' video, or showed her 'ow the cameras worked. We'd 'ave tea an' cakes an' she'd kiss me . . . Like 'er son, I was. Then you come, an' it was all, "Wolf do this" an' "Wolf do that" an' not a fuckin' word of fuckin' thanks. Like I was a fuckin' servant. Like when I was at 'ome, with me Dad: "Dave, do this now, an' I mean *now*, boy" – an' no thanks, no gratitude. Fuck *all*. But see 'ere, you go an' it suits us both, don't it, missie. Am I right?'

'Yeah, you're dead right. But when?'

'Now. Right now. Before your Kraut boyfriend comes visitin'. I know about 'im, too. Poor old Krautie-boy, no good to you, eh? Can't get it up . . .' He sniggered. 'I tried to tell yer, but that cowbag Rose stopped me. Well, yer know now – so it's not like you'll miss 'im or anyfing, is it? The fuckin' ponce. He's next, oh yes . . . Come on, get yer things – 'urry up.'

'Wolf, wait! My computer, my book – there's a bit of paper as well, it's very important, part of a letter, it's in a plastic baggie thing, in my bedside drawer . . .'

'Yeah, yeah, yeah. 'Ere, I checked your crappy machine once, did you know that? Just in case you was up to somethin'. Gotta be vigilant, ent yer? Not much of a book, though, is it? Who the fuck'd want to read that borin' bollocks? Oh, don't worry, I'll – I'll post it all to yer, at yer mummy and daddy's gaff, OK? Now, 'urry up. Don't yer want to get out of 'ere?'

Shaking violently, I put on my specs, wrapped myself in the sheet and, grabbing my things, went into the bathroom. I splashed my face with cold water to wake myself up, pissed, and got dressed. I pulled on my boots, slinging my ditty-bag across my shoulders, then crept towards the door where I bumped into Wolf as he stood looking down the corridor.

'Careful!'

'Sorry, sorry . . .' I could hardly breathe. Thank fuck my bag had an inhaler in it. I followed him as he picked up a big flashlight from where he'd left it outside my room and set off down through the house into the cellars. I felt a rush of panic as we went past a big door and he whispered, *'The Prophet's room.'* But he just snickered at me, and carried on.

The cellars at Soledad were ancient, part of the old Moorish lookout that had stood on the site before Math Griffiths bought the land and built the house. No one used the big, vaulted rooms except for storage; they were filthy with webby dust and years of neglect. The flashlight cast weird shadows as we threaded our way through old furniture and broken bits and pieces. An old tailor's dummy, a heap of gilt picture frames, a wooden hatstand. Family stuff; a battered old pram, a chipped and balding rocking horse.

Finally, in the furthest corner of the furthest cellar, we stopped in front of an empty wine rack that stood against the stone wall.

Wolf heaved it aside quite easily, the thick muscles bunching under his fat. I tried not to sneeze as the dust floated up in a dirty cloud.

There was a small, arched door behind it; a heavy wooden thing, studded and banded with iron. Wolf fumbled in his pocket and produced a big, rusty key. It turned quite easily; he must have oiled the lock when he planned this whole thing. I grabbed his arm.

'What's this? Where are you taking me – if you fuck me about . . .'

'Yeah, missie, you'll do *what,* exac'ly? Oh, don't fuckin' get in a state. You gotta trust me, 'aven't you? Look, it's an old escape tunnel, right? Leads out to – to the hillside above the village. No one else knows but me. I found it on the house plans. I like to know what's what, I do. Now, for fuck's sake, stop yatterin' and get movin' – go on. I'll light the way, it'll all be over soon, ten minutes, max. Now, get on with it –'

He opened the door and pushed me through into the pitch-black.

34

I stumbled along in the wavering shadows of Wolf's torch beam, my hand outspread on the rock wall nearest to me, trying to keep myself steady. I could hear Wolf's breathing behind me and an occasional burst of swearing as he tripped on the uneven floor.

'Why don't you go in front? It'd be easier.' I'd asked this several times, but he just grunted something about my shutting the fuck up and getting on with it. He said the same thing again this time. God, how I disliked him. One of the greatest pleasures of getting out of here would be never having to see his ugly face again. I swore at him under my breath as I shuffled along.

It was oddly warm in the tunnel. The air was moist, the walls damp and sometimes running with water. The further we went on, the more desperate with fear and claustrophobia I got. It was horrible, and everything about caves and tight places I hated most. The total blackness around me was terrifyingly disorientating, the distorted shadows thrown by the torch beam somehow making things even worse. I hated the stifling sense of unreality and the liquid horror of the dark. I kept thinking that Wolf had said it'd take no more than ten minutes. You could stand anything for ten minutes, surely? But I just couldn't bear caves, even big show caves like the Cueva de la Pileta scared me, and this tunnel was nowhere near that size. It was like being in the intestines of the earth.

We seemed to go on for hours. Then Wolf spoke, startling me.

''Old on a minute.'

I turned round to see what he wanted.

He hit me hard round the side of my head with the big flashlight.

It was like an explosion had gone off in my skull; blinding lights, a coppery taste in my mouth. Then a dull numbness behind my ear that I didn't have time to think about because, suddenly, I was on my hands and knees on the floor, retching and gasping for breath, the tunnel pitching and yawing like crazy in the spinning light of the torch.

Wolf strode over and kicked me in the ribs and then on the hip, knocking me over. It was all too quick for me to take in. I felt the blossoming pain and lay curled up, wrapping my hands round my head to protect myself while I wondered what the fuck was happening.

'Wha' – what you doin' . . . ?' I heard my own voice as if from very far away. It sounded weak, wavering.

He laughed, the light in his hands jiggling and strobing. 'You're so fuckin' stupid – did you think I'd just let you wander off and get the coppers an' fuck knows what else? Oh yeah, I know what you'd get up to, you stupid cunt. I heard you goin' on about murder – *murder*, for fuck's sake! As if them who went Home were murdered – shows how much you fuckin' know, you cow. It was an honour for 'em. They're queuing up to be Purified – not that a fuckin' scumbag user like you'd understand that. Now, you listen ter me, I gotta protect Mama Jay, protect the Foundation – it's my duty, d'you hear? I didn't want to do this, but you made me. I gotta save Mama Jay an' The Prophet from selfish fuckers like you. Yeah, just plain selfish, you are. See what you made me do?'

He kicked at me again, but I rolled away and he missed,

grunting as he tried to get his balance on the slippery floor.

Terror flooded my mind. 'Wolf – you can't – please, let me go. I won't tell anyone, I swear . . .' The pain in my head intensified tenfold as I tried to speak.

'Sorry, bitch. Gotta go. Oh, this ain't a tunnel, by the by. It's a cave system. You won't ever get outta here, there ain't no way out. I fibbed. Bit of a porky.' He giggled, like a child. 'There you go, all's fair, eh? You're Goin' Home quicker'n you thought, ent yer? I can't 'ave you out there in the world alive. They'd find yer, see, wherever you was, you being so God-almighty fuckin' *special,* bein' The *Bride* an' all. Well, not any more, oh no. You'll just be a bag of bones down 'ere, all alone. Ah – poor little fing. My heart pumps custard.' His inane giggle reverberated in the dark again. 'No, I'll tell 'em you got out y'self – maybe the Kraut dint lock the door after one of his little night-time visits. An' poof! You vanished inta thin air. Perfect. They can look all they like, but they won't ever find yer. Anyhow, fuck you, missie, I'm off.'

And before I could even get up, I heard him turn and go back down the passage we'd come up as fast as he could. I dragged myself on to my knees, terror and panic tearing at me as the light vanished round a corner and the dark fell on me like a suffocating blanket.

'Wolf! Wollllllfffff! Please! For God's sake! Please don't leave me here! Please! Please! Noooooo! God, *no* . . .' My screams echoed in the tunnel uselessly. He'd won.

I was all alone in the warm, still darkness.

I've forgotten a lot of what happened down there; apparently that's natural. Too traumatic, especially in view of everything else that had happened. The mind just packs in, locks the doors. Anyway, I think I passed out at first, my head hurt so badly; and my ribs – I could feel he'd damaged them because it hurt to breathe. I also think I went mad for a while, stark mad. I don't like to think of that. Screaming and screaming, clawing at the rock until my fingernails bled. I kept praying it was another dream and I'd wake up. Well, I did, but I was still in the tunnel, and it was pitch-black, too dark to see anything except the lights in my head, or the patterns in front of my eyes when I rubbed them. I'd lost my glasses, too. I fumbled around for them, but I dared not leave the wall in case I got lost. I couldn't see . . . I wanted my specs so badly, but I couldn't find them. Not that it mattered, down there . . .

I lay still after that, in my own waste; like a baby, crying. I should have killed myself while I'd had a chance, I thought, rather than die like this. Formless terrors crept up on me; things I knew were irrational but couldn't control. The boogie-men of childhood; the devil under the bed, the monster in the shadows. But in the end, the worst thing was how completely alone I was, how completely without hope. There was no chance of getting out of the caves. Even proper cavers sometimes got lost in caverns they knew well, I'd seen it on the news. I realized I'd probably starve to death, if I didn't fall into a crevasse and break my back. Or worse, I'd just break a few bones and have to lie there for days in hideous agony until . . . I mean, how long would you stay alive without food? Would I go insane and try and eat my own flesh? Oh, God, let me die quick, let me die quick . . .

Then, as I prayed and cried and tried to make myself as small as possible, my head throbbing and my body aching, something happened in my brain: a stillness, a perfect moment of clarity. I knew I was going to die, because even if I could retrace my steps, the heavy oak door would be locked and bolted, the wine rack pushed against it, and probably more bits of old furniture too, just to make sure. It wasn't like when you're in a fast car and you think, *'Oh, I'm going to die'*; I knew I was going to *die*, to stop existing. It was over and that was that. At first, I panicked about it, fighting it – it wasn't fair, it wasn't right – but then a great sense of calm and peace flooded me and I stopped struggling. The dying was almost a relief; it was the pain of it that frightened me. But I was grateful to know that at the end of those last, flickering spasms, death waited for me, patient and still.

Then it came to me that I could either wait for it here, lying in my own piss and shit, dying craven and weak like a beaten animal – or I could crawl off into the caves and die trying. Both options were hideous. It was my choice; my last choice. The dying I had accepted, it lay in my heart like the only certain thing I'd ever known, comforting me. I was sorry not to have been able to say goodbye to the people I loved, but that didn't really matter; we all died in the end, we were all equal in that. Huw had been right, in a way, it was like going home. Not, I thought grimly, that he'd been in a big hurry about it. Yeah, do as I say, not as I do, all right.

Nothing in the past mattered now. I had to decide the manner of my death; make the choice for myself, for my pride, my fury, the anger that had been my companion as long as I could remember. I would choose the way I died. And I did.

I sat up in the womb-like dark and let the rage make the choice. I started to crawl away into the caves. Fuck 'em – d'you hear? Fuck 'em all. I laughed and laughed and laughed; the sound echoing and re-echoing until the infinite silence returned, like the perfect calm a pool returns to after you throw a stone into it.

At first I kept crawling because I was afraid to stand, but eventually I got up. It was dreadful. I nearly threw up from terror when I lost touch with the wall at one point, because I seemed to float off into space. There was no up, no down and, without sight, my hearing became painfully acute, straining to pick up any possible sound, even though there were none. I was so happy – weird though that may seem – when I felt the gritty dampness of the wall under my hand again.

I had no idea how high the cave ceiling was either. Probably it varied, but I had no way of knowing. I moved an inch at a time, my feet never losing contact with the floor, my arms outstretched, always touching the left-hand wall. The idea I might fall into a pit, or get trapped in a narrow passage, dogged every step, so I sang songs to myself and recited poetry – not that I knew much off by heart. Children's rhymes, mostly, or things of Jack's. I only had one real thought, and that was to keep going. I'd die quicker that way, you see, because of using up energy.

I wasn't being brave; don't think that for a moment. I had no hope whatsoever of getting out. I just wanted it over as quick and painlessly as possible. I wished desperately that I would sort of pass out and just die in my sleep. That was the best possible thing I could pray for, and I did as I crept along, crying and shaking.

But the dark was so oppressive. Random thoughts came into my mind all the time and then flitted off; I couldn't hold on to any ideas for long. I remember feeling terribly sorry for anyone who lost their sight because the dark was like a living thing, breathing and warm, like flesh. Sometimes I wanted to hit out at it, to hurt it; it was my enemy. Every step was a battle and the war had barely begun.

I slept sometimes. Again, time had no meaning, so how long I dozed for doesn't matter. I'd always wake up with a start. Sometimes I thought I heard voices call my name, my heart hammering. Oddly enough, I never got wheezy, it was like that was too trivial now.

But I was so hungry, my stomach burned and spasmed

and I had the shits constantly until there was nothing left to pass; even then, the convulsive pushing of my bowels didn't stop. Pure fear, that, I think. I had dreadful stomach pains as well, from my chest to my hips. My whole body blazed with pain most of the time. Not like the Pain Offerings at the Meetings, because I'd have given anything for this to stop. I hadn't volunteered, it was out of my control, the body short-circuiting. I tried to ignore it, but that wasn't possible. Then I tried to remember what poor little Azul had said about the Sundance and his long fast. Nights of Power, he called those starving times. Well, this was a long, eternal Night of Power, then. He'd said you reach higher states, see more clearly, that bodily discomfort falls away. But not for me; my body dragged along like a lead weight, constantly nagging and ragging at me with its demands. I missed Azul, he'd been so devoted – yes, that was the right word – so devoted to me. That kind of love doesn't come along very often, if ever, and I hadn't taken him seriously. There was so much I hadn't understood.

Not just the language thing, either. The whole nature of having faith, or believing in something. I hadn't really taken in the idea that the Chelas genuinely meant what they said. That Rose had believed utterly in the things she'd told me. I suppose I'd imagined it was a bit like Cam and his drippy friends at Shambhala; nice to be 'spiritual', but not *real*, not serious. Deep down, I'd thought the Chelas would all get tired of it eventually and go off to be proper people with jobs and families, a mortgage, a car. It was all a passing phase. I mean, it was so medieval, the concept of withdrawing from the world to a life of prayer and stuff. You'd miss the telly, wouldn't you? And pubs and clubs and music and . . . wouldn't you? You would if you were normal, surely? That's what British culture told us all, anyway – I can't speak for the rest of the world. But Britain was wholly without any thought of anything that wasn't material. Completely secular. Only laughable weirdoes and possibly, backward foreigners, went in for religion. Didn't they say the two things you couldn't talk about in polite conversation in England were politics and religion? No, I'd had it all in front of me at the Foundation, but I hadn't imagined for an instant it was *real*. They'd never lied to me; I just hadn't heard them telling me the truth.

All this swirled around in my mind as I dragged myself on into the caves. It made me laugh. Too fucking late for all these brilliant insights now, girl. What would Phillip say if he could see you now? So much for anger management. What would Millie say? Or Maz – poor Maz. She must have been desperate, and I had let her go without even trying to sort it out. I ran off to some bloke again, hoping he'd make it all go away for me. What did it matter who Tatum's father was? Really, what the fuck did it matter? Maz was her mother, that was all that counted. Jack would never have acknowledged Tatum, I knew that. Oh, he'd have been flattered to think he had a kid – lads liked that, proved they were real men – but he'd still have fucked off to London, leaving Maz to shoulder the burden alone. No, she was worth ten of him, truth be told. Twenty, even. Maz wouldn't give up if she were here, she'd fight to the end. I learnt that off her, if nothing else. But Millie – I wished I'd said goodbye to my Mills . . .

The hunger dulled to a thick, brutal ache as I staggered on. I even stopped dreaming of food. I drank, though. In fact, I fell into a shallow pool, one of several that dotted the path like beads on a necklace. I lay in the water, my heart pounding with the shock, feeling around me in case it was bigger, or deeper than it seemed; but it was about the size of an ordinary dining table, as far as I could tell. I wondered if I could drown myself, but it was only a few inches deep. I dragged myself out and tripped over into the next one. I drank from that; the water was blood-temperature. I didn't want to, thinking it would spin the agony out, but I couldn't help it. Sometimes your body does what it wants. So I just let it, what did it matter?

Then after a time, I began to see things. I knew, in some part of my mind, that they were hallucinations, but I didn't care. I hoped it was a sign of the end. I saw my parents and Frankie; I babbled on as they hung in the dark, fading slowly into particles of light. I told them I loved them. They said they knew and it was OK. I said I was sorry, and they forgave me. I cried again after that.

Then Jack came, his ghost trailing through the caves – restless, angry. I told him I understood more, now; but he wouldn't look at me. He turned his head away like he used to when we argued. Then, I'd been frightened of him, but now – well, he couldn't hurt me. His rage was like mine; it came from the hurt of childhood. We were the invisible children who never get into the light. He was more like me than I'd ever thought. I'd seen him as so far above me, when really, he was only a furious boy, lashing out in his hurt and churning with the violence that never eased his aching heart. Repeating the lessons his daddy taught him; binding the past to the present in the blows that never satisfied.

In the end, he did look at me as I trudged slowly on to nowhere. He asked for my forgiveness in his surly, furious way. I forgave him because it was easy and I knew I still loved him, despite it all. Because of it all. My lost man-child. I should have stuck up for myself more; I should have left after the first hint of his violence. I should have given him the fight he wanted; not with fists, but with the strength of my will. I would have won. He wanted me to. But I had given in because I was so scared of losing him. Well, I suppose I couldn't help being me any more than he could help being him. I forgave myself, too; why not? There was no one else there to do it, here in the dark. Jack went, after that, and I was alone again for a long while. I got into a kind of dreary rhythm, like a trance that went on and on. Never knowing where I was, whether it was a huge chamber, or a small tunnel. Just knowing the wall, and sometimes, fluted, rippled rock formations that seemed to move under my hand. And once or twice, stalactites and stalagmites, like twisted umbilical cords winding off up to nowhere. They frightened me, though, because it was harder to keep hold of the wall, my security, my companion. I wondered if there were cave paintings, too, like at Pileta caverns. Probably not. I didn't think anyone had ever lived here.

Then, suddenly, shocking me out of my dreams, my outstretched hand touched stone in front of me. I froze. Was this it? The end of the caves, a blank wall? I forced back the fear and groped along it. Nothing. Solid rock. Crying, I stopped, terrified I'd fall into a crevasse. Then, a careful, sliding step, and another . . . My hand plunged into space. An entry! Shaking, I measured it with my hands.

It was just over three hand-spans wide.

The panic ripped through me before I could stop it. I gibbered in my head about getting stuck – getting stuck standing upright, the rock closing round my body, choking, suffocating . . .

It took a long, long time to get up off the floor and ease into the crack. I went in sideways, flat along the wall. My legs trembled as I felt my way ahead, the growing horror that it was getting narrower seizing hold of me. It *was* getting narrower – and it was *turning*; I could feel the shape of the corner jutting out.

I forced myself round the hairpin bend and, at the point of the turn, I stuck.

The rock had me caught at the chest; a projection behind and the narrow edge of the bend. It was over. This was it.

Suddenly, I found myself flailing wildly, smashing at the wet stone with my hands, screaming until my throat was raw. A strength I didn't know I had possessed me and I tore myself through; the stone grinding through the soft flesh at the top of my breasts, tearing my tunic and leaving a long, deep graze. But I was free and I fell to the floor, exhausted and gasping for breath. Stupid, stupid – why fight? Why? What did it matter where I died? But I couldn't help it, it was like drinking; my body did it, not me.

I didn't dare move after that. I sat against the rock, my feet touching the opposite wall, and felt the fiery new pain of the cut on my chest join the other old familiar pains I'd carried for so long. I touched the wound and brought my fingers up to my mouth, tasting the blood. I was still real, then. I licked the little rivulet of water that I could hear running down the wall next to me; I didn't want the taste of my own blood in my mouth . . .

I sat for ages; staring into nothing. Shapes came and went in the blackness. I felt myself drifting, exhausted, the pain of my injuries and my stomach coming together into one big throb of agony. Points of light like sequins twinkled and swarmed in front of me. Gold and red, coalescing, forming . . . A vision . . .

Rearing out of the dark, the Holy Mother gazed down at me, her wonderful, tender face suffused with love. I was dying. It was all over.

She hovered there, shifting and shimmering, filling the darkness. I knew what She was then and why I'd loved her so. She was the most ancient goddess, old beyond imagining, older than these caves: the most primitive and instinctive of our blind desires for something else. Something good, something powerful and strong. For a mother's unselfish, pure, fierce love. For warmth and comfort and a place to lay our burdens down. The Great Goddess, dressed in new clothes. Enduring through the aeons. I'd seen Her in the Virgin Mary, but She'd always been there and always would be. The Giver of Life.

And the bringer of Death. Maiden, Mother, Crone. She wore all these faces. Primitive and savage, gentle and loving. As She birthed, so She came and gave death, cutting the cord at last; leading us by the hand into the Mystery. Oh, it wasn't so bad. I was very, very tired, and She was so beautiful . . .

I felt the tears on my cheeks as the Virgin lifted Her pale hand in blessing; the sparkling glitter of Her robe, the heavy crown that rested on Her smooth, dark hair, the scattered roses that fell in fragrant showers from the thin crescent moon Her bare feet stood on. She was complete. Ineffable. Power glowed around Her like the shifting rays of the Aurora Borealis. She had come to take me home; Mother, Goddess, the symbol of my lost love; the healer of broken hearts.

I slipped to the floor and reached out my hand to Her as She floated in the darkness of what would be my tomb. I seemed to feel the breath of Her movement as She swayed in front of me, the prismatic crystal of Her robe shattering into the dark. Around Her, shapes formed in the blackness, lambs maybe, the Lamb . . .

Lambs didn't stink; didn't make that evil, guttural bleat – goats did.

I could smell it: feral, musky, rank. I could smell . . . I reached out again, to the animal shape that seemed no more than a black-on-black lump in the darkness . . .

And touched fur . . .

I fell back with a yell, my heart pounding so hard I thought it would burst. The goat – the real, live goat – shot off up the passage as frightened as I was. In a frenzy, I lurched after it and saw the dark was thinner, greyer. Frantically I scrabbled on, falling over, pulling myself up until I ran bang smack into a wall of rock. I fell backwards, stunned, my face exploding in pain. No, no, it didn't matter, go on – for fuck's sake, go on . . .

I crawled forward dizzily; where had the fucking goat gone? It *had* been real, it had – and I could feel a definite waft of air, a moving current, God . . . I stood up unsteadily and felt the rock I'd smacked into – there was an edge! Then a space, wide enough to let a goat through. I pulled myself round, it was like the protruding edge of a screen. I shoved myself through and stumbled into a pool of water . . . Cold water, not warm and dead like the cave pools; this was cold, that meant . . .

I was in a cave where grazing goats came to drink. I could see light, a few feet away. God! Light! The cave mouth, a ragged, overgrown slit, was directly in front of me, like a dazzling tear in the body of the earth. I flung myself at it sobbing and gasping.

And fell out into the world, on to a steep hillside carpeted with wild irises. I lay in that fragrant, perfect blue, blinking in the light of a sunny winter's day, the heat on my face, the clanking carillon of the goats' bells echoing off the hillside as they fled in panic. I lay spreadeagled and felt the light on me, and wept. Nothing had ever seemed so wonderful, so blessed as that light . . .

Oh, yes, yes, yes – the *light* . . .

Epilogue

'Finis coronat opus' Proverb

San Francisco's nice at this time of year; I like the warmth, though Thom says I should use a sunblock all the time, even just sitting out here on the balcony – sorry, *deck*. I'm sure he's right, but I keep forgetting. I forget things all the time at the moment – normal, apparently. Part of the recovery process, I'm told.

I have to say, Thom's been great; I'd never have thought it. I don't know why, but I suppose – well, we're not related or anything. Anyway, he's been fantastic. And Frankie, of course. But there's something about American courtesy, you know? Thom's so sweet, nothing's been too much trouble. He arranged everything: my counselling, my doctor. Helping me deal with my panic attacks. And he's spent hours talking to me about – stuff.

I do go out a bit now. At first, I could only manage to go swimming in the pool in the basement of the complex, but now, with Thom's help, I've even ventured out for walks. I still can't sleep without a night-light, though. I don't think I ever will. Thom and Frankie think I'm being brave, but I used up any bravery I ever had back then, in the caves. All gone now.

It's Post-Traumatic Stress Syndrome, they say. Not that I've told anyone the whole of what happened – they'd never understand. I told them I'd been in a cult, that my friend had committed suicide, that they'd tried to keep me there against my will but I escaped. Thom's the only one who really understands, even though he doesn't know the truth of it. He knows about 'New Religious Movements', as Dr Baker, my therapist, calls them. He was in one when he was a kid, knows all the jargon – 'love bombing', that sort of palaver. We talk sometimes, at night, while Frankie works . . . But I can't say much; I start crying and it's bad for me.

It's so good of them to have me here. As soon as I got out of hospital, Frankie sent me a ticket and I came over. They've been incredibly generous, paying for everything. Frankie says it's what brothers are for, but it's more than that. I think he feels guilty because he went off to America and kind of left me to it back home. He thinks he abandoned me. Silly. I've told him that's rubbish, but I think he wants to make it all better for me, like he did when we were kids. Bless him.

I don't have syphilis, by the way. I did, but I'm cured now. Only the thick white scar on my wrist is left. It was cured quite easily, the disease, just a course of pills. I've had so many pills, some for this, others for that. Now tranquillizers. I'd rattle, if you shook me.

I have had some very bad patches, I can't lie, but it's better now. I wrote to Millie and Maz; it's not great, but at least it's a start. Old arguments like that don't seem to matter any more. Only being alive matters now. I tried to tell them that.

Soledad burnt. Did you see in the papers? It was news all over the world. *Priceless Art Treasures Lost in Cult HQ Blaze*. That sort of thing. Solar Temple all over again. The media loved it. They found three bodies, together in the same room. Huw and Jane, I suppose – and who else . . . ? Wolf? Donner? I can't help hoping it wasn't Donner, despite everything. I could tell the authorities where to look, where to dig if it's bodies they want.

But I won't. It won't bring Rose back. The people who murdered her are dead, anyway.

It was murder, in my view. I know Rose went willingly, but they put it in her head, played on her weakness, her vulnerability. Like telling someone they can live on air alone, and then going, *'It's not my fault they starved to death. They didn't have to follow my ideas!'* Some people will always follow, however insane the theory. They want to – oh, to give themselves up to a higher power, even if that 'power' is a mad person. Just as long as that person seems certain. Absolutely, unshakeably certain. It's the certainty that draws the followers, you see. They want certainty in a fragile world like ours; they're desperate for it. It's more important to them than their own lives, the lives of their families, anyone. So if you spout off about your brilliant theories, if you declare with that grand, blind flourish egomaniacs have that *you and you alone know the truth* – you're responsible for the followers that will inevitably gravitate to you, like beads of mercury drawing together. You hold their lives in your hands. No point whining about it, that's how it is. You're responsible. Anyhow, that's what I think. I know not everyone agrees with me – but then, they haven't been through what I've been through, have they?

But Rose – oh, it was murder all right. I have no doubt about that. And the others. Murder wears different masks, you know. The Griffiths twins were responsible, they killed those Chelas the same as if they'd . . . *They* didn't live up to their responsibility, you see. It could have all been so different, so beautiful, so . . . Oh, well, no point going on. I chose not to go to the police, so you could say I was irresponsible, too. I often do.

The worst thing is, I miss them: Rose, Donner, Azul, Marigold. I never even knew their real names. They loved me so much, and I . . . I loved them. How could you not love someone who thought you were wonderful? Even Souris – we had a laugh. We had the work. All lost now; her perfect library and my book. My scrap of Charlotte's letter – all the other letters I never found – gone up in flames. Did the Chelas set that fire when Huw and Jane died? Did Wolf, or Donner, or whoever decide to Go Home with them? Who knows. It's the sort of thing they would do; like a Viking funeral.

I can't help it, I really miss them. The Chelas, God, they never slagged me off, or told me I was crap, immature, useless. It was unconditional love. Perfect love. I was special, at Soledad. Really special. I can't help thinking, if it hadn't been corrupted by money; if they'd just stuck to Huw's ideas, if Huw had had the courage of his convictions and Gone Home when his time came instead of clinging on so desperately, ruining everything . . . But that's what I did, isn't it? I hung on. I couldn't help it and neither could he, or Jane with her thwarted motherlove, I suppose. It's such a shame, don't you see? It was a brilliant philosophy, so pure . . . If you went back to the beginning, if you did it properly, it would be . . . Well, a better way of life.

Oh, everything is so mixed up in my mind. I know I'm supposed to think the Foundation was evil, wicked – but I can't. It went down the wrong path, that's all. Huw was too flawed a vessel, right from the start. If they'd had a leader who . . . See? I can't stop fretting about it. Thom understands, he says it was the same for him, even though he was just a disciple, not like me . . . Anyhow, he swears it fades in time . . . I nod at him, and smile. I don't like to tell him I hope it doesn't.

Because I know they're looking for me. They'd have to. Otherwise everything they went through would be for nothing. I'm not hard to find, if you tried. Not at all. And the other day, in the park, I thought I saw . . . But there's lots of Hispanic people in San Francisco, it was probably my imagination. Thom brought me straight home, bless him, no questions asked, and phoned Dr Baker. American medical care is excellent. If you've got the cash – which of course, Frankie does.

I'm really grateful. It's so nice and warm, here. I've got to get better, get strong again. Big strong Alma Greer, like I was. I must.

Because I am The Bride.